With the New Republic shattered and a Yuuzhan Vong conquest looming, it is up to Luke, Leia, and their loved ones to snatch victory from the jaws of defeat. . . .

Star Wars®
THE NEW JEDI ORDER

THE NEW JEDI ORDER

FORCE HERETIC I
REMNANT

SEAN WILLIAMS
AND
SHANE DIX

BALLANTINE BOOKS • NEW YORK

A Del Rey® Book
Published by The Random House Publishing Group

Copyright © 2003 by Lucasfilm Ltd. & ® or ™ where indicated. All Rights Reserved. Used Under Authorization.

All rights reserved.

Published in the United States by Del Rey Books, an imprint of The Random House Publishing Group, a division of Random House, Inc., New York, and simultaneously in Canada by Random House of Canada Limited, Toronto.

Del Rey is a registered trademark and the Del Rey colophon is a trademark of Random House, Inc.

www.starwars.com
www.starwarskids.com
www.delreybooks.com

ISBN 0-345-42870-6

Manufactured in the United States of America

First Edition: February 2003

9 8 7

For Nydia & Kirsty

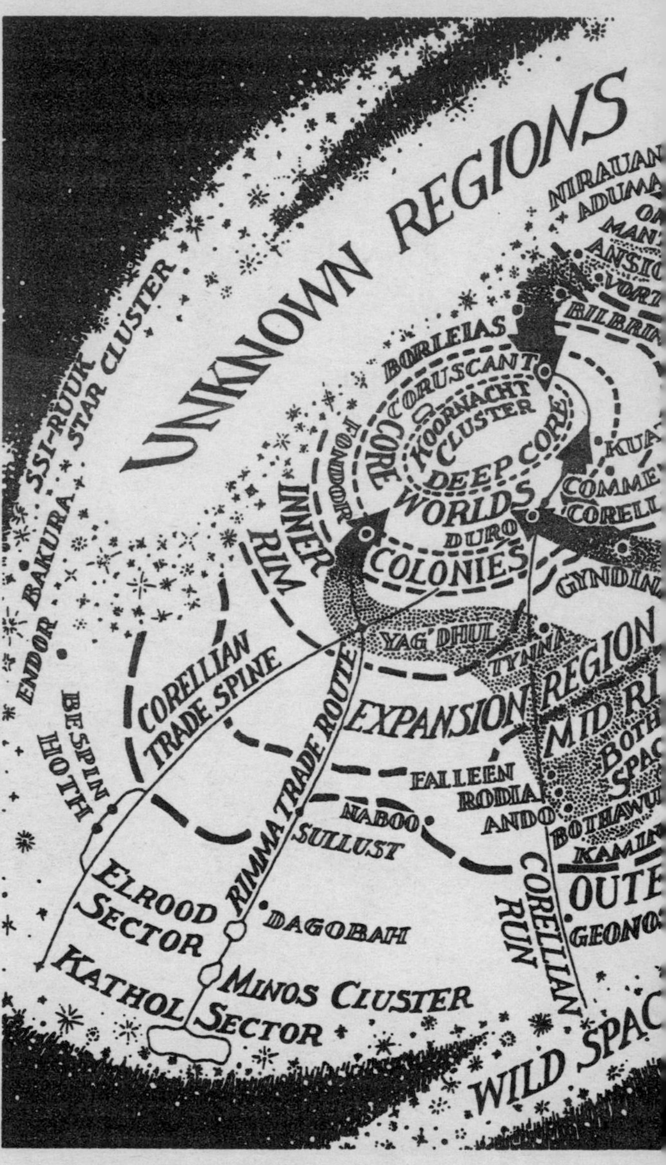
UNKNOWN REGIONS
SSI-RUUK STAR CLUSTER
BAKURA
ENDOR
BESPIN
HOTH
CORELLIAN TRADE SPINE
RIMMA TRADE ROUTE
INNER RIM
FONDOR
BORLEIAS
CORUSCANT
KOORNACHT CLUSTER
DEEP CORE
CORE WORLDS
DURO
COLONIES
YAG'DHUL
TYNNA
EXPANSION REGION
FALLEEN
RODIA
ANDO
NABOO
SULLUST
DAGOBAH
ELROOD SECTOR
KATHOL SECTOR
MINOS CLUSTER
CORELLIAN RUN
NIRAUAN

TINGEL ARM

EMPIRE • BASTION • HELSKA • BELKADAN

• DURRILLION

• DANTOOINE

• ORD BINIR • BIMMIEL

GAMAR

ATHOMIR

HOR • YAVIN

• WAYLAND

MERIDIAN
SECTOR

MYRKR

OBROA-SKAI

OSSUS

TION
CLUSTER

CRON
DRIFT

APES CLUSTER

KASHYYYK

CORPORATE
SECTOR

IMMISAARI • KUBINDI

HUTT
SPACE • KESSEL

NAL • YLESIA

HUTTA

M.

GAMORR

33 YEARS BEFORE STAR WARS: A New Hope

Darth Maul: Saboteur*

32.5 YEARS BEFORE STAR WARS: A New Hope

Cloak of Deception
Darth Maul: Shadow Hunter

32 YEARS BEFORE STAR WARS: A New Hope

STAR WARS: EPISODE I THE PHANTOM MENACE

29 YEARS BEFORE STAR WARS: A New Hope

Rogue Planet

27 YEARS BEFORE STAR WARS: A New Hope

Outbound Flight

22.5 YEARS BEFORE STAR WARS: A New Hope

The Approaching Storm

22 YEARS BEFORE STAR WARS: A New Hope

STAR WARS: EPISODE II ATTACK OF THE CLONES

Republic Commando: Hard Contact

21.5 YEARS BEFORE STAR WARS: A New Hope

Shatterpoint

21 YEARS BEFORE STAR WARS: A New Hope

The Cestus Deception
The Hive*

Republic Commando: Triple Zero

20 YEARS BEFORE STAR WARS: A New Hope

MedStar I: Battle Surgeons
MedStar II: Jedi Healer

19.5 YEARS BEFORE STAR WARS: A New Hope

Jedi Trial
Yoda: Dark Rendezvous

19 YEARS BEFORE STAR WARS: A New Hope

Labyrinth of Evil

STAR WARS: EPISODE III REVENGE OF THE SITH

Dark Lord: The Rise of Darth Vader

10-0 YEARS BEFORE STAR WARS: A New Hope

The Han Solo Trilogy:
The Paradise Snare
The Hutt Gambit
Rebel Dawn

5-2 YEARS BEFORE STAR WARS: A New Hope

The Adventures of Lando Calrissian

The Han Solo Adventures

 ## STAR WARS: A New Hope YEAR 0

STAR WARS: EPISODE IV A NEW HOPE

0-3 YEARS AFTER STAR WARS: A New Hope

Tales from the Mos Eisley Cantina
Galaxies: The Ruins of Dantooine
Splinter of the Mind's Eye

3 YEARS AFTER STAR WARS: A New Hope

STAR WARS: EPISODE V THE EMPIRE STRIKES BACK

Tales of the Bounty Hunters

3.5 YEARS AFTER STAR WARS: A New Hope

Shadows of the Empire

4 YEARS AFTER STAR WARS: A New Hope

STAR WARS: EPISODE VI RETURN OF THE JEDI

Tales from Jabba's Palace
Tales from the Empire
Tales from the New Republic

The Bounty Hunter Wars:
The Mandalorian Armor
Slave Ship
Hard Merchandise

The Truce at Bakura

*An ebook novella

6.5–7.5 YEARS AFTER STAR WARS: A New Hope

X-Wing:
Rogue Squadron
Wedge's Gamble
The Krytos Trap
The Bacta War
Wraith Squadron
Iron Fist
Solo Command

8 YEARS AFTER STAR WARS: A New Hope
The Courtship of Princess Leia
A Forest Apart*
Tatooine Ghost

9 YEARS AFTER STAR WARS: A New Hope
The Thrawn Trilogy:
Heir to the Empire
Dark Force Rising
The Last Command

X-Wing: Isard's Revenge

11 YEARS AFTER STAR WARS: A New Hope
The Jedi Academy Trilogy:
Jedi Search
Dark Apprentice
Champions of the Force

I, Jedi

12–13 YEARS AFTER STAR WARS: A New Hope
Children of the Jedi
Darksaber
Planet of Twilight
X-Wing: Starfighters of Adumar

14 YEARS AFTER STAR WARS: A New Hope
The Crystal Star

16–17 YEARS AFTER STAR WARS: A New Hope
The Black Fleet Crisis Trilogy:
Before the Storm
Shield of Lies
Tyrant's Test

17 YEARS AFTER STAR WARS: A New Hope
The New Rebellion

18 YEARS AFTER STAR WARS: A New Hope
The Corellian Trilogy:
Ambush at Corellia
Assault at Selonia
Showdown at Centerpoint

19 YEARS AFTER STAR WARS: A New Hope
The Hand of Thrawn Duology:
Specter of the Past
Vision of the Future

22 YEARS AFTER STAR WARS: A New Hope
Fool's Bargain*
Survivor's Quest

25 YEARS AFTER STAR WARS: A New Hope

The New Jedi Order:
Vector Prime
Dark Tide I: Onslaught
Dark Tide II: Ruin
Agents of Chaos I: Hero's Trial
Agents of Chaos II: Jedi Eclipse
Balance Point
Recovery*
Edge of Victory I: Conquest
Edge of Victory II: Rebirth
Star by Star
Dark Journey
Enemy Lines I: Rebel Dream
Enemy Lines II: Rebel Stand
Traitor
Destiny's Way
Ylesia*
Force Heretic I: Remnant
Force Heretic II: Refugee
Force Heretic III: Reunion
The Final Prophecy
The Unifying Force

35 YEARS AFTER STAR WARS: A New Hope
The Dark Nest Trilogy:
The Joiner King
The Unseen Queen
The Swarm War

40 YEARS AFTER STAR WARS: A New Hope

Legacy of the Force:
Betrayal
Bloodlines
Tempest

ACKNOWLEDGMENTS

We would like to thank, for their help in many different areas: Greg Bear, Ginjer Buchanan, Chris Cerasi, Leland Chee, Richard Curtis, Sam Dix, Jeff Harris, Nick Hess, Greg Keyes, Jim Luceno, Midge "McCool" McCall, Christopher McElroy, Ryan Pope, Michael Potts, Sue Rostoni, Shelly Shapiro, Walter Jon Williams, and Lucy Wilson. The Mount Lawley Mafia and the SA Writers' Centre provided, as always, valuable support. Our debt to all the previous authors in the series—and everyone whose creativity has ever enriched both The New Jedi Order series and the *Star Wars* universe—cannot be expressed in words. The warm reception we received upon joining the team is a tribute to the vibrancy of the community that has grown around these stories. We would particularly like to thank George Lucas for starting the story in the first place, and the fans for making the daunting task of continuing it not only easier but also incredibly enjoyable.

DRAMATIS PERSONAE

Arien Yage; captain, *Widowmaker* (female human)

Cal Omas; Chief of State, Galactic Federation of Free Alliances (male human)

Cilghal; Jedi Master (female Mon Calamari)

Danni Quee; scientist (female human)

Gilad Pellaeon; Imperial Grand Admiral (male human)

Han Solo; captain, *Millennium Falcon* (male human)

Jacen Solo; Jedi Knight (male human)

Jagged Fel; Chiss Squadron (male human)

Jaina Solo; Jedi Knight, Twin Suns Squadron (female human)

B'shith Vorrik; commander (male Yuuzhan Vong)

Kunra; former warrior (male Yuuzhan Vong)

Kyp Durron; Jedi Master (male human)

Leia Organa Solo; former New Republic diplomat (female human)

Luke Skywalker; Jedi Master (male human)

Mara Jade Skywalker; Jedi Master (female human)

Nom Anor; former executor (male Yuuzhan Vong)

Todra Mayn; captain, *Pride of Selonia* (female human)

Saba Sebatyne; Jedi Knight (female Barabel)

Shoon-mi Esh; Shamed One (male Yuuzhan Vong)

Tahiri Veila; Jedi Knight (female human)

Tekli; Jedi Knight (female Chadra-Fan)

Thrum; Assistant Primate, Galantos (male Fia)

Vuurok I'pan; Shamed One (male Yuuzhan Vong)

There are three ways to defeat your enemy. The first, and most obvious, is to better him in a trial of force. The best way is to have him destroy himself . . . The middle way is to destroy your enemy from within. Judicious application of the middle way shall make your blows more effective if you later take the way of force. From the middle way it is also possible to push your enemy onto the path of self-destruction.

—UUEG TCHING of Kitel Phard,
Fifty-fourth Emperor of Atrisia

PROLOGUE

Saba Sebatyne knew the moment she emerged from hyperspace that Barab I was burning. Where the planet normally displayed a cloudy, gray face lit by the glow of its primary, a sullen red dwarf, her infrared sensitive eyes now saw a fiery inferno. Smoke billowed high into the planet's atmosphere as the surface below boiled in outrage at some recent violation.

Wanting to suppress the dread welling up inside of her, wanting to deny what she was seeing, Saba banked her X-wing into a steep dive toward the surface so she could take a closer look.

This couldn't be happening, she told herself. There *had* to be someone left alive down there, surely.

But her monitors were empty. There were no ships in orbit; no transmission sources; no signs of life.

"This iz Saba Sebatyne," she spoke into the comm unit. "If anyone can hear this broadcast, please respond. *Anyone.*"

Silence was her only answer, scratched with static.

She shook her flattened, leathery head, hoping in vain to lose the vision, the thought, the truth. So many worlds had fallen since the Yuuzhan Vong had first invaded the galaxy—but not Barab I. While a part of her had always known it was a possibility, she hadn't really imagined that it would ever actually happen to her homeworld.

She clicked the comm to try again—not because she seriously expected a response, but because there seemed nothing else *to* do.

"Reswa?" Her voice broke on the emotions rising at the thought that her hatchmate might have perished in those cruel fires. It was for Reswa she had been returning to her home planet in the first place. Her hatchmate was to embark on her coming-of-age ritual shenbit bone-crusher hunt, and she had asked Saba to be her witness in this. It was an honor to be asked, and a rejection of the invitation was regarded as highly insulting—especially when the one asking was a close family member.

Family . . . the word had never sounded so empty as it did now. Friends, family—they were all gone. Nothing could have survived the flames that now ravaged her homeworld. And the closer she came to the surface of the planet, the more horror she saw. Alater-ka Spaceport was a smoldering crater; the shenbit reserves were now nothing but bubbling lava plains; the Shaka-ka memorial was sliding inexorably into a steaming sea . . .

She guided her X-wing through the upper reaches of the atmosphere, the ship buffeted by the upthrust of hot gases rising from the smoking ruins of her homeworld.

"This one should have been here," she whispered. It was a foolish notion, she knew. Even had she been here she wouldn't have made any difference to the—

All thoughts ceased.

She saw them.

Slipping around the limb of the planet, a small contingent of coralskippers—four in all—were breaking from low orbit, where they had been out of her scanning range. They were escorting a ship the likes of which she'd never seen before: a huge, vaguely ovoid mass, its movement slow as it labored against the pull of Barab I's gravity. It reminded Saba of a bloated balloon ready to burst.

Whatever the ship was, it and its escorts were all that remained insystem of the attack fleet that had destroyed her world. A mopping-up squadron, perhaps. Whatever. It didn't matter. If there had been a hundred Yuuzhan Vong battle cruisers out there, her response would have been the same . . .

She allowed the grief inside her to rise unfettered, feeling it blossom into a rage that felt perfectly satisfying, immediately easing her emotional pain. That pain, she knew, could be eased still further by action.

Gritting her razor-sharp teeth, Saba veered off to intercept the coralskippers. They didn't see her at first, clearly assuming that all resistance had been quashed. She was able to get in close before they realized she was even there. Only when she was practically on top of them did the skips break formation, three of them peeling away to come about on an attack vector. It was too late for the skip closest to the balloonlike ship: she emptied a round of laserfire into it, crying out in rage as she did so. She didn't really expect such a crude attack to achieve anything except to get their attention, so was surprised when the coralskipper exploded in a violent flash of crimson that flung shards of the craft far and wide.

The explosion had the unexpected effect of clearing her mind. The skip must have been already damaged, its dovin basal disabled from recent battle with the Barabels. Such a simple victory, so soon in the battle, startled her. Perhaps, she thought, she hadn't expected victory at all. She had simply gone into the fight expecting to die— no, *wanting* to die. Her people were dead, and so deep down she reasoned that she should be, too.

Now she was in a fix—and one she might not be able to get herself out of. Two of the remaining skips were coming at her from behind, unleashing streams of molten plasma in her direction. She didn't want to die, and her reflexes agreed. She avoided the fate of her fellow Barabels by rolling her X-wing and skewing down and around her attackers. Some of the plasma reached its target, however, instantly depleting her shields.

She didn't have time to check if the skip had stayed on her tail. Her R2 unit tootled an urgent warning: off to her port side another skip was coming in fast. She pulled up sharply, rocking unsteadily in her cockpit as plasma balls flickered past. Saba winced. That last shot must have sheared a millimeter of paint from her wing.

She barely had time to thank her droid for the headsup before the first two skips returned to make another pass at her. It was too much, she knew; if she remained on the defensive like this, then sooner or later they were going to get her—and out in the open, she had no choice but to *be* defensive.

With this in mind, she moved her X-wing nearer to the larger Yuuzhan Vong craft. She kept her flying tight, swooping in close to the massive, bulbous vessel, feeling the craft's dovin basals tugging at her shields. They weren't as effective as the dovin basals on the other ships she'd come across in action; these no doubt had a different purpose, although she couldn't guess what that might be.

Sweeping under the belly of the thing, confident that she was safe on at least one side, Saba gave pursuit to the skip whose buddy she had destroyed. It tried to shake her by swerving abruptly from side to side, but she was able to stay on it long enough to get a bead on its dovin basal. When her target-lock flashed, Saba loosed one of her torpedoes. She had done this enough times to sense when she'd fired a good shot, and the second her finger squeezed the trigger, she knew she had the skip beaten. The torpedo detonated on target, effectively downing the skip's defenses and allowing her to blast the rocky craft into oblivion with a hail of laserfire. She called out in delight as the coralskipper fell apart in a stutter of explosions.

She was quick to bring her emotions into check, however, when she banked her X-wing to come back around and once again saw her planet burning. This was not a time for celebrating, she reminded herself.

Another warning from her droid. This time she didn't even pause to check where the attack was coming from; she just rolled her X-wing in toward the main ship. The surface of the thing seemed to move in strange and subtle undulations as she passed near it—almost like a sac filled with water—although at all times it remained as rough as the exterior of the coralskippers. She noticed something else, too: huge tentacles that unfurled from the stern of the craft, flailing around as though reaching for Saba's ship.

"What iz this?" she said aloud, not really expecting a reply. Nevertheless, the R2 unit behind her tootled a response. She didn't need to check her translator to know that the droid didn't have enough information to be able to give her a proper answer.

She kept herself close in to the huge ship, veering constantly to avoid the writhing tentacles. She swung around the underside of the vessel when one of the skips came in too close and risked taking a couple of potshots at her. She avoided the attack easily enough, and the plasma shot harmlessly into the space away from the balloon-ship. The skips wouldn't fire if she stood between them and their charge.

What iz it? she asked herself again. And why were the skips being so careful around it? It had no defenses to speak of, except for the small escort of coralskippers, and its only weapon seemed to be the tentacles that constantly lashed out at her. If there *was* anything else, then why didn't they use it?

There was no time to dwell upon the matter, though. Time was running out for her. She couldn't stay defensive indefinitely. Others from the fleet would soon be making their way back to assist their comrades, she was sure.

She pitched the X-wing again, jinking to avoid one of the tentacles while at the same time spraying a cover of laserfire at one of the incoming skips. The shots were easily absorbed by the dovin basal's black hole, but it was enough to make the pilot swerve out of her way. That bought her a few valuable seconds to get herself into a better position. She pulled her fighter up into a backward arc, coming around the top of the massive saclike vessel and down onto the skip that had just swung past. She didn't wait to get the dovin basal properly in her sights this time; she simply fired. The torpedo detonated too soon to be of any use. Saba silently cursed her rashness; a wasted shot!

There was no time to bemoan her luck. She quickly brought her ship around again to pursue the lucky skip. It released blazing plasma from its side cannons. A handful of the globules struck her forward shields. The ship shuddered under the impact, and she snarled as her R2 unit reported a further 12 percent depletion to her shields.

Determined, Saba went after the skip, doggedly tailing it around the body of the larger vessel and keeping its dovin basal at all times in targeting reticle. Finally, with a lock on her target, she went to depress the firing trigger. At that moment the remaining skip crested the top of the main craft, loosing a volley of plasma. She brought the X-wing sharply around, heading directly for the incoming skip, her forward shields taking the full brunt of the hot plasma and being reduced still further as a result.

A tentacle whipped after her, snaking through the vacuum to strike. Instinctively, she pushed the nose of her ship down, leaving the coralskipper behind her to plunge broadside into the thick and unyielding appendage, effectively stripping half the craft's hull from nose to tail and causing it to spin out of control. Saba pursued it, pounding the damaged skip with laserfire, not stopping until it disintegrated into a ball of vapor.

An exclamation of joy died in her throat when, a split second later, she saw the remaining skip abruptly emerge from the vapor cloud of its fallen comrade. Saba moved easily enough to avoid it, missing the craft by about five meters. She swung her X-wing smoothly and deftly, a confidence returning in her that had been missing since the battle had begun. Now that she had reduced the odds, she felt she had a much better chance of survival. All she had to do was stay focused—and be mindful of those tentacles!

The skip tried to lead her away from the main craft. She didn't mind anymore. With only the one skip remaining, she no longer felt the need to use the huge vessel as a shield. Without the others around to trouble her, she could take this last one out with little difficulty.

She chased the skip for several thousand kilometers out from the tentacled vessel, waiting for a decent shot. The skip opened up with its plasma cannons, filling the space in its wake with streams of molten plasma that rained down upon Saba's X-wing.

Her R2 unit whistled a warning: her shields were totally depleted. It didn't matter; Saba had to stay on target until the opening came. When it did, she stutterfired at the skip's dovin basal and launched a single torpedo. A perfect shot, she knew—the instinct confirmed a moment later when the dovin basal overloaded and the skip was left defenseless. The alien pilot attempted desperately to evade Saba's pursuit. But it was no use. She depressed the firing button of her laser guns, and watched in satisfaction as the bolts made their way into the rear of the enemy craft, quickly tearing it apart with a blinding flash.

Saba found herself wanting to laugh out loud at the victory. It was an emotion empty of joy, containing only bitterness and grief. What was victory when her planet hung burning behind her and her people were dead?

She hissed savagely as she brought her X-wing around to attack the remaining Yuuzhan Vong vessel. It swelled before her like a hideous, living moon—a target almost impossible to miss. She didn't bother with her targeting computer. She simply aimed and fired, releasing her three remaining torpedoes into the huge ship with grim satisfaction.

They sank easily into the hide of the craft. Three detonations occurred in quick succession, deep within its belly. A rent appeared in its side, outgassing fire. The tentacles flailed crazily, as if in pain.

"For this one's home," she whispered. "For this one's people."

She banked for a final pass to finish off the ship, her heart racing as she thrilled at the thought of her impending revenge on the enemy. It was a moment she would savor for many years to come, even as she grieved for those she had lost.

Laser bolts peppered the side of the craft, widening the rent and creating numerous new ones. To Saba's surprise and disappointment, however, the ship didn't explode. Instead, the sac burst from top to bottom, stretching like a fruit left too long in the sun. From the tear poured a strange translucent gel, followed by what appeared to be a thousand six-pointed stars.

Stars? She relaxed her grip on the laser cannon trigger. How could that be? There were thousands of them, tumbling into space, glinting in infrared starlight. They couldn't be weapons, or the strange ship would have deployed them earlier. They couldn't be bounty, either, for nothing of value on Barab I matched those peculiar shapes . . .

She reduced speed, coming in cautiously for a better look. Her R2 unit plucked one star at random from the jumbled mass and brought it up on her display. A sickening sensation flowered in her gut as she saw just what the points of the "stars" were.

Two arms, two legs, a head, and a tail.

Nothing of value . . .

The thought rang in her mind as the horror of what had happened sank in. The Yuuzhan Vong didn't value metals or jewels. Their biological sciences had no use for Barab I's usual bounty. They did, however, take captives—and they had to transport them somehow.

My people!

Saba watched helplessly as the ship continued to spill its contents into the cold vacuum of space. Her entire being shuddered to a grief that burned more intensely than the fires raging on the planet below. Her last thought before tears obscured her vision was a despairing, soul-tearing cry:

What have I done?

PART ONE

INTERSECTION

Three Months Later

"I say we fight on!"

The voice echoed through the vast, domed hall that was serving as a replacement for the Grand Convocation Chamber on Coruscant, where the Senate had previously met. With Coruscant currently in the hands of the Yuuzhan Vong, Mon Calamari had been selected as a temporary capital and now played host to the representatives of the Galactic Alliance—a group much smaller than a full meeting of the Senate had once been, before the Yuuzhan Vong invasion, but still several hundred strong.

They responded to the call to fight in the fashion preferred by their individual species. There were whistles, grunts, shrieks, and subsonic rumbles. Some waved appendages; others stamped their feet. And others still, Leia Organa Solo among them, remained silent. She stood completely motionless, gently extending herself into the Force to feel it crackle and flare from the conflicting emotions of those gathered around her.

The speaker, a sour-faced Sullustan by the name of Niuk Niuv, paced the floor with an energy that belied his size. Clearly agitated by the sudden commotion, he lifted one hand to his ear to indicate his discomfort, while the other attempted to motion the crowd to silence. Even with his audio dampeners in place, the level of noise around the hall still hurt his sensitive ears.

"We have them on the back foot," he said, his large black eyes roaming the assembly. "They are overextended and ill prepared to defend themselves. They didn't expect to *have* to defend themselves so late in the game—which is precisely why we must drive home this advantage! To ignore the opportunity we have been given would be like putting our collective head back on the chopping block!"

"And who took it off the block in the first place?" The call came from the far side of the chamber. Leia immediately recognized the voice as belonging to Thuv Shinev of the Tion Hegemony.

Niuk Niuv's face contorted into a fleshy snarl. "That is irrelevant," he said irritably.

"Really?" Shinev bellowed. "I wouldn't have thought so. Too long have some among us treated the Jedi with contempt and suspicion. If we do have the chance now, finally, to force the Yuuzhan Vong back, then we should at least acknowledge their opinions on the subject!"

"If you think it necessary, then by all means thank them," the Sullustan retaliated. "I'm not saying they don't deserve that. But to do anything less than strike back at the Yuuzhan Vong would be madness, no matter what the Jedi say! We must prove to the Vong that we cannot be subjugated and will not tolerate their oppression! They have done enough. It is time for us to show them who this galaxy really belongs to! We must strike back hard, and we must do it *now*."

A scattered cheer rose up among the Senators. It was loud, but not as deafening as Leia had feared it might be. After so many crushing defeats, most of the representatives remained uncertain that the Yuuzhan Vong could be rolled back as easily as Niuk Niuv stated. But the willingness to try was undeniable.

As Leia's gaze swept the crowd, she caught the tall, long-faced figure of Kenth Hamner on the far side of the chamber. From the scowl on the Jedi Master's face, Leia felt sure he was about to speak out against Niuk Niuv. But it was another who voiced their concerns.

"What if you're right?" Leia identified Releqy A'Kla, daughter of Camaasi Senator Elegos A'Kla, who had been ritually murdered by the Yuuzhan Vong's Commander Shedao Shai in the early days of the war. Since she had already served in his stead during his absence, her people had voted her into her father's position for the duration of the crisis. "What if we *can* beat them?"

"Then we win!" Niuk Niuv's big, round eyes were bright with anticipated glory.

"But at what cost?" A'Kla's fine, golden down shivered with intense emotion. "The Yuuzhan Vong fight to the death, Senator. Admiral Ackbar used this very fact against them at Ebaq Nine. I don't think you truly realize what this means."

"I realize," the Sullustan said. "And I realize that it is not our responsibility. If the positions were reversed, they would undoubtedly do the same to us."

"I'm sorry, but my people cannot support such extermination under any circumstances," she said. She brought her long, three-fingered hands up to her chest. "We are pacifists, Senator. We do not wish such horrors on our consciences."

"And I respect your people's ethics," Niuk Niuv replied. Turning from her to address the entire chamber, he continued: "If there was an alternative, then I would consider it. But in the absence of any such alternative, I am not prepared to sit back with my neck out waiting for the Yuuzhan Vong to bring an amphistaff down upon it!"

Another cheer rippled around the room.

"It's all very good for the pacifists to argue about compassion and restraint, but it is *they* who will benefit from the ultimate peace that *we* will bring about with our actions!" Niuv faced Releqy A'Kla once again. "What good is pacifism if you are dead, Senator?"

Releqy A'Kla sank back into her chair, blinking in dismay.

"We will crush the Yuuzhan Vong," Niuk Niuv concluded to the Galactic Alliance representatives gathered, punching a fist into the air. "And we will send their remains back where they came from!"

The cheer was louder this time. Leia's fellow Alderaanian, Chief of State Cal Omas, said nothing. It would have been pointless at this stage, with the majority now so evidently behind Niuk Niuv's sentiments.

Across from her, Leia saw Hamner's scowl deepen as he shook his head and slipped silently from the huge hall.

"Finally, we are vindicated."

In a room not far from the domed hall in which the Senators met, a gathering of Jedi Knights and Masters looked similarly reduced in numbers but was no less passionate. Jedi Master Luke Skywalker had called the meeting to discuss strategies for the coming stages of the war with the Yuuzhan Vong. Waxarn Kel, the current speaker, paced in front of the gathering like a caged howlrunner. His face and hairless scalp were pink with fresh scars, indicating just how close he had come to being another victim of the Yuuzhan Vong anti-Jedi vendetta.

"Explain," Luke said. He sat on the stage at the front of the chamber, one knee raised to support the elbow of his right arm, and that hand supporting his chin. The unnatural coolness of the hand's artificial skin against his jaw helped keep his head clear.

Kel looked up at him with a frown. "Do I really need to?" he asked with a mix of irritation and surprise. Then, to the rest of the Jedi, he said, "We've been slandered, hunted, and butchered from one side of the galaxy to the other. We became the scapegoat for everything the New Republic brought upon itself because of its complacency and inability to act. We told them things they didn't want to hear, and what was our reward? We were damned for it, that's what. But now we *have* been vindicated. The trap on Ebaq Nine and the defeat of the Yuuzhan Vong have shown that we are a force to be reckoned with. Vergere's sacrifice will not be in vain."

"I hadn't realized that our fight was with the survivors of the New Republic," said Kyp Durron, leaning in flight uniform against one of the chamber's fluted walls, arms folded across his chest. "I thought our battle was with the Yuuzhan Vong."

"It is." Kel regarded Kyp with some annoyance. "The Yuuzhan Vong are our enemy—not just of every peaceful citizen of the galaxy, but of the Jedi in particular. That's been the frustrating thing about this war. The New Republic has thwarted our every attempt to defend ourselves. If it wasn't the Peace Brigade actually trapping us and selling us over, it was idiots like Borsk Fey'lya holding us back. Well, now we're free to act, and we can show them just what we are capable of doing!"

"I presume you have something in mind." Kyp's expression was neutral, but Luke sensed a cautious interest lurking behind it—like that of someone poking at a bug's nest with a stick to see what might emerge.

"Of course," Kel said. "We strike, and we strike *hard*."

"The Yuuzhan Vong?"

"Of course the Yuuzhan Vong!" Kel's eyes flashed anger. "We must act to ensure that public opinion doesn't turn against us once again."

"How might it do that, Waxarn?" Luke asked.

Kel glanced back up at Luke. The Master could feel the scarred young Jedi Knight consciously bringing his emotions into line.

"I fear it could happen all to easily, Master," he said, bowing slightly. "Unless we act decisively to reaffirm our usefulness and goodwill, to prove beyond the slightest doubt that the war can only be won with our assistance, then we risk looking weak. Or worse, looking as if our loyalty to the Galactic Alliance is weak."

Luke smiled sagely. "Surely our loyalty is to peace."

"First and foremost, yes, Master," Kel put in quickly. "But you have to be strong to protect peace from those who would destroy it. Sometimes it is necessary to fight in order to bring an end to fighting. Isn't that the way of the Jedi?"

Is it? Luke asked himself as he pondered the words of the young man before him. Luke himself had acted more than once on the philosophy espoused by Waxarn Kel and those like him. The cry had been taken up several times throughout the war with the Yuuzhan Vong by those tempted to take the seemingly easy route through the dark side rather than brave the ambiguities of the Force.

Luke didn't think Kel had fallen to the dark side, though. There was none of the anger and hatred in the young man that Luke could sense in a handful of others presently around him. They remained quiet, allowing Kel to speak their words for them. But it wasn't difficult for Luke to read their feelings. So many had been hurt by the Yuuzhan Vong and the Peace Brigaders that desiring retribution was, perhaps, only natural. Natural wasn't necessarily right, though, and part of Luke's job was to ensure that those in his charge weren't led astray.

None of the Jedi in the room had yet fallen to the dark

side, and for that he was thankful. Some of them had taken a wrong turning here and there, just as some were being tempted to do now. But Luke had faith in all of them—even those who disagreed vehemently with his own opinions. He was sure that the collective wisdom of the Jedi, their strong belief in the healing, sustaining energies of the Force, would gradually assuage the grief they all felt for loved ones who had died in the war—as well as for themselves.

Luke straightened and dropped down onto the floor of the room to face Waxarn Kel. Once considered handsome, he was now scarred almost beyond recognition. And it was from this that Luke felt the man's emotions stemmed. Every time Kel looked in the mirror, he would be reminded of what the war had done to him and those he loved, and his anger and hatred would grow.

The dark side can beckon to us from so many quarters, Luke thought.

"If we strike now," Kel said, undeterred by being eye to eye with the great Jedi Master, "we can do the most damage. But if we wait too long, our enemies will have time to recover and—"

"Do you believe that this is why we have survived as long as we have?" Luke interrupted calmly. "Because our enemies are weak? Did those of us who have fallen in battle do so because *they* were weak?"

Kel blinked as a look of uncertainty passed over his face. "Master, I would never think that—"

"Of course not," Luke continued smoothly. "The Yuuzhan Vong are a powerful species, and they have used our weaknesses against us just as we are learning to use theirs. No species is perfect, and no war is won purely by strength. There are many other factors that must be considered."

Kel nodded, lowering his eyes. "Yes, Master."

Luke inwardly cringed. Kel was addressing him as a droid would its owner.

"Under my leadership," Luke said, "we have seen special combat units trained and led by the Jedi making a decisive difference in battle—yet at the same time I refuse to allow a Jedi to stand for political office. So do you think me weak?"

The young Jedi was shocked at the suggestion. "Master, that's not what—"

Luke tried again. "I have formed a new Jedi council and placed non-Jedi upon it," he said. "Is *that* the action of a weak individual?"

"No, Master."

Before Luke could speak again, he was interrupted by a low chuckle from Kyp Durron. He faced him, lacing his hands together behind his back.

"Yes, Kyp?" he said.

"Master, I *know* you are weak." Durron bowed formally at the waist—but with respect, not sarcasm. "As am I." His hand lightly swept around to indicate the room. "As is everyone here. But I am proud of my weakness, for it makes me who I am. Forgetting one's weakness is a sure recipe for disaster."

The door to the chamber opened, and Luke turned to see Kenth Hamner step into the room. Luke nodded acknowledgment, hiding his disappointment that it wasn't Jaina. His niece was running late for the meeting, and he couldn't help but feel worried. The loss of Anakin, Jaina's younger brother, struck deep into the part of him that was all too human: the part that had turned away from Master Yoda's teaching to rescue his friends; the part that loved his wife, Mara, and his son, Ben, more deeply than anything else in the galaxy; the part that could fully understand the need to strike back at those who had hurt the ones he loved. He wouldn't blame himself for loving, or call it a weakness, but he would blame himself for not meeting his duty of care. Aside from Jaina, too many of the Jedi were missing from this meeting: Tam Azur-Jamin, Octa Ramis, Kyle Katarn, Tenel Ka, Tahiri Veila . . . If they were dead, he would feel as though he had failed each and every one of them.

Waxarn Kel had turned a faint crimson under his scars. Luke couldn't tell if Kyp Durron's point—the one Luke himself had been trying to make—had finally hit home, or if the young man was simply embarrassed for looking something of a fool in front of his colleagues. And some of those were becoming restless again; the tension in the air was palpable. Despite the recent turn-around in the fortunes of the Jedi, there were clearly still some who thought his leadership flawed.

"Thank you, Kyp," Luke said, reciprocating the bow. "There is more to winning this war than military might allows. Remember that, all of you, and we may yet win it in a way that saves us from ourselves, too."

He swung back up into his sitting position on the stage and caught Jacen's eye in the process. His nephew, standing apart from the others at the back of the hall, nodded slightly, then turned his attention forward as Waxarn Kel sat down and the next person stepped up to speak his mind.

"Same meat, different bantha."

Cal Omas snorted at Kenth Hamner's words. Although the Jedi physically towered over him and he found the man's dour expression impenetrable, the Chief of State of the Galactic Alliance had developed quite a liking for Hamner in recent weeks. Unlike most politicians, Omas had an appreciation for straight talking.

"We didn't have bantha on Alderaan." He was standing by the immense convex viewport of his office, staring out at the view. Beneath him, the terraced walls of the floating city swept away, merging into the mist thrown up by the mountainous waves far below. Beyond the mist there was only the tumultuous sea, stretching out to the horizon. He'd spent a lot of time at this view, hoping for a glimpse of the planet's legendary krakana coming to the surface. More often than not, though, he was too deep in thought to even notice if one had.

He glanced over his shoulder to Kenth Hamner and said, "But I do know what you mean."

A murmur of assent rolled through the small group of people seated before him.

Two hours had passed since the meetings of the Senate and the Jedi. Omas had called a select group of people together to discuss the outcomes of both meetings: apart from Hamner, both Skywalkers were there, along with Leia Organa Solo, Releqy A'Kla, and Sien Sovv, the Sullustan Supreme Commander of the slowly re-forming Galactic Alliance military. In other words, people he could trust—and people he could use, in the best possible sense of the word.

"I called you here to ask for your help." He turned now to face everyone in the room. "Because I have to tell you, I am altogether sick of fighting."

"The Yuuzhan Vong?" Mara Jade Skywalker asked. She was sitting at the long, oval transparisteel table, her husband standing beside her.

Omas shrugged noncommittally. "Borsk Fey'lya was bad enough. Fighting him every step of the way used to make me want to weep. The losses we incurred because of his stupidity . . ." He shook his head, wanting to lose the memory. "He's gone now, and I had the momentary foolishness to think that it would somehow make things easier. But I was wrong. His death has sent the Bothans on this crazy ar'krai war of theirs, and I have one of my senior admirals arguing for an all-out push to wipe out the Yuuzhan Vong once and for all. I take it to the Senate, and all I hear is more of the same from them. Even the Jedi—"

"Not all of us." Luke Skywalker's frown was deep, as though he'd been personally stung.

Omas respectfully inclined his head to the Jedi Master, and to A'Kla, who had stiffened in her seat. "Forgive me," he said. "No, not all of the Jedi, and not all of the Senate, either. But there's too much craziness out there for any real decisions to be made."

"Should I take it, then," Leia said, "that you don't approve of the final push?"

"You're asking a politician to buck the public's will?" Omas laughed lightly, humorlessly, as he returned to his seat. He sank into it with a sigh. "The truth is, I wouldn't commit our forces to attack at the moment, whether I wanted to or not. We've made some small progress against the Yuuzhan Vong, yes, and we seem to be holding our own at the moment, but if we overextend we'll just be putting ourselves in their position. Until we have enough in reserve to defend ourselves, should such a push go wrong, I'm not prepared to authorize anything dramatic. Otherwise, we run the risk of losing what small advantages we've gained, and maybe even ending up worse off. We need to consolidate first, *then* fight back."

"I wondered why Traest wasn't here for this," Hamner said. "He's not going to approve of this decision, is he?"

"He'll have to live with it. Kre'fey is a good strategist, and he stuck by us when we needed him, but he's not my Supreme Commander. I trust Sien on this."

Sien Sovv nodded, his big, black eyes blinking. "Consolidation is the key. I'm not going to stick my neck out until I'm sure my vibro-ax is bigger than the Vong's."

"Discretion is the better part of valor," Mara said.

"Perhaps. If I *had* the forces at my disposal right now, maybe I would feel differently." Sovv shrugged.

Skywalker nodded. "A push would be harder to argue against, in that case. I understand. It becomes a moral argument, then. If we do attack with intent to destroy, does that make us any better than the Yuuzhan Vong themselves?"

There was silence around the table. Omas studied each of them in turn. Skywalker looked worried, and his wife was watching him closely. His sister, Leia, had the tight-faced reserve he had learned meant that she was thinking carefully about everything going on around her. Kenth Hamner and Sien Sovv were military through and through, used to arguing in terms of resources and objectives, but on less firm footing when it came to philosophy. Senator A'Kla was the only one displaying any clear emotion. The Camaasi's golden fur was practically bristling with agitation.

"Yes, Releqy?" Omas knew what she was going to say before she had even opened her mouth. That was why he had invited her to the meeting in the first place.

"I hope to speak for all of us," she said, "when I say that our ultimate objective is peace. Not just an end to the war."

Again, a murmur of agreement swept around the table. Only Princess Leia voiced dissent.

"Peace at any cost," she said, "isn't peace."

Mara was quick to back her up. "At best it would only be a temporary cease-fire."

"We need something more permanent to base this new Galactic Alliance on apart from the defeat of an enemy," the Princess went on. "As well as a solid infrastructure and guaranteed supplies, ships to replace those destroyed and open hyperspace lanes, we need security and order, and—"

"What we need," Sien Sovv cut in, "is Coruscant back. It's a symbol of our authority, and without it everything we attempt is undermined."

"All valid points," Omas said, acknowledging his Supreme Commander with a curt nod. "But I fear we're reaching for stars when we've barely managed to get out of the gutter. Keeping things together on a daily basis, let alone rebuilding what we've lost or fighting back, is my most pressing concern at the moment. The subspace networks and HoloNet itself are a mess. Do you have any idea how hard it will be to put things back together when we don't even know which bit is doing what anymore? Half the pieces can no longer even talk to each other."

"It's not as though people haven't been trying," Leia began.

"I know, I know," he said. "You and Han have put in a lot of effort, and so has Mara. Marrab, too, is doing his best—"

"*Gron* Marrab?" Mara interrupted. "Surely there must be someone better for the job than that."

"Well, he's a Mon Cal, so he's local," Omas said, unable to help feeling defensive. "And besides, it's not as if I have much choice. That's my point, really. I don't *have* any choices. The intelligence community was routed when Coruscant fell, just like the Senate. All we have in its place is a lot of fine effort, but nothing coordinated. There are at least six chains of command out there, all feeding through to different people by different means. They don't talk to each other; I'd be surprised if there aren't still more that won't talk to me.

"And that's when they *can* talk," he went on. "There are parts of this galaxy as big as the Core that we haven't heard from for months. We don't know if this silence is self-imposed or due to infrastructure collapse. We don't know if it's a technical problem or deliberate sabotage. All we do know is that the communications we once took for granted have fallen into disrepair along with everything else."

"And in the absence of communications," Luke put in, "ferment breeds."

"Precisely," Omas said. "It's pointless to win a war only to watch the Galactic Alliance fall apart around us afterward."

"Then what is it you want, exactly?" Mara asked. "I presume it has something to do with us, otherwise we wouldn't be here."

"I need a group of people committed to bringing things back together," Omas said passionately. "A mobile task force traveling from place to place—reconnecting the dots, if you like. Familiar, trustworthy faces, symbols of peace and prosperity. That kind of thing. I thought of Master Skywalker first, of course. And Leia, too. A New Republic presence will certainly help things along."

"That's 'Galactic Alliance' now, Cal," Leia said.

"Yes, of course. That's going to take some getting used to." He continued: "The task force doesn't need specialist technical expertise to repair the networks where they're down; you can call for that sort of help if needed, when the problem has been isolated. Just in case it's a military problem, I'll provide a squadron or two for protection— but you shouldn't need anything more than that. You're not there to intimidate, but to communicate. Open up the black spots, whatever it takes, and bring them back into the fold. At least let them know we're paying attention, anyway."

He paused to allow others to comment. When no one did, he said, "Well, what do you think?"

Leia was the first to respond, nodding slowly and

thoughtfully. "In principle, I think it's a good idea," she said. "And I'm sure Han will agree, too."

Omas offered a faint smile in appreciation. "I was hoping this would be the case," he said. "The *Falcon* would make a great support vessel."

"And you don't really have many to spare," Leia said. "I understand."

Omas glanced at Luke and was surprised to see the Jedi Master frowning. That threw the Chief of State for a moment. What wasn't there to like about his plan? It gave the Jedi a chance to reestablish their peacekeeping role in the galaxy while at the same time tying them ever closer to the Galactic Alliance. If the mission was a success—and there was no reason Omas could see why it wouldn't be—then no one in the Senate would be able to argue about the worth of the Jedi again.

"Luke?" Mara prompted, also catching her husband's frown.

The Jedi Master remained silent for a while longer, as though mulling over everything Omas had just said. When he did speak, it was slowly, choosing each word with care.

"This would solve only half the problem," he said. "No matter how well we did our job, it would still leave the Yuuzhan Vong. That's a problem that isn't going to go away, no matter how much you stifle the agitators. But what if I told you I could solve your military problem *and* the moral problem in one operation?"

"I'd be interested, naturally," Omas said, then lifted his thin shoulders and spread his arms in a supplicating gesture. "But *how*?"

"The Imperial Remnant," Sovv said, answering for the Jedi Master.

Luke looked at the Supreme Commander, nodding. "The Empire."

"They turned us down," Leia said. "Pellaeon said that he had no interest in joining forces. As far as they're concerned, they've been holding their own perfectly well against the Yuuzhan Vong."

"And at that point, *we* weren't," Luke said. "But now that we're starting to hit back, they might change their mind."

"Well, it would certainly solve the military problem," Omas said. "It would also legitimize the name of our new government."

"The *Galactic* Federation of Free Alliances," A'Kla said.

"Exactly. There's not much meaning to it if entire chunks of the galaxy won't join."

Omas folded his hands before him, returning his attention to Luke. "You're proposing a diplomatic mission, Master Skywalker?"

"To the Imperial Remnant—and to the Chiss, too," he replied. "They're the ones who refined the toxin developed by Scaur's scientists—the Alpha Red bioweapons. That project is still hanging over us. We mustn't forget that.'"

"No. Admiral Kre'fey isn't letting me."

"I thought the project was on hold," A'Kla said, the purple fur above her eyes ruffling slightly beneath a frown.

" 'On hold' in military terms simply means that you're set on stun," the Supreme Commander said. "The blaster, however, is still powered and aimed."

"Or it would be, given just a few weeks' development time." Omas himself was deeply conflicted over the Chiss plan to use biological warfare to defeat the Yuuzhan Vong. On the one hand, he could see the military sense in wiping out the enemy with one strike—a strike that would cost nothing in terms of troops or fleet resources. But it smacked of using the enemy's own tactics against them. The Yuuzhan Vong had employed biological warfare on

Ithor—whose native bafforr trees, ironicallly, were the very source of the Alpha Red toxin—and many other worlds, destroying whole biospheres in the process. It was a dirty, demeaning tactic, and it could so easily be used against the wielder. In his nightmares he saw system after system falling to a gray plague while, at the same time, the Yuuzhan Vong were wiped out by the Chiss bioweapon. The end result would be a lifeless, sterile galaxy.

He didn't want *that* to be what his administration was remembered for—even if there was no one left to remember it.

"Destroying the research," Sovv said, "would meet with the strongest resistance from some under my command. I cannot guarantee that they wouldn't take independent action to stop you."

Luke nodded. "I'm aware of that, Commander. That's why I wouldn't be going to the Chiss to propose or attempt such a move. That's their decision, and I'll leave it up to them. I would only be extending the hand of peace."

"People will automatically assume a hidden agenda." Sovv turned to Omas. "If you're going to allow this, Cal, I'd advise that it be an informal mission. Unofficially sanctioned, top secret, hidden agenda—whatever you want to call it. The fewer people who know about it, the better."

"If it's not official," Omas said, "I'm not sure how much support I could lend it."

"That's okay," Luke said. "We'll have *Jade Shadow* and my X-wing, and we might even be able to call in a few favors on top of that. The only support I really want is an assurance that you won't try to stop us, and that you'll hold the warmongers back while we're gone."

"That shouldn't be a problem," Omas said. "There's

plenty to keep people busy." He leaned back into his chair, sensing more to Luke's request than appeared on the surface. "However, I doubt that the Yuuzhan Vong will make it as easy for us as Senator Niuv would have us believe."

"It's a long way to travel, isn't it?" Sovv asked. "I mean, I appreciate you going to such lengths to bring the Empire into the fold, but I'd have thought you'd be more needed here. Isn't there someone else you can send? Kenth, here, for instance, would be perfectly competent. The Empire and the Chiss would respect his background."

"You make a good point, Sien." Luke briefly exchanged a look with Mara and Leia that Omas couldn't interpret. "But those very same abilities you mention make him perfect for the job of keeping things calm here. Neither the Empire nor the Chiss will resolve the Yuuzhan Vong problem alone, even in a military sense. To be honest, they are only secondary objectives. There's something else I need to do while I'm gone."

"Ah." Omas pushed himself forward as the missing piece slowly became clear. "The Empire and the Chiss—both lie in or near the Unknown Regions."

A faint smile appeared at the edges of Luke's mouth. "That's true."

"What is it you're looking for, Master Skywalker?"

"If I told you, Cal, you wouldn't believe me."

"The moral solution to the war?"

"Perhaps. An alternative, anyway."

Luke raised a hand as Omas began to ask another question.

The Chief of State rested back into his chair again with a wry smile. "I guess I can't force you to tell me," he said. He glanced at Sovv. It was obvious that his Supreme Commander knew as little about Skywalker's plans as he did. "You've offered enough for me to give you my private assurance that I won't do anything to hinder your plans. Having the Empire and the Chiss aboard won't guarantee the security of the Galactic Alliance, but it'll help. If you think you can give me a long-term resolution to the war as well, then I shall do what I can to assist."

The Jedi Master kept his expression carefully composed, but the way his wife touched his arm suggested that she was happy with the outcome of the meeting. Like her husband, though, her face revealed nothing.

"What about you, Leia?" Omas asked. "Will you still do what I've asked of you?"

She nodded. "Of course," she said. "You can count on both Han and me to do whatever we can to help."

The Chief of State nodded in return. "I'm grateful," he said. "Make a time with Sien to discuss the logistics. We'll see what special operations can lend you. I know you have some connections down there." He stood with a smile, knowing perfectly well that Jaina Solo's Twin Suns Squadron was a sure bet for the mission—and if she was involved, Jag Fel wouldn't be far away. Together they would keep the military side of the mission covered, and possibly more than that: he was sure Sien Sovv wouldn't mind applying a little force to some of the more unruly sectors of the galaxy.

"Now, if you'll excuse me, I have a line of beings wanting to see me."

"We thank you for your time," Luke said, taking his wife's hand as she rose from the chair. "As well as your cooperation. May the Force guide us all."

"To peace," Releqy A'Kla said, standing with the others.

"To peace," Omas echoed wholeheartedly as they filed out of the room. He knew that only time would blunt the teeth of the Corellian sand panthers in the ranks of the Senate, the Defense Force, and the Jedi. Whatever Luke

Skywalker had up his sleeve, Omas only hoped he could give him enough time to bring it into effect before those sand panthers gathered outside his office door, hungry for *his* blood.

From space, the ocean world Mon Calamari shone a brilliant, peaceful blue. Under a sky that glinted like ice, curving cloud patterns traced words only stars could understand. All but the keenest of eyes would fail to see the coral outcrops, marshy islands, and floating cities that were scattered across the planet's often turbulent seas. But they were there: the provisional capital of the newly formed Galactic Alliance and birthplace of two intelligent species was called home by more than twenty-seven billion people, including the legendary Admiral Ackbar and Jedi Master Cilghal. From up on high it was impossible to appreciate the hard times Mon Calamari had seen under the resurrected clone of Emperor Palpatine and the renegade Admiral Daala—hard times that the inhabitants of the planet could well see again before this war with the Yuuzhan Vong was over.

That's the beauty of an ocean world, Jaina Solo thought as she guided her X-wing down to the port city Hikahi. *It shows no scars.*

"XJ-Three-Twenty-three, you're clear to dock," came the distinctive Mon Calamari voice. "Proceed to Bay DA-Forty-two."

She gritted her teeth as blast scoring on the fuselage of her X-wing caught the atmosphere on reentry, provoking a violent shudder that made her R2 unit squawk in alarm.

Moments later, as the X-wing glided in toward the docking bays, the droid tootled a short series of beeps and blips. She glanced at her craft's translator and smiled at her R2's message.

"No, I'm sure Mon Cal's high salinity levels won't be too good for your electronics," she said. "But it really shouldn't be too much of a problem, Cappie. I didn't bring you here to go swimming."

Kyp Durron met her when she landed. Her former squadron leader looked tired and drawn, seemingly much older than when she'd last seen him a couple of weeks earlier.

"Nice to see you, Colonel," he said.

"Sorry I'm late," she said, tugging off her flight helmet and slipping it under an arm. "There were delays making sure Twin Suns was adequately berthed. Did I miss the meeting?"

"Afraid so," he said as they walked together from the docking bays. "But that's okay. I get the feeling that everything's being decided behind the scenes. Gathering us together was just a formality—a way of reminding us that there's a bigger picture. You know?"

Jaina nodded absently, only half listening.

"Is Tahiri here?" she asked after a few paces.

Kyp looked at her, his brow wrinkling. "No. Why?"

She shrugged as she continued walking, not meeting his eyes. She didn't want him to see how deep her concern ran. "It's probably nothing," she lied. "She left a message for me for when I docked at *Ralroost*. She said she wanted to talk to me as soon as I arrived. She sounded . . ."

Kyp waited for her to continue, but when she didn't he asked, "What, Jaina? What did she say?"

Jaina struggled to remember just how the girl had sounded. "I don't know, Kyp," she said. "It wasn't so much what she said as the way she said it. I just got the impression that something was wrong."

"Well, if she is here on Mon Cal," he said, "she didn't come to the meeting."

An upwelling of concern for the girl—no, young *woman*, Jaina corrected herself; Tahiri was a Jedi Knight now—rushed through her. Tahiri had been close to Anakin. If dealing with his loss had been half as hard for Tahiri as it had been for Jaina, then she could certainly understand the odd note of grief that had been evident in her voice. But why now? Why did Tahiri want to speak to *her*?

"Jag's here," Kyp said, and the feeling those simple words inspired surprised her.

"Really? Where?" She kept her gaze ahead as they continued through the maze of corridors, hopeful that this would be enough to prevent him seeing how her cheeks had flushed at the mention of Jag's name.

"Right now he's in a meeting with your parents, actually," Kyp said. "They're hatching some sort of scheme." He stopped abruptly and turned to face her. "There's talk of winning this thing, Jaina," he said. "A *lot* of talk. It's almost hysterical. Before Ebaq Nine we were all but beaten; now you'd think we already had the Yuuzhan Vong on the run."

Jaina nodded. She understood perfectly what he was trying to tell her, and why. The politicians had no real idea what it was like on the battlefield. They were insulated by layers of command from the action, from how things really were. For all the losses they'd suffered, she'd always tried to maintain a sense of optimism, but even though they had recently made considerable headway, she knew they still had a long way to go. There were no certainties. There never was with war.

But she could sympathize with the politicians *wanting* to believe that victory was imminent. This war had been hard on everyone. Years of defeats, inexorable advances by the enemies, losses in every quarter—it had all taken its toll. She could see it in Kyp's eyes and in the way he seemed to have aged. She could feel it in herself, the grief for Chewbacca and Anakin still strong, her descent into the dark side painfully recent . . .

"I'll be careful," she said, vanquishing the memory with a firm nod. People would be taking sides everywhere in the makeshift capital. She wasn't going to commit to anything without first learning something of what was going on "behind the scenes," as Kyp had put it.

Kyp resumed their walk, moving confidently through the warren of tunnels. He had obviously been on Mon Cal long enough to familiarize himself with the city. The deeper into the city they went, the more crowded the corridors became, and the more hurried the activities of the people became. Jaina saw beings of varied species, sexes, and sizes going about all manner of duties. Technicians rubbed shoulders with bureaucrats while armed soldiers bumped into secretaries, and through it all trundled myriad droids. The air rang with industry and purpose, which was more than a little overwhelming for Jaina after the confines of her X-wing and only her R2 unit for conversation.

"I'm sorry," Kyp said, recognizing her discomfort. "Perhaps we should have taken a tunnel cab. I just thought you would have had enough of being cooped up in small spaces."

"No, that's okay," she said. "I did need to stretch my legs a little."

It wasn't just the exercise she was grateful for, though. It also gave her the opportunity to ground herself. Had she stepped off her X-wing and walked straight into a meeting, she would never have gained a feeling for the place. There was a vitality here that she found invigorating. Out of the chaos, some sense of order was returning, even if people couldn't agree on what to do with it. This was what she was fighting for; the future of her civilization was being decided in these halls as much as it was in the vast battlefields of space.

Finally the corridors widened and the crowds thinned slightly. There was space to walk abreast, and the noise level dropped enough for them to talk about the finer points of squadron command without having to shout to be heard. Kyp seemed to find a measure of comfort in relatively mundane talk of promising new tactics and pilots. Their ships, like the staff that flew them and maintained them, were showing signs of fatigue. Little repairs had to be constantly performed to ensure they didn't escalate into something more catastrophic: fatigue was insidious, be it metal or mental. The principle was the same, she supposed, at all levels of the resistance.

They eventually came to a door guarded by two Mon Calamari security staff. The guards brought their coral pikes up in a brief salute before guiding them through. Inside, leaning over a wide screen displaying dozens of detailed maps and charts, were Jaina's parents, Han Solo and Leia Organa Solo. Standing between them was a tall, dark-complexioned woman with her hair pulled back in a tight bun. Jaina recognized her as a former New Republic Intelligence officer. Also there, just as Kyp had said he would be, was Jag Fel. All looked up when they entered, but it was to Jag that Jaina's attention was drawn.

She was delighted to see his face break out into a smile upon seeing her, even if that smile was just as quickly stifled. She had learned early on in their friendship that he didn't approve of public displays of affection. When his time came to formally greet her, he would do so with a stiff nod and perhaps a tight handshake—but that was all. It didn't bother Jaina; just the knowledge that the affection was there at all was enough for her. She would carry that quick smile with her for the rest of the day, until they could find time to be alone later.

"Jaina." Her mother stepped over to enfold her in a tight, warm hug. Since Anakin's death, her mother's embraces had become more frequent and were delivered with more passion than ever before. It was almost as though every time she saw either Jacen or Jaina these days, she was overcome with relief.

Her father's large hand ran through her hair, stopping at her shoulder to squeeze gently. "Good to see you, kid," he said with a wry smile.

"You too, Dad." She reached up and kissed him on the cheek. The prickliness of his chin, the scent of his unkempt hair, and the sight of his lopsided smile—the familiarity of these simple aspects of her father brought with it a sense of comfort she had always felt around him. For all her mother's efforts, Han Solo still had a slightly disreputable air. Jaina had been told by some that she had inherited a portion of that, while her twin brother had gotten their mother's thoughtful nature.

"Where's Jacen?" she asked, taking a step back from both of them.

"Your uncle Luke has him working on something else," her mother explained. "He'll meet you when we're finished."

Jaina caught Jag's eye and was completely thrown for a second when he winked at her. For the second time that day she felt a blush forming, so she turned away, looking for a distraction in the Intelligence operative standing before the luminous star charts.

"Belindi, isn't it?" Jaina said, searching her memory. She stepped over to the woman and extended a hand.

The woman gave a single, respectful nod. "Belindi Kalenda, that's right," she said. "Chief Omas has asked me to coordinate an operation involving your parents—and you, if you're willing."

"And that's where I check out," Kyp said.

"You're leaving?" Jaina asked, surprised.

He nodded, shrugging, the flickering lights from the map painting his features with an assortment of colors. "My job was only to escort you here, I'm afraid," he said with exaggerated disappointment.

Jaina smiled at this. "The great Kyp Durron reduced to being a delivery boy, eh?" she teased. "Who'd have thought? And to think, you once offered to take me on as an apprentice, too! Glad I didn't take that route."

"You're a funny girl, you know that?" he said in return. "For a Solo, that is." He didn't give her chance to respond. "But listen, if you feel like catching up later, why not stop by at the Ocean's Floor café for a drink? Bring young Jag here along, too. He can show you the way." He offered a mock salute before turning to leave. Then, at the door, he faced her again. "And if you like, I'll make a few inquiries about Tahiri for you," he said more seriously.

She smiled her appreciation at him. "Thanks, Kyp," she said softly.

When he was gone, Belindi Kalenda quickly summarized the mission for Jaina's benefit. The others stood by patiently, interjecting a few words here and there to help clarify certain aspects of the plan. It sounded simple enough: travel the open hyperlanes fixing communications links and reminding the locals that they were still part of a galactic civilization. Jaina was sure it wouldn't be so easy in practice, though. The Yuuzhan Vong, by mining the major hyperspace routes, had left some areas isolated for as long as two years. No one knew with any certainty just what was happening inside such regions, but there had been rumors of local despots seizing control while attention was focused elsewhere. It was probably safe to assume that, in some places at least, their welcome wouldn't really be heartfelt.

She loosened the tabs on her flight uniform and participated in an hour or so of discussion regarding the mission objectives. There would be numerous opportunities to coordinate with local governments and such organizations as the Smugglers' Alliance along the way, although it was difficult to plan for anything in advance with so little known for certain about most areas.

At one point an orderly brought some refreshments for them: raw pointer fish cuts and lampfish tongue, along with tall glasses of chilled Calamarian water. Although she was hungry, Jaina only picked at the salty comestibles while she listened to her parents debate the best way to structure the mission itself. There was no bitterness or anger to the argument; they simply disagreed over the details and weren't afraid to say so. In the end, though, it was Leia whose opinion made the most sense, so Han backed down without acrimony. Where once he might have taken offense at the suggestion that the *Falcon* wouldn't be enough to ensure the safety and success of the mission, now he just shrugged and let common sense rule.

The mission, Jaina was told, would be comprised of one fighter squadron, the *Millennium Falcon,* and a recommissioned *Lancer*-class frigate called *Pride of Selonia* under the command of a Captain Todra Mayn, recently relegated to less active duties after being injured at Coruscant. Mayn would defer to Leia and Han in all matters regarding the mission, as would the leader of the fighter squadron. There didn't seem like much else left to decide upon, except, perhaps, for where exactly the mission would proceed first of all. Jaina felt as though there was little she could contribute. Jag, too, was quiet for the better part of the discussion, although she had no doubt that he was paying as close attention to everything that was being said as she was. The three people doing the talking, Belindi Kalenda and Jaina's parents, didn't seem to notice that their more youthful audience was remaining silent.

After several minutes spent discussing the relative benefits of Antar 4 and Melida/Daan, Jaina leaned across the screen and broke in. "Is there any particular reason that I'm here?" She kept the frustration from her tone as best she could. "It just seems to me that I have very little part to play in this plan of yours."

Leia looked at Han, who backed away from the screen with a gesture that implied the answer was obvious. "You're here because we want you here," he said.

Jaina had learned to mistrust any nonchalance her father displayed. It usually meant that he was uncomfortable about something.

"Why?" she pressed.

"Because we need a military escort," her mother explained. "That fighter squadron has to come from somewhere."

"Why Twin Suns, though? There must be others you could take."

"That's true, sweetheart," her father said. "But—"

"Don't 'sweetheart' me, Dad," she cut in irritably. "There's something you aren't telling me."

"Listen to what we *are* telling you," Leia said, taking a step toward her daughter. "This mission is important, and we want the best pilots accompanying us."

"But I have work to do *here*! There are the new pilots to train, new simulators to program. The war isn't going to stop just because you're off on a jaunt to reunite the galaxy, Mom. I can't just dump everything and leave!"

"Your training work will continue during the mission," her mother said calmly, moving in to place a reassuring hand on her shoulder. "I'm proposing to allow Lowbacca to form his own squadron with the pilots you've trained. The gaps left in Twin Suns you can make up from Chiss Squadron. There's still a lot to learn from each other."

"Yes, but—"

"What are you afraid of, Jaina?" her father joined in, moving to Leia's side. "The war's still going to be there when you get back. That much, at least, I can promise you."

Feeling set upon, she turned to Jag for support, but he just shrugged helplessly. For a split second she felt a rush of anger at him, too, but she knew that was ridiculous. He would never side against her out of spite; if he was backing her parents now then it was only because he believed they were right.

"Don't be too hard on your parents," Belindi Kalenda said, shifting awkwardly on the far side of the flat display. "This was my idea."

Jaina asked Jag, "I take it you'll be staying here, then?"

"Actually, no," he said. "I'll be going along with you."

She turned to her parents, then looked back at Jag. "As part of Twin Suns?"

"It's not the first time, and probably won't be the last."

"We like the idea of having two experienced squadron leaders," her father said, "especially with a mix of Chiss and your pilots in the air. This way we can have one leader groundside with us at all times, while the other remains up in orbit to keep an eye on things."

Jaina sighed in defeat.

Deep down, she knew it made good tactical sense, but she still didn't like it. She couldn't shake the feeling that her parents weren't telling her the whole truth. Part of her felt as though they were doing this to give her a rest, but weren't prepared to say so because they knew the reaction they'd receive. And if that was the case, they were right. The idea of being put out to pasture was offensive to her in the extreme.

But whatever their true motives were for wanting her along, the fact was that she was going. The only saving grace in all of this was the fact that Jag was going along also, which meant that they'd at least be able to spend more time together . . .

Her thoughts were distracted by the buzzing of her comlink. Turning away from the meeting, she pulled it from her uniform belt clip and raised it to her lips. Before she could even say a word, however, the panicked and choked-up voice of Tahiri issued from the small gadget in her hand.

"Jaina?"

Out of the corner of her eye, Jaina saw her mother's eyes widen in surprise.

"Tahiri, where are you?" Jaina asked, already reaching out into the Force in search of the girl. She was nearby, and for that, at least, Jaina was thankful. "You said you wanted to see me. You said it was urgent."

"Jaina, I'm so sorry. I was—I—he—"

Jaina was struck by a powerful psychic pain emanating from the girl—a pain so great that it had spilled over into the world around her. She attempted to offer comfort to Tahiri through the Force, extending herself so that she could mentally embrace her and ease her torment. But the emotions were too intense—too raw.

"Tahiri, what's wrong? What's happened?"

"It's Anakin."

"Anakin? What about Anakin?"

"He—" Again Tahiri's voice ceased in midsentence. It was almost as though something was stopping her from speaking. Then, all of a sudden, the words burst free from her: "He's trying to kill me, Jaina. Anakin wants me dead!"

The accompanying sensation of distress broadcast through the Force peaked, then abruptly disappeared. At the same time, the comlink signal ceased.

"Tahiri? *Tahiri?*" Jaina reattached her comlink to her belt and faced her mother, who was rubbing her forehead in obvious discomfort. "You felt it?" she asked.

Leia nodded in confirmation. "She's in trouble, Jaina."

Jaina didn't need her mother to tell her that. Even those not Force-sensitive could have figured it out just from the sound of Tahiri's voice.

She turned to Kalenda and said, "We need a trace on her comlink—and fast."

The Intelligence officer nodded and turned away to speak into her own comlink.

Jaina's father came up and put a reassuring hand on his daughter's shoulder. "It'll be all right, honey."

She nodded, but wasn't convinced.

"Tahiri's been missing for almost two weeks now," Leia said. "She didn't respond to Luke's call for a meeting of the Jedi. We didn't know where she'd gone or what she was doing."

"She called me." Jaina winced, remembering the pain she had just felt radiating from Tahiri's mind. She should have made more of an effort to contact the girl as soon as she arrived. She might have been able to prevent it—whatever it was that had happened.

"I have a location," Kalenda said shortly. "Lane eighteen-A, level three. I've sent someone to investigate."

"Do you know the way?"

"Yes, of course."

"Take me." Jaina was on her way to the door before the woman had time to respond. If there was one thing Jaina had learned about command, it was that you didn't give people the opportunity to argue—*especially* in emergencies.

The security officer took charge as soon as they left the conference room. Jaina was close on Kalenda's heels, with her parents and Jag not far behind. Moving with rapid steps through the wide corridors of the city, weaving naturally through the bustling crowds, Kalenda led them up a level and across several high and arched thoroughfares. Jaina resisted urging the woman to go faster. If Tahiri had already moved on from the source of the transmissions, then running wasn't going to change anything. Instead, Jaina reached into the Force to try and find the girl; to reassure her, help her . . . But she was unable to feel her anywhere, and that only heightened her concern.

Kalenda's comlink squawked. Still walking, she listened for a moment, then, after half a dozen steps, she faced Jaina. "What does your friend look like?"

Jaina pictured the young Jedi in her mind. "Human, blond hair, green eyes, a little shorter than me."

"I think they've got her," Kalenda said. "Security has found someone answering your friend's description near the site of the last transmission. A medical team is on the scene."

Jaina felt a chill run through her. "Medical team? Why? What's wrong? Is she—?"

"We're almost there," Kalenda said. "It's just up another couple of levels. Here, climb onto this."

The security officer commandeered a passing hovertaxi, quickly speaking her clearance and authority codes to the droid operating it.

"This will be quicker," she said. "The lanes tend to get more congested the higher up you go."

The narrow vehicle rocked as they all clambered in.

There was enough room for only four passengers; Han was forced to stand on the cab's outer footboard and hang on. He had to crouch down slightly when the droid guided the cab into one of the ducts reserved for emergency vehicles. Sometimes, Belindi Kalenda explained, it was the only way to ensure a quick and unobstructed passage to the city's higher levels.

As she sat in the front of the cab, staring vaguely as the damp and craggy walls of the duct raced by, Jaina felt her mother's hand squeeze her arm in reassurance. And while the gesture was appreciated, it didn't really help. The absence of Tahiri in the Force was making her sick with worry.

The cab spat out of the vent into a vast market area. The entire place was in a dome, the sides of which rippled and shimmered with golden water that cascaded gently, and impossibly, down its surface, while hanging from the uppermost section were thick, lush vines that swayed hypnotically in the humid air. Below, the area was heaving with activity as hundreds of individuals went about their everyday business of trading everything from food to parts of old household service droids. Among all the hustle and bustle, though, one section stood out from all the rest. A large crowd had gathered around an area that security officers and droids were attempting to cordon off so that the medical team Kalenda had mentioned could get in.

Unable to negotiate any closer to the scene because of the curious onlookers, the cab came to a halt and all five passengers quickly alighted, with Jaina roughly forcing her way through the crowd that stood between her and Tahiri. A security guard stopped her when she tried to cross the perimeter of the cordoned-off area, allowing her to pass only when Kalenda flashed her ID and instructed the guard to let them through.

Jaina froze when she saw the supine figure being attended to by the two members of the Mon Cal medical team and their MD-5 droid. At first she didn't even recognize her: Tahiri had cut her hair short, and she'd lost a lot of weight. There were bags under her eyes and a hollowness to her cheeks; her face looked as though it hadn't been washed in days. Worst of all, though, were her arms: they were covered in bloody slash marks.

"Is this her?" one of the medics asked.

She wanted to say yes, but the girl lying before her looked like a completely different person from the Tahiri she knew.

As Jaina watched, Tahiri stirred. From an apparent state of deep unconsciousness, she twitched and tried to roll over. The medics did their best to restrain her, but she was stronger than she looked. With arms flailing around and her eyes wide and unseeing, she tried to stand up, but was failed by her unsteady legs.

"Anakin?" she screamed. "Anakin!"

Her eyes caught Jaina's the same instant one of the medics stuck a spray hypo against her throat. The hiss of the spray coincided with an intense surge through the Force, as Jaina felt Tahiri's panic and terror rush into her all at once. Then Tahiri slumped face-forward into the embrace of the droid and the surge faded.

It was only when she exhaled that Jaina realized she had been holding her breath. She felt comforted and warmed by the presence of Jag at her side, but just for once she wished he would forget his ideas about displays of affection in public and simply hold her.

"*Is* this her?" the medical officer repeated, turning to Jaina now that they had managed to settle Tahiri.

Jaina nodded dumbly in response.

"You don't seem too sure," the officer said.

"No, I'm sure," she said. "That's her. Her name is

Tahiri Veila. I don't know what she might have done here, but she's not a criminal. She's a Jedi Knight."

The medic nodded his understanding. "We'll treat her gently, I promise."

Jaina watched on as Tahiri was placed onto a waiting hovercart and carried away.

"Please give us some space," she heard the droid instruct the crowd. "This is an emergency. Please make room."

Jaina backed away, clutching Jag's arm for support. A wave of dizziness rolled over her. From the other side of the city, she could feel her twin, Jacen, asking her what was wrong, but she didn't have an answer for him just yet. All she knew was the mixed-up jumble of feelings she had received from Tahiri's mind. The incredible, overwhelming sorrow she could understand; she invariably felt the same thing whenever she dwelled on the death of her brother. But below that had been something else—something that Jaina would have thought Tahiri incapable of. It was an emotion she had never felt from the girl before, and its intensity frightened her. But it was there, and it was real.

It was hatred—a deep and unremitting hatred . . .

The smell of burning flesh was the first thing she was able to clearly identify. It was unmistakable—a smell so caustic and pungent that it crept like a dung-worm through her nose, furiously writhing its way into her olfactory nerve center to ensure that she never forgot it. And how could she? It was so overwhelming that she felt sure she'd never be free of it, no matter how far she could get from this place.

It was close, too—so close, in fact, that she found herself checking her own arms to make sure her own skin wasn't smoldering. All she saw, though, was a layer of ash that had settled over her like a fine and gentle snow. And beneath that . . .

She hid her arms in the folds of her robes, looking again into the thick smoke. She could hear movement and voices, but no matter how much she squinted and strained, she couldn't make anything out through the haze. And constantly in the background came the *snap* and *fsst* of the fires consuming flesh, along with the occasional *crack* from what she imagined to be bones breaking in the extreme heat. But she still couldn't make anything out, no matter how much she squinted.

She took a couple of cautious steps forward until her feet came to the edge of the rocky outcrop upon which she was standing and was able to make out what was happening. Down below she could see a compound, and in it a ceremony was taking place. Those gathered there had their faces concealed beneath hoods, and they were all dressed in robes similar to the one she was wearing. They seemed to have been waiting for her arrival, for when they saw her emerge from the smoke they automatically began the ceremony proper, chanting as they marched around the compound. It was a language that was at once alien as it was familiar—a language that simultaneously terrified and comforted her. These emotions were not generated by the words themselves, however, but rather the culture this language was rooted in.

She ignored the proceedings, looking instead about the five-sided compound. In each corner there stood an immense effigy of a god, each one staring down toward a pit at its feet. The priests were filing past these pits in turn, casually tossing into the smoking holes what she instinctively knew to be various body parts. In accordance with her ambiguous emotions, she found herself both warmed and repulsed by the sight, with one part of her wishing to give thanks to the gods that accepted these offerings, while another, deeper part of her wanted to throw up from the smell emanating from the pits.

The effigies that rose into the shadows she knew well—all except one. The farthest one from where she stood was a god unlike any she had seen before; she felt it did not even belong here with the others. It was mostly hidden in the shadows, rising like a giant snake high above the other graven images around the compound. Its presence was a blasphemy she wanted to protest against, but she couldn't because she felt it was here *because* of her. Its eyes—they weren't staring into the pit like the other statues, they were staring at *her*. More than that: those immense, red eyes were *accusing* her.

Why did you leave me? she heard it whisper into her thoughts.

She wanted to flee. The part of her that had been comforted by the ceremony was suddenly panicked and scared. But there was nowhere for her to go. All the passages leading into the mortuary were closed, plugged up by yorik coral.

She didn't have time to dwell on it, however. One of the priests had caught her attention and was waving at her to watch the burning of the body parts in the pits. But whose body was it? And what was it? Human? Yuuzhan Vong? It was impossible to tell from such a distance.

Other priests motioned for her to watch. She frowned in confusion as she leaned precariously over the lip of the pit. What was it they wanted her to see?

She saw.

The body parts weren't being destroyed—they were being remade. They were crawling from their individual fires over to the unnaturally large pyre blazing in the compound's center, immersing themselves into the blue-and-orange flames. The fire licked at each of the parts—taking the quivering mat of skin and wrapping it around the pulsing organs, collecting the limbs and snapping them back into place in the appropriate socket.

She turned to the snake statue, beseeching it to stop. Through the choking smoke it no longer looked like a reptile, though. It looked like . . . But, no. The smoke was too thick by far to allow her to make anything out clearly. All she could discern was its eyes, red and penetrating in the oppressive gloom of the chamber—its stare no longer upon her, but rather focused on the events taking place in the compound below.

She looked down to see a figure stepping from the pyre, its skin blistering from the heat.

"Please," she whispered to the reptile, begging for forgiveness.

"Please," the figure from the flames echoed at the same time—also to the reptile, but for a different reason. It seemed to be pleading with the statue for life, as though the reptile had the power to grant or deny this.

Then suddenly, without warning, the figure from the flames turned to face her up on the rocks. The burns on the skin had vanished, and all that remained now were scars. But even with this disfigurement, she was still able to recognize the face. It was like looking directly into a mirror . . .

She turned and fled into the shadows and smoke, effortlessly smashing the yorik coral plug that had formed over the passage through which she'd initially entered, fleeing into the darkness of the tunnel, running from the abomination with her face . . .

"A living *planet*?" Danni Quee's voice possessed a rising tone of incredulity. "You're not talking about Zonama Sekot, are you?"

"Good," Master Luke said. "You've heard of it."

"I've also heard of the Algnadesh Ship Graveyards,

and the Lost Treasure of Boro-borosa, but that doesn't mean I'm going to go halfway around the galaxy looking for them. Every astronomer who's worked the Outer Rim knows about Zonama Sekot. They know it doesn't exist, for starters."

Saba Sebatyne tensed. In Barabel society, expressing doubts over a superior's decision in such an open manner would certainly result in a challenge, and a challenge meant a blood fight. Although she had turned her back on some of her people's more aggressive ways, she still found herself a prisoner to her upbringing. It was something she would probably battle the rest of her life—especially now that her people were no more. How, after all, was one to fight a ghost?

"I understand your reaction." Master Luke smiled patiently. "It's not the first time I've gotten this response, believe me. If you'll allow me to explain my reasons, though, I'm sure you'll come around . . ."

Jedi Master Luke Skywalker's explanation sent tingles of excitement through Saba's joy-starved brain. *A living world?* Her tail coiled and uncoiled reflexively from the excitement such a notion stirred. Of all the wonders she had seen since leaving Barab I, a sentient planet would have to be the most profound.

Her mind froze as another level of significance to the Master's words occurred to her. *He's telling me because he intends for this one to go with him,* she thought to herself, her slitlike eyes widening at the idea. She couldn't help but feel both wonder and despair at the thought. She would have to decline. She had no choice. And with that thought, her mind drifted . . .

The Master's office was not ostentatious. It contained a plain desk and three chairs suitable for people of various species. Occupying those chairs were Saba, Danni, and the healer Master Cilghal. A hologram of the Master's son, Ben, repeated every forty seconds in one corner of the desk. Saba's eyes were caught by it, entranced by the innocent play of the child. She vividly remembered the one time she had met him, while he was on a brief holiday from the Maw. The Jedi Master's son, although still very young, was already used to the many different shapes and sizes in which life presented itself in the galaxy, and so had displayed no alarm at the sight of Saba's naturally fierce demeanor. Quelling the grief at losing so many young of her own kind, Saba had flared her nostrils back and grinned with all her teeth unfolded. She was delighted to see the boy respond with a bright, wide smile that stretched from his mouth right up to his deep, steel-blue eyes.

Her eyebrow ridges drew closer together in a frown. The memory was a sobering one. Everyone, it seemed, had lost something during the war with the Yuuzhan Vong. Many people had lost their homes, their families, their lives. She herself had lost her Master and her apprentices before watching Barab I die. Her complicity in the destruction of her people slowed her recovery, made her doubt her own abilities as a fighter—but to be reminded of what she was supposed to be fighting for made her feel slightly better.

Life. The future. A single child's smile.

"Are you sure it's safe?" Master Cilghal asked from behind her. Woken from her daze, Saba turned slightly in her seat so she could watch both the Mon Calamari healer and Master Skywalker at the same time.

"Look at it this way," Master Luke said. "If we stay here on Mon Cal, we're at ground zero for Yuuzhan Vong retaliation. We're also prime targets for Peace Brigade action. I doubt there will be anything as dangerous as either of those possibilities in the Unknown Regions."

"With all due respect, Master Skywalker, we don't

know what's in there. That's why it's called 'Unknown.' "

Danni Quee would know, Saba assumed. The human scientist had started life as an astronomer and only by circumstance moved into specializing in the enemy's works.

"Exactly," Master Skywalker said, acknowledging the point with a patient nod. "But this is an exploratory mission, not a military one. We're not going to pick fights."

"You'll try to stop them if you find them, though."

"That is the nature of the job." Master Luke smiled. "Will you come?"

Danni shrugged in a way that implied she was helpless to make him see reason. "Of course. I wouldn't miss it for the world."

"And you, Master Cilghal, have you reconsidered your decision?"

"I have, Master Skywalker." The healer stood, bowing her head. "But I have not changed my mind. I am needed here. There is too much work for me to do, too many people to teach in the ways we have lost. It would be irresponsible of me to leave now."

The words implied another challenge, but the manner of neither Master acknowledged it.

"I understand," Master Skywalker said smoothly, "although I am sorry we won't have you with us."

"I recommend my apprentice, Tekli, to go in my place."

"Thank you, Cilghal. We would be delighted to have her aboard. With Danni, Mara, myself, and Jacen, our complement is almost complete." Master Skywalker turned to address Saba, presumably to invite her to join him and the others on the mission to the sentient planet. Saba's powerful heart raced—

—but before he could speak he frowned, and his attention turned inward for a moment. A look of concern flashed across his face.

"Master?" Saba said.

"I'm sorry," he said. "I thought—"

Master Cilghal's comlink buzzed at that moment. She answered it, listening intently to the tiny voice issuing from it. "Take her to the infirmary. I'll be there immediately." Standing, she said, "I'm sorry, Luke. It's Tahiri."

"Where is she?" asked Master Skywalker, also standing. "Is she hurt?"

"She's here in the city," Cilghal explained, moving hurriedly toward the door. "Medics found her a few moments ago, unconscious. I've advised Tekli to bring her in. I'll go there now to supervise her examination."

"I'll alert Mara," Master Skywalker said as Cilghal left the room. "She'll want to be there. And Jacen, too."

"What about you, Hisser?" Danni asked as the Master reached for his comlink to make the call. "Will you come?"

For a moment Saba was confused. "There iz little this one could do for Tahiri—"

"No, the mission." The young human woman reached across the space between them to touch her arm. "It sounds crazy, but Vergere knew what she was talking about. Are you going to come along?"

Saba froze, barely hearing Danni's words. Few humans touched her. Barabels were best known for their violent—some would even say barbarous—ways, and it was well known that a wrong gesture or word could be enough to provoke a challenge. Sometimes they became the target of status-proving assaults from other species— usually by adolescents going out of their way do so in order to prove that they weren't afraid of what might happen as a result. In days gone by she might have ruthlessly shown them that they *should* be afraid—but now she was a Jedi Knight, and she had learned to quell such automatic impulses. Or so she'd thought.

Danni was a friend. They had worked together in the past. She trusted Saba not to hurt her.

She quelled the reflex to strike out, but she couldn't quell the dismay that filled her at what might happen if she made the same mistake again. She had attacked the wrong people once already. How was she ever to make up for that?

"It would be an honor to accompany you on any mission," she said, "but it would be better if you found someone else. Someone whose judgment haz not proven to be so poor."

"It's not your fault—" Danni began.

"Their deathz were from this one's hands." Saba shook her head solemnly. "Their memory iz this one's accuzer. This one failed to feel the people trapped in that slaveship because of anger and hatred—blinded by dark emotions. If this one had shown more control, they might still be alive today."

"That's true," Master Skywalker said. Saba looked up. She hadn't noticed the Master finish his calls. "And they might be slaves of the Yuuzhan Vong, too. Or food. Wishing that things were otherwise does nothing to erase memories. Wounds do not heal by ignoring them."

"This one appreciatez what you are trying to do," she said with quiet regret, turning to face him, "but I cannot."

"We're not asking you to come out of sympathy, Saba. We—*I* am asking you to come because you are a Jedi Knight, and we need your help. Your life sensitivity has grown enormously since the loss of your people. You have to admit that we could use someone like that, where we're going." He watched her, gauging her reaction. "Do you really want me to *order* you along?"

The thick black plates covering her body stiffened. "I

would not like to fail you, Master. If I fail again, my people fail with me."

"So don't fail, Saba." The Master smiled. "Think of it as a hunt—one last hunt for the honor of your people. How better could they be remembered?"

That thought caught her. What the Master was proposing wasn't a battle in which victory meant instant death for one side. The quest to find Zonama Sekot would be played out over weeks, maybe months, through dangerous and uncharted territories. There would be clues to discover, trails to follow, traps to unravel. They would have to be stealthy, keen-sensed, and quick-witted. Who knew where it would lead them, or what they might find at the end of it?

Her tail thumped the floor. Part of her responded to the challenge—and there *was* a challenge implicit in the Master's voice. A reminder of who she had been, and still was on many levels. She was a hunter, the end result of generations of breeding and a lifetime of instincts. If anyone could hunt a living planet, it would be her.

How better could they be remembered?

"If you've no further objections," Master Luke said, "I'd call that settled. You'll come with us on the hunt for Zonama Sekot."

Saba vacillated for a few seconds longer, then acquiesced with a nod. A hunt was better than waiting around Mon Cal for the Yuuzhan Vong to attack.

"This one will come," she said.

His smile widened. "Thank you, Saba."

"I'm glad," Danni added, squeezing her arm tightly, then letting go.

Saba dipped her head in a gesture anyone familiar with Barabels would instantly recognize: honored obeisance with overtones of awe.

"Now," said the Master, standing, "let's go find out what happened to Tahiri."

Deep in the bowels of Yuuzhan'tar, a cloaked figure moved stealthily through the shadows. His ooglith masquer was failing, drying around the edges and beginning to peel away, rejecting the face beneath just as the society to which he had once belonged had rejected him. Those living above him—in that artificial landscape that had once been known as Coruscant but was now named after the legendary Yuuzhan Vong homeworld—they would surely kill him if they ever found him. He knew that without question. They had tried often enough in the last couple of months he'd been forced to live in the filthy underworld of this revolting planet. But Nom Anor had no intentions of letting them find him just yet. He had learned to hide well in these artificial caverns and tunnels, among the abandoned machines that littered the underworld. It made him sick to have to dwell among such abominations, but it was necessary if he was to survive—and he *would* survive.

He moved furtively along the artificial roads, cursing under his breath as he silently damned the one who had effectively destroyed him. He lashed out at one of the numerous droid husks standing in his way, not caring that the rusty metal gashed his fingers. His insides burned with anger at the contemplation of his fall. Should he remain down here another ten years, he knew he would never forget that betrayal, and *never* surrender his anger.

When the quiet had finally settled around the noisy clatter of the droid he had just smashed, he continued walking—a fugitive in this forsaken and forgotten underworld. He knew that his thoughts were slightly imbalanced, that isolation and near starvation were taking their toll. But that did nothing to undermine his determination to survive.

The deep, artificial caverns of Yuuzhan'tar were places he'd had no great wish to visit, let alone flee to. The invading armies of the Yuuzhan Vong had flushed all manner of vermin from them, including entire cultures that had existed in the crawlspaces of the original inhabitants' government. Strange, wild-eyed outcasts all, they had been either sacrificed as part of Warmaster Tsavong Lah's purification program, or turned into slaves or soldiers for use in further battles. Once the caverns had been declared empty, they had been abandoned, and ignored as irrelevant. The new warmaster, Nas Choka, recently recalled from Hutt space, had continued the purification campaign. Everyone had assumed that the underground ruins were empty still . . .

As he stood dripping blood from his cut fingers, he began to realize that a new sound had joined those far-off echoes—something other than just the sounds of dripping water and creaking of old metal. In fact, someone was coming toward him. A whispered voice was amplified by the walls around him into a faint susurrus, like that of a faint and distant wind.

Nom Anor wrapped his bleeding hand in the remains of his cloak to prevent it from leaving a trail and ducked into a nearby alcove. He strained to listen to what was being said by the approaching voice, but it was impossible to discern. He couldn't even decide how many there were. He presumed the voice had an audience, but could hear no other footfalls.

He tore off the dying ooglith masquer and tossed it to the ground. If it was another search party sent to find him, then the disguise would be of no use anyway. And if it wasn't a search party, then he would need every sense available to him. Either way, the masquer had become irrelevant to his needs.

A ragged figure carrying a dull, bioluminescent lamp came around the corner, heading in the opposite direction to Nom Anor. The figure was hunched and unkempt, its robes flapping around it like the wings of some uncoordinated flying beast. It was muttering one phrase over and over, hoarsely and under its breath:

"Sha grunnik ith-har Yun-Shuno. Sha grunnik ith-har Yun-Shuno."

He recognized the phrase. It was a simple incantation to the gods, asking for clemency. The incantation wasn't directed to one of the gods to whom the former acquaintances of Nom Anor had appealed. It was intended for Yun-Shuno, the thousand-eyed deity of those who had failed or been outcast from Yuuzhan Vong society—the Shamed Ones, as they were known.

With that realization, all worry of capture left him. The creature was a Shamed One, and he therefore had nothing to fear. Shimrra would never send a Shamed One to do a warrior's job—and even if the Shamed One guessed who he was, the lowly creature would have no reason to turn him in.

Nom Anor waited until the Shamed One came abreast of his hiding place, then stepped out in front of it, quickly and with menace. His sudden appearance had the desired effect: the Shamed One—a middle-aged male—reared back, flapping his robes in terror before collapsing to the ground, squealing as he begged for mercy.

"This place is forbidden to all of Yun-Yuuzhan's children!" Nom Anor boomed down to the prostrate figure. "Explain your presence here!"

"Have mercy, Master! I am nothing—not worthy even of your contempt! The gods have spurned me and I crawl like a worm through the belly of the world!"

"I know what you're doing," Nom Anor spat. "I'm not blind, fool! But you still haven't told me *why* you are doing it. Stand up and address my face!" The plaeryin bol in his left eye socket tensed, ready to spit venom should the Shamed One show any sign of recognizing him.

The scruffy creature raised himself to a hunched crouch, holding his lamp upward in supplication. His face in the dim light was lumpy and twisted; his eyes were crooked, and his nose seemed to be on the verge of sliding right off his face. The result of poor breeding practice, Nom Anor observed disgustedly to himself.

"I am lost, Master. That is all. I swear it! I was separated from my work detail and became confused. I tried to follow their voices, but the echoes confused me. I am worthless and humble and submit to your will in all things, Master."

The Shamed One bent low, still mumbling his apologies and supplications. Nom Anor pushed him roughly backward with one foot. The former executor knew a liar when he met one. The question was, *why* was the Shamed One lying? And, more importantly, what exactly was he lying *about*?

"What is your name?" he asked when the Shamed One fell silent.

"Vuurok I'pan, Master," the creature replied, barely looking up.

"How long have you been lost down here, I'pan?"

"I have lost track of time, Master," he said. "But it feels like hours."

"Do you have water on you?"

"No, Master," he answered, averting his stare to the ground. "There is no drinkable water down here that I have found."

"Really?" Nom Anor ran a thick finger over his painfully cracked lips. "It is odd, then, don't you think, that your lips do not seem as dry as mine?"

The Shamed One's eyes went wide as he stammered out a reply. "It *feels* like hours since I became lost, Master. But perhaps it hasn't been so long."

Nom Anor resisted the urge to smile in triumph. Poor liars tripped constantly over their untruths. "Tell me," he said, stepping over to I'pan. "What was the work detail you were assigned to? Who was your overseer? If it wasn't so long ago that you became lost, then they might not be too far away. Perhaps we can find them, yes?"

Vuurok I'pan whimpered. Nom Anor kicked him again, putting all his rage and frustration into the blow.

"Fool! Who do you think you are lying to? You have no tools and aren't even dressed for underground detail!"

"Please, Master! I am no one. I am nothing. I am *rishek olgrol immek'in inwey*—"

"Silence!" Another kick. "Your voice is an offense to my ears!"

The Shamed One became a bundle of quivering rags, face covered by sticklike arms and bony back upraised. Nom Anor thought rapidly to himself. If this Vuurok I'pan creature *was* a runaway, then he must have found some way to stay alive in the underground of Yuuzhan'tar. If Nom Anor could gain access to that means, he, too, might be able to live a little longer. That, for now, was all that mattered.

"Take me to the others," he snarled, putting every iota of command into his voice.

"Others?" the Shamed One squeaked. "What others?"

"Understand this, I'pan," Nom Anor said. "The only reason you have not died a coward's death is because you could be of value to me. Should it turn out that I have overestimated your worth, then I shall be sure to reconsider my actions."

"No, Master, please!" I'pan quickly withdrew on all fours, cowering a meter or so away. "I shall take you to the others, I swear! I swear it on the name of—"

"If your Shamed tongue so much as dares utter one more word, I shall rip it out and eat it for my sustenance."

I'pan fell silent without another word. Instead he stood and—slowly, as though wary of turning his back on Nom Anor—began hobbling back the way he had come. Nom Anor followed just as cautiously, aware that he had no particular reason to trust this broken spirit he had coerced into doing his will. For all he knew, I'pan could be leading him into a trap—or worse, if he was as foolish as he appeared, leading them both to their doom on the surface, convinced he might be able to bargain a pardon from the warmaster.

But what choice did he have? He had to go where the Shamed One led him. It was either that or continue wandering aimlessly through this gods-forsaken planet. He had survived this long, true, but how much longer could he last before he succumbed to thirst and hunger? Or before one of the search parties got lucky and found him?

No. He needed these "others" if he was to survive. If they were as pathetic as I'pan, he was sure he would be able to use them to his advantage . . .

I'pan began to relax as their journey progressed. His posture straightened and his voice became firmer, advising where to step cautiously and where to duck his head. He occasionally stole glances at Nom Anor as they walked, nervously at first, but then more boldly as they moved farther into the tunnels. The former executor could practically hear the other's mind turning over. He had no doubt that the Shamed One suspected now who he was.

"What?" he barked after I'pan turned around for the third time in as many paces.

"Nothing, Master." I'pan focused all his attention forward.

Nom Anor grabbed the neck of his flapping robe and hauled him off balance. "What is it you are thinking, my stinking worm?"

"I am wondering, Master . . ."

"Speak it!" Nom Anor shook him to loosen his tongue.

"Are you—are *you* a Shamed One like us?"

Nom Anor struck I'pan so hard that blood from his gashed fingers splashed in a wide arc across the metallic floor between them. I'pan bounced off a nearby wall and collapsed to the ground with a pained grunt. Before he had a chance to collect himself, Nom Anor picked him up again and hurled him into the opposite wall. This time I'pan could not hold on to the lamp, and it went flying down the corridor, its pale light reflecting briefly off abandoned machinery buried in the walls.

The moaning of the Shamed One as he again tried to pick himself up only incensed Nom Anor further, and the former executor's vision dissolved into spinning blotches as a torrent of rage exploded behind his eyes. He heard himself screaming words that even he couldn't understand as he pummeled I'pan again and again, the Shamed One curling around himself to protect his face from the assault, whimpering helplessly as blows and kicks were rained down upon him.

When the fit had passed, Nom Anor sagged into himself, his anger and energy spent. Leaning against the wall, still panting heavily, he forced himself to think rationally.

Vuurok I'pan was huddled in a corner, trembling with fear. Realizing just how close he had come to killing the Shamed One to assuage his rage, despite the fact that I'pan might yet prove to be of great assistance in keeping him alive, Nom Anor offered a hand to help him to his feet. The Shamed One took it apprehensively, clearly fearing another outburst.

Nom Anor pulled him in close, breathing steadily into his face.

Are you a Shamed One like us?

"Ask me that again, I'pan," he said, "and those will be your last words."

Nom Anor released I'pan, walked a few paces down the passage, and collected the lamp. Returning, he shoved it into I'pan's quivering hands.

"Show me the others," he said, gesturing for I'pan to continue walking. The Shamed One did so, and in silence, not looking back once for the remainder of their journey.

Master Cilghal's infirmary was a world unto its own. Large enough to hold three examination tables and a small audience, it was designed to be a classroom as well as a place of healing. Shelves of obscure remedies and arcane technologies lined every wall; an open door led to an herbarium for growing medicinal plants; and three full-sized bacta tanks off to one side took up almost a quarter of the room. Saba liked it because, unlike most surgeries or medic stations, this place was not sterile and lifeless. Thanks to the curved walls and undulating ceiling being layered with sopor-moss to aid the patients' recovery, the air in the room was both rich and invigorating.

The human Jedi Tahiri Veila lay unconscious on the center examination table. A small group had gathered around her, watching with concern as Master Cilghal examined her. Several of Saba's apprentices had spent time with Tahiri while on their mission to the Yuuzhan Vong worldship orbiting Myrkr, seeking out the voxyn queen. It had been a mission that had not gone smoothly, and had resulted in the loss of a number of their party—including Anakin Solo, Han and Leia's younger son. Only one of Saba's apprentices had survived. It had been a perilous mission, so she was lucky to have even that one survive. *Tesar*—

Saba stopped in midthought and brought herself to the present. *Hunt the moment,* one of the elders of her family had once told her. *Grip it in your claws and never let it go. Slip too far into the past or the future, and you will be lost.*

Such teachings arose from a barbarous past, in which grief and fear lurked everywhere one looked, but they had echoes in Jedi training. She had learned to strip herself back to a single point of consciousness, focused solely on the task at hand. Applying such meditation techniques was almost second nature to her. Indeed, they were arguably the only things that had saved her mind after the destruction of so much she had held dear.

Hunt the moment . . .

Saba had never regarded herself as being particularly close to Tahiri. They were different—they came from different worlds, had different backgrounds, and held different values. Nevertheless, they were bound simply by virtue of being Jedi. In the short time Saba had known Tahiri, she had struck Saba as a Jedi with a bright future ahead of her. She had come across as young and inexperienced but still full of potential. As with many Jedi, Tahiri was powered by an inner determination. A fire burned in her that had remained undiminished even by the death of the boy she'd loved, Anakin Solo.

She wondered where that fire was now, in the body of the frail, young human before her. If she, too, was trying in her own way to focus on what lay before her.

Anakin's parents were there, looking as concerned as they would for one of their own offspring. Outside, watching through the sterile barrier that cordoned off the room, were a number of other concerned individuals, Jag Fel and Belindi Kalenda among them.

All attention was on Jaina, as she tried to explain to Master Cilghal what had happened.

"She collapsed in one of the public halls," she said, her hands animated in front of her. She was clearly upset by the turn of events. "We traced her there after she called me on her comlink. She sounded—upset. She wasn't making much sense."

Master Cilghal gestured and Tekli handed her the instrument she required. Their unspoken communication was near perfect, obviously the result of a familiarity developed over years of working together.

"What was she saying?" the healer asked, her moist, webbed hands pressing a nutrient gel to Tahiri's forehead. Even Saba could tell that Tahiri was malnourished.

"She—" Again Jaina hesitated. "She said that Anakin was trying to kill her. Like I said, she wasn't making much sense."

Saba wasn't an expert at reading human body language, but she sensed that Jaina was hiding something.

"I felt her calling for Anakin through the Force," Master Skywalker was saying.

Jacen Solo nodded, exchanging glances with his twin sister. Saba suspected that Tahiri's grief was touching places uncomfortably close to their own.

"I see no reason for Tahiri's collapse," Master Cilghal concluded upon finishing her scan of the young woman. "Physically her body is under stress, but she isn't ill. As far as I can tell, all she needs is to rest and eat properly for a couple of weeks. I suggest we let her sleep for the moment. Until she wakes up and we can talk to her, there really is little else we can do."

Leia stood to one side, with her husband's arm around

her waist. Her eyes were glistening. "Do everything you can for her," she said. "I refuse to let her become another victim of this war."

Master Cilghal looked up and nodded her head. "I'll place her in a private ward, under full observation."

Leia turned and walked from the room. Han and Mara went with her, followed by Jaina and Jacen. Saba started to go also, but was stopped by Master Skywalker's voice.

"Not you, Saba." He spoke in a way that made it sound like a request, not a command. "Please, stay for a moment."

She obeyed, returning to stand with him and the two healers over the supine body of the human girl. Saba's eyes were most sensitive to the infrared part of the spectrum, so the finer details of Tahiri's face were lost to her. But something was burning deep within her, that much Saba could tell. Tahiri lay flat on her back, her chest gently rising and falling, eyes roving behind closed lids—to all appearances, the girl was sleeping. But Tahiri was radiating heat like a furnace, as though her body was working overtime even while lying still. And there was something about that fire that raged inside her . . .

Now that she was closer, Saba found herself intrigued by it. It wasn't a fire that needed fuel; if anything, it seemed to be burning *itself*, as strange as that sounded.

"What is it you see, Saba?" Master Skywalker asked.

"This one iz not sure," she replied.

"But there is something?" Master Cilghal pressed, her huge eyes rolling inquisitively.

Saba nodded uncertainly. "There seemz to be, yez."

She searched the young woman for any sign of what might be wrong. Her peculiar sensitivity to life wasn't the same gift as that possessed by Master Cilghal and the other healers. Saba wasn't attuned the same way they were. Disease, in the form of viruses and bacteria, was a sort of life, too, and deserved respect. She might flinch at a warrior beheading a shenbit and leaving its meat behind, but she could rejoice in the progress of a plague. That hadn't endeared her to some of her colleagues. The Jedi teachings told them that they should be devoted to preserving life—a philosophy to which she wholeheartedly subscribed. *Which* life, though, was the question that troubled Saba. Was an intelligent being such as herself, for example, of more intrinsic value to the Force than, say, a swarm of piranha-beetles? She wasn't as sure as her fellow students had seemed to be that that question had a simple answer.

This ability to sense life had grown since Barab I. It made her an asset when the healers failed; she saw something that they did not, when the flow of life was imperiled rather than life itself. Her frequenting of the medical wards of Mon Calamari had enabled her to exercise her gift more frequently than was possible on a battlefield, enabling it to grow stronger, more refined. When she looked at Tahiri—*really* looked at her, not just with her basic sense of smell and sight—she saw the usual human patterns of life swirling through her. If each cell was a star, then her veins were hyperspace trade routes and her nerves were HoloNet channels. What looked like a single, continuous body on the outside was in fact a joyfully chaotic community containing billions of components. The flow of information and energy among those components was what Saba saw when she looked at Tahiri—or anything living, for that matter. Life was a process, not a thing.

But in Tahiri she saw something else, too. There were disruptions to the flow, strange eddies where it would normally be still, and pools of calm in areas that she was used to seeing active. There was more to this young human than met the eye.

"I wonder," Master Skywalker mused. "Jaina is closest to Anakin in temperament, so perhaps that is why Tahiri came to her. And the Yuuzhan Vong have just suffered their greatest losses since the beginning of the war . . ."

Master Cilghal looked up inquiringly when he trailed off into silence. "You believe you know what afflicts her, Luke?"

"For certain?" He shook his head sadly. "No. But if we had the time, I think Saba here could figure it out. Unfortunately, there is vital work that needs to be done—by all of us." He turned to Saba. His eyes were deep and full of concern and determination in equal measures. "We leave tomorrow. You, too, Tekli." The healer's apprentice bowed solemnly and silently. "I would stay to be with Tahiri, given the choice, but . . ."

Again he let his words trail off, sentence unfinished.

Saba felt in Master Skywalker all the weariness of a man who had fought his own father—and a tempting journey to the dark side—for most of his life, and she understood. Sometimes *the moment* demanded too much of even the greatest hunter.

"War narrows our choices," Master Cilghal finished for him.

"Yes," Luke said. "Yes, it does."

Movement through the cramped tunnel was difficult, and made doubly so by the presence of the nutrient vines and cloning pods that were impeding her progress. But she kept going regardless of how hopeless she felt her situation was. She attacked the vines and pods falling around her with a vigor generated from desperation and fear. No matter what she did, though, they kept coming at her—they kept *growing* around her!

Breaking free of the restrictive passage, she risked a glance back into the dark mouth from which she had just emerged. The vines and pods continued to pulsate steadily, contracting and expanding like a fleshy sphincter. The fine ash pumping from the cave reminded her of blood cells, swirling around her in an almost threatening manner and carrying with it the terrible stench of burning flesh—a smell that served to remind her of what she was running from.

She fleetingly wondered if her stalkers had been caught in the tangle of vines in the tunnel; but it wasn't so much a serious thought as a hope—and an empty one at that. The thing with her face would chase her until its last dying breath, and the thing chasing *it* would never stop. The lizardine god-figure was hot on both their heels. She would never be able to face the two of them. Exhaustion wheezed in her chest with every breath she took. Until she found a chance to collect her strength, confronting these nameless horrors was an inconceivable option.

She urged herself away from the tunnel mouth, but found only darkness ahead. Taking tentative steps forward, she waved aside the ash that was getting into her eyes and mouth. She wanted to run, but without being able to see where she was going, it was too risky. Her footsteps vanished into the void, sucked away with the light. She stopped and peered ahead. It was only then that she noticed patches in the shadows that were actually darker than others—that there were *degrees* of blackness. When her eyes had adjusted fully, she could see more clearly the cavernous space she was in.

It was tall, with massive arches at either end and small alcoves lining the walls to either side of her, only meters away. From these she thought she could make out movement, like that of beasts shifting in their lair. She looked around her with nervous wonder. It all seemed terribly familiar, in a claustrophobic sort of way.

Before she could isolate the memory, though, the snout of one of the beasts emerged from the shadows, the rest of its lithe body following. She sucked in air, coughing on the ash that went into her throat, as the creature passed by close to her face, the eye on the side of its head glaring out of the dark, examining her as it swept by.

A voxyn, she was sure—and all alcoves around her were filled with them!

Her heart beat faster at the thought. As though in sympathy, the vines and pods in the tunnel behind her beat faster also, forcing out even more of the foul-smelling ash into the cavern.

She edged back from where she felt the voxyn to be, bumping into a ladder as she did so. Unable to go forward or back, she began to climb it. Her progress was hampered by the swirling ash, but the higher she climbed, the easier it seemed to become.

If I can climb high enough, she thought, *I will be free.*

She noticed as she climbed that the walls of the cavern began to glow from the lichen covering them. Dimly at first, but with each rung the luminosity of the lichen intensified, until it became so bright that everything below her was lost to the glare.

Was she safe now? she wondered. Was she finally free?

Her silent queries were answered by the ladder vibrating under her fingertips as the thing with her face began to climb after her. She forced back the tears of frustration and continued to ascend; there was no choice now but to go up and out. She climbed higher and higher, until the ash that was blowing about her face was no longer gray ash at all: it had become white, like snow.

She stretched out her tongue to collect some of the flakes, wanting its wetness to sate her growing thirst. But she winced and spat at the terrible taste. This wasn't snow; it was too dry. This was dust!

Her tears flowed unchecked as she continued her climb, disappointment gnawing at her heart. Disappointment quickly turned to terror, however, when the ladder shook again. The reptilian statue had begun its own ascent, roaring out its anger to those above. But there was something new about its roar that made her hesitate . . .

She hung there with arms wrapped tightly about the coarse wood of the ladder, listening as the reptile bellowed again. This time she realized it wasn't just a vague and angry roar as she'd first imagined it to be; it was something much more than that. This creature was crying out a single word over and over again.

Its howls echoed throughout the dusty cavern, and the ladder she stood on trembled from its bellows. The roar sounded as though its voice had been slowed a thousand times, until it became almost totally unintelligible. But the more intently she listened, the clearer it seemed to become, until she had no doubt whatsoever of what the creature was saying.

It wasn't a word. It was a *name*.

"Tahiri," it called out to her, its tone tugging at her heart and the guilt she carried. "Tahiri . . . Tahiri . . . Tahiri . . ."

Tahiri woke to the sound of someone screaming, realizing only when she found herself being restrained that it was, in fact, herself.

She felt something cool and scented being pressed against her forehead. Pushing the hand holding it aside, she tried to roll away, but restraints across her chest held her in place. Nevertheless, they didn't stop her from trying to wriggle free—even when a second hand joined the first, pushing her shoulders firmly back onto the bed. She desperately scrabbled at her side for her lightsaber, only to find it gone. Besides which, the hands were simply too strong. She would never have had the chance to use it even if it had been there.

"*Sith spawn!*" she shouted at her assailants. "Let me go!"

"*Tahiri!*" Beneath the whip crack of command to the voice, there was something unmistakably familiar to it. She stopped fighting for a moment, trying to make out the figure standing over her, all but blurred through her tears. It couldn't be, could it—? "Calm down, *please!*"

"Jacen?" The fight drained out of her like air from a punctured balloon, and she sagged back into the soft mattress, sobbing. "Oh, Jacen, I'm so sorry. I—I didn't know it was you. I thought it was—"

"It's okay," he said, his tone warm and reassuring. "Just let it out. Don't keep it inside where it can hurt you."

She frowned at him as he came slowly into focus. His words left her feeling oddly naked. "What do you mean?" she asked, wiping at her eyes with the backs of her hands.

"Bottling things up," he explained. "It doesn't help anyone. Trust me. I should know."

He smiled, but she found it difficult to reciprocate the gesture. The residue of the dream still lingered in her thoughts.

She sat up, this time finding no resistance from either Jacen or the restraints.

"You feeling any better?" he asked.

She wasn't, not really, but she didn't want to seem ungrateful. "I'll be fine," she said. "Thanks."

"You're welcome," he said, reaching behind her to ease the back of the bed up. It was only then that she looked around and recognized where she was.

Despite the absence of the usual sensors or equipment, there was no mistaking the small, circular room as belonging to a medical ward. The smell of sopor-moss lingered about her, despite the wide-open viewport off to her left that admitted the fresh air blowing off the Calamarian seas outside. There was a functional edge to the room's walls and furniture. Also, her own clothes were gone, replaced by a drab hospital smock. A thin sheet covered her on the bed.

"What am I doing here?" she asked, rubbing her hands across the bandages on her arms.

"You blacked out."

Jacen sat on the edge of the bed beside her, his own hands coming over hers to stop her self-conscious movements. Even though he didn't say anything, the message was obvious: she shouldn't worry about what was hidden there, yet.

"The medics found you in the Water's Edge market," he said.

She concentrated for a moment, staring at the folds in her sheet. She remembered contacting Jaina, remembered the uncontrollable panic that had disoriented her following the dream of the Yuuzhan Vong cemetery. Then she had found herself in the cavern where the voxyn lay hidden . . .

She shuddered at the memory. "What's wrong with me?" she asked, looking up at Jacen.

"It's a bit of a mystery, actually," he said. "They can't find anything."

His brown eyes were searching hers. She looked away, not sure if she was relieved or disappointed.

"I guess I must have just fainted, then."

"You've been unconscious for fifteen standard hours, Tahiri," he said. "You didn't just faint."

"I-I've not been sleeping well lately," she lied, looking away.

Fifteen hours? This was the worst episode yet. Maybe it would be for the best, she thought, if the truth finally came out. Even though she wanted to, however, she found she couldn't bring herself to say the words.

He'd hate me if he knew, she thought. *They would all hate me!*

"Tahiri?"

She looked up again. "I'm sorry," she said. "I don't know what's happening to me." That, at least, was partly true.

"That's okay," he reassured her. "I'm sure Master Cilghal will work it out sooner or later."

"I'm sorry to have been a burden, Jacen."

"You're not," he said. "Coming here to keep an eye on you was a good excuse to get out of some tedious meetings I'm supposed to attend. Besides, it gave me a chance to get a little bit of shut-eye myself. Things have been pretty hectic these last couple of days."

He did look tired, she noted. There were lines around his eyes that she hadn't noticed the last time she had seen him. But how long ago was that? After his return from Coruscant? During the battle at Ebaq 9? It dismayed her to realize that she couldn't remember just when that had been. In recent weeks—months, perhaps—her life had become a blur.

"Where's Jaina?" she asked.

"Sleeping. She said to say hi when you woke up."

Disappointed, Tahiri nodded and looked down at her folded hands. She didn't know why she wanted to talk to Jaina so badly, or what she would say when she did. That she was sorry she hadn't been able to save Anakin the way he had saved her? That she missed him as much as

Jaina did? No, what she wanted to say, what she *needed* to say, could never be said—not to Jaina, not to anyone.

She looked again to her arms, wondering at the wounds underneath the bandages. She remembered doing it to herself, remembered *seeing* herself do it, but she had been unable to stop herself.

She closed her eyes, wanting to shut out the thought. But it was impossible. The thoughts were always with her these days, waking or sleeping.

"Is Master Luke angry at me for missing the meeting of the Jedi?" she asked.

"No, of course not," he said, laughing lightly. "Uncle Luke isn't the sort to get angry about stuff like that. Trust me, he's more concerned about your well-being. Actually, he had been hoping to take you along on this new mission with us. He thought you could use some time away from all the action. But given your condition, it was decided that perhaps it would be best if you rested some more."

"Mission?" she asked, the beginnings of dismay creeping into her voice. "What mission?"

"We're looking for something," he said. "I don't know how long it will take us—or even where we're going, for that matter—but I do know it's something we have to do. If we don't, we could end up losing the war—even if we end up beating the Yuuzhan Vong."

She frowned. "That doesn't make sense."

"It depends on how you look at it," he said.

"And how do *you* look at it, Jacen?"

"Honestly?"

She nodded.

"Well, personally I think the worst thing we could do would be to wipe out the Yuuzhan Vong."

Her frown deepened at this. "Why?"

Jacen stood, running a hand through his shaggy

brown hair. "We already know that they'll never give up," he explained, moving around the bed. "They'll just keep fighting until they're all dead. But when they're gone, where does that leave us? I don't know about you, Tahiri, but I don't particularly want genocide on my conscience."

She opened her mouth to speak, but before she could, he went on.

"I know what you're probably thinking: if the Yuuzhan Vong don't register in the Force, then why should we care if we wiped them out? But I don't think it's that simple, Tahiri. The Force isn't just about what happens to living things; it's also about what living things do to one another. No matter how you look at it, if we win by military means alone, then we'll end up committing an atrocity, and there's no way I can explain such an action without resorting to the dark side. I refuse to accept that there is no alternative."

She stared at him, taken by the passion in his voice. This was a Jacen she had never seen before. Committed and sure of himself, he was no longer the teenager she had come to know. His experiences on Coruscant had changed him. He was so much more the adult now.

"Do you remember Vergere?" he asked after a few moments' silence.

"Of course." The change in subject puzzled her.

"She told me something before she died." There was a slight deepening of the lines around his eyes as he spoke, and his hands fiddled with the railing at the foot of the bed. "She told me about a place she once visited—long before you or I were ever born, Tahiri. It was a world unlike any other in the galaxy. The people who lived there had a reputation for building starships. But not just any starships. These were without equal—starships that could outperform anything built even today. She was sent by the Jedi Council on a mission to find the ship-builders, even though there were those who thought the planet little more than a myth. She was successful: she found the planet and its inhabitants; she saw the marvelous starships in operation—and many other things, for that matter, things the likes of which no one had ever dreamed possible. It had jungles and vast forests; but they were not shunted aside or eaten away in the name of industry. This was a world in balance."

His eyes gleamed with the wonder of this secondhand vision.

"Vergere fell in love with the place," he went on, "rejoicing in its jungles, its many forms of life, the way it seemed to her to be a living hymn to the Force. But she failed to guess the truth underlying what she saw—at first, anyway, even though it had been under her nose right from the beginning. The thing about those starships made on the planet, the thing that made them really special, is that they were alive."

Tahiri's eyes narrowed. "Like the Yuuzhan Vong ships?"

He nodded. "These were no ordinary ships, Tahiri," he said. "They lived and breathed and died just like any other being. They were alive like you and me, like any living thing. And so was the planet that made them."

"The *planet*—?" she started, incredulously. If it hadn't been Jacen telling her all this, and had he not been so earnest in his telling, she might have laughed the whole thing off as a joke. But he was serious; this was real.

"Its name was Zonama Sekot," he said. "It was a living being in its own right, one of the most wondrous things this galaxy has ever produced."

Tahiri felt a strange tingling sensation go through her. " 'Was'?" she echoed.

"Not long after Vergere arrived, aliens came and attacked it. Zonama Sekot referred to these aliens as 'Far Outsiders.' We know now that these Far Outsiders were the Yuuzhan Vong—possibly a reconnaissance party sent to explore the galaxy before the actual invasion. The planet had been negotiating with these Outsiders for months, Vergere learned. The Yuuzhan Vong were fascinated by it, as you can imagine. A living planet would not be so different from one of the worldships that they used to cross the great gulf between galaxies."

"So what happened?" Tahiri prompted when Jacen went quiet as if in thought.

He looked up. "The Yuuzhan Vong attacked and Zonama Sekot fled," he said. "The whole planet—moved. It changed systems, and hasn't been seen since."

"Moved?" Tahiri echoed. "Just like that?"

He nodded. "There's no mention of it in any records anywhere. It's as though it completely vanished."

"And you're going looking for it—this living planet?"

"Exciting, isn't it?" he said, coming back around to her side and sitting on her bed. "Vergere told me that the Yuuzhan Vong, in their own way, revere life. Not as a Jedi reveres life, cherishing each individual as a component of the Force that is both life and greater than life, but rather in their own perverse way. Their reverence for life, she said, is mixed with notions of pain and death. This fascinated me, and still does. It underpins their entire culture. I've always felt that if we could understand this ideology better, then we would understand *them* better.

"Call it an instinct," he went on. "Zonama Sekot is the key to the whole thing—to victory. I'm sure of it. That's why Vergere told me about it. It might help us find a way to turn back the Yuuzhan Vong. It did it once before, after all, if on a smaller scale."

"Maybe it can make us ships as good as or better than

the Yuuzhan Vong's coralskippers." Tahiri marveled at the thought. "How do you intend to find it?"

He shrugged. "That's the problem, isn't it? It's done a very good job of staying hidden all this time, so tracking it down isn't going to be easy. When I talked about it with Uncle Luke, there was only one conclusion we could come to: if it hasn't been seen, then it *has* to be in the Unknown Regions. There's nowhere else it could be. A fertile world is not exactly the sort of thing that would be omitted from a ship's log."

"Let alone a world that has appeared out of nowhere," Tahiri added. "Or has a mind of its own."

"Exactly," Jacen said. "It's literally the stuff of legends. And in the absence of rumors, we have to go chasing them ourselves. We're stopping at the Empire first, since their territory borders the Unknown Regions; they might have information we can use. And then there's the Chiss: they've explored the Unknown Regions much more than we have; they'll have access to a wealth of data—"

"If they'll share it with you. Either of them."

"We'll just have to talk them into it."

Jacen withdrew into himself for a moment, and Tahiri took the chance to collect her own thoughts. It all sounded very unlikely: living planets, old Jedi missions, wild crusades into the galaxy's darkest regions, Yuuzhan Vong prophecies. But she knew to keep an open mind. After all, stranger things had happened in his family's history . . .

A twinge of pain accompanied the thought. Had Anakin lived, it might have been *her* family, too, by now.

She pushed the thought down as far as it would go. It whispered that she should tell him everything, exactly how she felt and all she suspected was happening to her. But she couldn't. Jacen had more important things to worry about, even apart from Zonama Sekot; he had been grappling with Jedi philosophy so deeply and for so long that the smaller concerns of those around him might seem trivial, perhaps even silly. She had no evidence, after all, that the things she was experiencing *were* anything more than nightmares, even though they felt so real.

"Is Jaina going with you?" she asked, shrugging free of the uncomfortable train of thought.

"Hmm?" Jacen broke from his own reverie. "Oh, no. She has other work to do—with Mom and Dad. Sometimes it seems like we're spending most of the war apart." He looked sad. "But if you're worrying that you won't be seeing her, don't. She'll be in tomorrow, when she's caught up on her sleep. And speaking of which . . ."

"Oh, I'm sorry," she said. "I'm keeping you up. You already said that you wanted to get some—"

"No, Tahiri." He laughed. "Actually, I was meaning you. You said you've not been sleeping very well lately."

She nodded cautiously, not wanting to encourage questions along those lines.

"Okay," he said. "So relax for a moment and close your eyes." He edged closer as she did as he asked; at the same time the back of the bed lowered, and he placed his splayed his fingers across her forehead and temples. In the shadow of his hand, she smelled Anakin and bit her lip.

"I just want to try something," she heard him say.

And that was the last she knew for an endless, timeless moment.

She awoke again to sunlight streaming through the room's wide and opened viewport, the sound of water crashing against the city walls, and the smell of salt on the air. The transition from night to day was so jarring that, for a moment, she didn't know where she was. But with a quick glance around the med room, it all came rushing back.

What had Jacen done to her? She felt rested for the first time in weeks, certainly, but instead of gratitude, she was left with a sense of betrayal. There was a strange feeling behind her eyes, as though someone had been poking around in there while she slept.

Jacen was nowhere to be seen, which was only to be expected. On the bedside table, under a jug of blue milk, she noticed a small piece of flimsiplast. Taking it, she unfolded the note, immediately recognizing the neat, confident handwriting as belonging to Anakin's older brother.

It read, simply:

You will always be family to us. J.

Family. She sat up and hugged herself as though from a sudden chill. She had been thinking about family just before Jacen had put her to sleep, however he had done it. The reference seemed too pointed to be a coincidence. He must have taken the thought from her mind, and—

Did he see my dreams, too? she wondered, fearfully. *And if so, did he also see . . . ?*

She dispelled the disquieting thought by taking the piece of flimsi and tearing it into tiny pieces. Then, stepping over to the window, she released the pieces to the wind and watched them until they had all disappeared into the rough waters below.

The training mat took the bulk of the impact, but the fall still left Jagged Fel winded. He lay gasping on his back for a moment, then levered himself upright.

"Nice move," he said, massaging the muscles in his left shoulder. "For a scruffy rebel, anyway."

He stood, dropping into the classic Chiss "Forbelean Defense" stance. From such a position, virtually all forms of attack could be deflected. On the opposite side of the mat, Jaina Solo dusted off her loose-fitting training outfit.

"You aristocrats are all the same, aren't you?" she joked. "Underneath that tough exterior, you're all as soft as Mon Cal jellyfish."

"And that coming from the daughter of a *princess!*"

She opened her mouth to reply, but he didn't give her a chance to say anything. Instead he lunged at her for another attack. Two half paces forward took him within arm's reach. Ducking to avoid the defensive feint he knew she'd use, he brought one shoulder up to deflect her arm and his body and right leg around to sweep her off her feet. If he surprised her at all, she didn't let it show. Instead she jumped lightly as his sweeping kick caught her feet. Seemingly effortlessly, she used the momentum of his blow to spin her body around its center of mass, landing, in apparent defiance of gravity, on one hand, upside down. It lasted only a split second, but it was all she needed. Her left leg transferred her angular momentum *back* to him via his chest, sending him flying. Before he had even hit the mat again, she had cartwheeled back on to her feet and was standing, poised and at the ready, waiting patiently for him to recover.

He sat up, rubbing at his chest. "Sith spawn, Jaina!" His lungs felt like a clawcraft with a leak into vacuum. "That *hurt.*"

"It serves you right," she said, barely breathing heavily. "My dad always said you should never let someone get away with calling you 'scruffy.' " Seeing that he wasn't in a hurry to get up and retaliate, she relaxed her posture. "Besides, I thought the Chiss never attacked first."

"Yeah, well," he mumbled, propping himself up some more. "You insulted my father."

"I *also* thought they didn't let their hearts rule their heads during combat."

"That was for using the Force during an unarmed sparring match—"

"But I hadn't used it yet," Jaina quickly pointed out, stepping over to him.

"I could tell you were about to, though."

"Really? Then you must have the Force, too, my friend." She smiled down at him and offered a hand to help him up. "Can you tell what I'm thinking now?"

He took the hand and pulled her down onto the mat with him. "Can you tell me what *I'm* thinking?"

I want to be very much more than your friend, *Jaina Solo,* he thought.

Her smile widened as she entangled her legs in his and leaned in closer to him. "I don't need the Force to know that."

They kissed—only briefly, but it was enough so that when they pulled apart again, her breathing had quickened. It pleased Jag to know that while she could kick him halfway across the room and not break a sweat, it took a simple kiss from him to set her heart racing. So he kissed her again, longer this time, enjoying the feel of her lips against his. He didn't allow any thoughts of honor or propriety to get in the way of the moment, either. On this occasion he was more than happy to let his heart rule his head. Opportunities for the two of them to be alone were rare—*too* rare not to be taken advantage of.

He hadn't told her yet that this was the main reason why he had fought for their inclusion on her parents' mission. Yes, he was feeling like a finely spun wire, likely to break if stretched any tighter, but he knew he would keep fighting well beyond reason if the war demanded it. His Chiss training emphasized the need for regular rest in order to perform at one's best. All of the members of the Chiss Squadron knew that, too. But he could see the fatigue in their eyes, and even he had made mistakes recently. His second in command had pointed that out. She wasn't innocent herself, she had admitted, but it was his job to know better, she said. And, of course, she was right.

The diplomatic mission was a godsend, then—a way of making sure everyone got some rest while still performing a valuable duty, and at the same time it gave him a chance to spend more time with Jaina.

Jaina broke for air and sat back with her hands resting on his chest. Jag wondered if she could feel the beating of his heart through his thin training uniform.

"Duty calls," she said after a moment. "And I'd like to see Tahiri beforehand." She pulled a regretful face. "Sorry."

"The only thing you should feel sorry for, Jaina Solo, is cheating."

She playfully punched his shoulder before standing. "Winning is everything."

"Do you really believe that?"

Her expression turned serious for a moment. "I think I did, once," she said. Then she stretched out her hand once more. "Come on."

He took her proffered hand, this time allowing her to help him to his feet. Halfway up, however, she let go and he fell back with a thump onto the mat.

"You're far too trusting, Jag," she said, smiling. With a wink, she headed for the showers.

They briefly reconnected again afterward. Side by side, not touching, they walked toward the infirmary, where she was to see Tahiri before meeting with her parents to go over their plans one more time. He would go on to a meeting with her uncle and aunt. They would need all the information he could give them on the Chiss if they were seriously planning to go to the Unknown Regions expecting help.

As they walked, Jag rubbed at his breastbone. It was still tender from the last kick she had delivered.

"I'm sorry if I fought you hard today," she said, noting his discomfort. "I'm just . . ." She shrugged. "I don't know, Jag. I guess I'm a little angry about being put out of action."

"So you're fighting harder to prove you haven't lost your edge?" he said. She nodded. "Listen, Jaina, no one has said *that*."

"No, but it was implied. That's why they want me on this mission, I'm sure. They want to rest me up."

"Now you're just being paranoid," he said. "But anyway, so what if going on this mission *does* allow you to get in some rest? You've earned it, haven't you? I really don't see what the problem is, Jaina."

"I'm surprised you're taking it so well," she said as they rounded a corner, almost bumping into a couple of Ho'Din walking the other way. "I expected you to be as annoyed as I am about all this; in fact, I would have thought you'd be cursing and swearing!"

He shrugged. "You don't tend to learn too many swear words at the Chiss academy."

"Really?"

"Yeah, really. The worst insult I learned there was *moactan teel*."

"And what does that mean?"

"That you're fair-haired," he said with some embarrassment. It was an insult that only really worked in Chiss space where everyone had jet-black hair. Here, among so many variations of hair color, it seemed ridiculous. "Sorry," he added.

She laughed out loud. "Are you apologizing for the

insult to my own hair color, or the lameness of the insult itself?"

He felt himself blush, but didn't respond to her teasing.

"I tell you, if you want some good insults, you should listen to my father. I learned plenty from him over the years," she said. "And if you don't want them directed at you, then I suggest you take care."

They parted at the infirmary with no obvious display of affection. He was far too conscious of the people around them for that. He kept imagining what others would think if they were seen together: "What's the outsider doing with the Jedi today?" His upbringing with the Chiss had left him short on social mores when it came to public displays. He didn't want to be seen to do the wrong thing, and he was pretty sure Jaina wasn't mistaking his caution for disinterest.

He continued along the winding corridors to the meeting with the Skywalkers. Part of him wished that it was *this* mission he and Jaina were participating in. He would have loved for her to see the Chiss capital again: icebound Csillia, with its blue snowfields and clear skies. Since joining one of the phalanxes—the twenty-eight colonial units that comprised the domestic Chiss military force—at an early age, he had found few opportunities to return to the capital planet, let alone the estate on which his parents, General Baron Soontir Fel and Syal Antilles, had recently settled. The Yuuzhan Vong had been harrying the Unknown Regions as well as the rest of the galaxy. Life, even for a relatively young and untested starfighter pilot, had been hectic.

Untested no longer, he reminded himself as the door to the small, oval conference room slid open and he entered.

Inside the darkened room, Jag found Jedi Master Luke Skywalker and his wife, Mara, studying numerous maps and charts on a clear, vertical display screen. As he stepped in and the door behind him closed, the Jedi Master straightened, staring at him through an incomplete section of one of the maps. Jag instantly recognized this particular great swathe of the galaxy as the area that the New Republic and the Imperials called the Unknown Regions, and what he called *home*.

Luke acknowledged Jag with little more than a nod.

"We know very little about the Chiss," he said without preamble, stepping around the display screen toward Jag. "I like to think that this is a situation that can be rectified."

Jag studied the Jedi Master's face for any sign of duplicity. As always, he saw none. "Grand Admiral Thrawn's actions paint us in a dubious light," he said in response. "I understand the reluctance of many people to deal with us."

"And the reverse is probably true. No doubt you've met your fair share of people purporting to represent the New Republic. The Unknown Regions have always been a haven for criminals and outcasts, as well as renegade Imperials."

Jag inclined his head in acknowledgment of the point. "What is it you wish to know?"

"First of all, I'd like to know if the Chiss have any knowledge of a certain planet in the Unknown Regions."

"For that you would need to contact the Expansionary Defense Fleet."

"Is there anyone in particular there that I should be talking to?"

"I can't give you names."

Luke raised an eyebrow but didn't query his answer. "Okay," he said, placing his hands behind his back and pacing in front of the display screen. "Then second, I need to talk about closer ties between your people and the Galactic Alliance."

"The same department would handle those inquiries."

"But I wouldn't want them to end there," he said, stopping his pacing and facing Jag fully. "This isn't just a matter for the Nuruodo family to consider under the military and foreign affairs portfolio. It's also a communications and justice issue. The Inrokini and Sabosen families handle those affairs, if my information is correct. It's also a colonial issue, since the Yuuzhan Vong are affecting everyone, and that's overseen by the—"

"The Csapla, yes," Jag said. "Your sources are correct, whoever they are."

"A contact in any or all of these departments would be helpful, Jag," Mara said from the other side of the screen, the faint light from the maps flickering across the beautiful woman's red-gold hair.

"I'm sorry but, again, I cannot give you any names." He could sense their frustration and made a sincere effort to dispel it. "I do understand the reasons for you asking, and I assure you I am not trying to be obstructive. I simply cannot answer you."

"Why is that, Jag?" Mara asked.

"Two reasons, really," he answered. "One is that I'm not in a position to know who holds what rank in any of the appropriate families. I know who *represents* each, but they are just political positioning. Who actually *does* the work, I have no idea. It's these people you would need to speak to; and it is they who will seek you out when your intentions become known."

Luke nodded thoughtfully. "And the second reason?"

"Even if I did know," Jag said, maintaining steady eye contact with the Jedi Master, "I wouldn't tell you. You see, the Chiss are taught from the earliest days of training that it is not the person holding the position that is important, but rather the position itself. Individuals must allow themselves to be subsumed into the role society expects them to play. If you asked for someone by name, they would on principle not talk to you. If you asked for them by rank, however, they would not hesitate."

"Then what rank should I ask for?" Luke asked.

"In the first instance, the matter of this planet you seek, you should ask for the chief navigator of the Chiss Expansionary Defense Fleet. Regarding closer ties with the Galactic Alliance, you would need the assistant syndic in the same department."

"Isn't that the position currently held by your father?" Mara asked.

Jag didn't dignify the question with a response, even though it was correct. He was becoming increasingly irritated that they knew as much as they did. "If you address your inquiries through those avenues," he said, "then I am sure you will be heard."

"And in your opinion, will we get what we want?" Luke asked.

"It depends on too many factors to say for certain. Whether we've seen this planet you're looking for is an obvious one; how badly the Yuuzhan Vong are hurting us is another."

"I was under the impression they weren't hurting you at all."

Jag allowed himself a half smile at that. "I think it's safe to admit that the Yuuzhan Vong are hurting everyone to some degree or another. It's good that you are attempting to address this as a galaxywide problem, for that's precisely what it is."

Mara came around the display now, as though to look at him properly. "So you'd like our help, but you won't even tell us who to talk to in order to offer it to you? I find that—interesting."

Jag recognized the deliberate provocation, but wasn't offended by it. "I apologize if you think I'm being unreasonable."

"You are being unreasonable. But you're being what your culture expects of you, and to be honest, I admire you for that. It's just not how we would operate, that's all."

"No doubt time will reveal many such differences between our people."

Mara smiled; there were clearly no hard feelings there, either. "No doubt."

"There's one other question I'd like to ask, though," Luke said. "The Galactic Alliance doesn't have a vast amount of resources to spare at the moment, as you are surely aware. In fact, in places we're as thinly spread as the Yuuzhan Vong. What are the chances, do you think, of procuring aid from the CEDF?"

"I imagine that would depend on how your other negotiations went. If you can convince the Chiss Expansionary Defense Fleet that your mission is of strategic value to the Chiss, then they might give you an escort of some description. But then, they might not, also. If your mission is valuable *enough*, you might end up in competition with the CEDF."

Mara raised her eyebrows in mock alarm. "They'd steal it out from under us?"

"Depending on what *it* is," Jag shot back.

Luke chuckled. "Well put." He leaned against the transparent display and folded his arms across his stomach. "You're holding yourself very well here, Jagged. It can't be easy, caught between two different cultures like this— twice over, if you like: a human raised by the Chiss, then sent back to deal with the Galactic Alliance."

"No," he replied, thinking of Jaina. "Sometimes it isn't easy."

"But it's good, I think. For all of us. We need another example of the Chiss to help us judge their nature, and you are as good as one of them. Thrawn was brilliant, but not the best ambassador a culture could wish for."

Jag stiffened defensively. "The Chiss do not ask to be judged, Master Skywalker. Not by you; not by anyone."

"But you judge us." There was no acrimony in the Jedi Master's tone. "We all do it, Jag. It's only natural. And we know enough of your foreign policy to know your opinion of 'lesser' civilizations. We might be one of them."

Jag could feel himself being led out onto treacherously thin ice. "Neither Grand Admiral Thrawn nor myself was an ambassador, as I'm sure you both realize. He was simply doing what he thought most appropriate in a particular military situation."

"As are you. I understand," said Luke. "Thank you for your help, Jag. I appreciate it."

Jag was surprised that the meeting had taken so little time. He had expected a more determined interrogation. But as Luke guided him to the door, he realized it wasn't quite over yet. A small but strong hand gripped him by the shoulder, and Mara said: "Look after my apprentice, won't you?" Jag looked down into the startlingly green eyes of the woman beside him. "I know she's a Jedi Knight in her own right, but in some ways she's still very much a child—albeit a precocious one." The green eyes smiled. "I hope you can be a beneficial part of her education."

"I intend to be."

"Good," she said, withdrawing her hand and nodding. "I'm glad."

*   *   *

There were many other things Jag still had to organize with his second in command, and he went straight to the barracks she had been given to discuss them with her. Eprill was ready and waiting, in full uniform.

"What did you tell them?" she asked, almost reproachfully. She had known about the meeting with the Skywalkers and disapproved of their intentions.

"Nothing they didn't already know," he said.

"That alone might be too much." Red eyes blazed at him from a blue face.

He opened his mouth to snap at her, but discipline took over before the words emerged. He couldn't be angry at her for simply doing her job. The Chiss Squadron may have originally come on a fact-finding mission, but now it was here—at his instigation—to fight the Yuuzhan Vong. The negotiations and information bartering should be left to the Chiss Expansionary Defense Fleet.

But at the same time, he couldn't in good conscience let Jaina's uncle, aunt, and twin brother go blindly into a potentially tricky situation. They meant well, and their goals were admirable. Part of him wanted to give them every assistance he could, even if it did mean violating the oaths of secrecy he had sworn to the Chiss.

He didn't know what his father would think. The Baron was human, too, but he had embraced the Chiss culture as completely as it had embraced him. If his father *had* been in contact with the Skywalkers, then Jag doubted he would have told them anything of substance. They might simply have been bluffing to see what he would say in response. Jag wished he could ask his father what was going on—but that would have been seen as a sign of weakness. It had been his decision to keep the Chiss Squadron in Galactic Alliance space; he alone had to deal with the consequences of that decision. He hoped his father would be proud of the way he had handled himself.

But there was more to it than that. The military situation was too complex for one person alone to handle. He wanted his government involved, and he hoped that Master Skywalker would manage to achieve this.

Shrugging the problem aside, he sat down with Eprill, his second in command, and attempted to decide on a roster for the coming weeks. She would remain behind to take command of the Chiss Squadron. There would be six pilots left, enough to work as an independent unit alongside new pilots from the training program.

Jag knew that Eprill was as tired as he was. He also knew that she would be offended if he didn't leave her behind to take on the job. This was a big break for her, a chance to demonstrate her ability to command in combat, instead of just following orders. Looking at her now—at her pressed uniform, her perfectly straight posture, her black hair pulled severely back to the nape of her neck as per regulation standards for a Chiss soldier—he knew that she deserved every success. She was the epitome of what a Chiss officer should be.

She reminded him, in fact, of his childhood friend Shawnkyr, who had returned to Chiss space after Ebaq 9. Shawnkyr was almost *too* perfect—as a pilot, as an officer, and as a Chiss. She was exactly the sort of person he should have ended up with—not someone like Jaina, the headstrong, stubborn daughter of parents who openly spurned military authority. He had known Shawnkyr ever since their victory over looters during their academy training; he had known Jaina only a couple of years. Shawnkyr had a perfect understanding and acceptance of the chain of command; Jaina was known as something of a loose blaster, following orders only when they concurred with her own moral code. The contrast couldn't have been more extreme.

What his family would think of Jaina, he had no idea. Given their own background, they might accept her perfectly well. But then again, they might not. And if they didn't, then how would it affect his standing among the Chiss, that he had chosen one from outside? He wasn't certain which he would choose if forced to decide between Jaina and his own people. He envied Luke more than he could say; his heart ached to see the three moons of Csillia again. But would his heart have ached more to leave Jaina behind? He didn't know, and a large part of him didn't particularly want to find out, either.

"Jag?"

"Huh?" He snapped out of his thoughts. "Oh, I'm sorry, Eprill. My mind was elsewhere."

"Obviously." There was a hint of disapproval in her voice. "I asked if you thought Sumichan should go with you, or if you'd like me to keep her here to work on her maneuvers."

He sighed. Jaina occupied almost every thought these days. He doubted he could be rid of her, even if he wanted to be.

"She can come with me," he said. "She just needs time to practice—and where we're going, I'm sure we'll have plenty of spare time on our hands."

Then again, he added to himself, *the way the Solos operate, maybe not . . .*

In the previous years, much had been learned about the infidels who occupied the galaxy promised by the gods to the Yuuzhan Vong. Nom Anor had played an important part in gathering and interpreting that knowledge. As a result, he felt justified in thinking that he understood the enemy better than anyone else. But even he failed to get his mind around a culture that would allow a planet's natural surface to be buried under lifeless metal and transparisteel—and not just once, but thousands of times over, so that it was almost impossible for any living thing larger than a rodent or more persistent than moss to survive beneath it.

Yuuzhan'tar was not a world Nom Anor would have chosen to conquer. Had it not been the center of power in this galaxy, he would have happily left it to choke in its dust and smog while the rest of the galaxy came alive with the glorious Yuuzhan Vong invasion. The hardiness of the vile encrustations smothering the planet—the *built things* and the obscenities called *machines* so loved by the enemy—was such that the dhuryam responsible for turning it into a more suitable world seemed to be unable to overcome them. Hundreds of thousands of years of habitation had their own momentum, and mere klekkets of Yuuzhan Vong occupation couldn't turn that back overnight. The roots of these *built things* went deep into the planet, and it would take time to extract them fully.

Nowhere was this more obvious than underground. Buildings had been built upon older buildings, which in turn had been built upon buildings older still, until a crack in one's basement might open up on what had once been an attic in another. And since construction in this fashion was rarely seamless, there were millions of narrow paths that had never been mapped. It was through such ways that Vuurok I'pan led Nom Anor, descending carefully along steep traverses that appeared to be tiled underfoot, as though they had once been roofs. He took them through areas immensely wide, though barely high enough for them to crouch—areas compacted between enormous slabs of ferrocrete and time-flattened piles of rubble. None of which sat easily with Nom Anor. He was not a coward, but the idea of scuttling through such spaces was distinctly unnerving.

Soon they came to an impossibly large vertical tunnel that plunged into depths of darkness that Nom Anor hadn't imagined possible. They spiraled down the interior of this tunnel for what felt like an eternity, walking upon metal steps that constantly creaked and groaned under their weight. It was so large that it could have easily held an entire transport carrier, except that it was almost totally filled with a mysterious silvery column. The thing stretched up high into the darkness above them, taking up so much of the space that there seemed only enough room for the stairs on which they descended. What purpose the column served, exactly, Nom Anor couldn't tell. Perhaps it was the outside of another pipe built within the old one. It, too, was probably abandoned, like everything else in the empty spaces—dead metal left to die, left to *rust*.

Rust. Now that was a concept the Yuuzhan Vong knew about. The reaction between the elements iron and oxygen was an important one in biology. But the abhorrence with which the process was held by these machine builders had been unexpected. Sometimes Nom Anor thought it a good metaphor for how the Yuuzhan Vong invasion *should* have been conducted: slowly, insidiously, the machine builders could have been eroded from beneath until all their glittering, unnatural towers fell and crumbled to dust. But here, underground, he could see the fallacy of the plan. Rust took time, and the Yuuzhan Vong were not known for their patience. The worldships were dying; their people needed homes. If the basements of Yuuzhan'tar could still stand, even after being so long untended, then invasion by rust would simply be too slow.

Still, there was something in the concept, he was sure.

It nagged at him as he followed I'pan farther down into the depths of this abominable planet—so deep, in fact, that the coolness of the upper levels eventually became replaced by a stifling heat and smell not dissimilar to a coralskipper backwash.

Is this to be my tomb? he wondered. *The bowels of a planet whose very nature is blasphemous?*

No! He quickly reined in his thoughts. He would not die here like some worthless vermin, in some hole where even the gods could not find him, if they had ever existed. No matter how deep I'pan went, he would live. He had to. That he currently had no plan and no resources beyond his mind didn't bother him: any goal at all was better than just giving in—and the power of his mind wasn't to be scoffed at.

He didn't know how long they'd been moving, but eventually they emerged into the huge cavern that he knew instantly to be the refuge of the renegade Shamed Ones. He could smell them, their fear and their desperation. I'pan stopped a few paces ahead of him, facing Nom Anor with a newfound confidence—as well as relief, it seemed. He must have felt that here, at least, he had the support of his companions, and that Nom Anor was less likely to attack him than he had been earlier.

"This is it," I'pan said unnecessarily, his arm sweeping around the dusty area. Even with this newfound confidence, his voice still carried a habitual obsequious tone. "We have arrived, Master."

The area was wide and circular, with a high, domed ceiling arcing overhead. Across the ground were scattered numerous blisterlike structures that Nom Anor recognized as minshals, grown for temporary accommodation. The entire place was lit by bubbling, bioluminescent globes hanging from the ceiling high above.

Off to one side, a slanting airshaft led even farther

down into the seemingly endless city basement. Issuing from its wide throat were deep and rhythmic vibrations that made Nom Anor's calves vibrate. Moving over to the shaft he saw a chuk'a waste processor deep inside, its muscular segments busily ingesting rubble as it worked its way downward into the vent, turning it into the walls, ceilings, and floors of the new homes for the Shamed Ones, filling the empty spaces in much the same way that some insects built their nests.

"We found the chuk'a some levels above," I'pan said. "Mislaid for dead, we think, it has since come in handy for our needs."

In the strange, greenish light from the bioluminescent globes, Nom Anor could see I'pan's disfigurement much more clearly. Rejected by coral implants, the Shamed One's face lacked the brutal beauty of a true scarring. His skin was unnaturally smooth, and, apart from his nose, there was a symmetry to his features that offended Nom Anor's refined sense of aesthetic. No wonder I'pan had been outcast. The gods' shaming of him was visible for all to see.

"*We?*" Nom Anor asked, wasting no energy on sympathy. "I see no one other than yourself here, I'pan. Where are these others of whom you speak, and why do they hide?"

"We hide for the same reasons you do," said I'pan. There was no accusation in his tone, so Nom Anor felt no cause to lash out at him. "We have learned to do it out of necessity—for self-preservation." Then, ringing a bell that dangled from a tripod by the entrance to the shaft, he suddenly called out: "Ekma! Sh'roth! Niiriit! We have a visitor."

Muffled voices responded to I'pan's call and the sound of the chuk'a ebbed. Nom Anor straightened as footsteps sounded seemingly from all around him. The fear of capture returned to him. With the minshals and the chuk'a the Shamed Ones no longer seemed so helpless or liable to obey his will. Down here, in their world, he was just one individual among many.

Still, he thought, any number of Shamed Ones should be as nothing to one who defied the Supreme Overlord himself. He held himself as proudly as he could while awaiting his fate, his wounded hand hanging freely, still oozing blood.

A dozen figures appeared from the shadows around them; three more emerged from the entrance to the airshaft. The Shamed Ones surrounded him, studying him. All were ragged and misshapen, although few as severely as I'pan. Two, in fact, seemed perfectly healthy, tall and ritually scarred like warriors. Nom Anor had never seen warriors so filthy before, however, and their rags were a far cry from vonduun crab armor.

One of these two stepped forward. Her face was narrow and angular; scars traced deep crosshatched lines across her cheeks and temples.

"I know you," she said, barely a pace away from him. She displayed no fear whatsoever, only confidence, for which Nom Anor felt nothing but admiration. For a while he had thought they would all be like I'pan.

"Well, I don't know *you*," he responded evenly. Underneath his calm, he was tense, readying himself for attack. One dart from his plaeryin bol and she would suffer a quick and painful death.

"Does it matter who I am?" she snapped. "You have failed our warmaster many times, *Executor,* but I doubt you've ever noticed the ones who fell with you. There are many like me who suffered for your ineptitude. Not all of them found honor in death."

"You still might," Nom Anor said, on the verge of

using the plaeryin bol. But he held himself back. Killing her would set the rest against him. Until he was certain he was about to be betrayed, he would exercise restraint—uncharacteristic as it was for him.

"True," she said, the blue sacks beneath her eyes pulsing slightly from suppressed emotions that he could only guess at. "I still might."

She turned her back on him, and he bit down on his anger at the deliberately insulting gesture. After a few seconds, with those around silent in anticipation of Nom Anor's response, the female faced him again, her dirty teeth smiling at him.

"I am Niiriit," she said, "former warrior of Domain Esh. And you are the once-great Nom Anor." She looked him up and down briefly with a dismissive snort. "I presume you must have failed the warmaster once again. Why else would you be seen down here among the likes of us?"

She paced around him, putting on a show of superiority for her compatriots in Shame. Her garb was little more than tattered rags, but her bearing was strong and muscular. Nom Anor couldn't help his admiration for her—even as he contemplated her death.

"I have not failed." He answered the accusation leveled at him by Niiriit, but his good eye was directed at those huddled around him. It was these whom he needed to impress his authority upon.

"You measure success, then, differently from what I would've expected."

He showed her his teeth, then. "If you wish to mock me, do so openly, not as a coward."

"I'm sorry," she said, returning to stand in front of him again. "It wasn't my intention to mock, just to point out the reality of your situation. It must be faced. We have faced it in our own way, and as a result are doing well enough down here. We live, we are safe, and we are building a home for ourselves." She indicated the air-shaft. "Our lacks include reliable food supplies and adequate clothing, but what we cannot steal we will soon be able to grow. Sh'roth here used to be a shaper." Her hand fell upon the shoulder of one of the older ones in the group. "Many of us have worked in the fields in the past. Among us we have the knowledge to create a self-sustaining community that has no need of the dhuryam. What happens on the surface will be irrelevant here. We just want to be alone—to be left in peace to find our own sort of honor."

Niiriit's defiance struck a chord within Nom Anor. She was Shamed, but she was clearly not defeated.

"I'm impressed," he said, his own survival instincts rising to the fore. If they could survive down there, unnoticed by the cleanup crews and occasional security sweep, then it wasn't impossible that he could, too.

"We're not doing it to impress you," Niiriit said. "Nor did we seek your admiration."

"Nonetheless." Once he would have died rather than utter the words he was about to say, but he knew he had little choice in the matter. "I would stay with you a while, given your leave."

Her expression didn't change. "Why?"

"You need able bodies, and I am willing to work."

Again she asked, "Why?"

That was harder to answer. "The sun has not yet set on the fortune of Nom Anor," he said. "It will rise again, given time."

"And will we rise with it?" called out one of the Shamed Ones off to his left.

"Yes," he said, looking vaguely in their direction. "I give you my word that, should I return to my former position, I will restore your honor."

There was a murmur of consent that quickly rippled through the Shamed Ones. They were obviously taken with his offer.

"How can you listen to this?" The male ex-warrior standing just behind Niiriit stepped forward. "We have no reason to trust him!"

"I know that, Kunra," Niiriit said, her attention remaining fixed upon Nom Anor before her. "But he's one of us, now. If he betrays us, then he betrays himself. Isn't that right, Nom Anor?"

The former executor swallowed his pride, and it tasted of bile. Everything Niiriit said was true. They *could* trust him, because here in the depths of this offensive world, these Shamed Ones were all he had left. Yes, he had told them he would give them back their status if he were returned to his former position, and it was an offer he would happily keep his word on. For the chance to restore his own honor, Nom Anor would make any sacrifice necessary.

"We are allies, Niiriit Esh," he said, giving her full name in return. "I shall not betray you."

He raised his gashed fingers and steeled himself to reopen the wound in order to demonstrate by sacrifice that they could take him at his mercy. It was an instinctive gesture, drummed into him after years in Shimrra's court.

Niiriit stepped forward and stopped him. "That is not necessary down here," she said. "We recognize a different sort of honor, a different sort of gods."

"Different gods?" he repeated.

Niiriit nodded, grinning. "And I just know you'll like them," she said, her dark eyes glinting in the greenish light from the globes overhead. "In fact, you've met some of them in person. Spoken to them, even."

"You are talking about the *Jeedai*?" he asked, finding it impossible to contain his astonishment.

"That appalls you, Nom Anor?" She shook her head, as if disappointed in him. "Live and learn, my friend, or die with the others when their time comes. The choice is yours."

"And I make it freely," he said, bowing low to cover his surprise. The cult of the *Jeedai*? Here on Yuuzhan'tar? He'd heard whispers of it from his spies in the world-ships, but for it to have infiltrated so close to Shimrra was unthinkable. No, more than that. He would have thought it *impossible*.

And yet, impossibly, it was so. What was going on down in these dungeons of Yuuzhan'tar was more than just survival. It was heresy.

Live and learn, he told himself, repeating Niiriit's words as though they were a mantra. *Perhaps there is a way, after all.*

"Tell me about the Jedi," he said. "I am keen to know more . . ."

This is going to change everything, Jacen Solo thought as he stood beneath *Jade Shadow*'s tapered nose, watching from off to one side as his friends and family made their farewells to one another. *This is the beginning of something new.*

It was a very different kind of premonition that rolled through him as he stood there on the landing bay, pretending to busy himself with last-minute checks to the ship. It wasn't necessarily a sense of foreboding, but rather something deeper, more profound. It was as though he could vaguely make out the future, and it was a strange and alien place—somehow a consequence of *this* moment.

Then again, perhaps it wasn't a premonition at all. Perhaps the feeling was a direct result of all the stimcaf he'd been drinking, coupled with the fact that he hadn't been sleeping well of late. For the last few nights he'd been sitting in his room for hours on end, worrying—not just about the mission, either, but about leaving half the people he loved behind, as well.

He watched them now, hugging, shaking hands, kissing, laughing. For all the levity, one would think *Jade Shadow* and her crew were off on nothing more than a jaunt to the sunbaked moons of Calfa-5 rather than on a mission to the Unknown Regions. But he didn't need the Force to tell him that beneath the casual facade there simmered a somberness that would have been difficult for any of them to shake . . .

Just about everyone was there to see off *Jade Shadow*. His mother had come, shadowed once again by her Noghri bodyguards, Cakhmaim and Meewalh. Han clapped Luke on the shoulder and advised him to keep out of trouble. The well-meant hypocrisy provoked a light smile from the Jedi Master, who nodded and wrapped his old friend's hand in both of his and shook firmly.

To one side stood C-3PO, gleaming bronze in the arc lights illuminating the side of the armored transport looming over them, with R2-D2 beside him, whistling cheerfully to reassure his metal companion.

"It's not *you* I'm worried about," C-3PO returned. "It's me!"

R2's domed top turned as it issued another string of beeps and whistles.

"Well, at least you don't know what awaits you in the Unknown Regions," C-3PO said. "I know far too much about the place Mistress Leia intends to take me."

Jag Fel helped load the last of the supplies into the transport. Danni Quee was running late and had sent some equipment down ahead of her on a repulsor platform. When it was empty, it beeped to no one in particular and trundled away. Cilghal's apprentice, Tekli, had already loaded supplies the healer had insisted they

might need on their long journey. Luckily the giant reptilian Jedi, Saba Sebatyne, had brought less than half her
allocation, creating extra space. Like Jacen, the stoic
Barabel stood away from the others, her small eyes
blinking while her tail twitched restlessly about her feet.

Perhaps she senses it, too, he thought. *After all, those
of us leaving on* Jade Shadow *could be gone for months.
Who knows what we'll be returning to, or what we'll
even be bringing back with us?* Communications with
the Unknown Regions were notoriously unreliable, routed
through just one long-distance transceiver on the edge of
known space. After Anakin's death, he wasn't so naive as
to assume that he would ever again see any of these people
he was now saying good-bye to.

*But I have no choice. Like everyone else, I must do
what I must. The war with the Yuuzhan Vong might
be won without us, but there are many different kinds
of war.*

Jaina noticed him standing to one side and came to
join him.

"What's wrong, brother? Having second thoughts
about going?"

He turned to face her and was surprised by how grown-
up she looked. Although the age difference between them
was barely five standard minutes, she seemed so much
wiser and more mature than he pictured her in his mind.
Where was the child with whom he'd tormented C-3PO
on Coruscant? Or the teenager who had single-handedly
repaired a crashed TIE fighter on Yavin 4? The girl was
gone, replaced by this young woman standing now before him. Try as he might, though, he couldn't recall exactly when the transition had occurred.

"Not at all," he replied, forcing a smile. "Just a little
overwhelmed, I guess."

He looked at her again, still somewhat amazed by

the confident woman standing before him. They weren't kids anymore. The universe had taught them the hard way that the responsibilities of being an adult weren't always easy. But the Force connection between them was still strong, and this fact alone brought him great comfort.

"I hope you find what you're looking for," Jaina said, intruding upon his thoughts.

"I'm sure we will," Jacen said. "All available data suggest that the Unknown Regions are where—"

"I meant in your heart, brother."

His smile came easier this time. "I won't come back until I do."

"Is that a promise, Jacen?" she asked. "Or a prophecy?"

"Perhaps it's a little of both."

She embraced him, then, tightly and warmly. "Just make sure you *do* come back, okay?" she whispered close to his ear.

She winked at him as she pulled away, and before he could say anything more, the space she had just vacated was suddenly filled with other people wishing him well and bidding him good-bye.

Jag Fel shook his hand with a definite air of reassurance. Jacen forestalled his father's usual gruff attempts at farewells by cutting off whatever he'd been about to say and simply giving him a hug. His mother hugged Jacen, too. She didn't offer any words, though. She didn't need to; the emotion in her eyes spoke volumes.

Others appeared before him, taking his hand, patting his back, and speaking animatedly. He heard little of what was said; his attention kept going back to his sister, now standing at the back with Jag—who respectfully kept his hands to himself. Nevertheless, even though he didn't hear a lot of what was being said to him, Jacen could *feel* the sentiments expressed. The air was almost crackling with the Force as so many emotional Jedi clustered around him.

He would miss the ones who would remain behind, but he wouldn't grieve—no more than he would for Vergere. Even now, so many weeks after she died, he could still hear her voice in his mind as clearly as though she was one of those standing right there beside him.

"You have always been alone, Jacen Solo. Even in the midst of your family, and your friends. Even when you touched the Force. You have always been set apart, distanced, separated and alone, through no choice or action of your own."

He hadn't understood everything his teacher had said to him, and suspected he would be picking at the meaning of her words for many years to come—if not the rest of his life. Vergere had been a creature of contradictions, a pet of the Yuuzhan Vong at one moment, an ancient Jedi Knight in another.

"Everyone is part of you," she had said, "just as you are part of everyone."

It was a simple truth, and one he embraced now as he said good-bye to his friends and family. While his loved ones lived, wherever they were, he had no cause to grieve . . .

At that moment, Danni Quee bustled into the bay, her shoulders laden with bags. Following her, looking somewhat dazed and confused, was Tahiri.

"I found this one wandering in the corridors outside," Danni said.

Tahiri flushed pink. "I-I got lost on the way here," she stammered. "I'm sorry."

Jacen felt a wave of compassion for the girl. The three deep scars on her forehead stood out strongly against her blood-filled face. She still looked terribly thin and uncertain of herself; there was little in the girl's appearance and nervous manner to suggest the Jedi he knew her to be.

He reached out with the Force to touch her, comfort her. She glanced over at him, a faint trace of gratitude in her smiling eyes. But she turned away quickly, uneasily, back to the others.

"So this is it?" Danni said, her eyes bright, her curly blond hair standing in a nimbus around her head. "We're really going?"

"We're really going," Luke said. Mara went aboard *Jade Shadow* to prime the yacht's systems. Saba and Tekli followed. The sound of mechanical systems whirring into life gave the farewells a new urgency. The Solo/Skywalker clan gathered for one last moment while the others moved aboard. Jacen was unsurprised to see tears in Tahiri's eyes when she was invited to join in, but was glad she agreed.

"May the Force be with us all," Luke said after a moment.

"It always is," Jacen said automatically, paraphrasing another of Vergere's teachings. "The Force is everything, and everything is the Force. The only uncertainty lies in ourselves."

Jaina smiled at her brother; Leia did the same, and kissed his cheek.

Then it was time to go. Everything was loaded, and everyone was there. There was no point delaying any longer. As R2-D2 glided ahead of him up the ramp into *Jade Shadow*'s belly, Jacen felt the premonition rush through him once more. It prompted him to halt momentarily and cast a quick glance back to his parents and sister.

What if I'm wrong about Zonama Sekot? he wondered anxiously. *What if this grand quest is nothing more than an elaborate means of running away from conflict? What if I misunderstood Vergere completely?* Even if he *had* understood her perfectly and was doing exactly the right thing for the moment, it still wouldn't be easy. As she had said: "No lesson is truly learned until it is purchased with pain." The lesson the Galactic Alliance had to learn was a difficult one, and he was in no doubt that the people most likely to bear the cost would be those on *Jade Shadow*.

He offered a brief wave and then continued into the maw of the ship. At the top of the ramp he saw Danni standing there, waiting for him. Her smile did little to hide her own anxieties.

"There's nothing to be nervous about, Danni," he said, looking calmly and evenly into her eyes. "Everything is going to work out just fine."

"Really?" she said, shucking the larger of her bags. "Well, either you know something I don't, Jacen Solo, or you're one of the best liars I've ever met."

PART TWO

DESTINATION

The moment *Jade Shadow* dropped out of hyperspace near Bastion, capital of the Imperial Remnant, Saba Sebatyne knew something was wrong. Her mind rang with the distinctive and unsettling harmonics of life extinguished in great amounts. But it was more than that—this was the *absence* of life itself, as though chunks of the vital universe had been hollowed out, deeper than vacuum.

She roared at the same time Mara announced: "Yuuzhan Vong!"

"Where?" Luke asked from the copilot's seat.

"Everywhere!" Mara's hands played across the controls. "Hold on, everybody. This could get rough!"

The ship lurched violently. Saba didn't need viewscreens to tell her that they'd been seen by the enemy. The empty points that were the Yuuzhan Vong and their strange, living vessels spun around her like pollen in a miniature hurricane. *Jade Shadow* danced among them, weaving in and out of confrontations, desperately trying to shake off any enemy craft they picked up on their trail. The ship rang with the sound of weapons fire, both incoming and outgoing.

Saba's blunted claws left great dents in the fabric of the navigator's chair she occupied. She wasn't aware of the low rumbling coming from her throat until Jacen Solo braved the shaking deck to come and crouch down next to her.

"Do you feel it, Saba?" he asked. "Can you tell through the Force what's going on?"

"I feel . . ." Her teeth clenched tight as another wave of death rolled over her. Bastion was being pummeled by the Yuuzhan Vong; lives were being extinguished by the millions. She didn't have words.

"I'm sensing life here," Jacen said, "but in great disarray."

Saba agreed. She could sense the life energies scattered around the system: some on the planet, panicked, trying to escape the invaders; some in orbit, pulling back before an overwhelming invasion; and several other clusters throughout the system where forces were attempting to regroup. They were outnumbered by the Yuuzhan Vong, but they *were* there.

"I can make out at least fifteen capital ships!" Mara shouted from her position at the controls. "Big ones, too!" She shook her head in frustration. "Bastion is going to take a pummeling, no matter what we do."

"It looks to me like they're pulling out," Luke said. "Falling back to regroup elsewhere. Look." One figure stabbed at a screen. "They're civilian ships. They've evacuated Bastion."

There was a moment of tense silence as the significance of that statement sunk in. To evacuate Bastion, the Empire must have been hit hard. But it wasn't finished. As galling as a retreat was, sometimes it made the best tactical sense. The ships flooding in waves from Bastion were getting out under cover of the planetary shields. It looked like they would hold long enough to save much of the population. If the population had stayed put, however, the concentrated fire of the Yuuzhan Vong would have eventually overwhelmed them.

That portion of the battle was already decided. Saba sent her mind out across the system, to where life-lights clustered in smaller groups. The largest, she guessed, contained the equivalent of two Star Destroyers as well as a number of support vessels. They were swinging around the back of a gas giant, caught in its gravity shadow and harried by a powerful enemy contingent.

Saba focused on the viewscreens before her, trying to match what she'd seen against the coordinates in the real world. *Jade Shadow* was too small to affect what happened on Bastion, but it might make a difference in a smaller arena.

"There," she growled, pointing with a thick finger. "That section there. But you must be quick. They're in trouble."

Jacen stood and stepped over to his aunt to relay the information. Saba shut her eyes as *Jade Shadow* leapt forward, ducking and weaving. Mara made a short hyperspace jump to take it closer to the gas giant, and for one brief and blessed moment there was nothing but silence.

Just another planet attacked by the Yuuzhan Vong, she told herself. *Hunt the moment.*

A small, furred hand grabbed Saba's scaly wrist. Opening her eyes again, she saw that Tekli now occupied the space that Jacen had just vacated. The diminutive Chadra-Fan emitted a wave of pheromones that Saba found soothing. She knew that the healer's apprentice had learned how to control her chemical scents to produce compounds with properties therapeutic to various species, but she hadn't realized that the Barabels were included among those.

Although it might once have seemed strange to her to be comforted by a creature that looked more like a meal than an equal, she sighed gratefully, allowing herself to relax and be taken by the peaceful scent. A moment later, all too soon, it was back to the fighting.

The screen was filled with a bloated, orange-yellow gas giant. Numerous rings and moons crowded around it, as if for safety; many already showed signs of disruption as warring fleets plowed past or sometimes even directly into them. Far below, through the dense atmosphere, Saba felt alarm spreading through a colony of balloonlike life-forms; similar to the giant beldons of Bespin, they were too primitive to understand the meaning of the disturbances taking place in the sky.

Jade Shadow came around the planet as though intending to ram the remains of the Imperial fleet, trailing two determined coralskippers. As Mara neared the two Star Destroyers that Saba had sensed, she performed a deft gravitational whip around one of the gas giant's larger moons. The coralskippers followed, tugging at *Jade Shadow*'s shields with their dovin basals. Plasma fire peppered at their rear until, when *Jade Shadow*'s vector had matched that of the Imperial fleet and it was in full view of the Star Destroyers, Mara stutterfired to distract them, then used the Force to drop two shadow bombs under their guard. The coralskippers blossomed into energy. Once the afterwash of the explosion had passed, *Jade Shadow* slowed and leveled out.

"This is Mara Jade Skywalker, captain of the Galactic Alliance transport *Jade Shadow*, hailing Imperial Star Destroyer *Chimaera*. Are you receiving me, *Chimaera*?"

The subspace receiver crackled before a reply came in: "You're a long way from home, Captain Skywalker."

"Just thought we'd drop in to see how you guys were doing," she said sardonically. "And from the looks of things, I'm guessing not so good."

"Your timing could be better." The comm operator sounded weary. "I don't suppose you've brought a fleet with you."

"I'm afraid not, *Chimaera*, but you could do worse than concentrating your fire on that cruiser lurking at the back. It's holding a yammosk. Take it out, and you might find your luck changing."

"A yammosk? . . . How could you possibly know that?"

"Ask questions later, when you know I'm right."

"Understood, Captain Skywalker. Passing on the information now."

"Before you do that, I need to speak to Grand Admiral Pellaeon."

"Patching you through to the bridge now, Captain Skywalker."

The line went dead and, barely seconds later, a squadron of TIE fighters left the launching bays of *Chimaera*, angling away from the gas giant below to target the yammosk-bearing cruiser. Although the Yuuzhan Vong had eased off their attack for the moment, it was obvious that prior to *Jade Shadow*'s arrival the fighting had been intense. Both Star Destroyers were scarred from weapons fire; black gashes had been torn through *Chimaera*'s underside, exposing a large number of decks to naked space. Saba could feel its crew fighting to stay alive, along with the fading traces of those who had failed. She couldn't tell exactly how many were injured or dying, only that there were many.

"If you've come to say *I told you so*, Skywalker, then I'm not interested," the Grand Admiral announced curtly. "This isn't the time for—"

"I'm not known for gloating, Gilad," Luke said, leaning past Mara to speak into the comm. "No more than you are for giving up."

"*Both* Skywalkers? To what do we owe this honor?"

"Call it destiny, or good luck. Either way, your forces are taking a pounding. Can you tell us what went wrong? Considering the size of your home fleet, I would have thought you'd be able to hold your own."

"They took us by surprise," the Grand Admiral said irritably. "We *were* holding our own to begin with. Then the Vong pulled back. We thought we had them on the run, but they were just getting out of the way."

Mara nodded in understanding. "Grutchins?"

"Thousands of them," the admiral said. "Once they'd punched a hole in our defenses, the Yuuzhan Vong came back into the fray. We've been on the back foot ever since."

Saba hissed at the mention of the hideous, insectoid creatures. Swarms of grutchins had laid waste to too many defenses during the war with the Yuuzhan Vong for her to doubt that the same had happened here.

"Admiral," Master Skywalker said, "the offer to join forces is still open."

"Your sister was up here a while back, trying to sell us on that idea. I thought the Moffs made it quite clear then that your help wasn't required."

"And where are the Moffs now, Gilad?"

Saba noticed Pellaeon's hesitation. He may have been a commander with pride, but he was also smart enough to acknowledge when he needed help, no matter how much it hurt to do so.

"Okay, Skywalker," the Grand Admiral said after a moment. "We'll discuss this later, if there *is* a later. I understand you've given us some telemetry that might shift the balance here. If that works, we'll regroup with the rest of the fleet at Yaga Minor. Civilian refugees are heading for Muunilinst, but we suspect the Vong will follow our forces, to keep us off balance. If you beat us there, look for Captain Arien Yage of the frigate *Widow-maker*. She used to serve with me on the *Chimaera*; if she survived Bastion, she'll listen to you."

"Understood." Mara and Luke exchanged glances. "Good luck."

The Grand Admiral closed the line. For a moment, no one on *Jade Shadow* spoke. It was Jacen who finally stated the obvious.

"It had to happen," he said. "We knew it was inevitable, even if they didn't want to admit it."

"That doesn't make it any easier to watch." Luke's voice was slightly reproving. His eyes were haunted by the deaths everyone was feeling.

"I wish there was something we could do," Tekli muttered.

"Unless it's likely to create a fleet out of thin air, you're better off not wishing," Mara said, glancing back at her briefly. "They had their chance to join with us, and they didn't take it. I'll bet the Yuuzhan Vong left them alone, knowing the Imperials would never join in—not until provoked, anyway. When their spies said they'd had just enough time to get over Ithor, to relax the defenses, the Vong hit them with everything they could spare. It's what I would have done in their shoes. Flatten the Empire with whatever resources they can get, this far out, and get rid of a niggling irritant. Then put those resources back into the real battle, elsewhere. Do it quickly enough and those forces won't be missed."

"If the Empire survives, it may prove to be more than just an irritant," Luke said. He backed away to give his wife clear access to the controls. "What's the name of that other Star Destroyer? Do you recognize it?"

"It's pretty banged up, but I think it's the *Superior*."

"The Yuuzhan Vong aren't going to let them wander around here forever."

"Your guess at how much longer they can last is as good as mine, Luke. Pellaeon can probably handle this lot, if they take out the yammosk, but anything tougher will turn him into metal rain for that moon over there."

"And us with him, if we stick around." Master Skywalker was clearly unhappy about the decision he was being forced to make. On the one hand, Saba guessed, he wanted to stay and add the *Jade Shadow* to the Imperial forces withdrawing from Bastion. On the other, he had the mission itself to think of: the hunt for Zonama Sekot. Being destroyed wouldn't solve anything.

Her claws itched at the thought of running from battle, at leaving another planet to the nonexistent mercy of the Yuuzhan Vong. But harsh though it sounded, it seemed that leaving Bastion in favor of the mission *did* make the most sense.

"We'll meet them at Yaga Minor," Master Luke said, sighing heavily.

"The old stomping ground."

"Can you get us safely out of the giant's gravity well?"

Mara responded unhesitatingly. "Of course. I can outfly the scarheads with my eyes closed."

"Then do it," her husband said.

"Better strap in. This isn't going to be the gentle scenic stroll we were promised."

Saba left them to handle *Jade Shadow* and strapped herself into a seat in the passenger bay. Danni Quee, who had sat pale-faced and silent through the entire encounter, remained in position to Saba's right, next to Jacen Solo and Tekli. This was a familiar configuration. They had spent much of their voyage in readiness for mishap, despite Mara's words. Every time they had come out of hyperspace—and even during longer jumps, for the Yuuzhan Vong interdictor ships were an ever-present concern—they had been safely strapped in, just in case.

Now that "in case" had happened, Saba found the familiarity soothing. The hunt had begun. All that remained was to see if the prey perished, or if the hunter went hungry. The matter of who out of the Yuuzhan Vong and the Empire was the hunter, and who was the prey, she hadn't decided yet. But even from what little she had experienced of Grand Admiral Pellaeon, she already knew that he was not the sort to be readily preyed upon. He would have surprised many would-be hunters by turning on them at the last moment and showing unsuspected teeth. Perhaps this time would be another.

The niggling thought that even the sharpest teeth could be blunted with time followed her as *Jade Shadow* raced through hyperspace to the rendezvous point.

Jacen took the navigator's seat in *Jade Shadow*'s cockpit when they emerged from hyperspace a discreet distance from Yaga Minor. The planet was known for shipyards that serviced the Imperial Remnant, and via the screens he looked on, impressed, at the vast orbital frameworks that dwarfed Yaga Minor's single, small moon. Everything from microwelders to self-contained ore smelters was being used to create ships for the ever-growing fleet. Two half-completed Star Destroyers hung in the spindly embrace of one of the shipyards; the others were in the process of building various freighters, frigates, tugs, and TIE fighters. An engine-testing range near one of the yards flashed every color of the rainbow—and beyond— as vessels ran through their paces before being released into service.

When *Jade Shadow* arrived, the remains of the fleet

stationed around the Imperial capital and its neighbor, Muunilinst, were slowly coming into orbit around Yaga Minor—disheartened by the retreat but determined to fight back. The first of the survivors docked their ships alongside the Golan III Defense Platforms orbiting the planet, while those needing repairs headed for the yards. It wasn't long, though, before the available berths were full. Yaga Minor wasn't designed to accommodate the entire fleet at once, not even one reduced by the surprise attack on Bastion.

Jade Shadow's long-range sensors detected three Star Destroyers arriving from Bastion, neither of them *Chimaera* or *Superior*. Jacen waited anxiously for any sign of Gilad Pellaeon. If the Grand Admiral didn't survive the battle of Bastion, Jacen didn't fancy their chances of bringing around the Imperials. Pellaeon had so often been the voice of reason in the proud isolationist state. If anyone was going to convince the Moffs to join the Galactic Alliance, it was going to have to be him.

"How long do we wait for him to appear?" Danni asked Jacen quietly from behind, not wanting to startle him. She still looked nervous. Their escape from Bastion had been much narrower than Mara had let on, he knew, and Danni was Force-sensitive enough to have guessed it. Indeed, their trip thus far, from Mon Calamari across Yuuzhan Vong–occupied territory, had been enough to put anyone on edge. Once he would have felt safe upon reaching the Imperial Remnant, but the attack on Bastion had dispelled that comfort.

"To be honest," he said, "I don't know. What I do know, though, is that Gilad Pellaeon is a survivor. If he can get out of there, he will."

Proximity alarms bleeped and Jacen turned his attention to his aunt's voice as she explained who they were to a squadron of TIE fighters that had noticed *Jade Shadow* lurking in the planet's outer orbits. But there was none of the usual Imperial hostility in the squadron leader's voice, as he was expecting. If anything, the pilot seemed relieved that *Jade Shadow* wasn't an advance vessel from the Yuuzhan Vong, scoping out Yaga Minor for the next wave.

My enemy's enemy is my friend, Jacen reminded himself. If Gilad Pellaeon didn't make it, then at least they would have that going in their favor.

His relief was short-lived, however, when another call came over the subspace band.

"Unauthorized vehicle identifying itself as *Jade Shadow*," said the deep, guttural voice through the comm unit. In his voice Jacen detected nothing but officiousness. "Please respond."

"This is *Jade Shadow*," Mara replied. "What is it now?"

"You are required to state your intentions and prepare to be boarded."

"What? We're on a peaceful mission."

"That remains to be seen," the voice continued. "Do as you're told immediately or your engines will be disabled."

"I'd like to see you try," Mara snarled. "Who am I talking to? Which idiot sent you?"

"I am Commander Keten and I represent Moff Flennic of Yaga Minor. You are violating Imperial space and will be fired upon if you do not obey its regulations."

Now *this* was more what Jacen had come to expect of the Imperials. He moved back through to the cockpit to find Luke and Mara conferring over how to respond to the commander's demands. Through the massive transparisteel canopy, Jacen saw an armed Imperial transport moving to match orbits, accompanied by a dozen TIE fighters.

"What do you want to do?" Luke was saying.

Mara looked uncertain. "I don't know. I need time to think."

"Time we don't have, my love," Luke said.

"I don't see what the problem is," Jacen put in. "Why not just let them board? It's not as though we have anything to hide."

Luke nodded. "He's right, Mara. And it will be a gesture of goodwill, besides."

Jacen felt warmed by his uncle's support. Mara, however, was not as convinced. She shook her head, rejecting the idea.

"I know Flennic's type," she said. "He'll have a chip on his shoulder bigger than a Super Star Destroyer. Let him get ahold of us and we'll end up in some shipyard sweatshop for the rest of our lives."

"Which might not be that long if the Yuuzhan Vong keep coming this way," Luke returned wryly.

"Please respond immediately," the commander said shortly. "Or we will be forced to take action."

A smile touched Mara's lips as an idea sprang to mind. "With the Jedi we have on board, all we have to do is get Keten here and we can make the problem go away."

Into the comm unit, she said: "We see your point, Commander. Our passenger space is limited, but we'd be pleased to welcome you aboard. When you see for your own eyes that—"

Keten cut her off with a chuckle. "You don't honestly think that I'd be the one coming aboard, do you? I'd sooner stick my head in a drive tube than take my chances with your Jedi mind tricks. No, the boarding party will consist solely of Mark Five security droids."

Mara cursed under her breath. "Well, there goes that idea."

"You can hardly blame him for being suspicious," Jacen said. "You were intending to use those Jedi mind tricks, after all."

His uncle sighed. "Well, we can't very well turn him down now," he said. "Not after agreeing to be boarded."

The communicator bleeped. Another transport was edging closer.

"This is Captain Yage of *Widowmaker*," a woman's voice said over the comm. "Commander Keten, you may stand down. I shall be boarding this vessel myself, seeing as you will not."

"But Captain—" Keten started.

Yage cut him off sharply. "May I remind you, Commander, that right here and now I outrank you," she said. "I am ordering you to stand down, and I expect you to comply without debate."

There was a long pause before Keten finally came back with, "I shall submit to your authority, Captain, but I would like it to go on record that I do so under protest."

"Duly noted, Commander," Yage said. "Yage out."

The armed transport and its contingent of fighters accelerated to a lower orbit, leaving *Jade Shadow* to face the new arrival.

"Requesting permission to dock, *Jade Shadow*," Captain Yage said over the comm.

"The same Captain Yage Pellaeon told us to look out for," Luke reminded Mara.

"That's not the highest recommendation," Mara said, "but it will have to do." Speaking into the communicator, she said: "Feel free to match velocities and extend your umbilical, Captain. Welcome aboard."

Jacen went back through the ship to ready the air lock. *Jade Shadow* was relatively cramped, given the extra

equipment she had been fitted with along with the supplies required for their extended mission. There were five
staterooms, a passenger bay, a galley, and a common
area leading off a central, looping corridor. The bridge
and common room were the diamonds in the corridor's
ring. The main air lock hatch with its dummy door was
located on the port side.

As he passed through the passenger bay, he was met by
Danni coming the other way.

"Is everything okay?" she asked quickly as he passed.

"Better than it could have been," he said. "I'm just
going to greet the locals now."

He hesitated at the entrance to the main corridor,
looking back at the scientist. So far throughout the
trip, Danni hadn't really had a chance to contribute in
any way. He couldn't blame her for looking and sounding so anxious.

"I don't suppose you'd like to join me, would you?" he
asked.

Her worried expression dissolved into a grateful smile
as she followed him out of the passenger bay, obviously
pleased to be finally doing something. When they reached
the air lock, Jacen double-checked that his lightsaber
was at his side, just in case this Captain Yage was not as
reliable as Pellaeon had suggested she would be. From the
corner of his eye he caught Danni watching him. He faced
her fully when he saw the apprehension on her face.

"Are you okay?" he asked.

She shook her head. "Why do I keep allowing myself
to get talked into these things, Jacen?"

He frowned, confused. "I didn't think I talked you
into anything," he said. "I just thought you might like to
come along and greet—"

"No, not here!" she said. "*Here*—on this mission."

Jacen nodded, understanding the core of her reservations. "The locals can't be that bad, can they?" He tried to ease her concerns with a smile.

She shrugged. "I've never actually met Imperials before. But I do remember the stories my parents used to tell me." She paused, her eyes flitting nervously from the air lock to Jacen. "They can't *all* be monsters, can they?"

"No. They're human, Danni, just like us." He leaned against the bulkhead next to her, enjoying the momentary quiet the two of them had been granted. "You know, I wonder sometimes what it'll be like when the war is over. What do you suppose we'll do when we're not being asked to do stuff like this?"

"We'll go back to doing whatever it was we did before all of this started, I guess," she said.

He laughed a little at this. "It's been so long now that those days before the Yuuzhan Vong arrived are starting to blur. It gets harder and harder each day to recall just what it was like back then."

"Maybe that's a good thing," she said. "A break with the past. If we can get the Empire to join up, that'll make the Galactic Alliance something truly new. Who knows? We might just find galactic unity yet."

"That's all well and good," he said, "but I wonder about the small things, too. What *I'll* do, not just what happens to the galaxy."

"You'll do what Jedi Knights seem to do best," she said.

He studied her for a second. "Which is?"

"Get into trouble, of course," she said. Despite her nervousness, she forced a smile.

He smiled in return, glad that her mood had lightened. "I'd just as happily settle for a quiet life somewhere. There's a lot left to think about. A lifetime or two's worth, in fact."

"It could get lonely."

"It could indeed." He thought it nothing more than a flip comment until his gaze met hers. Suddenly he found it hard to look away.

"Jacen?" Mara's voice from his comlink snapped him out of it.

"Yeah," he said, straightening. "I'm here."

"Ten seconds," she said. "I'll disarm the outer hatch when the umbilical is pressurized."

A moment later a dull thud echoed through the hull as the Imperial transport sealed an umbilical to attach the two craft. Pressure readings on the far side of the air lock rose steadily once the noise died away. Less than a minute later, Jacen heard a gentle hiss as the air lock broke its seal and swung open.

He glanced at Danni. Her face was set in a determined mask, with no sign of the vulnerability he had sensed a moment before. But she tensed noticeably as three people in Imperial uniform stepped through the air lock. The one in the lead, a solidly built woman in her forties with black hair bound tightly into a bun, Jacen assumed to be Captain Yage, with the two male officers following close behind, their blaster rifles at the ready, her bodyguards.

"Welcome aboard *Jade Shadow*," Jacen said pleasantly, stepping forward. He introduced himself and Danni, keeping his hands respectfully behind his back at all times. Yage bowed perfunctorily to each of them in turn, but made no effort to introduce her male companions. "We'd like to thank you for your assistance back there."

"Not at all," the captain said. "I have never been fond of time-wasting bureaucracy—particularly from the likes of officious idiots like Keten." She smiled tightly. "That's off the record, of course."

"Of course." Jacen waved the guests through to the

common area, where Mara and Luke stood, ready to greet them. Off to one side stood Saba and Tekli. Jacen noted the way Yage's bodyguards started in alarm at the sight of the enormous Barabel, their rifles rising slightly. Yage was startled also, he was sure, but she was professional enough to suppress any sign of her surprise. Saba rumbled slightly in her throat, and the troopers lowered their weapons.

Yage inclined her head politely to the two nonhumans when introduced, but quickly returned her attention to Luke and Mara.

"So at last I meet the legendary Skywalkers," she said, stepping forward to shake their hands. "I've certainly heard a lot about you."

"All untrue, I'm sure," Mara said pleasantly.

"I hope not. Gilad speaks very highly of you both."

"I don't suppose you've heard if Grand Admiral Pellaeon has returned from Bastion," Luke said.

A shadow seemed to pass across Captain Yage's face. "I'm afraid that Fleet Intelligence is in disarray following the Yuuzhan Vong's attack."

"Have you learned anything more about how the enemy managed to do so much damage so quickly?"

"I already know why. We were taken disgracefully off guard by the attack. Our spies had reported that the fleet approaching us was headed for Nirauan, not here at all, but I guess our spies weren't as reliable as we'd thought. Even so, we should have been ready. Anyone with half a brain should have seen the flaw in the reasoning that, if we hadn't been attacked yet, we were unlikely to be attacked at all. Our refusal to join with the rest of the galaxy in resisting didn't make us safe. That type of logic didn't work for the Hutts, so why should it have worked for us?"

"It seems to me," Mara said, "that you're paying the price for the council's lack of foresight."

"Perhaps now the Moffs will see reason," Jacen added.

Yage half turned to look at him. "You think so? You've already seen what Moff Flennic thinks of you. He might try to resist the Yuuzhan Vong, but he'll never join the people who took the Empire away from him." She looked at each of them in turn, her gaze finally coming to rest on Luke. "That's why you're here, isn't it? To try again to get us to join you. We already have a treaty. What more do you want?"

"Ideally," Luke said, "we'd like the Empire to become part of the Galactic Alliance—but that's one for our respective legal representatives to argue out. For now we'd simply like us to agree to help each other before we continue on with—"

"We can fight well enough without your help," Yage quickly pointed out. She may have been more courteous and diplomatic than Keten, but she still carried the Imperial pride. "We're ready for them now."

"You won't get far using your existing techniques," Mara said. "Our greatest minds have been working on a way to counterattack using the yammosks that make the Yuuzhan Vong so hard to beat. We can give you those techniques—"

"In exchange for what?" the captain interrupted, a slight suspicion gently curling the corners of her mouth.

"Absolutely nothing," Luke said. "I'm not a diplomat, Captain. I'm a Jedi, I stand for life and peace, and I would never hold anything back for the sake of political point scoring. I'd rather get about the business of saving lives."

A thrill went through Jacen at his uncle and former teacher's words. They rang true to the new philosophy of the Force that he was trying to determine. Captain Yage, however, was not as easily impressed, and raised a skeptical eyebrow at the Jedi Master.

"Don't Yuuzhan Vong lives count to you, Jedi?" she asked.

Luke didn't recoil from her response. "The Yuuzhan Vong are the aggressors, and our help won't guarantee their defeat. What you do with this information is up to you."

"To be honest, Skywalker, if it *was* up to me, I'd use it quite happily," she said. "But things will be grim without Gilad to champion your cause. The hard-liners will always believe that the Empire in its glory days could have withstood the invaders with ease, and that your weakening of our strength has led directly to our destruction. If destroyed we must be, then we will go down with pride." Her voice was steeped in bitterness. "The last refugees from Bastion arrived some time ago. We're not expecting any more. If Gilad had survived, I'm sure he would have been here by now. With that in mind, you might be better off assuming that he won't be here to help you."

The mood in *Jade Shadow* turned instantly grim. "Then we shall need to make alternative plans," Luke said. "We'll need to talk to Flennic, even if he's not prepared to listen to us. Can you get us to him without turning us over to the likes of Keten?"

She pursed her lips thoughtfully. "I can try," she said. "With Gilad out of the way, the anti–Galactic Alliance forces will be in ascendance. Add to that the fact that the Moff Council will be in tatters after the attacks on Bastion and Muunilinst, and you'll see why I hesitate to guarantee you anything at the—" She stopped as her comlink buzzed. "Excuse me."

Captain Yage turned away to take the call, exchanging a few simple words with the person on the other end. Before she had finished talking, before he had even seen her face, Jacen knew something was wrong. He could sense a powerful emotion radiating from her.

"What's gone wrong?" he asked when she clipped the comlink back on her belt.

"That was my second in command on *Widowmaker*," she said. "A shuttle just made it from Bastion containing injured ferried from *Chimaera*." Her troubled eyes met Luke's. "Gilad was on board."

"That's good news, isn't it?" Jacen said.

She shook her head. "Not really," she said. "He's in a coma, and he's not expected to live."

Anakin's mother came to see Tahiri the day before the *Millennium Falcon* was due to leave on its mission to patch up the communications gaps in Galactic Alliance space. Jacen and the others had left two days earlier, leaving a surprising hole in Tahiri's life. Since she'd learned that she had been intended for that mission, she felt as though she had let everyone down. She wasn't doing much to help the war effort by huddling in Master Cilghal's infirmary, that was for sure. Jaina came when she could, but she was too busy organizing Twin Suns' departure to be wasting time with the sick. Anakin's sister had said it was not a problem, and that she didn't mind taking time out to visit Tahiri, but Tahiri felt guilty nonetheless for inconveniencing her. She had caused Jaina enough trouble as it was.

So when the Mon Calamari nurse announced that Princess Leia herself had dropped by to visit, Tahiri was more than a little surprised—as well as embarrassed.

"How are you feeling?" Anakin's mother pulled up a

seat and sat close to the edge of Tahiri's bed. Mon Cal's sun was setting, sending brilliant colors through the window and across the middle-aged stateswoman. There were many lines on her face, but they came from laughter and kindness and compassion. It was easy to see why Han Solo loved her. She was still very much a beautiful woman, with her eyes being her most outstanding feature. And whenever Tahiri looked into those eyes, she felt she could see Anakin staring back at her.

"I'm fine, thank you," Tahiri lied, blinking back the tears that were welling up.

Leia narrowed her eyes in friendly accusation.

Tahiri relented with a smile. "Okay," she said. "It's true that I have seen better days. I'll admit that much. But I'm just more tired than anything else. Even the small trip to see *Jade Shadow* off kind of took it out of me." She shrugged. "Other than that, I think I'm doing all right."

"There's no rush," Leia said. "The important thing is that you get well. Cilghal tells me that you've put on weight, which is good news. She believes that your weight loss constitutes the total of your physical symptoms. Once you think you're ready, you're free to leave." She paused, allowing space for Tahiri to speak. When nothing was said after a few seconds, Leia asked, "Do you think you're ready?"

Tahiri didn't know how to answer. She knew that she could get up and walk out of the door anytime she wanted, but she didn't know what would happen after. The dreams hadn't stopped; if anything they'd become worse. If she left now, they would gnaw at her as they had before, and before she knew it she would be back in the infirmary again, still unable to explain to everyone just what was happening to her.

She didn't want to leave; she felt safe here. But she also

couldn't stay forever. The infirmary was for sick people, and she was—

What? What *was* she, exactly? She didn't know, and that was the problem.

Leia placed a hand on her arm, and Tahiri realized that she still hadn't replied to the question.

"I want you with us when we leave," Leia said softly.

Tahiri felt herself recoil in surprise. "You can't be serious."

Leia frowned. "Why wouldn't I be?"

Tahiri struggled for the words that would help make sense of everything that was happening in her head, but none were forthcoming. So she made excuses instead. "I'm not a very good pilot," she said. "Or a politician!"

"But you are a Jedi Knight, Tahiri," said Leia. "And that is something else entirely."

"You have Jaina," Tahiri pointed out.

"Who is also a colonel, and has other responsibilities."

Tahiri didn't know what to say. *You're a Jedi Knight.* The words didn't sound right, didn't *feel* right, and that only renewed her guilt and reinforced her belief that she had betrayed her friends. Worse, she had betrayed the memory of Anakin.

Had he *ever felt such self-doubts?* she wondered.

It was unlikely. None of the Solos seemed to be burdened with such a weakness. They always knew exactly who they were and what they were doing. They were the most focused people she had ever met. The most *sure* of themselves.

Except for Jacen. He had doubts. She knew that he was still wrestling with his relationship with the Force and the council that Luke Skywalker had formed. Perhaps she should have spoken to him while she'd had the chance. But it was too late now. He was in a completely different part of the galaxy, and who knew when he was coming back?

"We all have doubts about ourselves, sometimes," Leia said, and Tahiri was appalled to realize that she had fallen silent again. "It's part of what makes us sentient beings, Tahiri. Doubt makes us examine ourselves and all that we do. And without the ability to do that, we become nothing short of monsters. I had doubts when I joined the Rebellion, all those years ago, and I had doubts when I married Han. But it's unlikely that Grand Moff Tarkin had doubts about destroying Alderaan." She paused for a moment, reflectively. "Don't be ashamed of doubt, Tahiri; it's a perfectly acceptable feeling."

Tahiri was surprised to see tears sparkling in Leia's brown eyes, although whether they were for her destroyed home, she couldn't be sure. Then Leia reached out a hand and placed it over Tahiri's.

"I think," Leia said, "that you need the chance to find out who you are, Tahiri Veila, and I'd like to give that chance to you. What do you say?"

A chance to find out who she was . . . For a moment, Tahiri froze, wondering what Jacen had told his mother. Was this some kind of game? But when she looked into Leia's eyes, all she saw was softness and sympathy. There were no games. This was real.

You will always be family to us, Jacen had written. The notion of family tugged strongly at her. Her parents had been killed in a raid by Sand People on Tatooine when she was a toddler. She was taken in by Tusken Raiders and raised by Sliven, who had died not long after she had been taken to the Jedi academy. She had no one else in the universe, except—

No, she told herself, forcing down the darkness that rose like a tide inside her. *I will not think these thoughts!*

So she nodded. "Thank you," she said, forcing a smile. "And I'll try not to be too much of a burden on you all."

Leia smiled back and squeezed her hand. "You will be an asset, Tahiri. More than you realize."

Some of Leia's warmth stayed with Tahiri after she had gone, but not for long. Night had fallen, and there was a slight chill to the air stealing through the open viewport. Tahiri closed it and curled under the covers, shivering. The scars on her forehead were aching, as though a vise was tightening around her skull. She sensed someone else in the room with her, but was too afraid to lift her head and look.

If I ignore her, she told herself, *maybe she'll just go away.*

"Tell me more," Nom Anor said. He stared across at I'pan sitting opposite him, the light from the fire flickering on his haggard features.

I'pan nodded eagerly and did as he was told. "As they near the end of their quest, the Shamed One Vua Rapuung and the *Jeedai* Anakin Solo are stopped by another group of warriors—this one even larger than the one before. This group once served under Rapuung himself, before he was Shamed. They challenge Rapuung and question why he is consorting with an infidel.

" 'I have nothing to be redeemed for,' Rapuung tells them proudly.

" 'We know your claims,' the warriors respond.

" 'You believe me cursed by the gods?'

" 'Whatever you are, whether cursed or not, you have clearly gone mad. You fight with an infidel against your own kind!'

"Now, Rapuung can understand why these warriors would think him gone mad—he would have surely felt the same had he seen another warrior fighting against him with an infidel at their side! But his circumstances allow him no choice; this is his only way to fight for the truth.

"So, Rapuung challenges the warriors to defeat him alone, without the *Jeedai* at his side, so that he may prove his worthiness."

Nom Anor narrowed his eyes. "But did you not say before that he had no amphistaff?"

I'pan nodded, standing to give his retelling more impact, his arms gesturing with theatrical flair. " 'Take up a weapon, Rapuung,' the warriors insist. 'Do not make us kill an unarmed man.'

"But Rapuung is determined. 'I have triumphed thus far without weapons,' he says. 'If the gods hated me so, would they have allowed this?'

"The warriors have no good answer to this, nor to his skill in battle, and, with the *Jeedai's* blessing, Vua Rapuung defeats them single-handedly."

Nom Anor listened with the same rapt attentiveness as the others in the small fugitive group, huddling around the heat radiating from the fire. In the story, which took place on the captured world Yavin 4, Vua Rapuung was supposedly Shamed by the gods and therefore his implants wouldn't take. Believing that he had in fact been betrayed by his former lover, the shaper Mezhan Kwaad, he sought revenge on her. Along the way, he came across the Jedi Anakin Solo who assisted him in his quest, teaching Rapuung the Jedi heresy as he went. Initially reluctant, the Shamed One had been converted, much to the horror of those who had once known him. Even the Shamed Ones didn't defy the gods.

What happened next was quite unknown to Nom Anor, even though he had studied the events that had taken place on Yavin 4 in some detail, analyzing the details of a quite different heresy: that of the shaper Nen

Yim, who had also been stationed there. She, along with Mezhan Kwaad, the same woman in I'pan's story, had been trying to bend the mind of a young Jedi girl over to the ways of the Yuuzhan Vong. Ultimately, the experiment had failed, and both Mezhan Kwaad and Commander Tsaak Vootuh had been killed in the girl's escape. Nom Anor knew all this; he had seen recordings of some of the events I'pan was relating; he had even met the Jedi Anakin Solo briefly while in the Yag'Dhul system. His spies had brought word of various versions of this story circulating through the lower castes. But he had never heard anything like the rest of the story that I'pan was relating to the attentive group.

"Go on," said Niiriit Esh, the former warrior who governed the small band of underground dwellers that Nom Anor had come to call his companions.

I'pan crouched down again to take up his tale, every eye present fixed unflinchingly upon him as they waited for him to continue. He was a good storyteller, and was clearly in his element relating the adventures of Vua Rapuung and the Jedi.

"On the landing ramp of the ship that would take them to safety, Commander Vootuh and shaper Mezhan Kwaad are forced to confront Vua Rapuung and the *Jeedai*," he went on. "Out of respect for what he once was, Rapuung demands that he be allowed to question his former lover in order to clear his name.

" 'I see no 'Vua Rapuung,' Commander Vootuh says. 'Only a Shamed One who does not know his place.'

" 'It is not I who is Shamed,' Rapuung replies. 'Do as the *Jeedai* says, and know the truth.'

"But shaper Mezhan Kwaad only sneers at this, saying that there is no sense in listening to the demented lies of Rapuung. 'He fights by the side of an infidel,' she says. 'What more do you need to hear?'

"Then from the crowd that has gathered by the ramp steps Hul Rapuung, Vua's brother. He is a proud warrior with no stain upon his honor. 'Do you fear the truth, Mezhan Kwaad?' he asks. 'If he is mad, then what harm will speaking to him do?'

"Mezhan Kwaad has no good reply to this, and Commander Vootuh, having already exposed the shaper in treachery, allows Rapuung one question of his former lover. But he informs her that she must answer truthfully, for the truth hearer will surely detect any lies uttered.

"Vua Rapuung stands tall among those who revile him and asks his question."

The chamber in which they sat was silent as they waited for I'pan to reveal Rapuung's question. He paused deliberately, dramatically, his gaze flitting briefly to each one sitting there before speaking again.

" 'Mezhan Kwaad,' Rapuung says, 'did you intentionally rob me of my implants, ruin my scars, and give me the appearance of being Shamed? Did *you* do these things to me, Mezhan Kwaad, or did the gods?'

"The shaper is silent for a moment, the look on her face too horrible to behold. She has been trapped, and all present know it.

" 'There are no gods!' she cries." I'pan stood tall, his hands reaching for the ceiling, as if this in some way would make the shaper's exclamation more powerful than it already was. " 'This wretched thing that stands before me is *my* doing!' "

Everyone gasped at this—all except Nom Anor who, while intrigued by the story, was not as easily impressed by I'pan's histrionics.

"Then," I'pan said, lowering his arms to his side, "with a base treachery that overshadows any she has shown before, she strikes Commander Vootuh and Rapuung, killing them both."

A sigh of remorse and disappointment went up from the group listening to the story. Nom Anor could empathize. The Shamed One Vua Rapuung had been vindicated at last, only to die an animal's death moments later, unable to defend himself against the biological trickery of the shaper.

"There the matter might have rested," I'pan said, "but for the *Jeedai*. Before the treacherous Mezhan Kwaad can escape, she is slain by the infidels. They defend Vua Rapuung's honor at great risk to their own lives. They are alone on this world, surrounded by an army of mighty Yuuzhan Vong warriors who even now move in around them. Not even their superior powers—their *Force*—can possibly save them.

"As a group of warriors loyal to the old gods move forward to do battle with the brave but doomed *Jeedai*, another group confronts them, led by Hul Rapuung, the redeemed Shamed One's brother. Out of respect for Vua's memory, he says, the *Jeedai* should be allowed to go free. They saved one of the warriors' own number from shame and dishonor; do they not, then, deserve to live?

"No, say the ones who cling to the old ways. The *Jeedai* are infidels. They defy the gods.

"Pointing at his brother's cooling body, Hul Rapuung responds: 'How many of you fought with him? Who ever questioned the courage of Vua Rapuung? Who ever doubted the gods loved him?'

"A muttering rises from the ranks of warriors gathered around him, and the two factions grip their amphistaffs tightly.

" 'You will die,' say those who stand before Hul Rapuung. 'What is the point of that?'

" 'A salute to the *Jeedai*!' cries Hul Rapuung in defiance, striking at the air with his spitting amphistaff. 'A salute of blood!'

"The two parties clash, Yuuzhan Vong fighting Yuuzhan Vong, old teachings versus the new. Amphistaffs rise and fall, whipping and snapping at vonduun crab armor. Warriors die at the hands of those they once called allies—and it is those touched by the *Jeedai* heresy who fall. Outnumbered by the followers of the old way, of Yun-Yuuzhan and his servant, Supreme Overlord Shimrra, those who stood for the honor of Vua Rapuung fall to the last warrior.

"But their sacrifice has not been in vain. When the victors turn from battling their fellows to destroy the infidels, they find that both the *Jeedai* Anakin Solo and his companion have escaped."

I'pan paused to sip from a cup of water. His audience sat in silence, caught in the events of that distant day on Yavin 4.

"Then the Jedi heresy should have ended there," Nom Anor said. He scanned the faces of those around him. "But you are all the spawn of that heresy, are you not?"

I'pan nodded, taking his place in the circle around the fire. "It *would* have ended," he said, "had it not been witnessed by the Shamed Ones watching from the edge of the battle, by the shapers' damutek. They spread the word, and that word continues to spread—from mouth to ear among those like us. There *is* another way for us Shamed Ones, a way that leads to redemption. We have found a new hope, and the word for that new hope is *Jeedai*."

I'pan bowed slightly to indicate the completion of the tale. Although those gathered had probably heard the story many times over, they had sat entranced throughout the telling as though listening to the words for the first time. There was a smattering of shoulder slapping from around the group, while a couple of others stood and moved away to perform other duties.

Those remaining turned their attention to Nom Anor. This was the first time he had heard the story in its entirety, and they were curious to see what his reaction would be. If he was as moved by the story as they obviously were, then he was clearly one of them. Even though he had been with them a couple of weeks now, helping them establish their new home and working around the camp as needed, he had still not been fully embraced into the fold. He had learned very quickly that trust among the Shamed Ones was more important than virtually anything else, and their sharing of the tale with him was the first indication of that trust being extended to him.

The former warrior Niiriit Esh was watching for his response more than anyone else, studying him closely through the thin flames from the fire that licked at the darkness. He stared back at her, unsure of how the tale had made him feel. The story was without doubt different from the one he had taken from his research on the Yavin 4 shaper heresy. The order of events was wrong in places, and some words had been said by others than those they were attributed to. Even the very essence of the story had changed. This story had resonance, clearly— a resonance that even he was not immune to. And perhaps that might explain how it had spread, despite the odds. Hearing that a pro-Jedi sentiment was spreading through the ranks of the Shamed Ones on Yavin 4, Warmaster Tsavong Lah had ordered all the Shamed Ones sacrificed in order to cleanse the world of heresy. And yet, somehow, the story had still managed to get out.

The thing that struck Nom Anor most about the story was that he himself, who had studied the incident in some detail, and who had access to the recordings of the original events, had not remembered the disgraced warrior at the center of it. Rapuung was just a Shamed One who'd been betrayed by his ex-lover, the shaper who had feared he might expose her heresy to her superiors. But now she was dead, while his name continued to live in the whispers of all Shamed Ones across the galaxy. His deeds had given hope to all those like him. Vua Rapuung was a legend.

As were the Jedi. Somehow their passive role in Rapuung's death had been transformed into a myth of hope for the Shamed Ones. If they ever knew . . .

"I can tell that you are moved," Niiriit said to him. "Do you see now why we live as we do?"

He nodded, understanding for the first time that it was more than simply preferring squalor to indignity. "It is a powerful message." He looked over to I'pan. "How did you come to hear it?"

"It was first told to me by one in my work detail on Duro," he answered, picking at the stringy meat of a partially cooked hawk-bat. "Varesh had heard it from his crèche-mate who in turn had heard it from one of her friends shipped here from Sriluur. Since then I have heard it many times from many people—each time slightly different from the last." Without the animation of his storytelling to hide behind, I'pan appeared once again awkward and self-conscious. "The version I have told is but one of many."

"Then how can you be sure it is the truth?" Nom Anor asked.

"I cannot," I'pan admitted. "I have no way of knowing whether the version I first heard, the one I have related to you, is more true than any of the others." He paused to spit a bit of gristle into the fire, glancing up to

Nom Anor as it sizzled in the flames. "But it is the one that feels right to me."

There was a murmur of assent from those remaining. By the reddish light of the fire, Nom Anor could see their unblinking eyes still filled with the scenes that I'pan had related. The misshapen, dirty, rejected band clearly *wanted* the story to be true. If there was hope for Vua Rapuung, then there might be hope for them, too. Exactly what the hope was for, Nom Anor couldn't tell. He didn't know if the Shamed Ones expected the Jedi to swoop in and rescue them from their pitiful lives; perhaps they believed that by consciously mimicking the characteristics of the abominable enemy they might somehow become worthy of their farcical Force—whatever *that* was.

"Well?" Kunra asked in a challenging voice, from the far side of the circle. The disgraced warrior still didn't fully trust the group's latest addition, even though Nom Anor had gone out of his way to demonstrate nothing but worthiness in the time he'd spent with them. "What do you say, *Executor?*"

Nom Anor's eye found Niiriit's; they were shining almost supernaturally bright. There was an expression of such intensity on her face that he found it almost impossible to resist. "I say thank you, I'pan, for sharing your words with me. I am honored that you think me worthy of it. I would like very much to hear more about Vua Rapuung and the Jedi, when we have the opportunity."

Niiriit smiled, her gaze still locked on his. He offered a smile in return, and realized only as he did that it was genuine. Of all the small band living in this underground camp, Niiriit was the only one with a mind keen enough to interest him. In the weeks since his arrival, he had enjoyed his talks with this ex-warrior the most.

Kunra, on the other hand, offered nothing more than a contemptuous grunt as he stood to leave the fireside group. As he watched him move away to the shadows, Nom Anor understood that Kunra might very well be jealous of the fact that a higher-ranking male was entering the group, thus usurping his own position. If this was true then it was stupid, although not unexpected.

And perhaps, Nom Anor thought, with so many gathered, now might be the best time to address the matter . . .

"You do not want me here, do you, Kunra?" he called after the ex-warrior. "You do not believe I am worthy of having Vua Rapuung's tale entrusted to me."

Kunra stopped and faced him, his body language defensive. "I merely reserve my judgment, Executor," he said. "As is my right."

"Your judgment of me?"

"Of you," Kunra confirmed, nodding. "I argued against you hearing the story of Vua Rapuung. It is the one thing in our lives that gives us hope. Our faith that the way of the *Jeedai* is a better one—a fairer one for all, not just those enslaved by the old gods—sustains us when all reason tells us that we should have given up long ago. Perhaps one day, by virtue of that faith, we will have the chance to regain our self-respect and emerge from the holes in which we cower. But you—given half a chance, I am sure you would defile it in a second if you thought it would help restore you to power."

"Are you suggesting that I would betray you?" Nom Anor asked. "You and all of those here who have taken me in and helped me?"

The ex-warrior's muscles tensed, his scars glistening in the light. "That is exactly what I am saying, Nom Anor."

Nom Anor stood now, also, and the Shamed Ones closest to him took an unsteady step back. Although much older and smaller than Kunra, he couldn't back down now. To do so would be to admit that he was lying. Unfortunately, he had few other options. If he couldn't talk the ex-warrior out of a fight—and he wouldn't have lasted as long as he had in Shimrra's court without being able to do *that*—there was always the plaeryin bol. Or if he hadn't misjudged the leader of the Shamed Ones . . .

She rose to her feet and stepped between the two. "I will not allow this," she said, her voice firm and deadly as an amphistaff.

"It's my right to challenge him," Kunra hissed through his teeth.

"I thought we had abandoned the old ways, Kunra," Niiriit said. "Now you wish to embrace them again? You cannot have it both ways."

"I understand that, but—"

"No buts, Kunra. Which is it to be? You are either with us or against us. And the same goes for you, Nom Anor," she said, suddenly turning on him. "We are too few to fight among ourselves."

Nom Anor bowed his head to her, partly to hide a smile of triumph. No, he hadn't misjudged Niiriit at all. "I apologize," he said to her. He then turned to his challenger and did the same. Playing the part of peacemaker was a new experience for him, but it was no different from any other role he had played in the past. He was a good actor. "It appears to be your right to mistrust me, Kunra. Instead of fighting you, I shall do all in my power to convince you that you are mistaken in your mistrust. Is that enough to at least allow peace between us?"

"For now," the warrior growled.

Niiriit nodded. "Good enough," she said. "Now sit, both of you. You're making me weary just looking at you."

"I think," Nom Anor said, "that I might use this excuse to retire for the night. I have heard much that requires consideration, and I am not as young as our friend here."

"Of course. Sleep well, Nom Anor. We shall discuss the *Jeedai* on another occasion."

"I hope so." He glanced quickly at Kunra as he spoke; the ex-warrior was grumpily thoughtful, but his anger had been successfully defused by Niiriit. That was good; Nom Anor didn't want to be stabbed in his sleep. Nodding good night to those still around the fire, he picked his way to the top of the ventilation shaft and descended the spiraling ramp they had built within it. The gradient wasn't steep, and the curvature was such that he completed a circle once every thirty meters or so. Within the circle of the walkway, rooms had been fashioned, two per level, that served as either crude quarters for the Shamed Ones or storerooms for the goods they had pilfered from the surface. The way was lit by the occasional lambent nest anchored to the shiny, layered surface that had been laid down by the chuk'a waste processor. It felt as if he were walking down the inside of an enormous shell.

He descended until he reached his room. Being the latest addition to the group, he lived in the quarters that had been most recently completed. There was still a tang in the air of the organic processes that had created the structure, and inside he had only the most rudimentary furniture: a rounded chest he had carved from a chuk'a egg and a dirt mattress. Nevertheless, it was still more comfortable than anything else he'd had since entering Yuuzhan'tar's underworld.

Nom Anor waved the lights out and lay on the bed, still clothed in the ragged remains of the cloak and uniform he'd been wearing when he had arrived. He hadn't been lying when he'd said that he had much to think about. The story of Vua Rapuung and the Jedi was an opportunity he had never dreamed of finding in the depths of Yuuzhan'tar. The strange, forbidden notions passing from mouth to ear offered him hope in the most unlikely of places. The whispers circulating through the Yuuzhan Vong underground did so like an asteroid orbiting a black hole, gaining momentum with each revolution, propelled by nothing more than the need to have something to believe in. The Shamed Ones might have brought this whisper into existence spontaneously, with nothing to back it up, simply to satisfy their terrible need for direction. But he knew the events of the Vua Rapuung story were based broadly in truth, and that made them so much stronger.

The Jedi aren't necessarily abominations. They can redeem as easily as they could kill.

He would never have heard such whispers from his usual vantage point, far above the forlorn creatures he currently associated with. Shimrra had no idea just how close to his heart the heresy was stabbing. If Nom Anor could follow the whispers to their source, if he could expose the heresy and bring to justice the person or persons responsible for spreading the word about Yavin 4, maybe then he could regain his previous standing—and perhaps be stronger than ever.

Thank you, Vua Rapuung, for giving me hope.

Nom Anor smiled into the darkness as he thought about Kunra's accusation that he would sell out his fellow Shamed Ones and all they stood for in a second if he thought it would help him achieve his goals. The ex-warrior was right, of course—except, perhaps, that he wouldn't need an entire second to do it.

*   *   *

"You can't be serious, Leia!"

Jaina rolled her eyes as she walked in on yet another of her parents' arguments—this one, it seemed, about the mission's itinerary. They were in the *Millennium Falcon*'s main hold, poring over charts.

"We have to start somewhere," her mother responded. "And this seems as good a place as any."

"But couldn't the decision have been made based on the toss of a credit or something, rather than some obscure and anonymous message?"

"What's going on?" Jaina asked, her curiosity piqued.

"Someone managed to get into the *Falcon*'s computers and leave us instructions on where to go if we want to walk into a trap," her father said hotly. "Your mother has taken it as some kind of portent and has decided to make it our first port of call."

"Well, I'm glad to see you're not lowering the discussion by resorting to sarcasm," Leia shot back with some of her own. "And I admit that it's all very suspicious, but that just makes me all the more curious to follow it up."

"But there's no sense to it!" Han went on. "I mean, are you *trying* to get us all killed?"

Leia scowled at her husband, but she ignored the remark. "Of course it makes sense, Han. The Galactic Alliance has lost contact with the Koornacht Cluster, and someone needs to check it out. That's exactly our brief, isn't it? So where's the problem?"

"Where's the problem?" Jaina's father leaned heavily over the map displays, his jaw tightening. "We've lost contact with Galantos and Whettam because the Yevetha have taken advantage of our little distraction and are on the move again. And you want us to go barging in there with a handful of X-wings and a rusty old frigate? *There's* the problem, Leia."

Jaina bristled at Twin Suns Squadron being described as a "handful of X-wings," but she didn't say anything. Her parents needed to fight this one out, and it was better if she stayed out of the line of fire.

Leia straightened, folding her arms in front of her. It was a clear message: she had no intentions of backing down.

"They're fine words coming from Han Solo," she said. "And do you have any better suggestions to go with your derision, Han?"

"Sure I have," he said, but with less self-assuredness than a moment earlier. "What's happening in Corellia is still anyone's guess—and then there's the Corporate Sector. That's practically next door to Mon Cal, and—"

"So the Senate hardly needs to send us, then, do they?"

"Maybe, Leia, but . . ." Han raised his hands in frustration and turned away. "Anywhere but N'zoth!"

Facing her husband's back, Leia's stony determination faltered. Jaina was surprised to see it, but she could understand why. The intensely xenophobic Yevetha had kidnapped and tortured her father for weeks, some years back, and would have killed him had he not been rescued by Chewbacca and Chewie's son Lumpawarrump.

"The last we heard, their shipyard was fully functional," Leia said, adopting a more diplomatic tone. "They're extremely capable engineers. They'll fight the Yuuzhan Vong, if they're not fighting them already."

"And then they'll turn on us," Han said, facing her again. "And the Fia, if they haven't already been exterminated. Why not send someone from the Smugglers' Alliance?"

"We need someone we can trust to do the Galactic Alliance's work, Han, not someone who will be looking for a quick profit."

Han looked as though he wanted to protest this, but he knew he didn't have much of an argument on this score.

Leia put her hands on her hips and sighed. "Look, Han, I've discussed the security aspects with Captain Mayn and—"

"You asked Todra before you brought it up with me?"

"*And,*" Leia continued without answering the question, "it's not like last time. We're not going to pick a fight with them, and if they try it with us, then we'll just leave."

Han sighed now. "All right, Leia. I can see how it makes sense from your point of view. It's a flashpoint, and we need to be there to make sure it doesn't spread. Perfectly understandable. But what if it's Jaina they capture, this time? Or you?"

"It won't be me, Dad," Jaina said softly, confidently. "I'm quite capable of looking after myself."

Han stared at his wife and daughter, wanting to argue but realizing he couldn't win this one. "All right," he said after a few seconds, his eyes narrowing sternly as he pointed his finger to each of them, "but you just remember that this wasn't *my* idea."

"I'm sure you'll be quick to remind us, should something go wrong." Leia smiled, kissing her husband's cheek briefly before getting back to work. There were many details to finalize before their departure.

Barely had she taken half a dozen steps from Han when the sound of boots could be heard clomping up the landing ramp and into the *Falcon*.

"Anyone home?" a male voice called.

"In here, Kenth," Leia said, recognizing the Jedi's voice.

Kenth Hamner stooped slightly as he came into the room. "I thought I'd find you here."

Seeing his somber expression, Leia stepped over to him and placed a hand on his shoulder. "What's wrong, Kenth? What's happened?"

"Not Kashyyyk," Han said, going pale. The Wookiee homeworld had recently been under threat by the Yuuzhan Vong.

"No, not Kashyyyk, I'm pleased to say." Hamner's expression didn't look particularly pleased. "We've just heard that the Imperial Remnant is under attack. Bastion and Muunilinst have been devastated. The offensive is expected to continue toward Yaga Minor as soon as the captured territories have been secured. Subspace and HoloNet networks are down." He turned to Leia when she opened her mouth to interrupt, as if knowing what she was about to ask. "We have no news of survivors, I'm afraid."

Leia's mouth closed in a thin line as she looked at her husband. "*Jade Shadow* jumped right into a war zone."

"They had no way of knowing," Han said. "It was just dumb luck."

"All we can do," Hamner said soberly, "is hope they weren't caught in the battle. If they managed to retreat to a safe distance, then there's no reason why their mission should be endangered."

Jaina closed her eyes, her mind reaching out through the Force, seeking her twin brother. The distance between them was almost incomprehensible, but they'd felt each other before across far greater gulfs. When she called his name, she didn't receive a reply, but she did feel an echo. He was there.

She opened her eyes and faced her mother. "Jacen's alive," she said.

Leia nodded. "Yes. And I would've felt it if anything had happened to Luke. But what about the others? And the Empire itself? If the Yuuzhan Vong have finally made a move on it, then that entire area is now unsafe. With the fleet at Bastion out of the way, they can push on into the Unknown Regions unchecked. From now on, noplace will be safe."

"Not even the Chiss," Jaina said. "We know the Vong have been harrying them from the outer edges of the galaxy. Now they'll be caught in a pincer grip."

"Only *if* the Empire falls," Hamner said. "It's too soon to say for sure one way or the other. This might only be a preemptive strike, simply warning us against using the Imperial Remnant in some sort of rearguard action against them."

"Which is precisely what we were thinking of doing," Han said with a grimace.

"Preemptive doesn't necessarily mean decisive," Hamner responded. "We know the Vong are stretched thin. To mount a major attack like this must have cost them dearly elsewhere."

"Perhaps we should step up our strike-and-run tactics in other areas," Leia said. "It might encourage them to withdraw the offensive."

Hamner nodded. "I know Cal and Sien are doing just that. It will also help take the hysterical edge off some of the calls to step up the attack, too."

"As long as we don't play into their hands." Leia nodded unhappily. "I just hate not knowing what's happened to *Jade Shadow*. We could help them if we knew they were in trouble."

"That in part is why I'm here," Hamner said. "Cal sent me to make sure you wouldn't go rushing after your brother on some foolish rescue attempt. We need you where you can do the most good."

"He's right, Leia," Han said, coming up behind her and taking her shoulders in both of his large hands. "Luke and Mara can look after themselves."

"And Jacen's no slouch, either, Mom," Jaina reassured her with a broad smile. "In fact, the three of them will probably send the Yuuzhan Vong packing in a day or two!"

The attempt at levity seemed to work. Jaina's mother took a deep breath and let it out in a gust. "You're right, of course," she said, patting her husband's hand as he squeezed her shoulders. "There's a bigger picture we need to consider. Until we know for certain that there's something wrong, we keep going as planned. To the Koornacht Cluster."

"What was I thinking?" Han exclaimed. "If it's not too late to change my mind, I'd like to put in a vote for Bastion. The middle of a Yuuzhan Vong war fleet *has* to be better than a Yevethan cell."

"The only cell there's likely to be," Leia said, with a faint smile returning to her attractive features, "is the one *we* put you in—for disobeying orders."

"*Whose* orders exactly?" Han said with mock indignation. "I'm the captain of this ship, remember?"

"You just keep telling yourself that, dear," Leia said.

"What does that mean?" Han returned.

Jaina left them to it, confident that the argument had moved from something serious to just play-fighting. She envied them the ease with which they talked to each other now. Chewbacca and Anakin's deaths seemed to have cemented their relationship stronger than ever. For all their sharp-sounding words, she knew they were really on the same side.

Not paying attention to where she was going, she didn't see C-3PO coming around the *Falcon*'s corridor until it was too late. With a cry, the golden droid staggered backward, tripping over a carton of rations on the floor and dropping the stack of Yuuzhan Vong–detecting mouse droids he'd been balancing, scattering them over the deck. Startled by the impact, many of them bleeped in distress, scurrying off in all directions. C-3PO flailed helplessly in an attempt to right himself, but the droids kept getting under his feet and hands, keeping him off balance.

"Oh, thank you, Mistress Jaina," he said as she grabbed him under the arms and helped him to his feet. "Beastly things! I don't understand why Captain Solo would need so many of them."

Jaina snatched at one of the agitated droids as it went past, but it managed to evade her grasp. Catching these things was harder than getting drewood mites from a womp rat!

"Because, Threepio," she said, grabbing for another droid and failing again as it darted between her legs, "they're programmed to look out for Yuuzhan Vong. Wherever we go, we can seed these droids to make sure there are no—*spies.*"

This last part was called out as she lunged again, this time managing to scoop one of the mouse droids off its runners. She pressed the shutdown switch on its belly, then pushed the inanimate droid into C-3PO's arms.

"Here you go."

"Thank you again, Mistress Jaina. But you really shouldn't trouble yourself with this. I'm sure you must have much more important tasks to do."

"No, not really," she said, sticking out a foot to head off another one. "Besides, it was my fault that you dropped them in the first place."

The job was made easier when Kenth Hamner pitched in to help, stopping on his way back from his meeting with her parents. His age made him less nimble than Jaina, but his longer reach easily compensated. Within minutes, they handed the last of the droids to C-3PO, whose thanks as he ambled off were muffled by the stack of droids once again in his arms.

"Thanks," Jaina said to Hamner as Threepio disappeared around a corner.

"My pleasure," he replied, dusting himself off. Then, just as she was about to continue on her way, he said, "You know, just between you and me, Cal's more worried about the Empire than he's letting on." He glanced at her wryly. "You'll let us know if you hear anything more definite from Jacen, won't you?"

Jaina frowned, confused by Hamner's conspiratorial tone. "Of course."

Hamner hesitated for a moment, then nodded his thanks and continued on his way to the ramp and out of the ship.

Jaina was about to go and do a double check on the welds of a bank stabilizer her father had installed for the trip when she heard footsteps coming from the common area. She paused, waiting to see if it was her parents coming to find her. Two seconds later, though, there was the sound of her father crying out followed by a loud metallic crash.

"Oh, my," she heard C-3PO say from down the corridor.

"Threepio!" her father yelled, as a handful of mouse droids scooted across the deck from around the corner.

Gilad Pellaeon had seen too many people die young to feel that he was, or ever would be, too old to live.

His memories came and went in flashes, as though a searchlight had briefly found them in a thick fog. His life had become a series of fragments, and he could no longer recall how the pieces fit together. There were images of his birthplace, Corellia, and Coruscant, his home during his youth, but these were swamped beneath hundreds of other memories of other worlds he had visited throughout the years; these in turn were buried beneath thousands of memories of the empty gulfs that separated these planets. He had spent almost a century in space, rarely setting foot on solid ground unless circumstances absolutely demanded it. Deep inside, his heart recognized no world as his home—not even Coruscant, which at best he had endured while there, always glad to leave. No, the closest thing to home he'd ever had was the bridge of a starship—and he'd been on too many of those to feel affection for any particular vessel. Even *Chimaera*, the Star Destroyer that had served him so faithfully for so long, was, in the end, just another ship.

He frowned, puzzled. The Battle of Bastion, like the rest of his life, lay in pieces in his mind. The sharpest of these pieces, the most painful, was the image of the destruction of the Star Destroyer *Superior*—riddled with fires and craters, tumbling to its inexorable and terrible fate in the gas giant below. *Chimaera* had been in almost as bad shape. His last intact memory was of a coral-skipper coming in low and fast to ram the bridge. He recalled nothing after that. How had he survived? No matter how hard he tried, he could find no memory to quell the confusion that throbbed at his temples. There was just blackness and pain.

Pellaeon's childhood memories were lost in that same blackness. He had been born before the Empire, before the anti-alien propaganda, before the fall of the Jedi—even before the birth of the child who would grow to become Darth Vader. His first military role had been with the Judicial Forces, which he had joined at the age of fifteen, having lied about his age. From the vantage point of a ship's deck, he had watched the tide rise and fall on so many politicians, and he had learned to be cynical about all of them—just as he had learned over the years to trust only in himself and his own judgments. That was how he had survived so many dramatic reversals. He was rarely the one at the front of the army, waving the sword and leading the charge. Gilad Pellaeon was the one more often than not standing back, ensuring his soldiers were well fed, well trained, and, above all, content. He had respect for everyone under his command—and for his enemy, too. That, above all, he thought, was why he was still alive today when so many others around him had fallen. You never knew when your enemy would become your new boss.

And that, ultimately, was the trouble with the Yuuzhan Vong. They didn't fit into this picture at all. He'd seen what they could do firsthand at Ithor, the forest world that had been utterly destroyed by the invader. He had argued with the Moffs that they should lend all support possible to the defense of the galaxy. They, however, had resisted the idea of fighting alongside the New Republic and had proposed instead to huddle in their own corner of the galaxy and watch as those worlds around them crumbled and fell to the alien intruders, all the while remaining blithely confident that they were somehow immune.

But that confidence, that arrogance, had been effectively shaken with Bastion. Ah, yes. Bastion . . .

Other details emerged from the fog as the searchlight of his memory flashed across them: the first alarms as the coralskippers and strange, alien capital vessels had appeared in the system, tearing through planetary defenses as though they were made of paper. The surprise couldn't have been more total. The disorganized way the Imperial

Navy had responded to the grutchins had appalled him. After Ithor, he had done his best to ready the Empire for a Yuuzhan Vong attack, but only his Star Destroyer, *Chimaera*, had responded efficiently and effectively at short notice. His crew had done everything he could have asked of them.

Pain stabbed through him, as though someone had rammed a force pike into his side. The memories fled as his insides exploded with fire. His back arched, his mouth opened wide to scream out his protest at the terrible agony flaring through him. He bucked and writhed to try to reposition himself in such a manner that the pain might stop, but nothing seemed to help. Nothing, that is, except for the voice calling out to him. It wasn't necessarily what the voice said, either, just the distraction it offered.

But then the pain closed in again, accompanied now by images of the Yuuzhan Vong's weapons flashing murderously around his ship, and the brilliant, almost blinding explosion of TIE fighters against the night sky.

Eventually these horrific images dissolved back into the blackness, leaving just the scattered pinpoint lights of the galaxy shining against the infinite darkness of space. The sight was one he had seen many times before, and one he'd thought he could never get tired of. He had always believed the idea of a galactic empire to be slightly ludicrous, since so much of it was empty space. The planets, moons, and asteroids comprising such an empire were just handfuls of sand thrown into a vast ocean of nothingness. No emperor could rule such an ocean, no matter how many of those grains of sand he might call his own. Such vastness defied capture by any means.

And yet this time, he sensed a difference. The gulfs didn't seem so empty anymore. There was *something*—something he couldn't find words to describe. A web, perhaps, stretching from system to system. A halo. A current running deeper than what lay visible on the surface. A *truth*, maybe?

Whatever it was, it made it seem as if the galaxy itself was *alive*.

Then even that began to fade as darkness crept in at the edges of his vision, taking the pain away along with everything else that had ever been him. Part of him fought it, as was his nature, but another part was happy to let it go. He had fought so hard and for so long against death that he had, perhaps, not spent enough time really living. He had no family apart from the navy; he had no home beyond the bridge of *Chimaera*. What was the point of living when he had nothing to live *for*?

The darkness opened up beneath him and he fell into it like a stone sinking into the depths of an impossibly deep sea. He could feel fluid all around him, and in his lungs; and yet, strangely, he wasn't drowning.

Bacta, he managed to think. *They've got me in a bacta tank.*

Then that voice again, calling to him.

Gilad Pellaeon, it said. *Admiral, can you hear me?*

He struggled to reply, fighting the darkness that pulled him down like thick tangles of seaweed. All he could manage was a single, choked syllable:

"I—"

Is that you, Admiral? Can you talk to me?

"I-I'm here."

With every word, the darkness receded just a little bit more. And as it ebbed, the pain returned.

"It . . . hurts."

I know, said the voice.

"Where—?" He wanted to ask where he was, but it didn't seem as appropriate as, "—are you?"

I have installed a neural shunt into your inner ear, the voice explained. *My voice is coming to you directly through your auditory nerve. Please forgive the intrusion, but we had to take drastic steps to keep you alive.*

"Who—are you?"

My name is Tekli, Admiral. I am a healer.

Agony ripped through him like a solar flare, burning every nerve fiber to cinders. Or so it felt.

"Are you healing me," he gasped, "or killing me?"

The pain is unavoidable. The only way to avoid it now would be for you to die. But you must stay with your body, no matter what it's telling you.

"I—can't—"

Yes you can, Admiral. We need you. If you die now, many others will follow. I'm not about to let that happen.

He wasn't used to being spoken to that way, as though by an insistent schoolteacher. "*You're* not—?"

I'm sorry. There are times when we all must endure the hurt in order to survive. Yours is now. The Force requires it.

Realization came to him then. *The Force.* This Tekli was a Jedi! But what was a Jedi doing in the Empire? And where—?

Another memory came to him. He had spoken to the Skywalkers in Bastion shortly before trying to break out of the gas giant's mass shadow. He remembered they had shown him some new tactics they believed would help in his fight against the Yuuzhan Vong. This Tekli, she must have come with them.

But what was he doing here with her? *Superior* was destroyed. He recalled ordering the evacuation of the dying hulk as it plunged into the gas giant. How had *Chimaera* avoided the same fate? If he had been injured and his crew had evacuated him to safety while they died, he couldn't live with himself. A good captain went down with the ship. He should be dead.

You're not dead, Admiral. Tekli's voice was compassionate but firm. *Like I said, I'm not going to let that happen. You and* Chimaera *are both banged around a little, but recoverable. Just hang in there a little longer, okay?*

He gritted his teeth and resigned himself to living a little longer yet. After all, what choice did he have?

When Jacen felt some of the tension ease in the tiny Chadra-Fan healer, he leaned forward expectantly.

"He fights with us now," she said, her soft voice barely audible over the mechanical buzzing of the droids assisting her. "He no longer works against us."

"You're sure he will live?" he asked, needing something more definite before he would allow himself to feel relief.

She craned her neck to look up at Jacen, something approximating annoyance in her dark eyes.

"Yes," she said simply. "But not if I continue to be interrupted. I need to concentrate to help him."

Her head dropped, and she fell silent again to devote her attention fully to healing the Grand Admiral of the Imperial Navy. Jacen felt subtle movements in the Force around her. He backed away in order to avoid disrupting her concentration further. The Chadra-Fan were renowned for their short attention spans as it was, without his interference making matters worse.

He stayed close enough to lend her a hand if needed— shoring up her relatively weak Force sensitivity with his own—but he did keep to the rear of the small medical bay, just to stay out of Tekli's fur.

Pellaeon had been removed from the bacta tank and now lay on his back on the room's operating table, attended by the frigate's 2-1B medical droid as well as Tekli. His numerous wounds stood out starkly in the harsh white light. Jacen could see far more than he actually needed to know that the man before him had come extremely close to death. His hips and abdomen had been half impaled, half crushed upon a control console when *Chimaera*'s bridge had been rammed by an enemy fighter. One of his junior officers had pulled him from the wreckage and into a medical frigate with survivors of *Superior*. Under cover of wreckage from the dying Star Destroyer, the frigate had managed to slip away relatively unharmed—although not before a dozen TIE fighters had sacrificed themselves to ensure the Grand Admiral's escape. The commander of the shuttle who had brought him to Yaga Minor didn't doubt that it was worth it.

For a while, though, it had seemed a meaningless sacrifice, for Pellaeon had very nearly died anyway. Sizing up the situation in Yaga Minor with admirable speed, the shuttle's commander had contacted Captain Yage rather than his direct superior in the navy. Yage had ordered the shuttle to dock with *Widowmaker* immediately to transfer the patient. Tekli and Jacen, weighed down by the healer's equipment, had stayed with the Imperial commander while *Jade Shadow* withdrew to a discreet distance. As soon as Pellaeon had arrived, wrapped tightly in a life-preserving cocoon, the Chadra-Fan had gone to work.

Jacen marveled how close it had been. First, the shock of removing the ageing admiral from the cocoon had stopped his heart. Then his body had failed to respond to bacta when they had finally gotten him into the tank. Tekli had ordered him to be removed so they could go to work directly on his more serious injuries, such as the ragged gashes and splintered bones of his abdomen and upper legs. Dripping blood and fluid, the old man on the operating table had seemed to deflate under the bright lights, losing substance with every second, until, finally, he began to respond to Tekli's treatment.

The pilot of the shuttle who had brought the admiral from Bastion had stayed with him throughout. A lean young man by the name of Vitor Reige, he looked exhausted and drawn. His left arm was clearly injured, but he refused to have any treatment until Pellaeon was stable, insisting that all attention be focused upon the admiral.

After a few minutes, when it was clear that Pellaeon's condition was going to continue to improve, the pilot exhaled heavily, gratefully, as if he had been holding his breath the entire time he'd been standing there.

He looked over to Jacen. "He told me to find you," he said. "Before he passed out the last time, he insisted I should find you Jedi, if you had come here."

Jacen frowned. "Because he thought we could save him?"

The man's expression became instantly pinched, as if he was offended by the very notion. "He wanted you to know that we were grateful," he said stiffly. "If anyone should bear a grudge against the Empire, it would be you. But you helped us, and he appreciated that. We all did. I wouldn't be here now if you hadn't risked your own lives to show us how to fight those . . ."

He fell quiet, biting down on the words. The memories of the recent battle were obviously still vivid in his mind.

Sensing the man's embarrassment, Jacen quietly changed the subject by pointing to the arm that Reige was cradling. "You really should get that looked at," he said. Before the pilot could voice the same objections that he had earlier, Jacen quickly added, "He's going to be okay. Really. Tekli will take care of him."

Vitor Reige nodded his appreciation. "You saved my life, as well as the life of the admiral. I shall forever be in your debt for that."

Jacen wanted to say that he didn't believe in debt, that people should just do what they thought was right regardless of obligation, but at that moment Tekli stepped back from the table and approached the two of them.

"I have done all that needs to be done," she said, her thin shoulders shrugging. "The rest is up to him, now, and how he responds to the bacta."

Jacen watched as the medical droids maneuvered Pellaeon back into the tank. The Grand Admiral twitched as if in a dream as the powerful healing fluids went to work, then settled down into the tank's warm embrace. Convinced there was nothing more that could be done at the moment, Tekli gathered her equipment to leave. Helping her carry her tools, Jacen led her from the infirmary, leaving the droid to tend to Reige. Immediately outside the medical bay they found Captain Yage pacing back and forth in front of the doors. She came to a halt the moment the door slid open and Jacen and Tekli stepped out.

Her anxious gaze fell upon Jacen, who nodded in response to her unvoiced question.

"He'll live," he said.

Like a balloon releasing its air, the tension seemed to evaporate from the captain, dissolving her concerned expression. "I didn't think it could be done," she said, dropping her stare to the Chadra-Fan standing silently and respectfully beside Jacen. "I'm sorry for doubting you. I offer the appreciation of all my people for saving the admiral's life."

The Chadra-Fan bowed her head. "I did not do it alone," she said. "Your admiral's determination to stay alive had a lot to do with it. With the will to live, anything is possible."

"And Gilad Pellaeon certainly has that," Yage said.

The fur around Tekli's mouth parted as she smiled at the captain. "He still has some recuperating to do," she said, "but he should be out of the bacta tank in about six standard days."

Yage's expression turned from relief to concern again. "Six days? That's too long!"

"Why?" Jacen asked.

"As far as the Moffs know," she explained, "Gilad died in Bastion. Flennic has had time to put himself in power, assuming control of *Stalwart* and the rest of the fleet. I wouldn't put it beyond him to do anything to avoid having to relinquish that power, now he's got it. While Gilad is weak, he is vulnerable, and we can't keep the secret of his survival to ourselves forever. Word is already spreading that one more shuttle made it out of Bastion before the battle's end. It won't be much longer before people know who was on that shuttle and where it docked."

"What will happen when they find out?"

She shrugged. "I don't know. That'll be up to Moff Flennic and his underlings." Her comlink bleeped. Listening to the short message, she nodded and answered that she would be there immediately. "I guess we won't have to wait long to find out. We've just received a recall order."

"Can't you disobey it?" asked Jacen.

"If we do, then we're going to have to have a *very* good reason."

"Perhaps you should let me talk to them," he said. "Maybe we can work something out."

The captain stared at him for a moment in obvious discomfort and embarrassment. Jacen understood exactly what she was thinking. Here was Yage, a captain of many years' experience from a diametrically opposed military force, and he was expecting her to hand over to him the explanation of why she intended to defy a direct order. But he could see how tempted she was. A Jedi Knight had saved the admiral; perhaps another would take this difficult choice away from her. At the very least, it might absolve her of a wrong decision.

Jacen carefully neglected to mention that his experience with Imperials was virtually nonexistent.

After a few moments' consideration she raised her voice to address the empty corridor: "I don't suppose anyone has any better ideas?"

She waited a moment until the silence was as deep as it was ever going to get on an Imperial war vessel.

"Well, I asked," she said, waving Jacen to follow her as she moved off. "Now let's see if you can make this situation any worse for us than it already is."

"Twin Suns Squadron, stand down," came the voice of Captain Mayn over Jag Fel's helmet comlink. "We have attained our orbital insertion and are go for satellite deployment. You may revert to internal command."

"Copy that," he replied briskly before switching to the squadron's internal subspace frequency. To the rest of the squadron he said, "You heard the captain: we made it safe and sound. Let's check out the neighborhood before getting too comfy."

Twin Suns Squadron peeled apart into quarters, each accelerating to cover different segments of the world below. From orbit, Galantos possessed an uninviting boggy brown-green color, and at first glance showed little signs of advanced civilization. It didn't take long, however, before the inhabitants of Galantos, the Fia, became aware of the ships in orbit about their planet.

"Unidentified vehicles," came a voice over subspace, "this is Al'solib'minet'ri City Control. Please identify yourselves and state your intentions."

"This is Captain Todra Mayn of the Galactic Federation of Free Alliances' navy frigate *Pride of Selonia*. Our mission is a peaceful and diplomatic one. We're here to talk to Councilor Jobath."

"Not so fast, Captain Mayn." The voice of the Fia was patient and steady. "You've only identified one ship. I count fourteen."

"That's correct, Control. There's *Pride of Selonia*, *Millennium Falcon*, and Twin Suns Squadron."

"And you command this mission, Captain?"

"Only when it comes to logistical issues such as these. Otherwise, I am under the orders of Leia Organa Solo."

"Beneath the Multitude! Leia Organa Solo?"

"That's correct, Control."

"Then we extend our warmest welcome to you, Captain," the Fia said effusively. "And, indeed, to all of her companions! And I am sure that Councilor Jobath would be delighted to speak with her once these formalities are out of the way."

"What formalities, Control? We've identified ourselves and stated our intentions. What more—?"

"Captain, we on Galantos believe in doing things the proper way." The voice of Al'solib'minet'ri City Control was polite but firm. "We still don't know how long you intend to stay, how many people intend descending to the surface, what the precise purpose of their visit is, where they intend to travel, and so on."

There was a slight pause from *Selonia*. "Very well, Control," Captain Mayn said wearily. It had been a long journey, literally from one side of the galaxy to the other. "We'll fill you in. Where do you want us to start?"

"Thank you, Captain." Jag could almost hear the prim and smug little smile in the Fia's voice over the comm unit. "First of all, can I have your exact mission designation for our records, please?"

Jag mentally switched off the conversation, leaving those in charge to work out the details. He had enough to think about as it was. As that day's Twin Suns Leader, he was responsible for the smooth running of the squadron on its arrival at a new system. Although he considered that he and Jaina had done a good job on short notice, small wrinkles in their procedures were still being ironed out. His clawcraft had an X-wing on each side, while two claws tailed Jaina's fighter; the same pattern was repeated by the remaining half of the squadron to ensure the components were mixed. This, they knew, would result in some initial awkwardness, but in the long run would ensure that the squadron knit together as a whole.

He banked in a smooth arc, powering for the southern pole over the planet's gelatinous green pond-seas. There was the occasional town and scientific outpost on some of the more firm, rockier areas, but nothing out of the ordinary that he could see.

"All clear at our end, Twin Leader," came Jaina's voice over his comlink.

"Thanks, Two. How about you, Three and Four?"

"Clear skies, Twin Leader."

"Easy picking," added Twin Suns Four, originally from Jag's Chiss Squadron.

"We're not here to stir up any trouble," he reminded his pilots. "So no showing off for the locals."

"From the looks of things, they could use some livening up," Seven commented dryly.

Al'solib'minet'ri City Control was still requesting information from Captain Mayn.

"Do you really need to know the *precise* location where the *Millennium Falcon* intends to land?"

"I'm afraid so, Captain Mayn. It'll save trouble in the long run, trust me. And you might also like to tell me who exactly will be comprising the landing party."

The captain sighed; Jag smiled. He was normally something of a stickler for procedures, but the Fia had a tendency to take protocol to ridiculous extremes. If he'd been in Mayn's position right now, he would have just gone ahead and landed anyway, regardless of what Al'solib'minet'ri City Control said. He doubted the consequences would have been too severe. The Fia' had no planetary defenses to speak of, so what were they going to do if Captain Mayn decided to disregard their precious procedures?

But then, diplomacy wasn't his strong point. He was quite happy to leave that side of politics to people like Jaina's parents—although he got the distinct feeling that Han Solo would have agreed with him, if pushed.

Captain Mayn's bored reply filled the airwaves: ". . . Cybot Galactica protocol droid See-Threepio, Jedi Knight Tahiri Veila . . ."

Tahiri's name caught his ear. He switched to another channel so he could talk to Jaina without being overheard.

"Did you know Tahiri was going with your parents?"

"No," Jaina replied. "But it's not a problem, is it?"

Jag didn't answer immediately. He knew that Tahiri was a friend of Jaina's and had been close to her brother, Anakin, but that wouldn't have stopped him from expressing a suspicion had he something definite to back him up. But he didn't. There was just her breakdown at Mon Calamari, and something about her behavior. He couldn't put a finger on it, but he felt that something was just not quite right about her.

"I guess not," he said eventually.

He hadn't even been aware that he regarded her any differently than the other members of the mission until the day they left Mon Cal. The departure of the mission had been decidedly more low-key than that of *Jade Shadow*, even though Leia and Han did have official recognition as envoys of the Galactic Alliance. Chief of State Cal Omas, Supreme Commander Sien Sovv, and Kenth Hamner had all put in an appearance to bid them farewell, thankfully without fanfare or speeches. With the Galactic Alliance in good hands, the *Millennium Falcon* had ferried the pilots of Twin Suns Squadron who weren't already in orbit up to *Pride of Selonia*, and a brief shaking of hands was held there. Jaina embraced her parents; Jag awkwardly accepted a pat on the shoulder from Han; Captain Todra Mayn, a tall, thin woman with a slight limp, had saluted the assembly with due respect. And that was it, except for a glimpse of Tahiri that Jag had stolen as everyone moved off to their ships. She had been standing at the back of the gathering, carefully removed from the activity. She was still thin, and very pale; the scars from her torture at the hands of the Yuuzhan Vong stood out vividly on her forehead. And her eyes . . .

Jag Fel wasn't one for flights of fancy, but he also wasn't one for ignoring what his senses told him, either— so when he saw the look of disgust on Tahiri's face and the intense hatred in her eyes, his hand had reached automatically for the blaster at his side. If she was to make any move whatsoever for Jaina or her family, he wanted to be ready. Had she shown any indication of attacking, he would have shot her down without hesitation.

She didn't, though, and the moment had passed uneventfully—but he had still been reluctant to remove his hand from the weapon at his side. It almost seemed to Jag that she had sensed him looking at her, and her gaze had swung over to him. When their stares locked, she was suddenly herself again, and he was left feeling slightly foolish. Whatever it was he had seen in her eyes had gone, replaced with a soft and subtle uncertainty.

Shoot Tahiri? What had he been thinking? She was just a sick teenager in desperate need of some rest, tagging along on the mission with lots of other tired warriors. Leia and Jaina thought she was having trouble getting over Anakin's death, that she had bottled up her grief so long and so hard that it was bursting out of her now in twisted, dark forms. When he had raised his concerns about her being on the mission, Leia had said firmly that it was just what Tahiri needed: a clear sense of direction provided by people she could trust. If something else went wrong, they would be there for her without hesitation. End of story.

Jag had no reason to doubt that it *was* the story's end. Nevertheless, that look he had thought he'd seen on Tahiri's face stuck with him, and he found himself repeatedly thinking about it throughout the long jump to Galantos. He didn't know exactly what the Yuuzhan Vong had done to her on Yavin 4, but he did know the enemy employed biological technologies far in advance of anything the Galactic Alliance had. Was it possible that the malevolent flash he'd glimpsed in her was in some way connected to this? It was impossible to say for sure. But whatever was going on behind Tahiri's fragile facade, he was going to need more information before he could take any action. And to do that, he was going to have to keep a very close eye on her at all times . . .

"I'm thinking of volunteering for ground duty," he told Jaina over the private line. "I haven't seen much of the Galactic Alliance, except from orbit."

"You couldn't have picked a worse place to start taking an interest, Jag," she said. "It looks like someone dumped an ore hauler full of sludge from orbit!"

He laughed. "Yeah, well, it makes a change, anyway. Care to join me?"

"Tempting, but no thanks. If it's all the same to you, I'd rather follow procedures from up here. Someone has to mind the baby, just in case the Yevetha come calling."

He thought he detected a mild rebuke in her voice. "I'm not off to a good start, am I?" he said, unwilling to give the real reason for going down to the surface. "Only a few days into our arrangement and I'm already trying to shuffle the roster around."

"No, that's okay, Jag. You should feel free to volunteer for these things, if that's what you really want to do. I was hoping we could jiggle the roster a little myself, to make sure we got a chance to be off duty and on *Selonia* at the same time." A note of teasing replaced the rebuke. "But if wading around in sludge is more your idea of a good time than hanging out with me . . ."

He smiled to himself. "You know that isn't the case," he said. "I was just hoping we could combine the two."

Her laugh was part shocked, part delighted. "You've been too long in that crash couch, spaceboy. I'll be sure to report you to your superior officer, next time I'm Twin Leader."

The line clicked off. Satisfied that he would be able to put his name down for the landing party without arousing her suspicion—or her ire—he turned his thoughts to regrouping with the rest of the squadron. Jaina was absolutely right in that respect: whatever his suspicions were regarding Tahiri, his job, first and foremost, was to look after the squadron and ensure the external security of the mission. The well-being of Tahiri was ultimately the responsibility of the person who had invited her aboard—and if he couldn't trust Leia Organa Solo, then whom *could* he trust?

Nonetheless, he decided to volunteer. Just to be sure.

"You're *what*?" The red face of General Berrida glowered at Jacen from the *Widowmaker*'s hologram.

"A Jedi Knight, sir," Jacen repeated steadily. "I've come to help you."

"*Help* us—?" The overweight general spluttered for a second. "And what exactly makes you think we need your help, Jedi Knight? All I see is an overgrown boy in robes."

"Appearances can be deceptive," Jacen said, refusing to wilt beneath the general's blustering and outrage.

Berrida laughed derisively. "So where *is* this help you offer us, Jedi? Where's your support vessel?"

"*Jade Shadow* has retreated to a safe distance." Jacen had spoken to Uncle Luke and ensured that the rest of the mission stayed well out of sight until his gambit had paid off—or not, as the case might be. "You don't have to worry about it."

"Don't tell me what I do or do not need to worry about, boy," Berrida growled. His holographic image flickered momentarily. "I don't like having unknown vessels lurking around my system."

"A sentiment I understand completely, General. Which is why I've come to offer my help."

"We don't *need* your help," Berrida said obstinately.

"I think you do." Jacen paced around *Widowmaker*'s cramped bridge, trying his best to radiate a sense of calm control. Inside, though, he was thinking faster than he had during any lightsaber battle. "Tell me, why do you think the Yuuzhan Vong attacked Bastion?"

"They have issued no explanation."

"Nor will they, probably," Jacen said. "Nonetheless, they must have one. No one risks resources in war without a reason. Now, I know you're not a fool, General, so I'm pretty sure you would have some idea as to their reasons. Why don't you share it with us?"

Berrida straightened, the corner of his mouth twitching irritably. "The Yuuzhan Vong attacked us in retaliation."

"For?" Jacen pressed.

"For Garqi, Ithor, Exodo Two—"

"And for supplying information to the New Republic—specifically, information on hyperspace routes to the Galactic Alliance, which enabled it to turn the tide of the battle and, for the first time, hurt the Yuuzhan Vong." Jacen enjoyed the surprised look on Berrida's face. On *Widowmaker*'s bridge, Captain Yage raised her eyebrows. "My mother negotiated that deal with the Empire, General. That's how I know about it. And I can assure you that not many other people do. There are people on our side as reluctant to deal with you as you are to deal with us."

"So?" Berrida snapped. The general made no attempt to hide his growing irritation with Jacen. "What are you driving at, *boy*? Speak plainly before I have you arrested for obstructing the Imperial war effort."

"It's really quite simple, General." Jacen smiled as sweetly as he could. "If the deal between the Empire and the Galactic Alliance was such a secret, then how do you think the Yuuzhan Vong ever learned about it? I mean, only your highest-ranking officers and my mother knew about it at the time. She passed it on to *our* military leaders, who employed it in our war effort. We know there's no leak at our end, because the new routes worked. If the Yuuzhan Vong had infiltrated our chain of command, the information you gave us would have done us no good whatsoever. The only way, therefore, that the Yuuzhan Vong could have known that the Empire had given the Galactic Alliance information that hurt them is if the leak was at your end." Jacen paused before pronouncing his conclusion. "You have a spy, General."

"Nonsense!" Berrida's denial was mixed with just enough shock for Jacen to realize that his reasoning had hit home. "That's impossible!"

"It's not impossible at all." Jacen changed his tone to one of sympathy. He'd attacked enough; the general's defenses had been breached. It was Jacen's task now to turn Berrida into an ally, not to keep attacking and make him even more of an enemy. "The fact is, we've had problems with infiltration ourselves. First with the Yuuzhan Vong, and then with the Peace Brigade. Your staff could be riddled with alien impersonators and sympathizers, and you would never know. They have living disguises called ooglith masquers that allow them to impersonate anyone."

"We'll conduct security sweeps, random checks," Berrida said, but Jacen could tell that the man's self-assurance was flagging.

"All useless, I'm afraid, unless you know what it is you're looking for."

Berrida glared balefully at him. "And you *do* know what to look for, I suppose?"

Jacen nodded. "My companions and I have had a great deal of experience with the Yuuzhan Vong. We don't profess to understand them, but I do feel that we are slowly coming to. And that, I believe, is the most important thing at the moment."

More important than destroying them, he thought to himself. But he doubted that the general was ready for such philosophy. *Be patient,* he told himself. *One step at a time.*

"Let's assume I believe you," Berrida said, "and that I take you on your word that—"

"You don't have to take my word, General," Jacen interrupted. "The evidence speaks for itself."

"Assuming I accept the argument, then," Berrida pressed on. "What next? Are you asking me to open my staff to your influence? How will I know then that I'm not trading one form of infiltration for another? I don't have to trust you, Jedi, just because you appear to be beating my enemy."

"I'm not asking you to do that, General. All I am doing is offering you and the Empire advice. You can take it or leave it. Just give me the opportunity to present it properly, and then you can decide what to do about it."

"Precisely what sort of advice are we talking about here?"

Jacen ticked several items off on his fingers: "First, we can advise you on how to detect and eliminate Yuuzhan Vong spies within your ranks. Second, we can teach your pilots new tactics that will help you fight more effectively on the front. And third, I can offer you my opinion of what you should do next."

The general grumbled disdainfully. "Which is?"

"That we should leave Yaga Minor as soon as possible," Jacen said. "Any spies you have will already have reported to their superiors that this is where the fleet has regrouped. If your destruction is their aim, then it would be reasonable to assume that they'll attack here soon, before you have a chance to get your act together."

The general grunted. "Anything else?"

"Only one other thing: we cordially invite you to join the Galactic Alliance to enable a continuation of this dialogue. We could have used your help many times over the course of the war, and I know that you can use ours now.

We're not supplying anything with strings attached, General, but we do offer the hand of peace. All we ask is that you at least think about taking it in return."

Jacen brought his own hands behind his back as he waited for the general's reply.

The holographic image of the general was motionless for a long time—long enough for Jacen to wonder if the image hadn't frozen. Then Berrida moved, tilting his head to one side with a grimace.

"I'll get back to you," he said, before his image abruptly dissolved.

Jacen let out his breath in a trembling rush, for the first time realizing how damp with perspiration his palms were. "I'm not sure if that went better than expected or worse than I could have imagined."

"Better," Yage said, stepping up beside him. "It's not in that fat fool's nature to negotiate, or to entertain an original thought, so to get him halfway there is something of a major coup. If I know him, he'll already be on the line to Moff Flennic—who'll tell him to stop listening to such nonsense and impound us before we waste any more time. But by the time he acts on it, the situation might have changed." She looked around her bridge, her expression concerned. "It really depends on what's happened to the chain of command."

"Who's filled the power vacuum, you mean?" Jacen asked.

Yage nodded. "Exactly. With *Chimaera* still missing, the Moffs will assume that Gilad Pellaeon is dead, but until they know for sure either way, they won't stick their necks out. And Flennic might not make any bold moves until he's certain of how the council will fall out. If he's got the support, he may even take the opportunity to make a move for leadership."

"That wouldn't be good."

"Not for you, no," Yage said. "And probably not for our chances of survival."

Jacen didn't say anything; it wasn't her he needed to convince.

Later, when Tekli and her gear were settled in one of the frigate's empty berths and the subspace channels were free, Jacen commandeered a line to talk to *Jade Shadow*.

"Do you want to come back?" Mara asked, her voice conveying the worry she felt for him and the diminutive Chadra-Fan. "We can slip back insystem and—"

"I'd advise against that," he said. "They're going to be looking for you, so I think you'd be better off staying where you are. And wherever it is you're hidden, don't tell me. It's probably best I don't know."

"That's not your only concern, is it?" Luke said.

"Well, no," he admitted with some embarrassment. "The thing is, Uncle Luke, I don't know much about Imperials, but I *do* know that they know you. I think they'd feel a lot more relaxed about negotiating with some young upstart than the man who brought down their Emperor."

"I totally agree with you, Jacen," Luke said. "And I know that you'll do the job right. You seem to have a natural strength when it comes to negotiating. Your mother will be proud. Not even she was able to talk the Imperials around, and she's one of the best diplomats the New Republic has ever seen."

Jacen smiled at his uncle's praise. "That's kind of you," he said. "Although to be fair to my mother, the last time she was here the Imperials didn't have the Yuuzhan Vong snapping at their heels. Things like that tend to make people easier to persuade."

"That's nothing but false modesty, Jacen, and you know it," Mara said. "Be sure to keep us updated on how negotiations proceed, as well as Gilad's condition. And don't forget that you can call on us for anything, anytime. We'll be flight- and fight-ready around the chrono if you need us."

"I hope it won't come to that. It could be hours before we hear back from Berrida or Flennic. And you'll know if they decide not to talk at all and make a move on us instead."

"Or if the Yuuzhan Vong come."

There was a small silence after Mara's words. Jacen had proposed the possibility of another advance by the Yuuzhan Vong fleet simply as a bargaining chip, but the more he thought about it, the more likely it seemed. He was less worried now about the Imperials than he was about being caught in an old frigate on the front line.

Still, the kind of work he was doing certainly felt a lot more faithful to his path than wielding a lightsaber or flying an X-wing in battle. He'd originally thought the stopover in the Imperial Remnant little more than a distraction on the way to finding Zonama Sekot, but perhaps it would prove to be something much more than that. Perhaps he had found another calling where he had least expected it.

But not even he thought that he could bring the Imperials around without Gilad Pellaeon behind him. Whoever filled the admiral's place while he was unconscious would be too busy watching their back to listen to Jacen—and the longer they were in that position of power, the less likely they would be to give it up.

Get well soon, old man, Jacen thought as he wrapped up the conversation with *Jade Shadow* and went off to find somewhere he could wait in peace. *Enjoy the quiet while you can. It may just be the calm before a terrible storm.*

"It's changed."

The voice of Anakin's mother snapped Tahiri out of her daydream. She'd been staring out at the gelatinous oceans of Galantos as the *Millennium Falcon* descended rapidly through the planet's atmosphere. She dragged her eyes from the view through the cockpit viewport to where Leia sat in the *Falcon*'s copilot seat next to Han's.

"I'm sorry?"

"Galantos," she said. "It's changed since I last saw it."

Tahiri glanced again at the view. "I didn't know you'd been here."

"I haven't. Borsk Fey'lya toured here briefly a while ago. He sent back some reports while I was still on the council. He didn't like it much, if I recall. Didn't get on with the locals."

"I can't understand why," Han grumbled sarcastically, flicking switches with exaggerated impatience. "These people could out-talk a Toydarian trader."

"It's just their way of going about things," Leia placated him. "I'm sure they'd find your ways equally as odd."

"Yeah, well, at least I get things *done*. I'm amazed anything's changed around here—ever! They'd discuss any proposals to death before they ever started building."

"Well, *somehow* they're getting things done," Leia said, pointing at the screens before her. "That city there isn't on any of the maps we have. Or that one."

Tahiri had boned up on Galantos's geography while in transit from Mon Calamari. She knew that the landscape below was inherently unstable, so the Fian cities were built to ride out seismic vibrations. Shaped like flattened spheres with stabilizing spikes beneath, they floated heavily on the many organic seas dotting the surface. Tahiri wondered if people would feel the movement of the cities as they wobbled beneath them. The very idea made her feel motion-sick. Hopefully, she thought, they had dampeners like the cities on Mon Calamari.

"So they've been building," Han said. "Joining the New Republic worked for them, obviously, even if it didn't teach them how to talk properly."

The *Falcon* swooped out of the sky, guided by navigational beacons to a circular landing field at the summit of Al'solib'minet'ri City. There was no evidence of any other starships, but there were a number of aircraft. Ground transport had been made difficult by the instability of the planet's crust; this had held back the development of the Fia until they had stumbled on balloons almost two centuries earlier. Now enormous vert'bo airships regularly carried livestock and other material goods across the shattered wastelands between the oases floating on the seas, while the Fia themselves took to speeders and suborbital shuttles. The sky was a maze of contrails near a busy town, punctuated by the enormous blimps, lazy dots drifting across a vibrant blue.

A celebration had gathered to greet the *Falcon* when it touched down. A band struck up when the engine noise died away and the landing ramp was extended. The music was strange to Tahiri's ears—a mixture of high-pitched whistles and hollow drones—but it gave the scene a festive air as she followed Anakin's parents down the ramp. Leia's Noghri bodyguards followed at a discreet distance, carefully eyeing the gathering for any activity that might be considered a danger to the Princess.

Not far away, Jag Fel's clawcraft had also touched down. Al'solib'minet'ri City Control had accepted his addition to the landing party, but only after confirming the details at length with Captain Mayn, for whom Tahiri couldn't help but feel sorry. Watched curiously by the crowd, the Chiss-trained pilot strode confidently to join the other humans at the center of the crowd of short, long-featured, web-footed Fia.

"Welcome to Galantos!" one of the Fia cried, moving forward and waving its long arms in apparent agitation. Although not much larger than an Ewok, the alien's gesticulating startled Tahiri, making her take a cautious step back. Then she realized that the gestures were only meant to convey excitement and delight.

"I am Primate Persha." The Fia's voice was high-pitched, but musical rather than irritating. She spoke loudly to be heard over the muted squeaks of the other Fia around them. "On behalf of Councilor Jobath, I'd like to welcome you to Galantos, Leia Organa Solo, Han Solo, Tahiri Veila, Jagged Fel, and protocol droid See-Threepio. It is an unexpected honor and a privilege for us all!"

Leia smiled and bowed courteously. "Councilor Jobath could not attend?"

"Unfortunately, no," the Fia said, her eyes looking somehow even more melancholy than they already were. "He had a pressing engagement in Gal'fian'deprisi City. But he promises to be here as soon as physically possible, and wishes me to convey his warmest and most respectful greetings and hopes that your stay will be an enjoyable and fruitful one. We have made our finest diplomatic facilities available to you and will strive to fulfill your every request. Please don't hesitate to ask for anything you require or desire at any point in your stay, day or night. Either myself or my assistant, Thrum, will be only too happy to accommodate you."

With one of her small, web-fingered hands, the Fia

waved them to follow her as she led them from their ships, waddling away on her wide, bell-shaped legs. A path opened up for them through a disconcertingly ecstatic crowd. The Fia were a small, inoffensive people whose wild arm gesticulations belied their otherwise placid nature. As Primate Persha kept up a steady stream of detailed instructions on how she or her assistant could be contacted over the next two days, Tahiri felt herself begin to lose track of the words. All meaning seemed to fade from them as the rising and falling of Persha's voice became notes of a complicated melody. Tahiri doubted that she was missing much by hearing only one word in three.

Persha led them into an ornate turbolift. C-3PO bumped into Tahiri's back as the doors slid shut.

"Forgive me, Mistress Tahiri," the golden droid said. "This sort of fuss is all a bit overwhelming for the likes of a protocol droid like myself."

"That's okay, Threepio," she whispered back so as not to interrupt the steady flow of Primate Persha's ongoing speech, which had now moved on to express the Fia's joy at having such visitors on their usually unnoticed world—especially in such times of trouble and hardship that the galaxy was seeing. "I never thought I'd meet someone who talked as much as you, either."

She knew the components of C-3PO's face never changed, but by the way he tilted his head at this comment Tahiri could tell that he hadn't really understood her little joke.

The diplomatic quarters in Al'solib'minet'ri City were expansive and well appointed. For all their isolation and other drawbacks, the Fia didn't skimp when it came to fittings and hospitality. Tahiri's room was decorated with white, bonelike panels ornately carved in the likeness of local life-forms; the images were peculiar looking, as befitted their environment, but stunningly crafted. The furniture was fashioned from a local, broad-grained wood, with some of the items so seamless that they looked as if they'd been grown that way rather than artfully cobbled together from various pieces. All in all, the room was both comfortable and luxurious—even if the bed was a little too short for her legs.

After checking out their quarters, the visitors reconvened in the anteroom at the heart of the diplomatic residence. Primate Persha had left them alone for the time being, graciously accepting their pleas to relax and unwind for a while—although not before reiterating her instructions, again in meticulous detail, on how to ask for anything at all they might require.

"I'll just be glad when we're off this rock," Anakin's father was saying when Tahiri walked in. He looked more flustered than Tahiri had ever seen him. She wasn't sure if it was because of the Fia or their proximity to the Koornacht Cluster—or perhaps it was a little of both.

"Don't tell me," Leia said with a half smile. "You're getting a bad feeling about this place, right?"

He shot her a dirty look before turning beseechingly to Jag Fel. "*Please* tell me there's a reason we shouldn't stay, Jag. Please. *Anything*."

"Sorry," said the tall, handsome pilot. "Can't help you, I'm afraid." Shrugging off his backpack containing equipment he'd brought with him and placing it on the table in the middle of the room, Jag turned to Leia and said, "I've patched us into the planetary comm network and have opened a link to *Selonia*. I think we're safe in assuming that our encryption is light-years ahead of what these guys have here."

"And the rooms?" Leia asked.

"Bugged, of course," he said. "But it's okay; I've jammed them. We're clean." Jag glanced at Tahiri when he said that, then quickly looked away. "We should be safe here now."

"You wouldn't think these people would have a need for listening devices," Han said. "They're so busy talking all the time."

Leia ignored his griping. "The Fia are all right," she said. "Actually, it makes a nice change from people who don't talk enough. But then, that's not to say that I'm entirely happy with what I see here, either." She fixed her husband with a sober stare. "*I'm* getting a bad feeling about all of this, although I hate to say it."

"About what?" Tahiri asked.

Leia paused as if reaching out into the Force for an answer. "I'm not sure," she said shortly, shaking her head. "Everyone seems happy enough to see us, and Galantos is obviously a fairly peaceful place, but—"

"But it's almost *too* peaceful, right?" Han offered.

"Maybe," Leia said. "And there's still the question of the communications blackout. Jag, will you contact Captain Mayn and ask her try to patch into the planetary transceiver? Galantos had one when it joined the New Republic; if it doesn't anymore, I want to know what happened to it. Failing that, have her attempt to contact the nearest intersector network and see if she can get a message to Mon Calamari directly. We might be able to fix the problem locally, if it's just a technical hitch, and move on elsewhere without wasting too much time."

"I'll second that," Han muttered.

"In the meantime, Tahiri and I are going for a walk."

C-3PO instantly shuffled forward, only to be stopped by Leia putting a hand to his metal chest.

"Alone, Threepio," she said.

"I do not think that this is advisable, Mistress Leia," Threepio squawked in protest. "For just the two of you to be out there alone—"

"Someone has to talk to our hosts," she cut in gently but firmly. "Otherwise we shall appear rude." When he started to voice his objections again, Leia said, "I appreciate your concerns, Threepio, but they're not necessary. We'll be fine. And besides, Han and Jag will need you to talk to the planetary transceiver—that's if they can get it on-line."

"But Mistress, I really must—"

"The Princess will be safe," rumbled Cakhmaim, one of the Noghri bodyguards who escorted Leia everywhere she went.

"See?" Leia said, not just to C-3PO but also to Han, who was looking as dubious about his wife's plan as the droid sounded. "And anyway, I'll have Tahiri with me to keep an eye out for anything out of the ordinary." The Princess winked at her. "That's if the conversation doesn't put her to sleep, of course."

Warmed by Leia's trust in her, Tahiri smiled. "I'll try extra hard to stay awake."

"Just be careful," Jag said. "And call us if you need *any* assistance, okay?"

"Stop worrying," Tahiri insisted, thinking: *Why does he keep looking at me like that?* It was difficult, she found, to regain self-confidence when those around seemed to have their own doubts about her. "You just concentrate on the housekeeping while we get on with the serious work."

She and Leia left the anteroom with the Noghri in tow, startling the small contingent of Fia who were huddled together outside in the hallway, whispering animatedly among one another.

"Oh, Princess Leia," exclaimed a relatively broad-faced Fia with orange robes and pointy elbows. They all took a step back as Leia stepped out into the hall. "You surprised us! I am Assistant Primate Thrum. I was discussing a matter of some minor importance with the diplomatic staff here. I apologize if we disturbed you in any way."

"Not at all," Leia said, stopping directly in front of Thrum. "May I ask the nature of the matter you were—discussing?"

"It is nothing," Thrum said, glancing awkwardly to the other Fia around him. "It is just that there appears to be an electrical fault in the quarters we have given you and we must ask—"

"Regretfully ask," put in one of the others leaning in close to Thrum.

"*Regretfully* ask," Thrum corrected himself, "that you consider moving—"

"We have noticed no such faults," Leia said imperiously. "My husband is sleeping. When he wakes, though, I shall have him look more closely. Until then, I'd appreciate if he were left in peace. He is extremely tired after our long journey."

"Ah, yes, of course, Princess, of course." Thrum bowed low, sweeping his spindly arms in undulating movements that Tahiri suspected were meant to indicate abasement. "We would never dream of disturbing the great Han Solo during a rare moment of rest."

Tahiri hid a smile. She had no doubt that the "minor electrical fault" they were talking about lay in the listening bugs that Jag had jammed. It must have frustrated the Fia no end that the only way they would find out what Leia and her entourage wanted was by good old-fashioned questions and answers.

"Thank you," Leia said, casting a brief and conspiratorial smile in Tahiri's direction. "I know he will appreciate that. For now, though, I was hoping that if it wasn't inconvenient, perhaps my friend and I could have a tour of your city."

Thrum straightened almost with a snap, his face beaming with pride. "Of course, Princess! We would like nothing more than to show off our magnificent home." He snapped his fingers twice and his fellow conspirators quickly scattered. "I shall arrange immediately for someone to notify Councilor—"

"That will take time," Leia said, sweeping forward and forcing the fussing Fia to half run just to keep up. "And I'm really not in the mood for waiting. Like I said, it's been a long journey, and I need to stretch my legs. Why don't *you* just take me around, Assistant Primate Thrum? It will make things so much easier."

He nervously followed along, clearly agitated. "But what of Councilor Jobath and Primate Persha?" he babbled. "I shall need to inform them—"

"I'm sure they can catch up in their own time," Leia went on, not even slowing her pace. "You know, they say that travel broadens the mind, and after a few days cooped up in an old freighter, I can assure you that mine is in some serious need of broadening. Now," she said, turning a corner at random, "what do we have down here? I don't think we came this way before. I must say, I like the architecture. Simple yet elegant. Are these corridors deliberately reminiscent of the Old Republic style, or did that come about purely . . ."

And so it went on, with Leia rarely giving the Fia a chance to speak—or, indeed, to protest that he simply didn't have time to escort them at the moment.

Tahiri let herself fall behind, enjoying the sight of

Assistant Primate Thrum trying to get a word in edge-wise. Glancing over the Fia's flat head, the Princess caught her eye and indicated for Tahiri to take another corridor. Tahiri hesitated, then inconspicuously slipped away, her bare feet padding silently along the stone floor.

She felt slightly guilty going off on her own in this manner. And nervous. As Leia's voice slowly faded, Tahiri put her hand on the lightsaber at her hip and attuned her senses to the world around her. The diplomatic quarter of the city was extremely quiet, and for the most part deserted. This didn't overly surprise her, though. Galantos wouldn't receive many visitors, despite the mineral wealth of its soils, so she imagined that this section of the city was probably empty most of the time. Borsk Fey'lya's dismissal of Galantos many years ago had led to an avoidance of the place by New Republic officialdom. No other councilors had visited the planet and, following the Yevethan crisis, it seemed that Galantos had, for all intents and purposes, fallen off the map.

It was odd, then, Tahiri thought, that the Fia had invested so much money in opulent quarters for guests who never came. And it wasn't just that the buildings and rooms were well maintained; it was more that they were actually *brand new*. Why would they build them now? Tahiri wondered. In the middle of a war?

Assuming she was being watched, Tahiri resisted her urge to break into some of the other guest rooms. She suspected that someone, recently, had stayed in the newly built quarters, and she would have loved for the chance to find out exactly who that had been. It was only a gut instinct, but she had learned to pay attention to her gut feelings—especially those originating in the Force, as this one seemed to. Someone *had* been here; she was sure of it. If not within the last few days, then certainly within the last month or two. Perhaps on her way back, she decided, when she had scoped out the rest of the place and getting caught wouldn't be so much of a problem, she would chance taking a closer look.

Following her instincts, she wove her way through numerous corridors until she reached a guard station separating the rest of the city from the diplomats' quarters. Two guards were busy discussing the details of a recent regulation change. They didn't seem to have been alerted to her presence. She gently reached out with the Force and encouraged them to leave their post for a moment, chasing a suspicion that they had perhaps seen someone lurking around a corner. While they were gone, she walked through their post as nonchalantly as she could.

The city outside the security perimeter was noisier than the guests' section. The corridors were plainer here, but had numerous skylights or light-tubes allowing natural daylight to filter throughout. She noticed species other than the Fia about the place, too—a couple of mournful Gran and a group of Sullustans chattering among themselves. She presumed this area of the city contained government offices of some kind, since most of the Fia she passed wore similar clothes: not uniforms, but more the conservative kind of garb one might find in an office anywhere. They noticed her, too, but did nothing to stop her. In fact, some even went out of their way to avoid her, almost as if alarmed to see her walking these corridors.

This troubled her as much as the newness of the diplomatic quarters. Why should they be so frightened of her? Perhaps it wasn't of *her* as such, she thought, but of a human loose in the city. But still, what had they seen to encourage such ill feeling? A Yevetha she could understand, but Gran and Sullustans?

Tahiri set aside the thought for now; she would address it later, with the others in the security of their quarters. For now she concentrated on looking both lost and curious, choosing routes with the least pedestrian traffic, and constantly checking over her shoulder for a sign of the guards she felt sure would by now be coming after her . . .

Her comlink bleeped. Without breaking stride, she raised her wrist and said, "Hello?"

"This is Leia. Where are you, Tahiri? Assistant Primate Thrum pointed out that we seem to have lost you. To be honest, I hadn't noticed. I was so wrapped up in the tour."

Tahiri smiled to herself. "Sorry," she said, playing along with the charade. "I should have called you before now. I went to go back to my room to get something and must have taken a wrong turn along the way."

"Would you like us to send someone to fetch you?"

"No, that's all right. I can find my way back."

"Are you sure?" Tahiri could hear Thrum babbling something behind Leia's words, but couldn't quite make it out.

"I'll call you if I can't retrace my steps. Until then, I'm sure I'll be perfectly safe."

There was no good argument to that. It wasn't as if she was out on the streets where a criminal element might threaten her; she was inside a government building populated by clerks. And Thrum could hardly insist that she return because *they* were nervous about *her*.

"That's fine, Tahiri," Leia said. "Come back when you're ready. Have fun while you're young, that's what I say. And I'm sure Assistant Primate Thrum would agree."

The line went dead. Tahiri smiled even wider, imagining the frustration Thrum must have been feeling in the face of Leia's incessant chattering.

The thought of the talkative locals brought something home to her then. The Fia around here were conversing with none of the driven intensity of Primate Persha or her assistant. They were discussing the everyday occurrences of their lives in some detail, yes, but nothing more than that. She couldn't help wonder if the endless chattering of the Fia she had been formally introduced to was the nervous prattle of someone hoping to avoid awkward questions.

She continued through the building for a while longer before coming to the realization that she wasn't about to learn anything new this way. The corridors were remarkable only in that they all appeared almost exactly the same, and the only doors she found to be open led to nothing more interesting than storerooms or offices, often occupied by gossiping bureaucrats. Because she didn't know what exactly to look for, beyond anything that might explain the communications blackout to Galantos, she didn't have any clear objectives. And besides which, after an hour or more, she was starting to get a little bored with the game.

Deciding to make her way back to the others, she found a turbolift and dropped ten floors; she walked around briefly before going back up the same shaft to the floor she had started on. Then, figuring that if she had any pursuers on her tail, this would set them back a little, she wound her way back to the security post she had snuck through earlier. The same guards were there when she returned, both looking tremendously relieved to see her.

"Mistress Veila! You have returned!"

"Please forgive our lack of courtesy when you came by earlier," said one, approaching her. "It was remiss of us not to be here to give you directions."

"It's really nothing," she said breezily. "I had a nice stroll."

"Please allow me to escort you back to your rooms," he said obsequiously. "We would hate for you to become lost again."

"That won't be necessary," Tahiri said, with a small wave of her hand. "I can find my own way back."

"I'm sure that won't be necessary," the second guard said, stepping up beside the first.

His partner nodded. "She can find her own way back," he said, and gestured her through without another word.

In fact, Tahiri did know her way back to her rooms, but that wasn't where she was heading. She was letting her instincts, not her head, guide her again. Someone else had stayed in these rooms—she was more convinced of this now than she had been before. She half closed her eyes to shut out the distraction of her physical senses, walking where her feelings led her, reaching out with the Force to make sense of her suspicions. Whoever it was who had been the Fia's guest, she could feel their echoes and shadows all around her: in the walls, the carpets, the gilt-edged cornices, the carvings . . .

She moved along the corridors, the feelings becoming stronger with each step she took, finally reaching their peak when she turned into one long passage leading to a wide viewport. The viewport itself looked directly out into the clear skies of Galantos, the sunlight through the decorative and colored glass casting rainbow hues across the numerous doors that lined the passage.

She stepped uneasily forward, her hands reaching out to touch each door in turn as she passed. They all seemed devoid of anything out of the ordinary, and yet the corridor rang with an odd, discordant resonance. The feeling was so strong now, in fact, it was almost tangible. Someone—

She stopped abruptly. Her entire body tingled as her fingertips came into contact with the door at the far end of the corridor. She wasn't normally able to sense individuals so strongly, particularly in the ambience of an unfamiliar world. So what made this one so special? Why was her stomach churning at the thought of opening this door? What exactly was it in these echoes that disturbed her so intensely?

You are being foolish, she chided herself. *You are a Jedi Knight and that is an empty room. There's nothing in there to be frightened of, but fear itself.*

The door slid open when she touched the keypad: nothing to hide, it would seem, or else the door would have been locked. But the mysterious presence hit her like a wave of stale air, making her flinch.

Somewhere in the distance she thought she heard voices calling her, so, despite her apprehensions, she stepped into the room. Her movements were slow and awkward, as though she were trying to take strides in a Mimban swamp.

As expected, the room was unoccupied. It was far from being empty, though. The feelings were so strong now that her entire body felt as though it was about to explode—and, such was the discomfort they were giving her, right then she would have been happy if it *had*.

Still allowing her instincts to guide her, Tahiri stepped over to the bed, lifting the quilt covering it to look underneath. Finding nothing, she lifted the entire mattress.

There.

At full stretch, she could just manage to get her fingers on the tiny silver object that lay on the dusty floor. And the moment she touched it, a shock went through her that sent her reeling. She lay on the floor, clutching the object, panting to catch her breath and fighting to hold the darkness at the back of her mind from sweeping in.

This was it: this was what had been calling to her. Just like the voices were calling to her now . . .

"Mistress Veila! Are you all right?"

Was it a Fia who had called her name? She couldn't be sure; she was too busy trying to stay conscious.

"You must come with us, please," the owner of the voice continued. "You should not be here!"

She felt herself actively complying with the request, even though she seemed to have no real control over her body. It was as if she were lost in a vague fog, her movements as clumsy as a puppet's.

Turning, she saw three Fia guards at the door, one stepping in to take her arm and guide her out into the corridor. There, the other two took position close behind her. They were speaking, but she couldn't quite make out the words, as though she were disassociated completely from her body, looking down from above on all that was happening. And it was all because of the thing in her hand . . .

She brought the pendant up to examine it more closely. It was silver in appearance, but fashioned from a substance unfamiliar to her, and molded in the shape of a bulbous-headed, many-tentacled jellyfish—a bizarre cross between an Umgullian blob and a Sarlacc.

But she knew what it was. Although she'd never seen anything quite like it before, she recognized it immediately.

It was an image of the Yuuzhan Vong deity Yun-Yammka, the Slayer.

A wail came bubbling up from inside her, crying out in a language she wasn't supposed to know: *Ukla-na vissa crai!*

Tahiri clutched the totem to her chest as the world grayed around her and plunged her, finally, into black.

*　　*　　*

In the week following the telling of the Rapuung story, Nom Anor accompanied I'pan on his missions to the upper levels. Using his knowledge of security codes and resource management, he was able to appropriate many of the raw materials the Shamed Ones needed to build their new home, things they hadn't previously been able to gain access to. Slowly but surely this ragtag bunch of Shamed Ones was becoming indebted to him, living a life they would not have been able to had he not been introduced to them. He had given them the lambents that supplied them light when the bioluminescent globes failed, and the arksh that gave them warmth during those colder nights, as well as the h'merrig, the biological processor that produced a significant percentage of their daily food. He had stolen the materials in good conscience, not caring how the thefts might hurt Shimrra's war effort. For now, all that concerned him was engendering the trust of his new companions. And while his small contributions had helped in this, it hadn't been enough to win over everyone—especially the likes of Kunra, who remained suspicious of his motives.

None of that mattered right now, though. He was on another mission with I'pan, and this time collecting equipment and gaining the Shamed Ones' trust was far from his mind. This time, he had a different agenda.

"How much farther?" His tone was full of irritation as he squeezed himself between two enormous conduits.

"Almost there." I'pan looked around to get his bearings, then headed for a small hole in one of the walls. On the other side was a ferrocrete tunnel originally intended to give maintenance droids access to a seemingly endless stream of cables and pipes bunched overhead. The tunnel curved away slightly to the left and had no entrances or exits other than those that had been knocked through the ferrocrete by other explorers. For all Nom Anor could tell, it might have circumnavigated the entire wretched planet.

They came across the corroded remains of a droid halfway along their journey. It was slumped on its side, burned out and stripped of all its useful parts. The expression on its blackened, empty face was a hideous parody of life. Nom Anor kicked it over, stepping on the fragments for good measure as he passed.

Soon they reached a narrow crack in the side of the tunnel, and I'pan put a knobby finger to his lips, calling for quiet. Then he slipped awkwardly but soundlessly through the crack. Nom Anor waited anxiously in the tunnel, fearing a trap. There was nowhere to hide in this endless, abominable place.

I'pan's hand suddenly reemerged from the crack and waved him through. "They're not here yet," he said. "We'll have to wait."

Nom Anor followed I'pan into the sub-basement. Despite years of infiltrating the infidel societies, he still felt slightly hemmed in by the sharp edges, flat planes, and impossibly perfect corners that characterized such rooms. Nothing in nature exhibited such properties as these artificial monstrosities—or at least not simultaneously, anyway. It felt as though their very design was intended to suck the life out of those who occupied them, as if in some vain attempt to fill their terrible emptiness.

The room's only door was locked from the outside. If he was patient, he told himself, he would soon be safely back in the reassuring jumble of the deepest levels, where the weight of all the buildings above warped the edges, bowed the planes, and thwarted the corners sufficiently to fool the mind into thinking it might almost be natural. *Almost.*

I'pan collapsed bonelessly into a corner, appearing in the shadows to be little more than a pile of rubbish under all the rags. Finding a spot in the center of the room, where someone had unsuccessfully attempted to soften the room's harshness by planting a vurruk carpet, Nom Anor concentrated on breathing exercises to pass the time. He was much fitter than he had been before Ebaq 9. He hadn't noticed how the years of stress had racked his body until a few weeks of a solid, simple exercise regime washed it clean. His pulse was again strong, and the gash across his fingers had healed perfectly into a ragged, attractive scar. He felt younger than he had in decades. Nom Anor's self-imposed exile may not have advanced his return with any great speed, but physically it was doing him a world of good.

The sound of scuffling from the far side of the basement's door broke his meditation. Nom Anor and I'pan rose to their feet together as the lock clunked, the door opened, and three people stepped through. The leader, a tall man with no eyesacks to speak of, stopped in front of I'pan but stared critically over at Nom Anor. He held a sack in one hand, which he passed to I'pan without a word.

I'pan took it. "Aarn, T'less, Shoon-mi," he said when the door was safely shut, addressing each of the strangers in turn. "I have brought someone who wishes to learn more about the *Jeedai*."

The three Shamed Ones studied Nom Anor closely. It was clear they didn't recognize him. He knew their type well. They carried an air of toil with them, as though subservience was an atmosphere that could be bottled. I'pan had explained in advance that these three didn't belong to a rogue group such as the one Nom Anor had stumbled across; such were rare, even following the spread of the Jedi heresy. These three were properly employed workers operating under cover.

"His name is—" I'pan started, but was stopped as Nom Anor stepped forward, pushing his companion aside.

"I am Amorrn," he said. The false name was intended ostensibly to avoid alarm over his former existence, but mainly to reduce the chances that word of his survival would reach Shimrra.

The tall one nodded. "I am Shoon-mi," he said, "Niiriit's crèche-brother. When she fell from grace, it was I who freed her from the priests' cells and allowed her to escape. She has told you about me?"

Niiriit hadn't, but Nom Anor could see in the man's sad eyes a yearning for acknowledgment. He knew this sort, too: his immediate family would have been Shamed along with Niiriit, and he was brave enough as a result to resist the established order in small ways, yet too cowardly to abandon it entirely.

"She has told me many things," he said. "She tells me that you, too, follow the ways of the Jedi."

This was mostly true; she *had* spoken of a person closer to the surface who believed in a slightly different version of the heresy. She and Nom Anor had had many conversations on the topic of the Jedi, but she had never once mentioned her relationship to Shoon-mi. He wondered if her devotion to the heresy had burned out all other concerns—perhaps even any feelings for Kunra that might once have existed.

"I pay heed to what I hear," Shoon-mi said cautiously.

"Will you tell me what that is?"

One of Shoon-mi's companions looked nervous. "This is neither the place nor the time," she said. "We are due back in—"

"You go, T'less," Shoon-mi said with an edge as sharp as the room's corners. "Tell Sh'simm we were held up in the yorik nursery. This is more important." He looked directly at Nom Anor, his narrow eyes studying the ex-executor intensely. "And this is as good a place as any."

The one called T'less nodded, glancing at Nom Anor before hastily slipping out of the room.

"Don't let us get you into any trouble," Nom Anor said ingratiatingly.

"We won't be missed," said the Shamed One I'pan had named Aarn. "Things are chaotic on the surface. Whatever it is that afflicts the dhuryam still causes great discomfort. There is confusion and instability. Many are joining our ranks as they are blamed for mistakes or inefficiencies caused by those higher up, and this influx makes it easier for us to slip through the cracks."

Nom Anor listened with stunned amazement. Aarn clearly suffered from a different kind of heresy: that of rebellion. He'd had no idea that such things were discussed at any level of Yuuzhan Vong society, even among the Shamed Ones.

"I'pan has told me the story he heard on Duro," Nom Anor said, swallowing his surprise. "But he tells me also that there are differences between his story and yours."

Shoon-mi nodded. "In the version he tells, it was Mezhan Kwaad who killed Vua Rapuung. But I have heard that he survived her blow, and that he sacrificed himself directly so that the *Jeedai* could escape. And I also heard that it was his brother who killed him. Hul Rapuung was willing to consider that Mezhan Kwaad had Shamed him intentionally, but could not go so far as to accept the *Jeedai* as allies. When Vua died, his supporters fell on Hul and killed him, and it was during this confusion that the *Jeedai* escaped."

"Even so," Nom Anor said, "the message is essentially the same, is it not?"

Shoon-mi shook his head. "There are differences there, too. The *Jeedai* stands accused of using fire in his attack on the Yavin Four installation. That is an abomination of the first order. Most people who hear the story shy away from it, preferring to ignore it as an awkward detail rather than try to examine it and thereby come to a better understanding of the *Jeedai*'s way. But understanding is the key. Anakin Solo proved himself to be more than just an infidel tool user. Later, when his créche-mates were in danger, he sacrificed himself in glorious combat so that they might live. He did not shy away from death. You and I both know that these are not the actions of primitive infidels. They are adaptive strategies—strategies we can learn from."

Nom Anor nodded, absorbing what he'd been told. This story of Vua Rapuung's death rang closer to his memories. There was no mass uprising in the records, no clash between warriors with different ideologies, as I'pan had related it. But Shoon-mi had not mentioned the slaughter of the Shamed Ones on Yavin 4, either. In the mythic sense, clearly the deaths of a thousand Shamed Ones were irrelevant compared to the death of a single significant one.

The fact that Nom Anor had once turned down an invitation to duel with the great Anakin Solo would never be known. The executor had killed an entire squad of warriors with an infidel's blaster in order to keep that particular secret from getting out.

"Where did you hear this story?" he asked.

"From me," Aarn said, stepping forward.

The relatively youthful Shamed One had narrow features that spoke of generations of Shame before him—so much so, in fact, that Nom Anor found it an affront to his dignity even to be in the same room as the man, let alone talk to him.

"I heard it from one of us who served on Garqi."

"And where did they hear it?"

Aarn shrugged, his craggy face pinched into a frown. "I'm not sure," he said. "Why do you need to know?"

Nom Anor shrugged this time. "I am merely curious how there came to be two stories that differ so dramatically about the same event," he said. "It's not as if it happened that long ago. One of the stories must be partly false—but that doesn't necessarily mean that the other is entirely true. If one should be false, why not the other, too?"

"They overlap enough to convince me that the foundations, at least, are true," Shoon-mi said. "You know how quickly rumors change. Word of mouth can distort truth in a very short space of time. But that does not change the *essence* of the story."

Nom Anor nodded thoughtfully, pretending to consider the point Shoon-mi had made. "But which, then, is the *most* true? Which Jedi do I listen to? The one who uses fire, or the one who doesn't?"

"You must follow your instincts," Aarn said.

Nom Anor glanced at the Shamed One, briefly and with a hint of a snarl at the corner of his mouth. It incensed him to have to associate with the likes of the man, when a few months back it would have been beneath him to even waste a thought on his kind.

"I'd rather hoped to follow the story back to its source," he said, speaking directly to Shoon-mi. "To the one who took it off Yavin Four in the first place—the one who saw it with his own eyes and was brave enough to repeat it."

"I don't have that one's name," Shoon-mi said. "I don't know that anyone does, either."

"He was never named in your version of the story?"

Niiriit's brother shook his head. "I'd remember if he had been. That person would be as famous as Vua Rapuung."

He'd also be dead, Nom Anor thought to himself. Going around telling stories about heretics was one thing, but admitting who it was who disobeyed Warmaster Tsavong Lah's direct order was another thing altogether. It could have been anyone, though: a warrior might have smuggled out a favorite slave; the shaper Nen Yim might have spoken of her experiences on Yavin 4; or someone belonging to a domain rivaling Kwaad might have even spread such rumors. The possibilities were numerous.

"Are there any other differences between the stories, then?" he asked, hoping to sound more like an innocent student of the Jedi rather than someone with an ulterior motive.

"There's some discrepancy over when the events occurred," Aarn said.

"Yes, I know. One version suggests that all this happened when Yavin Four was still in the hands of the Jedi. Doesn't that bother you?"

"Not really," Aarn said. "Stories do change of their own accord. I would be more suspicious if all the versions were exactly the same."

"Do you know of any others who tell tales like this, then?" Nom Anor asked.

"A few," Shoon-mi said. "Everyone tells a handful of trusted friends, and each of those in turn tells another handful. That is the manner by which rumors spread. Not knowing who told who more than one or two reiterations ago may be frustrating, but it certainly makes things safer for all of us."

That much was true, at least, Nom Anor thought. Without that fact working in its favor, the Jedi myth wouldn't have filtered far enough to reach his ears. At the same time, though, not being able to trace it back would hardly work in his favor. Shimrra wouldn't be happy with only half the information, if Nom Anor decided to divulge it. Unless the Supreme Overlord could be assured of wiping it out at its source, he would never believe that it had been completely eradicated. This would undoubtedly frustrate him, and that would make Nom Anor the source of this frustration.

The heresy was like disease eating away at the underside of Yuuzhan Vong culture. Beneath the surface, as he had always thought of it, beneath the warrior, shaper, and intendant castes, lay the foundations built by the workers. The efforts of the workers were sustained by the priests, who shored up any weak areas with babble that would barely hold water if one poked a single claw at it. The priests made everything possible because, without gods demanding sacrifice and servitude, what was there to stop the workers from rising up? Or the warriors from turning on the weak? The intendants from stealing from anyone they felt like? It was the glue of the gods that kept not just the Yuuzhan Vong invasion on course but the Yuuzhan Vong race as a whole together.

If something were to supplant the gods—new gods, or no gods at all—Nom Anor suspected that Yuuzhan Vong society would fly apart like a shattered planet. There would be no center left to hold it together; it would be eaten away, *decayed*. He knew it was his duty to report the extent of the heresy to Shimrra. To do otherwise would be to actively participate in the destruction of everything he had worked toward for decades. Yet part of him still wondered if there might not be some way he could turn all of this around to work in his favor, without bringing everything down around him. And wouldn't that be the greatest irony of all? To use his enemies, the Jedi, as the means to his own victory?

"Amorrn?"

He realized that he had been too preoccupied with his thoughts to notice the conversation taking place around him.

"I'm sorry," he said, gritting his teeth on the false camaraderie. "I was thinking of how strange it must have been for Vua Rapuung to be so close to a Jedi for so long."

"There have been others," Aarn asserted. "I heard of a *Jeedai* who allowed himself to be captured, and he couldn't be broken."

I'pan nodded. "I've heard of him, too," he said. "His name was Wurth Skidder. He seduced a yammosk with his mind and then killed it."

Nom Anor said nothing, although he was certain he knew more about the incident than the Shamed Ones relating it to him. The Jedi Wurth Skidder had been a prisoner on *Créche,* a yammosk-carrying clustership destroyed at Fondor. Its commander, Chine-kal, had been circumspect in reports prior to his death, but what seemed certain was that Skidder had been close to the breaking point before an attempted rescue by one of the New Republic's most daring irritants, Kyp Durron's so-called Dozen. One member of this group, a Jedi by the name of Ganner, managed to kill the yammosk, but he had been unable to rescue his friend. The galling thing was that, although Wurth Skidder had died, it was true he had never been broken.

"Mezhan Kwaad couldn't break the *Jeedai*-who-was shaped," Aarn said.

"And then there are the Twins, also," Shoon-mi said. "Both have been captured, and both have escaped. Yun-Yammka has never been able to break them, either."

"So you are saying that they are even more powerful than the gods?" Nom Anor asked.

The question seemed to make Shoon-mi nervous. "Not necessarily," he said. "But perhaps the *Jeedai* know more about the gods than the priests do."

And there it was, stated boldly: the true heresy that had the potential to bring the Yuuzhan Vong species to its knees. Once the workers stopped listening to the priests, what would fill the vacuum? The warriors? The intendants? The *Jedi*?

The latter truly would be an abomination, Nom Anor knew. He would *never* allow himself to be dictated to by an infidel. But he would use them to get what he wanted: either news of the heresy could regain his favor with Shimrra, or the heresy itself could destabilize the Supreme Overlord's rule. That seemed a simple enough progression. It wasn't the normal way an ambitious Yuuzhan Vong climbed the ranks—but since the ladder one would normally ascend to further one's status in the Yuuzhan Vong hierarchy had effectively been kicked out from under him, he was forced to resort to other methods. It wasn't something he was particularly proud of, but it was necessary.

"We must return." Aarn shuffled about on his feet. Nom Anor wondered if Shoon-mi's blatant statement of faith had unsettled him, too.

"I understand," Nom Anor said. "But I would very much like to talk to you again. The notion of truth intrigues me, and I'd like to hear as many different versions of Vua Rapuung's story as possible. If you hear it from anyone else—"

"Then we shall tell you, Amorrn," Shoon-mi said, nodding. "I'pan should take you to see Hrannik, too. I've heard she is also busy spreading the message."

"I will," I'pan said. "I know a couple of others, as well. The truth is spreading."

"The truth is spreading," Shoon-mi repeated, as though by rote.

Bidding a quick farewell, the two from the surface exited via the abominably right-angled door, leaving I'pan and Nom Anor alone again. His deformed companion opened the sack Shoon-mi had given him and looked inside.

"What is it?" Nom Anor asked.

"Food, some old clothes," I'pan answered. "The usual stuff. Shoon-mi likes to look after his sister."

"Why doesn't she talk about him?"

"Because she believes he is a traitor to the truth," I'pan said as though the answer should have been obvious. "As far as she is concerned, he should leave his unit and join her rather than paying lip service to the old gods. Until he does this, she will not even acknowledge his existence."

"But she will accept his gifts," Nom Anor observed wryly.

I'pan laughed at this. "She is not so proud that she will refuse help," he said. "Survival is her priority; changing her brother is secondary."

Nom Anor remembered the way Niiriit's eyes had glowed in the light during the telling of I'pan's story. She was a true fanatic, more dangerous to the system than any of the others. There was nothing more lethal than a trained warrior who had turned against her old leaders.

He smiled to himself, confident with the beginnings of a plan that was slowly forming in his head. All he needed now was the source of the Vua Rapuung rumor.

"Are you coming?" I'pan said, breaking into his thoughts.

Nom Anor smiled again, wider this time. "Time to go home, I'pan," he said, nodding.

I'pan climbed through the fissure in the wall they had entered through earlier, leading him in the direction of the "home" he thought Nom Anor had been referring to.

Jaina watched the holo through a third time. She still couldn't believe what she was seeing—although the heavy feeling in her gut suggested that part of her was at least beginning to.

The holo came from Al'solib'minet'ri City Control, piped up to *Pride of Selonia* on a secure line. Jaina had returned to the frigate specifically to view it, at the request of her parents who felt she needed to see what had happened to Tahiri. It also gave her the opportunity to get her X-wing serviced and diagnostic checks done on her craft's weapon systems while things were quiet.

The holo had been taken two hours before in the diplomatic quarters where her parents were staying with Jag, Tahiri, and C-3PO. It showed Tahiri being guided along a corridor by a small contingent of Fian security guards. According to the report Jaina had received from her mother, Tahiri had gone on a brief exploratory mission through the city, after slipping away, with Leia's assistance, from the Fian escort. It seemed that she had led the guards on a merry chase before they had finally managed to track her down to one particular room where they'd found her lying on the floor in a seemingly dazed state. She had accompanied them without protest, allowing them to return her to the others in her party.

From the casual manner that they carried their blasters, and from their unconcerned expressions, it was obvious that the guards were not expecting any kind of trouble whatsoever. Nevertheless, their leader appeared less than impressed by the runaround that Tahiri had given them.

Jaina watched as Tahiri looked down at something she had clutched in her hand. The cam angle didn't allow a good shot of what the object was, exactly, but Tahiri's reaction upon seeing it was both startling and disturbing. The girl recoiled as though struck by a blaster bolt to the forehead, her expression one of absolute horror. In an instant, too fast for the cam to follow, her ice-blue lightsaber was out and at the ready, sweeping to cover her from any attack. The security guards fell back, themselves startled, bringing their blasters up to the ready. The leader barked a warning, but Tahiri didn't seem to hear or see him. Her eyes were wide as they darted manically from side to side, exactly as if she was expecting an attack. Her lightsaber whipped around in a bright arc as she pirouetted to cover herself from some nonexistent attack from the rear. The guards jumped back a step or two farther at this, confused by the sudden change in the situation. Jaina could understand their fear, too. There was a look on Tahiri's face that warned of what might happen if she was provoked.

The ranking security guard was marginally braver than the others. Despite his own obvious apprehensions regarding Tahiri, he cautiously stepped forward and demanded she deactivate her lightsaber. If she didn't, he said, he would be forced to open fire upon her.

Jaina slowed the playback at that point, watching closely as Tahiri listened to the guard's request. The girl half turned; her expression changed to one of alarm, as though seeing the guards around her for the first time. A procession of emotions flashed across her delicate fea tures: dismay, regret, fear, and, finally, despair. For a split second, Jaina even thought Tahiri might attack the leader who had approached her. Then, as though struck from behind by a stun baton, her eyes rolled back into her head and her legs folded beneath her. Her lightsaber died the instant she released it, the handgrip clattering across the floor and into a wall.

Even then, with Tahiri seemingly unconscious and her weapon nowhere near her, the guards remained wary, keeping their distance with their blasters trained on Tahiri's prostrate figure. The leader was also reluctant to approach, nervously calling for backup on his comlink. Even when they did find the courage to step up to her and prod her with their feet, Tahiri didn't respond. It was only when the reinforcements arrived that the girl finally stirred, sitting up with obvious bewilderment. But she didn't protest against the weapons being leveled at her, or resist when she was loaded aboard a hovercart and examined by a medic. A short time later, she fell into what appeared to be a deep sleep from which she couldn't be awakened.

By then, the others had been notified and were arriving on the scene. Jaina's mother came first, along with a Fia who was later identified as Assistant Primate Thrum, followed closely by Jag.

"Is she hurt?" Leia asked the paramedic leaning over Tahiri.

"No," she was told. "She simply appears to have fainted."

The leader of the security guards explained how Tahiri had drawn her lightsaber. When pushed on the matter of why she should do something like this, the Fian security guard replied, "That's just it—I don't think it was *us* she was attacking." When asked to explain, however, the guard was unable to do so. Nonetheless, Jaina knew what he meant.

Even though the holo had been taken at awkward angles that often didn't allow her to see Tahiri's face, Jaina could tell that whoever Tahiri had been fighting, it *hadn't* been those guards. Her lightsaber was swinging, yes, but her attention had been on something else, something unseen. What that something was, Jaina had no way of telling.

Her mother, using every bit of leverage her diplomatic weight afforded her, convinced the medic, guards, and Assistant Primate that Tahiri would be better off in her own quarters, where she could be examined properly. The anxious procession had wound its way through the empty corridors of the diplomatic quarters to where Jaina's father and C-3PO were waiting. There, Leia had insisted they be left alone so that they might tend to the girl in peace and quiet. The Fia had agreed to allow this, but clearly with reservations. Even from her position in orbit, Jaina could see that Assistant Primate Thrum was not overly convinced that this was the right thing to do. His job had been to keep an eye on the visitors; what with Tahiri's unauthorized jaunt and the jamming of the bugs in the diplomatic suites, he wasn't really having much success at it.

Jaina's mother had called her as soon as they'd determined that Tahiri wasn't in any immediate danger and was, as the Fia in charge of the medical droid had diagnosed, simply unconscious. Jaina's first thoughts were concern that Tahiri's illness—whatever it was—hadn't been relieved by leaving Coruscant. Leia agreed: she had hoped that keeping her busy would be enough to clear the angst that seemed to have taken hold of her.

"But perhaps I'm hoping for too much," Leia said, frowning. "It's still early."

Jaina wasn't convinced it could all be put down to stress. "Whatever's going on, Mom, I don't think it's entirely in her head."

"Something in the Force, you think?"

"I honestly don't know. If it is, then it's something subtle that you're not picking up." She shrugged, feeling frustrated at being so far away from her sick friend. "She was a long time without a Master, after Ikrit died. Who knows what's been going through her mind?"

"Luke wouldn't have made her a Jedi Knight without being certain she was all right," Leia said, but something in her expression told Jaina that her mother didn't really believe it could be dismissed so easily.

Midway through the conversation, C-3PO announced that he'd managed to access a security holo showing what had happened to her before her collapse. The droid succeeded just in time; barely had he appropriated the holo when it was snatched out from under him and secured in a domain he had no access to. The Fia were clearly becoming sensitive to the overactive curiosity of their guests.

Jaina and the others watched the holo, increasingly mystified.

"Tahiri looks terrified," she said over the secure link with her family.

"Of what, though?" Han asked. "There's nothing there but the guards. And the most they would've done is bore her with details of procedures she should have followed."

"Well, *something* upset her," Leia said.

"Something that none of us can even see," Jaina mused.

And there the matter rested. Leia insisted that the best thing for Tahiri right now was to let her sleep. She hadn't been harmed by the Fia; there was nothing out of the ordinary on any of the scans C-3PO took of her. They would have to wait until she woke up to find out exactly what had happened.

"Here's another mystery," Jaina's mother said after a few moments' silence. "The Fia aren't afraid of the Yevetha anymore."

"What?" Han exclaimed. "That's like standing on the Jundland Wastes in high summer and not being afraid of krayt dragons."

"You'd think so, wouldn't you?" Leia agreed. "But that's what I was told by Thrum. When I asked him what precautions they're taking against the threat of another Yevethan attack, he said they didn't need to take precautions, as N'zoth was no longer a problem."

"Just like that?" said Han.

Leia nodded. "I asked him about diplomatic ties, thinking that maybe the Yevetha have had a change of heart about alien species. He said that they didn't exist. There's no embassy on Galantos; no negotiated peace settlement. It's like—" She paused, as if unable to find the words to express her thoughts. "I don't know—it's like the Yevetha simply gave up and decided to stay at home from now on."

"I don't believe that for a second," Han said. "It'd be like them to lie low for years while secretly rebuilding and plotting their revenge." He shook his head. "Mark my words: they have to be up to something. I tell you, if *my* home was on Galantos, I wouldn't be taking my eyes off that cluster for a second."

Leia nodded again and, far above in the ship, Jaina had to agree with the suspicion. Vicious xenophobes didn't just roll over after a sound beating; they came back twice as nasty and three times as determined. The

Yevetha were liable to come bursting out of the Koornacht Cluster at any time.

"Do you want me to take a look?" she asked down the subspace link.

She caught the momentary hesitation on both her parents' faces as they glanced at each other; but then, equally as fast, their expressions softened.

"Don't stick around to make any enemies," Han said. "Just get in and get out again, understood? Don't make me have to come in there after you."

Jaina smiled at this.

"And get back to us in one piece," Leia added.

The only dissenting voice came from Jag. "This is crazy," he said to her parents. "You can't be seriously considering sending Jaina off into unknown territory like this."

"We're not sending her," Leia said. "She volunteered."

"Besides, if the Fia are telling the truth," Han put in, "then the territory's likely to be safer now than it ever was."

"And if they're *not* telling the truth?" Jag asked.

"What's your problem, Jag?" Jaina piped up frostily.

"Look, I don't mean to imply that you couldn't handle it," Jag said. He looked uncomfortable confronting the combined Solo family. "I'm just thinking of the squadron, that's all. Who's going to run it with you gone?"

"You, of course," she said, surprised that she should even have to point this out. "It'll take me a couple of hours or more to prep for the mission. That'll give you time to get back up here and take over, won't it?"

"I guess so," he said. There was a look of uncertainty on his face that she wasn't used to seeing. He was clearly uneasy with this whole idea. "But there's something I want to do here, first, if that's all right."

"Of course," Jaina said.

He nodded, still without conviction. "And you'll take some backup with you, right, Jaina?"

She smiled, suddenly realizing the source of his concern. He wasn't thinking about the squadron at all; he was thinking about *her*. He was worried about her well-being, and the fact that he cared so much for her filled her with a warm satisfaction.

"If it makes you feel any better," she said, "then I'll take Miza and Jocell along with me."

She knew that would ease his mind on at least one score. They were two pilots from his Chiss Squadron, so he knew he could trust them.

"Okay, so that's settled," Han put in with a look she couldn't quite fathom. "When you're ready, Jag, I'd like to go with you to check on the *Falcon*, to make sure she hasn't been interfered with. I doubt we've given these guys enough time to plan anything like sabotage, but we can't afford to take any chances."

"I'll stay here with Tahiri and Threepio," Leia said with a slight frown. "Good luck, dear. And do as your father says: don't ruffle any crests, all right? If the Yevetha *have* softened, we could really use their help against the Yuuzhan Vong."

"Understood, Mom." The sight of Tahiri in the background, unconscious, pale, and vulnerable, gave Jaina a twinge of guilt for leaving. "I'll be back soon."

Jacen reached deep inside himself, searching for the wisdom of his last teacher's words.

"The Force is everything, and everything is the Force," Vergere had said, shortly before she died. "There is no dark side. The Force is one, eternal and indivisible. You need worry about no darkness save that in your own heart."

Not even the darkness of others? he wanted to ask her as he stood listening to Moff Flennic's ranting. The terrible, anti-life obscenities dripping from the mouth of this self-styled savior of the Imperial Remnant was almost more than Jacen could bear.

"Retreat?" the man was growling. "*Retreat?* I hear that word and I think of cowards; I think of cowards and I find myself reaching for my blaster." He paused to fix Jacen with a baleful glare, presumably to let him know he wasn't exaggerating. "There's not one man under my command who would accept an order to retreat from me without questioning my sanity. They'd sooner relieve me of my command than follow such an order—and they'd have every right to!"

"Moff Flennic," Jacen said as placatingly as he could, "if you'll just listen to what I have to say—"

Moff Flennic snorted. "And give you the opportunity to plant your thoughts in my head? I'm not stupid, boy. I'm not *senile*. Who do you take me for? I was hunting Eloms decades before you were even born."

Finding solace and strength in the memory of Vergere's wisdom, Jacen found an island of calm within himself and relaxed his clenched hands.

The solidly built man paced the flight deck in full uniform, waiting out Jacen's silence with tense energy.

"Well?" he snapped after a moment. "Aren't you going to tell me that hunting intelligent life-forms constitutes some violation of your weak Jedi sensibilities?"

Jacen shrugged philosophically. "My sensibilities are my own, sir, and I have no wish to impose them upon you."

"And yet you want me to do what you tell me," the man scoffed. "Isn't that the same thing, boy?"

"Not at all. I am merely explaining what, to me,

would be your most prudent course of action at this moment. How you choose to respond to my opinion, of course, is entirely up to you."

"But you won't like it if I ignore you, will you?"

"If you ignore me, your people will be slaughtered," Jacen said softly. "And no, I would not like that at all."

Flennic hesitated, something approximating amusement flickering behind his keen eyes. Then he resumed his pacing, slower, each step more deliberate than the last. "You know, boy, if you were one of my officers, I would have had you shot for speaking to me the way you just did."

Jacen fought to maintain calm. For all the Moff's abhorrence at the idea of Jacen implanting ideas in his head, he seemed to have no problem in practicing a few mind games of his own. The constant use of the word *boy* was no doubt intended to make Jacen feel small and inadequate. It was lame at best, and served only to further Jacen's frustration.

"Moff Flennic," he started tiredly.

The Moff raised a hand to silence Jacen. "I know what you're going to say," he said. "That you're *not* one of my officers—nor would you want to be, I imagine. But I wouldn't take you even if you wanted me to. And do you know why?"

"It's not relevant, sir," Jacen said, trying to maintain his tone of respect even though all he wanted to do was grab the man by the collar of his uniform and shout at him to just *listen*.

The man stopped pacing and turned to face him. "I have no idea why you're bothering to talk to me, boy. I'm clearly wasting your time. That's what you're thinking, isn't it?"

"Actually, sir, I don't believe for a second that I'm

wasting my time," Jacen said. "If anything, I think you know that what I'm saying makes sense, but you're just too proud to admit it. You're desperately trying to convince yourself that I'm wrong."

"Really?" The word was more of a challenge than a question.

"You're no fool, sir," Jacen said smoothly. "Convene the other Moffs, if you want to. Tell them what I've told you and see what they have to say. I'd be particularly interested in speaking to Moff Crowal of Valc Seven, since she might have access to something I'm looking for."

"And what might that be?" asked Flennic.

Jacen smiled slightly at the suspicion that suddenly pinched the man's face. "Information, of course," he said. "Understand, sir, that our time in the Empire is limited; our mission lies elsewhere. When we have what we need, we will be leaving."

Flennic's eyes narrowed. "And you think Valc Seven would be an ideal fallback position for our fleet when we retreat from Yaga Minor?"

"Actually, that's the last thing you'd want to do. Valc Seven is on the edge of the Unknown Regions. Fall back that far, and you've already lost the Empire. No, my choice of fallback—the place you would do best to lay a trap, if you prefer—would be Borosk."

The Moff was silent for a long moment. Jacen knew what he was thinking. Borosk was one of several small, fortified worlds guarding the edge of the Empire. The Moff would be wondering if this was part of some convoluted plot on behalf of the Galactic Alliance to gain territory from an old enemy.

But Jacen hoped that even Flennic would see that that was just ridiculous. If the Imperial Remnant lost such a stand, Borosk would fall to the Yuuzhan Vong, not the

Galactic Alliance. And the Galactic Alliance had more important things to worry about than a small system on the edge of its territory.

The continuing silence suggested that Flennic was unable, for the moment at least, to fault the plan. Pressing home his advantage, Jacen went on:

"Moff Flennic, if you move quickly enough, you might save Yaga Minor."

This got a reaction. Yaga Minor was the Moff's personal holding. When it fell—as it surely would, if the fleet stayed where it was—Flennic would have nothing, regardless of what happened to the Empire as a whole.

"Explain," Flennic demanded.

"The Yuuzhan Vong are stretched to the limit right now. Thanks to our hit-and-run campaigns, the forces they've assembled to knock out the Empire are badly needed elsewhere. They can't afford to commit here for too long. Knocking out your fleet quickly is their priority. Wherever it is, they'll go. Once it's destroyed, they figure they can wipe out your shipyards at their leisure."

"So if we send them packing now," Flennic put in, "you're saying they won't come back?"

Jacen shook his head. "I can't guarantee that," he said. "But if they did come back, it certainly wouldn't be in such numbers."

Flennic was pacing again. "And what makes you so sure staging a counterattack at Borosk will work?" he asked, his attention directed to the floor ahead of him.

"Two reasons," Jacen replied. "One, the spies infiltrating your staff will make sure their warmasters know about the move. And two, we'll teach you how to fight the Yuuzhan Vong more effectively."

That pulled the Moff up to a complete halt, swinging

his full attention around to Jacen. "In exchange for what?"

"Nothing, actually. My only interest is in saving lives and maintaining the stability of this region. We can haggle over information with Moff Crowal when this matter is resolved."

Moff Flennic grunted. " 'This matter'?" he echoed incredulously. "You make it sound like we're in the middle of a minor squabble over an asteroid!"

"Please don't take offense, sir, but from the point of view of the galaxy, that's more or less what this is. The Empire has dominion over a few thousand systems out of hundreds of thousands of millions. Yes, you have tactical significance, and no, I do not like to see lives wasted unnecessarily; but your failure to survive will make little difference in the greater scheme of things."

Flennic's face filled with blood. His jowls quivered from the rage building up inside him. Jacen had gotten the reaction he'd hoped for. Through the Force he could feel the pressure rising like stresses in a neutron star. Any moment now, something would give. The question was: would he explode or implode?

The answer never came. The comm on Flennic's desk buzzed and the Moff vented his anger on it.

"I told you, no interruptions!" he bellowed into the comm unit.

"But, sir, there's an incoming call from—"

"I don't care who it's from, you fool. Get rid of them now, or so help me I'll have you ejected into space without—"

He stopped short when another voice issued from the comm unit. "That's hardly the way to speak to a subordinate officer," the voice said. "Especially when you're on *my* ship."

Flennic's features went from startlingly purple to deathly white in the time it would have taken light to cross the room.

"Grand Admiral?" he said unbelievingly. "You're— *alive*?"

"Of course I'm alive," Pellaeon said, his voice oddly muffled but clear. "It will take more than a bunch of overeager Yuuzhan Vong to put me out of the picture."

"But—"

"What's the matter, Kurlen? You don't sound as over-joyed to hear my voice as I'd thought you might."

"No, that's not it at all. It's just—that is, I'm—" The man stammered awkwardly for a moment, then straightened and returned his glare to Jacen. "How do I know this isn't one of your mind tricks, Jedi?"

It was Pellaeon who answered. "Just take a look at him, Kurlen. He's as surprised about this as you are."

That was true. The last thing Jacen had expected was assistance from the man he had last seen unconscious in a bacta tank, looking as though death was but a few short breaths away. It also confirmed something he had been wondering: that Pellaeon had access to more than just audio via his comlink, but was hiding his own visuals.

"It's nice to hear your voice, Grand Admiral Pellaeon," Jacen said with absolute honesty.

"Under better circumstances, Jacen Solo, I would say the same." There was the hint of a smile in the man's voice. "Thank you for your help at Bastion. I owe the Jedi my life, and I never forget my debts. You can safely assume I shall listen to your thoughts on the Yuuzhan Vong with far more interest than some of my colleagues."

"It would be my pleasure to discuss them with you, sir," Jacen said, mindful to keep any conceit from his tone. Even though he would be dealing with Grand Admiral Pellaeon, he still didn't want to get on Flennic's bad side. The future was full of unseen waters; it was important to leave as many means of crossing those waters open to him as possible.

"Another time, perhaps," the Grand Admiral said. "I've been a little out of touch these past couple of days, and right now I have a strategic withdrawal to discuss with Moff Flennic."

"We were just discussing that very thing," the Moff said, licking his lips nervously.

"Were you, indeed?" Pellaeon asked. "And have you issued directives to the surviving officers?"

"Well, no, but—"

"Assessed possible locations for a more substantial regroup?"

"Borosk was one location that came to mind," Flennic said, shooting Jacen a warning look.

"A good choice, Kurlen. I suggest you get onto it straight away. The longer we sit here, the more stupid we'll look when the next wave arrives. Capital ships should start moving within the hour, leaving a small defense force behind. I trust I can leave the arrangements in your hands? I have business elsewhere that needs attending."

"Uh, Grand Admiral—"

"Yes, Kurlen?"

"Don't you think this deserves a little more discussion?"

There was a long silence. Jacen maintained an expression of serene patience while Moff Flennic looked increasingly nervous.

When Pellaeon spoke again, it was in a voice with all the cold clarity of a hydrogen bath.

"Understand this, Kurlen: what I just gave you was an

order, not an invitation. While I command the Imperial Navy, you *will* do as I say, regardless of whether or not you agree with those orders. Otherwise—and believe me when I say this—if I have to secede from the Empire in order to ensure this navy's survival, then I shall do so without hesitation—and I guarantee that we won't be back to pick up the pieces of your shipyards afterward."

"I understand, Grand Admiral," the Moff stammered.

"Good," Pellaeon returned crisply. "But I'm not finished. This is just the beginning. You will also issue orders to allow *Jade Shadow* free access to this system, and any system within the Empire. The Moff Council has gravely underestimated the threat of the Yuuzhan Vong against my advice one too many times, and it won't happen again. I won't *let* it happen again. The time has come to take what few assets we have left and ensure that nothing like this ever recurs. If we survive Borosk, the Galactic Alliance and the Jedi will be our best hope of long-term survival, and I intend to take advantage of them while the Empire still exists. Is that understood?"

The large but temporarily cowed man just nodded.

"The connection must be poor, Kurlen, because I didn't quite catch what you said."

"I understand perfectly, Grand Admiral Pellaeon."

"Excellent. Now, send our young friend back to *Widowmaker*. I want to pick his brain about the Yuuzhan Vong while I still have the opportunity to do so."

Flennic didn't look at Jacen as he pushed a button for the door to open. It did so with a faint hiss. Jacen bowed in farewell, but the Moff turned away as though he wasn't even there.

Hiding his relief to be out of the man's presence, Jacen walked rapidly down to the docks where the *Lambda*-class shuttle waited to take him back.

* * *

Jaina took her time prepping for launch, hoping to catch Jag when he arrived. But a suspicious-looking scuff mark on the *Falcon* held him up on the surface and she couldn't delay forever. As soon as she and her two wingmates were kitted up and had clearance authorization from *Pride of Selonia*, she launched her X-wing and powered away from Galantos.

The sight of two clawcraft shadowing her was still a little unnerving. It wasn't all that long ago that craft with similar cockpits—TIE fighters—had represented fear and hostility for those who had survived the Rebellion and the tumultuous years that had followed. She was too young herself to have any firsthand memories of that time, but Jaina had heard enough stories and seen sufficient footage to have had the same instinct instilled in her. She didn't know how many times the Empire had tried to kill her parents in all, but she was sure it was in double figures, at least.

At the same time, though, the clawcraft's four sweeping weapon arms resembled an X-wing's S-foils. Sometimes she wondered if the Chiss hadn't deliberately designed their fighters to unsettle and reassure both New Republic and Empire. It was like sitting on the fence, giving the impression that they might have allegiance to either power.

"Locking on to your navicomputer," Jocell said. A brisk, efficient woman from Csilla, homeworld of the Chiss, she was easy to work with. Miza was the better pilot of the two, but less reliable, as far as Jaina was concerned.

"Last one there's a flat-lined drebin," came Miza over the comm unit.

The decidedly non-Chiss phrase immediately caught

Jaina's attention. "Jump laid in," she replied, figuring she knew where the pilot had picked it up. The frigate accompanying the mission was staffed by navy personnel from all across the galaxy; when Twin Suns Squadron wasn't on patrol, there was plenty of time for socializing in the mess and picking up on some of the native lingo.

"Be on your guard for when we arrive," she said. "I'm bringing us in at the edge of the system, but you never know what might be waiting for us. Even if the Yevetha have embraced the idea of peaceful coexistence with their neighbors, they're not likely to welcome someone barging in through their shipping lanes."

"Understood," Jocell said.

"Discretion is my middle name," Miza added.

"Ready, Cappie?" Jaina asked. Her R2 unit whistled cheerfully as her forward view swung around to face the bright cloud of the Koornacht Cluster. "Then into the Multitude we go."

Stars suddenly extended into streaks of light as she and her wingmates blasted into hyperspace. From there on it would be up to her navicomputer and R2 unit to ensure that the three vessels reached their destination safely, leaving her with nothing more to do in the cramped cockpit than sit and wait and think . . .

Tahiri's frailty worried her more than she was prepared to admit—at least to others. Back on Mon Calamari, the girl had called her that one time before collapsing, but since then she'd barely said a word to her when Jaina had visited her in Master Cilghal's infirmary. Tahiri had been glad to see her, there was no question about that, but she had been uneasy and troubled at the same time—and maybe even a little embarrassed.

Tahiri had always been so fiery and independent, defying conventional sensibilities in numerous ways, from insisting on bare feet to disobeying direct orders. Showing off for Anakin had been part of the latter, Jaina was sure, but if the impulse hadn't been there in the first place, then her little brother would never have had such a willing sidekick.

No, Jaina thought. *Not sidekick.* She really had to dispel the image of Anakin and Tahiri as perfectly matched pals getting into harmless scrapes. Those "scrapes" they'd been involved in could hardly be regarded as harmless. If anything, some of them, such as their adventure with Corran Horn at Yag'Dhul, had been outright dangerous. And their last one together had been fatal, culminating in Anakin's death . . .

No, Anakin and Tahiri had definitely been more than just kids, and their relationship had been advancing toward something more than just friends near the end, too. The grief that Tahiri had been suffering was not for the loss of a friend, but for the loss of a loved one. Even if that love never had a chance to fully blossom, it didn't diminish Tahiri's pain. The *potential* for a relationship had been there, and it was for this that Tahiri grieved—a love not fully realized. Jaina imagined that the grief Tahiri suffered was on a par with her own, but at least she had the benefit of being able to focus her grief on what had been lost; Tahiri's grief was for something that could never be. It was, and might forever be, completely intangible.

Jaina wondered if her mother's decision to invite Tahiri along on the mission had been entirely sensible. Yes, the girl would do better kept busy rather than lying around in an infirmary, alone and dwelling on her grief. But was being surrounded by the Solo family the right thing for her? If Jag died, Jaina was certain she wouldn't want to be stuck in the company of General Baron Soontir Fel and Syal Antilles for too long. They would only serve as reminders of what she'd lost.

The image of Tahiri unconscious on Galantos, as pale and thin as she'd been on Mon Calamari, made Jaina's heart ache. After several awkward visits to the infirmary and a number of silences during the mission so far, Jaina still had no idea what it was Tahiri had wanted when she'd called her that day after Uncle Luke's meeting of the Jedi. To say she was sorry? To blame Jaina for letting Anakin die? She didn't know. The black tide of grief made people do crazy things. She knew that firsthand, and so did her parents. But if there was anything she could do to make life easier for Tahiri, she would do it in an instant. The problem was that she doubted even Tahiri herself knew what that might be. All they could do was hope that they could work it out before something else happened . . .

Too many hours, two system checks, a detailed scan of her R2's files regarding the N'zoth system, and a half-hearted attempt to learn some words in the fiendishly difficult Chiss native tongue later, her navicomputer bleeped to warn her that they were about to emerge from hyperspace.

"Heads up," she said to her wingmates. "We're there. And remember, this is just a surveillance sweep, so don't provoke anything unless you absolutely have to. Is that clear?"

"Understood, Colonel," Jocell said. "Preparing to disengage navigational lock."

"I don't know about you," Miza said, "but I'm becoming a little sluggish from all this rest we're supposed to be enjoying. I'll almost be *glad* if we could find something to shoot at."

"I know what you mean," Jaina said. "But I don't want you using so much as a hard stare without my direct authority, Miza. Clear?"

Miza chuckled. "I'll keep my hands safely in my lap."

"You do that." Her R2 unit bleeped again; Jaina glanced at the translator to learn they had five seconds before arrival. "Okay, guys, here we go."

The first thing that struck her as her X-wing rattled back into realspace was the brightness of the sky. She'd been in close clusters before, but it was easy to forget just how much of a difference it made when a large number of hot, young stars clustered so closely together—especially after spending so much time at the edges of the galaxy, avoiding the Yuuzhan Vong. Because she had brought them in at the outskirts of the system, N'zoth's primary was hidden in the radiance from the many other suns, and it took her some moments to actually locate it. Bright and blue-tinged, it burned at her with an almost forbidding glare.

Her wingmates dropped out of hyperspace beside her, and immediately peeled away into formation. Sensors swept the space around them; astromech droids chattered via comlinks; intrasystem landmarks were confirmed. According to New Republic records, no one had been to N'zoth since the Yevethan crisis, twelve years earlier. Then, the Yevethan Black Fleet had been routed by New Republic forces after it attempted a genocidal cleansing of the area around the Koornacht Cluster. Jaina agreed with her father that the silence since was probably an indication of frantic retooling rather than peaceful reconsideration. This would be the first opportunity anyone had to find out one way or the other.

"I'm picking up extensive mass readings," Miza said. "Judging by the uneven distribution, I'd say we have at least three fleets massed in orbit around worlds two and five."

"Which one's N'zoth?" Jocell asked.

"Two," Jaina supplied. "I'm not picking up signatures consistent with old Imperial designs, but that's not unexpected. The Yevetha were quick to learn, and they would have had to start again from scratch. Why not redesign at the same time?"

"No capital ships that I can see," Miza said. "Just plenty of small ones, easy pickings."

Jaina didn't caution him again; she knew it was just his sense of humor. Still, she would have preferred it if he remained serious like Jocell.

"There are no thrustship exhaust traces, either," Jocell said. "Rad and IR readings are—odd." After a brief pause, she added, "Jaina, are you seeing what I'm seeing?"

Jaina studied her screen. The mass shadows were exactly where Miza had said: clumped in broad orbital corridors around the rocky second planet and a bloated gas giant on the far side of the system. It made sense, she thought, to keep your fleets close to both home and a refueling base. You wouldn't put them all in one spot. That would be tactically unsound. Just because you weren't expecting trouble didn't mean it wouldn't come to find you.

The probing triangle of ships continued their surveillance of the system. From the Yevetha's point of view, she supposed, *they* were trouble, and she didn't doubt that the xenophobes would have monitoring stations all around the system, ready to spot just such an intrusion as theirs. But where were the flashes of engine exhausts as interceptors launched? Where were the echoes of hyperspace distortions as squadrons of updated thrustships rushed to confront them? Why was there nothing but diffuse mass and heat appearing on the scanners, nothing concentrated in any particular place?

N'zoth was radiating heat like a small sun. Not surprising for a desert world, perhaps, but why wasn't the heat concentrated around the cities?

Sithspawn, she silently cursed. If her father had been here, she knew just what he would have said.

"We're going in closer," she said. "And I have a feeling I know what we're going to find."

Neither of the Chiss pilots asked her to elaborate, suggesting that perhaps they had had the same feeling. Instead they silently slaved their clawcraft to her X-wing as she laid in a course for N'zoth.

The hyperspace jump was mercifully short. When they arrived where the two fleets had been in orbit around the Yevethan homeworld, Jaina found the reality of the situation much worse than she had imagined. There was nothing but wreckage. Thousands of thrustships, dozens of capital vessels, and one battle station capable of maintaining the entire lot floated in pieces around the planet below. The wreckage was still hot—it could take months for excess heat to radiate through vacuum—and it was this that had shown up on the scopes. Jaina took her small contingent on a wide parabola around the deathly silent wreckage, moving them in closer to the planet itself.

She didn't need to look, but she had to. N'zoth had been pounded from orbit, possibly by chunks torn from the wreckage of the fleet above. Lava and sulfuric clouds belched from the bottom of a score of new craters around the globe, and the atmosphere was filled with ash. Where there had once been cities, there were now only great holes in the crust. Every trace of the Yevethan civilization had been reduced to atoms.

For once, Miza didn't have any smart comments; he was as quiet as the others as they swung around N'zoth's equator. Jaina turned her sensors toward the distant gas giant, not doubting what she would find there. Someone had attacked the Yevetha, taking them unawares and totally decimating a fleet of considerable size. The Fia stood to benefit most from the destruction of the Yevetha—and it would certainly explain why they no longer seemed to care about the xenophobes in their backyard—but there was no way they could have come by this sort of firepower. No, this could have only been the work of the Yuuzhan Vong.

A cold and uncomfortable feeling spread through Jaina's stomach as she thought of her parents and Jag back on Galantos—little knowing what she'd found. She reached out with the Force to find her mother, but the distance was too great. And with communications down in the sector, there was no other way to warn them.

She was about to order their immediate return to Galantos when Miza messaged her. "Jaina, I'm picking up a transmission from that small moon we passed a moment ago."

"Put it on the air," she ordered.

There was a pause followed by some cold static. Jaina tried to boost the signal, but no amount of switches flicked would clean up the noise.

"Miza? Jocell? Either of you getting anything?"

"Nothing," Jocell replied.

"Likewise," Miza said. "It's like they're trying to open a line, but for some reason they're not saying anything."

"Maybe they can't," Jocell suggested. "They might be too badly injured."

Jaina nodded thoughtfully to herself. It was a possibility, she supposed. Flicking her own comm unit, she said, "Whoever you are, if you can hear this, click your mike twice."

There was a slight delay, followed by a distinct double click.

"Okay. Now, if you're injured, click twice again."

Another delay, followed by two clicks.

"I'm picking up a weak power reading from the bottom of a crater," Miza said. "It's consistent with that of a small vessel. I guess he's been hiding there in the ruins of his thrustship. He probably survived by laying low until whoever did this had passed on."

Jaina considered this, but quickly dismissed it. It didn't ring true, somehow. "No, that's not the Yevethan way. They don't hide from fights. My guess is he crashed there and was knocked unconscious, awakening only when the battle was over."

"That's if he *is* a Yevetha," Jocell said.

"What else would he be?" Jaina asked. "You're not suggesting he might be one of the Yuuzhan Vong, are you?"

"I don't know. But without a visual, we have no way of knowing."

"Miza? What do you think?"

"My gut instinct tells me it's a Yevetha—and an injured one at that. Like you said, Jaina, it's not in their nature to hide, so why else would he be down there? And it makes no sense for it to be a Vong, either. Whatever caused this was a big fleet. They came in, hit hard, and moved on. What would it serve them to leave a single small ship behind?"

"I agree," Jaina said. "But I also agree with Jocell that we're going to need a visual—especially if we're to rescue the pilot."

Miza's clawcraft was veering off before she could give

the order. "Already on my way. This shouldn't take too long."

"Jocell, keep an eye out for anything unusual. If we have to get out of here in a hurry, then I want plenty of warning."

"Understood, Colonel."

Jaina watched Miza's ship shrink to a tiny speck of light shooting across the face of the moon. She felt uneasy having her wingmate so far away, even though there seemed to be no overt threat anywhere in the system right now. Or maybe she was nervous *because* there was no overt threat around. It was too quiet for her liking.

To take her mind off everything, she opened a line with the Yevethan pilot.

"We're going to try to get you out of there. Do you copy?"

Two clicks.

"Hang in there. One of my pilots is on the way down now. He'll be passing over your head in a matter of seconds. Then we'll—"

This time a low, malevolent chuckle came over the comm unit, followed by a raspy, fluidy cough.

"Your optimism is as shallow as your compassion," said the voice—definitely Yevethan, and male. "You care no more for me than I do for you."

"Not quite the response I was expecting," Jocell muttered.

Jaina ignored her wingmate. "We do care—why do you think we're trying to—?"

"Soon I shall join my people," the Yevetha continued. "Soon the Yevetha shall be no more. But we shall not go down quietly."

"There is no reason to go down at all! Just let us—"

"In the face of death's bright dawn," the Yevetha went

on, "I shall offer one final act of defiance, so that when we are talked about in times to come, they will say that the Yevetha were warriors to the end!"

Jaina felt a cold discomfort pulse through her. "Miza, get out of there!"

"Way ahead of you, Jaina!"

"There is nowhere to run," the Yevetha said. "The galaxy belongs only to those who had the power to destroy our once-mighty race!" A faint and disturbing hiss issued from the comm unit. "Die with me, won't you?"

"Miza! Talk to me!"

"Almost—"

A powerful flash of energy lashed out from the ball of rock. Miza's clawcraft vanished into it a split instant before reaching Jaina's X-wing, sending her tumbling end over end, shields down and cockpit dead.

"You did it!"

Jacen found himself enveloped in a hug the moment he stepped off the shuttle's boarding ramp. Taken by surprise, he automatically returned the hug before realizing who was giving it to him. The warm, petite body pressed against his; the hair; the delicate yet very female scent . . .

"I always knew you would," Danni said, pulling away slightly. "But I was still worried about you. You Solos have a knack for doing things the hard way."

"It was Admiral Pellaeon, really," Jacen protested. "If he hadn't woken up when he did, I doubt I could have convinced Flennic of anything."

"You're just being modest." Danni laughed, playfully punching his shoulder. "I bet Jacen Solo could convince a Selonian to lie if he really wanted it to."

Footsteps approaching from the docking bay's main entrance prevented him from responding to this. Danni stepped back, looking embarrassed, as Luke walked around the corner.

"I thought I felt you come aboard," said Jacen's uncle, dressed in his customary Jedi robes.

"How long have you been here?" Jacen asked both of them. He hadn't seen *Jade Shadow* anywhere near *Widowmaker* on his return flight.

"Captain Yage sent a shuttle when Gilad woke up," Luke explained. "By the time Danni and I arrived, they'd used his codes to patch into the Imperial security network without being noticed, and from there eavesdropped on your conversation with Flennic. He insisted on interrupting. I hope you don't mind us doing that. It wasn't that we thought you couldn't manage on your own, Jacen. It just seemed simpler this way, and a chance to prove to Flennic that the Empire's Supreme Commander is still alive."

"I'm just relieved that the admiral came out of this all right," Jacen said. "Can I talk to him?"

"That will be up to Tekli," Danni said. "He's still recuperating in the bacta tank. That talk with Moff Flennic tired him out, short though it was." Then, leaning in slightly toward Jacen, she added, "You know, for someone normally so quiet, she certainly has a lot to say when it comes to her patients."

Jacen smiled. He had developed a great deal of respect for Master Cilghal's apprentice. Although not strong in the Force, her knowledge of healing was extensive, and she had clearly demonstrated the ability to handle herself during recent emergencies.

The three of them walked unimpeded through the corridors of *Widowmaker*. Luke seemed perfectly at ease, explaining as they went that Mara and Saba had stayed behind to keep an eye on events from afar. Jacen had to admire his uncle's poise. Even surrounded as he was by Imperial trappings, the Jedi Master moved and talked with an air that suggested this ship could have been his own rather than one that belonged to a once-formidable enemy.

They reached the medical bay and were automatically waved through by the stormtrooper guards. Inside they found Tekli studying reports on her patient's progress while a weary-looking Captain Yage talked to him.

Gilad Pellaeon looked better than when Jacen had last seen him, but not as recovered from his injuries as Jacen would have liked. He was still immersed in the bacta tank, and looked just as terribly thin and pale as before. He was communicating solely via attachments to his breath mask, which gave his voice the faintly muffled tone Jacen had noticed while dealing with Flennic.

"And what about Screed? Is he still alive?"

"Admiral Screed was executed by Warlord Zsinj," Yage said.

"Really?" As if in thought, Pellaeon paused for the time it took a few handfuls of bubbles to float up past his body. "My memory must be going to have forgotten that. I always had a soft spot for that old hawk-bat."

Yage glanced at Luke and his companions, realizing for the first time they had company. "You have visitors, sir," she said.

Pellaeon opened his eyes to peer through the thick nutrient filling the tank, then closed them again. His face was distorted by the curved, transparent wall enclosing him, making it impossible to read his expression with any accuracy.

"Ah, yes," he said. "Skywalker." There followed a sound like a grunt, but it could just as easily have been a short bleat of amusement. "Come to view the relic, have you?"

Jacen glanced at his uncle. The Jedi Master's face was calm and unruffled. He offered no response because clearly the comment didn't deserve one.

"How are things proceeding, then?" the Grand Admiral asked after a few seconds.

"Mara reports that ships are moving in ways consistent with the withdrawal you ordered," Luke replied. "The jump points are filling up fast."

"Good." He nodded slowly, the movement causing his body to swivel gently in the fluid. "It's nice to know that what Flennic is telling me is the truth. Nevertheless, I'll wager that he is skimming a percentage off the top to defend his holdings here."

"I wouldn't take that bet," Jacen said. "I don't think Flennic is going to like sitting here defenseless while the fleet abandons him."

"You're probably right," Pellaeon said. "He'll be snug and safe where the concentration of firepower is greatest. He wouldn't do anything that might risk his life. That won't stop him doing what he can to protect his investment, though." The Grand Admiral's eyes opened again, fixing directly upon Jacen. "You did well back there, young Solo, but reason and common sense were never going to bring Flennic around. He understands nothing but force—and I'm not talking about the one you Jedi regard so highly, either. I'm talking about the brute sort." His eyes closed once more, as if irritated by the solution. "Reminding him of his insignificance, unless he joined the greater scheme of things, might have done the trick, but in the end I'd rather have him angry with me than you. I'm used to it."

Jacen bowed slightly, even though he was aware that Pellaeon wouldn't see the gesture. "Moff Flennic is someone whose displeasure I wouldn't wish to cultivate,

Admiral," he said. "But I wouldn't lose any sleep over it, either."

Pellaeon laughed. "Well put, lad. As indeed was your argument back there. We really do find ourselves in a difficult place at the moment. I fear we won't have much time to practice the new maneuvers while relocating the fleet—or afterward, for that matter. If what you say is true, then the Yuuzhan Vong will be sure to strike when we are least able to defend ourselves. They'll want to strike hard and fast like they did in Bastion and leave us too battered to be of any use to anyone. I doubt they'll be converting our worlds just yet; they'll come back for those when they have both the time and resources to do so."

"It could be resources they're after," Danni said, "as well as neutralizing a threat."

"They could get resources from anywhere," Pellaeon said. "There are millions of uninhabited chunks of rock out there just brimming with raw materials. And they wouldn't require an army to take them, either."

"They don't use them the way we do, Admiral," Danni explained. "They still need planets for their plantations. But that's not what I meant, anyway. I was thinking of armies. Coralskippers and yammosks they might need to grow from scratch, but cannon fodder is much easier to come by."

There was a small silence. "You're talking about combat slaves?" Pellaeon said. "That would explain why they hit Bastion first, not Yaga Minor. If it had been me ordering the attack, I would've done it the other way around. And it also explains something else. Arien, that holo you showed me earlier. Put it back up on the screen."

Captain Yage tapped at a keyboard and instantly one

of the monitors displaying Pellaeon's vital signs was replaced by a patchy view of the Bastion system. The distributions of Imperial and Yuuzhan Vong forces were marked with sweeping schematics containing thousands of minute details. By scrolling the diagram forward through time, Yage could show how the battle had progressed on any number of fronts, as collated from information gleaned by sensors on all the Imperial vessels.

Jacen noted that the map became patchier as the battle progressed. Great empty spaces appeared in the intelligence as ship after ship was destroyed, along with observational satellites and beacons. Soon it was like trying to watch stars through storm clouds: apart from the area around the gas giant where Pellaeon had made his last stand, the rest of the system was visible only through infrequent, incomplete glimpses.

When she reached the point in the analysis she was looking for, Yage froze the image and zoomed in close on one of Bastion's poles. There, designated by a ringed dot, was a single ship.

"We don't know where this came from," she said. "The last survivors only caught a glimpse of it. Its vector suggests that it came in late into the battle, when the planet was all but taken. That didn't seem to make sense, since it's so big."

She called up some sketchy schematics. The vessel was shaped like a flattened sphere with five trailing stalks of various lengths. It was large enough to hold several of the Yuuzhan Vong carrier analogs Jacen was all too familiar with.

"If it was a military vessel," Yage concluded, "then why did they wait until the end of the battle to utilize it? But if it *wasn't* a military vessel, then what's it doing there at all?"

"It has to be a slave carrier," Pellaeon said. "They wiped out the fleets in orbit around Bastion, and that gave them an entire population ripe for capture. Those who couldn't get away in time are probably already on their way to the nearest processing plant to be turned into mindless drones willing to sacrifice themselves for the warmaster. I saw creatures similar to them at work on Duro."

"They have been used in many other places since," Luke said. "In fact, I'm sure that this was the same kind of ship that Saba encountered a few months back at Barab One."

Pellaeon nodded grimly. "Citizens of the Empire—*all* people—deserve better than this. Had we known that this was what they were after . . ." He trailed off, the thought as obviously disturbing for him as it was for everyone else in the room.

"You were outgunned, Admiral," Jacen offered. "There was nothing else you could have done."

"Outgunned and poorly organized," Pellaeon agreed. "Wherever that ship came from, the chances are it's probably hundreds of light-years away from us by now. The only thing we can think about now is how to stop it from happening again. At Borosk, or anywhere. To anyone."

As far as Jag Fel was concerned, very little was going right on Galantos. Councilor Jobath was still tied up somewhere on the other side of the planet, Tahiri remained unconscious, and he and C-3PO had yet to determine precisely why communications with Galantos had been disrupted. On top of that, Jaina, the one person he would have liked to have with him right now, was on her way to N'zoth, while he was still stuck on the planet. All in all, Jag felt he'd seen better days—*and* been on more successful missions.

Finally, after an hour pacing the common room of their diplomatic quarters, he decided that enough was enough. He had to do *something*. He couldn't delay rejoining Twin Suns Squadron any longer.

"I'm going for a walk," he said brusquely.

Thrum stood in alarm from the table at which he was showing Leia plans of recent additions to the planet's infrastructure. "I don't think that would—"

"It's okay," he cut off the nervous Fia. "I won't be that long. And I don't mind if I'm shadowed, either."

A guard, recently assigned to their door, accompanied him as he strolled through the wide, luxurious corridors, trying to remember the way to where Tahiri had collapsed. There was something about the recording of that moment that had been bothering him. Just before she'd drawn her lightsaber she had looked down. At first he had thought she might have been dizzy and had brought up her hand in the typical response people had to such spells. But then he realized that she'd been holding something, and it was possibly this that had triggered her reaction. No one else had mentioned it, which surprised him, but he had to check for his own peace of mind.

There had been nothing on the holo to indicate what it might have been, though, which meant he had no real idea what he would even be looking for. He still had to try. He'd already checked the pockets of Tahiri's robes, which had been empty, and he certainly couldn't ask her directly; so the only chance of finding out just what it might have been was to examine where it had all happened.

He reached the right corridor and strode along it to roughly where he thought the incident had occurred. Sweeping his gaze along the ground, he began a methodical search of the area while his guard watched on curiously.

"My friend lost something," Jag explained when he saw the deep furrows in the Fia's brow press down upon his melancholy eyes. "I just wanted to see if she dropped it here when she fell. It could have been overlooked in all the excitement."

The guard nodded his understanding, but the expression of confusion remained.

After a couple more minutes scouring the corridor, Jag said, "I don't suppose you could help me look, could you? It might help things along a little."

"What does it look like?" the guard asked.

That stumped him for a second. The Fia would probably want a detailed description, and he didn't have the faintest idea what it was.

"You'll know when you see it," he said elusively, adding under his breath, "I hope."

Their search was hampered by the thick weave of the carpet, along with the fact that the ambient light of the corridor wasn't particularly bright. His back soon ached, and he found himself wondering if he might not have imagined the whole thing. If there *was* anything there, it was proving harder to find than a flea on a bantha.

"Is this it?" the guard asked after a while. He held out a small piece of transparent plastic for Jag to examine.

Jag climbed to his feet and stepped over to the guard. As he took the proffered object and examined it, he tried not to look as though he had no more of a clue than the guard himself. The object, it turned out, was nothing more than a scrap of packaging missed by the cleaning droids. He didn't see how it could have provoked such an extreme reaction from Tahiri.

"No, that's not it," he said, hoping he was right. Nevertheless, he slipped it into his pocket just in case. "Let's keep looking."

Even as he said this, already bending over again to continue his search, he caught a glint of something silver in the carpet farther along the corridor. Cautiously, so as not to lose sight of it, he walked toward it. There, at the edge of the corridor fully four meters from where they'd been looking, was a small object poking out of the carpet. If it was the thing that Tahiri had been holding, then she must have flung it when spinning around defensively with her lightsaber; then, he imagined, it had been pushed deeper into the pile by the large feet of one of the Fia. Otherwise it would have surely been spotted before now.

He reached down and plucked it from the carpet. It was small, about half the size of his thumb joint, and looked to him to be a pendant or charm of some kind. It was metallic in nature, but with a *grown* texture, rather than forged. There was a hole through which a chain or thong might have been threaded, and on the face were carvings in an unknown language. It was surprisingly heavy.

The creature it portrayed was hideous and completely unfamiliar, but that wasn't so surprising, Jag thought. There were many different types of creature in the Galactic Alliance, and most of them were unfamiliar to him—just as the various cultures of the Unknown Regions would be unfamiliar to them. One thing about the creature portrayed did trouble him, though: It seemed to be covered in scars.

"Is that it?" the guard asked, peering over his shoulder.

"Yes," Jag said, quickly tucking the object into one of

his flight suit's pockets. "I'm sure my friend will be glad to see it again. She thought she'd lost it."

Thanking the guard for his help, Jag let himself be led back to the diplomatic quarters. Nothing had changed: Tahiri was still unconscious, and C-3PO couldn't give an estimate as to how long she might remain like this.

He sighed wearily. He really couldn't delay any longer. Jaina was long gone, and he had to get back to his squadron. Being accused of dereliction of duty was, at the moment, more of a concern to him than any of the uneasy feelings he had about the small, silvery object in his pocket and its relevance to the mission.

His clawcraft had been refueled by Al'solib'minet'ri City's landing field technicians. As he ran through the craft's maintenance records to double-check what exactly had been done in his absence, a brief note appeared on the computer screen:

YOU MUST LEAVE HERE IMMEDIATELY.

Jag stared at it for a long moment, startled. He quickly surveyed the bay for signs of someone watching him, but saw no one suspicious lurking about. Then, when he looked back at the screen, the message had disappeared. He tried to access it again, but the maintenance logs showed no record of it ever having existed in the first place. Whoever had left the message for him had made sure it would be erased as soon it had been read.

But why? And if the sender had been so keen to have him leave, then why put the message in such an inaccessible spot? Placing it in the flight systems, where he wasn't likely to see it until he was *already* leaving anyway, seemed redundant. Unless, maybe, the person responsible for the message had no choice but to use this means. Or perhaps the message was intended for him alone, and this was the only way to ensure that no one else saw or heard it.

He fought a growing sense of unease. Tahiri, the pendant, this message . . . There were too many questions without answers, and none of them sat easily with him. He fleetingly considered staying behind to help Leia and Han, but quickly dismissed the idea. There was no actual evidence that anything was up; there were just a couple of hints and warnings, as well as the workings of his suspicious mind. Besides, Han and Leia could look after themselves; they had had plenty of practice at it, after all.

"This is Twin Suns Leader, Al'solib'minet'ri Control," he said into the comm unit. "Preparing for ascent to orbit. Do you have a preferred corridor?"

"Not so fast, Twin Suns Leader," came the patient Fian voice from the other end. "There are still some questions we need to ask before—"

Jag rolled his eyes and activated the clawcraft's engines. Confident he could avoid any Fian vessels that might get in his way, he ignored the squawking of Al'solib'minet'ri City Control and roared up into the atmosphere.

As he matched orbits with *Pride of Selonia*, he contacted the two pilots Jaina had left on patrol when she left.

"Nice move, Jag," Seven said. "Captain Mayn's been itching to thumb her nose at all of these Fian formalities since we arrived. They've been hailing her every time our orbit drifts by so much as a *meter*."

There was amusement in Seven's tone, but Jag remained serious.

"Has there been anything more than that?" he asked. "Anything unusual at all?"

"Are you kidding?" she shot back. "Apart from all the chatter, it's been quiet. No incoming; no outgoing; nothing. The communications blackout is still in place. Beats me what people do around here."

Jag focused on that problem instead of the many others batting at him. He had initially assumed that the communications fault would be easily fixed, so they could move on to their second port of call. But when he and C-3PO had analyzed the records automatically kept by the planetary transceiver serving Galantos and the rest of the system, he had found that there was no fault at all. From there they had contacted the nearest intersector network and ascertained that communications between Galantos and the rest of the galaxy could be easily re-established, once a small routing correction was made. The fact that it *hadn't* been made was suggestive, but Jag hadn't decided of exactly what, yet. It was almost as though the Fia had deliberately cut themselves off.

But why would they do that? With the Yevetha at their back door, along with a wealth of minerals the rest of the galaxy would surely be interested in, contact with the outside would be exactly what they'd want. Except, Jag thought, that the Fia claimed that the Yevetha were no longer a threat, and they seemed to be turning a tidy profit from someone, anyway.

There *was* something afoot on Galantos, and he'd work it out sooner or later. All he needed was another couple of those puzzle segments . . .

An urgent bleeping issued from his instrument panel. "Twin Suns," came the voice of *Selonia*'s duty officer. "We're picking up hyperspace disturbances in sector twelve. It looks like we have company. Want to check them out?"

"Twin Seven, on my way."

"What sort of company?" Jag asked the duty officer as

he watched Seven's X-wing sweep out of formation and accelerate away from the planet.

"It's hard to tell," the duty officer returned after a moment's consideration. "They're still a long way out. But there appears to be a number of smaller vessels accompanying two much larger ones."

"Can you at least determine the *type* of vessel they are?" Jag pressed.

"No can do, I'm afraid," came the reply. "They could be—"

Another bleeping cut him off.

"Hang on, Twin Leader," the duty officer said. "More ships. Sector six this time, on the other side of the system. Two small vessels only, and one of them's an X-wing. The other could be a clawcraft, but its emissions are strange. It's almost as though—"

"Emergency!" came Jaina's voice suddenly over the subspace link. "I have an emergency situation. I've lost Twin Eight, and Nine isn't going to last much longer. I need immediate assistance. I repeat, *immediate* assistance!"

Jag's mind worked overtime. Eight was Miza, a Chiss Squadron pilot.

"What happened, Jaina? Did the Yevetha attack you?"

"Not quite," she said, sounding weary. "They were all dead when we arrived, bar one. He chose to blow his drive rather than talk to us, and that's what did all the damage. I only just managed to patch things together enough to get back here. But this will have to wait, Jag. You'd better watch your back to make sure what happened to N'zoth doesn't happen here, too."

"This is Seven," came the voice of the pilot scouting the far side of the system. "I have a positive ID on those incoming vessels. They're Yuuzhan Vong—two squadrons of skips and a blastboat analog escorting two larger types I've never seen before. They've spotted me and have started in pursuit. I need help out here, guys!"

Jag urged his clawcraft up and away from *Selonia*. "All right, Twin Suns Squadron," he broadcast to the rest of his pilots. "Let's scramble!"

PART THREE

INTERVENTION

She stood on the rise of a dune staring into the swirling white dust, trying to make out the object in the distance. Behind her, not far away, the thing with her face continued to come after her. She knew she should keep moving, but she simply didn't have the energy to do so anymore. It felt hopeless. Sooner or later the thing would catch up with her. It was inevitable, so why even bother trying to run? She may as well just stop here and accept it.

She silently chided herself for the defeatist attitude. She knew she shouldn't be so fatalistic, but she couldn't help it. It was just that there was never going to be a time when this thing *wasn't* going to be after her; it would never rest until it had taken her. The only question was, would it get to her before the reptile got to it?

She peered again into the dust and found her eyes stinging from the effort. She blinked away some of the particles, straining to see the something in the distance, something that towered high above the ground. She was almost relieved when the dust cleared enough for her to see that the object was in fact an immobile AT-AT looming over the tops of the dunes.

Around the base of the vehicle she could make out several standing figures, their identities obscured by dust and distance. She knew them; that much she was sure of, even if she didn't know exactly who they were.

"Lowbacca?" she called. "Jacen?"

No one responded. It was as if they couldn't see her waving at them, and everything she yelled was carried away from their ears by the wind.

Suddenly she saw the head of the AT-AT swivel around to face her, the rusted metal groaning with the effort. It stopped with a resounding *clank*, its guns now trained upon her.

"No, wait!" she called. "It's me! Please!"

It fired once, loudly, but there was no resulting explosion. Instead, from the weapons emerged a black ball that came toward her with slow precision, its edges shimmering. She watched helplessly as it approached, wondering what it might be that her friends had fired at her. There was nothing to do: she couldn't turn back, and she obviously couldn't go forward. This created in her a sense of hopelessness that made her cry. The tears fell from her cheeks into the dust, creating a sticky paste that collected about the soles of her feet.

"They think you are me," said a voice close to her ear.

She held her breath, afraid to look back to see who was standing behind her. But in her heart she knew it to be the thing with her own face. And it was close, too; she could feel its breath on her neck.

She lifted a hand to touch her forehead, feeling the scars there. Then she looked down to see the fresh ones on her arms. She pressed her fingertips into the suppurating wounds, and was surprised at how soft and wet they were. When she raised her hand to look at what came away from the deep cuts, she saw blood dripping from her fingers like tiny, perfect tears. In each one was a reflection—although whether the scarred face she saw in it belonged to herself or the thing behind her, she couldn't tell.

"You do remember me, don't you?" said the voice at

her shoulder. "You can't have forgotten me so soon. You left me just as you did him, didn't you?"

A recently scarred arm reached past her face, pointing in the direction of the AT-AT. She forced back the tears to look, and saw the figures still standing around the vehicle, in exactly the same position as they had been before—except now one of them was lying on the ground.

"I didn't leave him!" There was conflict in her thoughts, as memories clashed clumsily against one another. She was losing all hope of finding some purchase on reality. "*Did* I?"

"*Remember* me!" This time it wasn't a question, but a growled command, which effectively brought a name from the tangle of thoughts in her mind.

"Riina?" she said, still reluctant to look around.

But there was no reply, only the distant roar of the reptile calling her name from somewhere far behind.

The sound of the AT-AT firing again dragged her attention back to her friends. The black sphere had arrived, and she could now see that it was a swarm of flitnats come to engulf her. She stood firmly in the face of the incoming wave of insects, determined not to turn away, but nevertheless feeling the weight of futility tugging at her very soul.

"Why can't the Force be with me for once?" she said. The words were whispered, and yet their echo boomed around the dunes.

Deciding that there was really nowhere else to go but to her friends, she threw herself forward. The task was made difficult, however, by the paste caked to her feet. No matter how fast she tried to run, she didn't seem to be making any progress; no matter how many dunes she scaled, her friends stayed the same distance away from her; no matter how much she wanted to shake it, the thing with her face remained at her shoulder, whispering words that nurtured the guilt and regret that she had kept buried deep inside.

She summoned what strength was left in her to move faster. The whining from the flitnats rose and fell in pitch as they continued to sweep past her ears . . .

Tahiri woke with a jerk to the sounds of shouting and sirens. Her head spun dizzily when she sat up, and her vision was hazy.

"What's going on?" she asked anxiously.

A golden blur appeared before her. "Oh, Mistress Tahiri. Thank goodness you've finally awoken!"

"Threepio?" The siren was joined by a voice booming for attention. She rubbed at her temples, wishing that everything would settle down long enough for her to at least get her bearings. "Is that you?"

"I wish it wasn't, Mistress Tahiri, given our circumstances," came the droid's fretful reply. "I'd much rather be anywhere else than—"

"Don't panic, Threepio," Tahiri said, forcing herself to sit upright. "Everything's going to be fine, I'm sure."

It seemed strange to be offering reassurances when she herself was in need of them. An explanation as to what was happening wouldn't have hurt, either. But she knew that she was going to need the protocol droid's help right now, so it was a priority to calm him down before worrying about anything else. Besides which, his fretting would only exacerbate her confusion.

"Help me stand, Threepio."

The room swayed around her as the droid levered her upright, but she managed to remain on her feet with C-3PO's help. Outside the room she could hear voices arguing; focusing on these, she recognized Anakin's parents remonstrating with one of the Fia.

"I said, unlock this door!"

"I'm sorry, Captain Solo, but that won't be possible." There was no mistaking the wheedling tones of Assistant Primate Thrum. "We're in the middle of a state emergency and—"

"What sort of emergency?" Han's voice was rising sharply with each syllable uttered.

"As I have already stated, I really don't know what—"

"Then get someone down here who *does* know," Han bellowed. "Or so help me, I'm going to use your head as a batt—"

"Assistant Primate," Princess Leia cut in quickly over her husband's threat. Her tone was soothing, but there was no mistaking the note of steel beneath. "We are very concerned that we have lost contact with the rest of our mission. It seems that all communications from ground to orbit are being jammed—"

"That is part of the emergency!" the exasperated Fia said.

"We gathered *that* much," Han said. "But if you'll just let us get to the *Falcon*, we can—"

"That is not *possible*!" Thrum shot back, his frustration causing his voice to come across louder than he had probably intended. "I am not authorized!"

The voices were coming from the common area, through the door to her right. Snatching her lightsaber from the cabinet beside her bed, Tahiri moved unsteadily toward the door.

"What's going on, Threepio?" she hissed.

"There was a terrible commotion," the droid said. "Mistress Jaina returned to inform us that the Yevetha have been destroyed! But at the same time as her return, a number of other ships also arrived in the system. And now it seems that our communications have been jammed and we can't—"

"Ships?" she asked. "What sort of ships? Were they Yuuzhan Vong?"

"I believe so, Mistress," the droid said. "Although there was some uncertainty—"

"It's them," Tahiri said. "I know it is."

A disconcerting feeling spread through her, like ice crystallizing. It *had* to be the Yuuzhan Vong. She was as sure of it as she was of her own name. They or their representatives had been on Galantos before—the totem of Yun-Yammka proved that. They had probably struck a deal with the Fia: protection from the Yevetha in exchange for resources. The Fia would have assumed that they meant the minerals brought to the surface of their planet by its restless crust—but Tahiri knew better. The Fia were going to learn the hard way that the resource the Yuuzhan Vong valued most was living tissue.

She took a deep breath to steady her nerves, then stepped through the doorway and into the common area. Thrum had positioned himself in front of the door leading from their suite. Leia gently restrained Han, who was towering angrily over the Fia. The Noghri guards stood nearby, silently overseeing the exchange.

"I'm sorry." The assistant primate was apologizing again to Anakin's parents. He seemed to be in a state of almost absolute panic. "But there are no regulations to cover such circumstances!"

"We don't need your regulations," Tahiri said, influencing her words with the Force as she took a couple of steps toward the Fia. Leia and Han were as surprised to see her as Thrum. "Open the door and let us through."

Something shifted behind Thrum's eyes, and for a moment it seemed as though he might concede to Tahiri's demand. But protocol, in this instance anyway, was stronger than Force suggestion.

"I cannot," he insisted, shaking his head violently as

though to shake loose the unwanted thought. "I have already said that I don't have the authorization to—"

He trailed off in midsentence as Tahiri's lightsaber hissed to life, its bright blue blade reflecting in his wide and frightened eyes.

"*This* is all the authorization you require," she said, brandishing the weapon close to his face. "Now, please, open this door."

"Why didn't you think of doing that, Leia?" she heard Han whisper to his wife.

"I would," Thrum said, flustered, "but—"

Tahiri cocked her eyebrows. "But?"

The soft features of the Fia looked as though they were about to melt from the heat of Tahiri's saber. "But there are guards—"

The crackle of blasterfire from the other side of the wall interrupted him. There was a click, followed by the door sliding open. Han stepped forward with his own blaster at the ready, past Thrum and into the hallway outside. Tahiri could see the two guards who had been stationed outside lying dead across the entrance, one with a hole smoking in his back, the other with one in their chest. Han took one look at them and turned to face Tahiri.

"How did you do *that*?" he asked her.

"It—it wasn't me," she stammered, too surprised by the sudden turn of events to realize that he was only joking.

She removed her thumb from the activation stud of her lightsaber, extinguishing the blade. Then she stepped over to the doorway to look outside. Apart from the bodies of the guards and Han standing over them, the corridor was empty. But there was a smell there that immediately caught her attention—and it wasn't just the tang of blasterfire, either. This was something else altogether . . .

"There's no one here," Leia said as she came up beside her husband, the two of them glancing up and down the passageway. "So who shot them?"

Han shrugged. "Maybe they fell on their own blaster bolts."

"It doesn't matter," Leia said. "We're out, and that's the main thing. We can worry about the hows and whys later. Let's just get off this planet before we become prisoners of Fian regulations again."

Everyone made to move, except for Thrum, who held back within the room. Leia stepped up to him and grabbed him by the arm.

"You're coming with us," she said, leading the quivering Fia firmly out of the room and into the corridor with the others.

"But . . ." he started, shuffling forward on his big, flat feet. He quickly dropped his protests, however, when he realized that nobody was bothering to listen to him anymore.

Han led the way through the diplomatic section, with Thrum close behind. Leia and her Noghri bodyguards followed him, while Tahiri brought up the rear. She was still a little dizzy, but could feel her old self quickly returning.

The voice booming over the intercom continued to warn people to stay indoors and remain calm. The disruption was temporary, the voice assured, and would soon be sorted out. The howling of the sirens, however, contradicted this, and Tahiri could feel a great hysteria and dread lifting around her in the Force.

"I don't think this was a trap," she whispered to Leia. "They're as surprised as we are."

"I agree," Leia responded. "The Fia didn't know in advance that we were coming, and no ships or transmissions have left the system since we arrived. But that doesn't mean they won't take advantage of us being here, now that something has happened. I'm sure that the life of a Jedi still has some currency with the Yuuzhan Vong."

Tahiri nodded, firmly realizing that it was more likely *her* than Han and Leia that had resulted in them being locked up in their luxurious suites. The Fia would never downplay the roles Anakin's parents had in the liberation of the galaxy from the Empire, but as far as they knew, it was only the Jedi that the Yuuzhan Vong were interested in. If she hadn't been here, they might have been able to leave unobstructed.

As expected, when they reached the exit to the diplomatic quarters, they found a couple of guards stationed there. Han drew them all to a halt around a corner and turned his blaster on Thrum.

"Okay, flatfoot," he said, pushing the barrel of his weapon into the small of the Fia's back. "You're going to take us through here and to the landing field. Got it? We're your guests and they're just guards, so I'm sure regulations will cover it."

"Y-yes, of course," Thrum said as he was nudged forward.

Tahiri sent a command through the Force to give the nervous Fia the confidence he needed to pull off this simple task. She watched as in midstride the assistant primate seemed to summon a strength from within himself, straightening his clothes haughtily as he led the group forward.

Han holstered his blaster as they followed Thrum, while Tahiri hid the handgrip of her lightsaber in the folds of her clothes.

"I am taking the prisoners to interrogation!" Thrum announced loudly. *Too* loudly, Tahiri thought, realizing she might have overdone it with her Force command on the Fia.

"Interrogation?" one of the guards asked dubiously. He seemed a little taken back by Thrum's belligerence. "Where?"

"Section C," Thrum said curtly.

"For how long?" the other guard asked.

"Two hours."

"And will you accompany them on your return?"

"It doesn't *matter*," Thrum replied irritably. "It's not important. None of this is! All that matters is that I am *authorized*. I have jurisdiction here, and I will not have you questioning me like this!"

The guards, stunned by Thrum's uncustomary outburst, waved them through without further questioning.

"You know, that felt surprisingly good," Thrum said as they headed off down the corridor.

He seemed genuinely pleased with his performance, but Tahiri could tell that it had taken a lot out of him. His skin was moist and his hands were trembling almost uncontrollably.

"I'm proud of you," Han said, patting Thrum's sloping shoulder. "But you're not out of this yet."

Assistant Primate Thrum faced Han as they walked, detecting the unstated threat in the man's tone.

"Wh-what do you mean?" he asked, his nervous disposition returning to the fore.

"I mean that you'd better hope no one's touched the *Falcon*," Han said. "Because if they have, I'm going to take those long arms of yours and tie them in a bow around your head."

Thrum shuddered noticeably as he turned imploringly

to Leia, who simply rolled her eyes and shook her head at her husband's lack of diplomatic skills.

They made it almost as far as the landing field without being obstructed. Whatever was going on above the planet seemed to have distracted the security forces on the surface to the point that the absence of their prisoners wasn't even noticed until they had almost escaped.

The slap of footfalls alerted Tahiri to the fact that they were being followed. As Thrum pointed excitedly to the exit to the landing field, a squad of Fian security guards rounded the corner behind them. Seeing the fugitives, they began firing immediately. Their blasters were set for stun, but that only delayed their hostile intent. Tahiri ignited her lightsaber, effortlessly blocking the shots and sending them ricocheting back at the guards. Three fell immediately to the ground, causing the remaining guard to beat a hasty retreat around a corner. It was enough of a delay to allow everyone in her party to get safely through the exit.

Outside, the sky was uncannily blue. A tremor rocked the ground beneath her feet as they ran out onto the stressed ferrocrete—the first she had noticed since arriving on the unsteady planet. Either her senses were more highly attuned than before, or the city's stabilizers weren't being properly tended. With death about to rain down on the planet from above, she supposed that the usual perils of life on Galantos weren't as important right now.

The others ducked and ran for cover as another wave of blasterfire came from a building across the landing field. Tahiri sent a telekinetic punch to bring down a wall in front of the new threat, and their path was temporarily clear again.

"This way!" Han shouted, leading them from cover across the flat field.

Tahiri noted that where it had been empty before, there were now several small spacefaring vessels in various stages of warming up. Ground crews watched nervously as they ran among the ships, fleeing new shouts from behind. The occasional bolt of energy bounced off armored hulls, sending innocent bystanders diving for cover.

"This is all too much," C-3PO complained, the sound of the servomotors that moved his limbs a constant whine as he hurried to keep up.

Amid the confusion on the landing field, Tahiri's attention was drawn to one man who appeared to be pursuing them. A lean, vaguely nonhuman figure dressed in a dark blue flight suit, with a breath mask obscuring his face, he tagged them closely as Tahiri and the others dodged between the other vessels. He kept up with them easily enough, too, unencumbered as he was by the need to avoid pursuit or ambushes. He simply followed along, with his easy, loping strides, casually monitoring their progress.

When they were within a sprinting dash of the *Falcon*, Tahiri peeled away from the others to intercept their pursuer. She had no idea if he meant them harm or not, but she had no intentions of leaving her back exposed to him.

"Tahiri!" Leia called out. Han had the boarding ramp already lowered and they were all about to run in.

Tahiri ignored the calls; she had only about three minutes before the *Falcon* would be ready to launch, so every second counted.

The mysterious figure didn't run away as she approached. Quite the opposite, in fact. Waving, he indicated for her to join him behind the curved hull of a small yacht. She did so, realizing as she did what it was about him that had drawn her to him.

"It was you," she muttered breathlessly as a tingle of recognition ran through her, courtesy of the Force, first, then via her nose: his smell was strong and familiar. "You're the one who killed the guards and let us out!"

He nodded. "And one good turn deserves another, wouldn't you say?"

Tahiri's eyes narrowed, wondering what he was getting at. "You want our help?"

"I've been looking for a way off this rock ever since the Fia made their deal with the Brigaders."

"You want to come with us, is that it?"

"Not quite," he replied. He patted the hull of the yacht they were standing beside. "I want you to use your powers of persuasion to get the air lock of this thing open for me. After that, I can do the rest."

Tahiri was naturally wary of using her Force powers to help a complete stranger steal a ship. "Why should I do that?"

"You're just going to have to trust me," the masked being said. "I'm one of the ones who brought you here. That must count for something."

"Yeah, thanks a whole bunch." She glanced over her shoulder at where the *Falcon* was prepping up. Princess Leia called urgently to her from the ramp, an edge of something more than concern creeping into her voice.

"I can explain everything later," the stranger said, "if I survive. Right now there simply isn't any time."

Tahiri vacillated only for a moment, curiosity warring with caution. Then she reached out through the Force, feeling for the yacht's pilot. It was a Fian woman, and she was rushing through her preflight checks with terrified haste. A quick glance, however, told Tahiri that the pilot had missed a crucial stage in her engine warm-ups; the first atmospheric punch would overload the yacht's repulsors and cripple them forever. With that in mind, she felt more reassured that intervening with the Force in this instance was acceptable. If it meant saving this pilot's life, then that had to be a positive thing, surely?

Tahiri implanted a thought in the pilot's mind; she had forgotten to secure the tail hatches and needed to do it manually, and the only way to do it was to unseal the air lock. Cursing, the pilot smacked her forehead and came through the yacht to fix the problem.

Tahiri faced her masked companion evenly. "The rest is up to you," she said.

Her mystery man bowed slightly. "My thanks, Tahiri Veila." He moved around to the air lock, waiting for it to open.

"When—" she began.

"We will speak again when I reach orbit," he shouted, waving her away.

There was no time to argue with the stranger; she could already hear the rising wail of the *Falcon*'s engines. Han would be cursing her if she held them up any longer. Taking a deep breath, she gathered the Force around her like an invisible shield and braved the empty space between her and the unlikely-looking freighter. She ignited her lightsaber to build a wall of energy between her and the Fian security forces, moving the lightsaber in graceful, confident arcs around her, easily deflecting the blaster bolts as she backed her way toward the ramp. The joy of the fight rose within her, as she reveled in her skill with the blade and the failure of her enemies.

I am a Jedi Knight, she thought. *I am invincible!*

Then a strong hand grabbed her by the shoulder and dragged her onto the ramp just as the *Falcon* lifted from the ground. There was a rush of air around her as the ramp lifted.

She collapsed onto the metal decking, her lightsaber's energy beam retracting with a crackle.

"Tahiri," Leia said, edging aside her bodyguard and leaning over her. "Are you all right? What happened?"

"I had to help someone escape," Tahiri managed breathlessly, surprised just how quickly the feeling of invincibility gave way to exhaustion. "The person who helped us with the guards outside the room."

Leia frowned dubiously. "Who was it?"

"I'm not sure," she admitted with a shrug.

"But you're sure it was the same person?" Leia asked.

Tahiri nodded. Her confidence came more from gut instinct than anything else; she could *feel* that he was the one. And then there was the smell, although she still couldn't identify the source. "He said he would contact us from orbit."

"That's fine, if we make it to orbit." Leia looked forward, concerned. "I'm going back to the cockpit. Are you sure you're okay?"

"Never been better," Tahiri said, pulling herself up to a sitting position. And it wasn't a lie. She had helped Anakin's family escape capture on Galantos. Whatever her other failings were, she could be proud of that, at least.

Leia nodded uncertainly as she made to leave.

"I am all right, too, Princess Leia," C-3PO chirped as Leia passed him, his photoreceptor eyes watching her back as she hurried off to the cockpit. "In case you were wondering."

The Noghri guards left to follow Leia, leaving Tahiri alone with C-3PO. The golden droid let her use him as a counterweight to help her get to her feet, then staggered back as some sort of energy weapon discharged against the ship's shields.

"Goodness," he exclaimed. "Will this fighting never end?"

I hope not, part of her thought, but she was too frightened of what that meant to say it aloud.

Jaina brought her X-wing around in as tight a turn as it could manage. Although charred by the self-destruction of the Yevetha's ship near N'zoth, her X-wing still had enough maneuverability to run down the alien fighter she had clipped on her first pass. Stuttering her lasers, she trusted her instincts to tell her when its dovin basals were close to overload. Then, with a flick of her wrist, she issued a proton torpedo to dispatch the Yuuzhan Vong ship along with its pilot to oblivion.

Fighting off exhaustion, she targeted another skip, this one daring to come in too close behind Twin Eleven. A dozen warning shots were enough to change its mind, although her follow-up torpedo failed to reach its mark. She gladly gave up the chase when her R2 unit warned that her stabilizers were overheating again and advised that she pull back for a while. The brief respite gave her a chance to observe the battle from a distance, a luxury she couldn't afford when she was down in the thick of it.

Twin Suns Squadron was outnumbered three to one, but holding well against an enemy that hadn't expected such determined—if indeed *any*—resistance in the system. Although both sides had been taken by surprise, Jaina was pleased to see that it was the Galactic Alliance and Chiss pilots who were adjusting the quickest. That made sense; with the Yuuzhan Vong's yammosk suffering attempts to jam it while it dealt with the unexpected development, the individual pilots weren't trained to think independently, and therefore floundered.

The two larger, circular ships were not designed for war, but they weren't easy picking, either. Their yorik coral shells were tough, and the five long tentacles that dangled from their sterns were strongly muscled, lashing out with surprising speed at anything that came within reach. At the end of each serpentine arm was a toothless maw that opened and closed in the vacuum as though attempting to suck in passing ships.

Although Jaina had never seen anything quite like them before, the sucking tentacles—each several meters across—put her in mind of something her father had described seeing at Ord Mantell. He and Droma, the Ryn who had served briefly as his copilot after Chewie's death, had almost been sucked into the mouth by just such a giant tentacle.

"Slaveships," she said, voicing her thoughts.

"Empty or full?" asked Todra Mayn on *Selonia*. The frigate was slowly breaking orbit to lend its twenty quad laser cannons to the task of knocking out the incoming coralskippers.

"They're heading in toward Galantos, so empty would be my bet," Jag said as he pulled his clawcraft out of a tight roll. "After all, you wouldn't send a household droid in to clean a place with its waste-storage bin already full, right?"

She had to agree that it made sense. There was a world full of Fia down on the planet that was barely in a position to defend itself. The entire planetary defense force consisted of five squadrons of old Y-wings, none of which had yet even managed to reach vacuum. But for Twin Suns Squadron and *Selonia*, the planet's major cities would already have been under attack. Once this line of defense was gone, the entire population would become easy targets for those slaveships.

"How many people do you think they'd fit in one of those things?" Twin Three asked, swooping around the back of the nearest slave freighter and peppering its trailing tentacles with laserfire.

"Hundreds of thousands, maybe more," Captain Mayn said grimly, "if they packed them in tight enough."

"Enough for a disposable army," Jaina said, revolted by the thought. "If this is what came for the Yevetha, it's hardly surprising they decided to fight to the very end."

Cappie bleeped to inform her that her stabilizers were back in working order. Ramping her inertial compensators down another notch, to give her flagging reflexes as much information as she could, she immediately powered to join Three, whose insistent pounding of the slaveship had resulted in one of its tentacles being completely severed. She was doing her best to cut through a second, all the while avoiding the sucking maws of the others. It was like attempting to dodge three amphistaffs all at once.

There was no time for talking, then, as she concentrated on helping maim the slaveship. It was a cumbersome vessel, clearly relying on its escort for defense and not intended for combat. Although it was equipped with dovin basals capable of absorbing enemy fire, she suspected that the primary function of these was to enable the large mass of the ship to hover over a city while it ingested its prey. When it was full, it could return to wherever the slaves were being processed, dump its load, and head out for another.

It was a typically revolting biological solution to a problem she knew the Yuuzhan Vong were suffering from. They were short of warriors, and they needed replacements. No one had imagined that they had been preparing for a wave of mass enslavement for so long. They should have, though. It was exactly the sort of fate

Tsavong Lah would have gleefully imposed on the infidels: divide and conquer had always been his modus operandi, closely followed by enslave and murder. That Lah was no longer around to see the results of his vile plan was little consolation.

A voice crackled over the open subspace link. "Anyone looking for reinforcements?"

"Dad?" Jaina peeled away from a wildly flailing tentacle, too tired to concentrate on two things simultaneously. "Is that you?"

"None other," he announced cockily. "Hey, I hope you've saved some of those Vong ships for us."

Jaina felt a wave of relief wash a heavy weight from her shoulders as she spotted the battered, black disk of the *Millennium Falcon* rising rapidly from Galantos. She was suddenly battle-ready again as a new energy rushed through her.

"I'm glad you made it out okay," she said. "How did you swing it?"

"We had a hand," he said simply. "Hang in there, kid. Help's on its way."

A quick scan of her telemetry confirmed that there was still no sign of the Galantos defense force. There were a few hot spots on the planet indicating isolated launches, but these were mainly from the major cities. Private craft, she assumed, probably taking the rich and the prestigious away from the Yuuzhan Vong attack.

Like mynocks fleeing a disintegrating asteroid, she thought ruefully.

There was one ship, however, that didn't immediately break orbit for the nearest hyperspace jump point. A small yacht of Corellian manufacture, it seemed to be. hanging back as if waiting for something. The *Falcon* abruptly changed course to intercept it, and together they vanished around the back of the planet.

Odd, she thought. Jaina had no time to ponder it any further, though. The coralskippers were gradually getting themselves organized, and *Selonia* was still some distance away. Twin Suns Three was forced to withdraw from the slave freighter whose tentacles she was harassing, and Jaina found herself the target of a trio of determined skips. She ducked and wove through the wildly disorienting tangle of fighters, ion washes, and particulate debris, hoping that the slightest distraction to the skips would afford her some breathing space until some help arrived. But no matter what she did, they doggedly stuck to her tail, until soon her stabilizers were beginning to overheat again. Frustration and anger welled within her and she fought them as grimly as she fought the Yuuzhan Vong: being tired and uncomfortable was no excuse to give in to the dark side.

Her R2 unit squealed as two plasma volleys reduced her shields to dangerous levels. Just as she was seriously beginning to worry, a flurry of laserfire arced from behind her, scattering her three pursuers. Only one clung on after that, and the pilot who had saved her life soon dispatched it.

"Thanks," she said over the comlink as the coralskipper evaporated back to its component molecules. "I owe you one."

"I'll hold you to that, Sticks," Jag said.

She smiled to herself; she was so relieved to hear his voice that everything else assumed secondary importance. For a moment he came alongside her new XJ3, and she imagined that she could see him through the faceted visor of his clawcraft.

"Let me ask you a question," he said after a moment. "If you were the Fia and you'd done a deal with the Yuuzhan Vong, but *we* showed up and started fighting your allies, whose side would you fight on?"

"I don't know, Jag." She wiped sweat from her eyes with the back of her gloved hand. "Why? Does it matter?"

He paused slightly before answering. "Take a look at your telemetry," he said.

She did so, and saw multiple launches from three locations across Galantos, followed by formations of ion engine signatures thrusting for space. She couldn't help it: she felt fatigued all over again.

"Whichever side they're on," said Jag, "here they come . . ."

"Here they come!"

Gilad Pellaeon heard the words a split second before he felt a vibration run through *Widowmaker* as the frigate's ion engines engaged. Powerful enough to override inertial dampers and communicated via the hull to the fluid in his bacta tank, the vibration made him feel as though the whole world was shaking. He reached out to steady himself against the transparent shell containing the healing fluid, trying to concentrate on the good things about his situation. Yes, his injured body was confined to a bacta tank on an ageing frigate during what might possibly be the most important battle he would ever fight, but at least he still had his faculties about him. His mind was clear; he needed nothing more than that, really.

"Enemy fleet concentrated in sectors three through eight," said the voice of *Widowmaker*'s duty officer in his ear. He didn't need the running commentary, but he kept it going when he wasn't using the communicator in his breath mask to make sure he wasn't missing anything locally. The mask's modified visor showed him crisp, three-dimensional views of the action as it unfolded in the system, while sensor pads attached to his hands and wrists enabled him to switch views at will.

"Changing course to adopt primary position."

Widowmaker swung about to put the planet of Borosk between itself and the incoming Yuuzhan Vong fleet. A relatively small world, it would have been entirely unremarkable but for its role in the defense of the Empire. A symbolic retention after numerous retreats, it had been heavily armed to ensure it wasn't retaken by the New Republic, which had in turn armed its own neighboring worlds in case Borosk turned out to be the beginning of another invasion. As a result, the planet was heavily stocked with partially automated planetary turbolasers, ion cannons, and shields, and surrounded by extensive rings of space-based ion mines, all in a constant state of battle readiness. The planet was, in its own way, better defended than Bastion had been—since, in a sane universe, no one would have attacked there *first*.

The Imperial Navy Fleet now gathered around Borosk had had just enough time to organize into new task forces and squadrons. The losses in Bastion had been high, and the shock enormous, but discipline was still strong among the corps. Once Flennic had started issuing orders in Pellaeon's name, all thoughts of dissolution had temporarily vanished, and the command chain had been quickly reestablished. There were enough Star Destroyers left to consolidate the defense around four distinct battle groups, designated by their command vessel names: *Stalwart,* which Pellaeon had not permitted Flennic to retain, had the vanguard of the defense; *Relentless* and *Protector* protected the flanks; and the rear was maintained by *Right to Rule*. There were five other Star Destroyers committed to the defense of Borosk, making nine altogether. The remainder of the navy had stayed with Flennic around Yaga Minor, just in case the Yuuzhan Vong attacked there anyway. *Chimaera* was there, too, undergoing repairs, having finally limped into Yaga

Minor with a severely damaged hyperdrive and numerous other scars—but at least intact.

Despite the absence of his command vessel, Pellaeon felt an old excitement rise in him as he watched the battle groups deploy. That moment immediately prior to battle was simultaneously the most wonderful and the most terrifying. Everything was in place: ships were at the peak of their performance, while pilots were at their sharpest; he could almost tell who was going to win before a single shot had been fired, simply based on the disposition of forces. Sometimes he wished victories could be awarded so easily, without lives lost or resources wasted, or grudges formed . . .

This was not such a time. In this instance he wanted nothing more than to fight, to quash the enemy's attack, reduce them to their basic component molecules. And, watching the incoming fleets, he knew they desired the same for their enemy. The Yuuzhan Vong would never share in Gilad Pellaeon's wish for victory without loss. For them, sacrifice—glorious or otherwise—was fundamental to their belief system. Trying to imagine them without it was like trying to picture Coruscant without buildings.

Stalwart sent four TIE fighter squadrons to engage the lead ships while they were still recovering from the hyperspace jump. Pellaeon counted two enemy warships at the head of that particular attack—giant ovoids as long as a Star Destroyer with huge coral arms near the nose that sprouted coralskippers like pollen. There were three carrier analogs toward the rear, also branched and budded with coralskippers; these were accompanied by numerous gunships capable of spraying volleys of plasma at anything daring to come too close. There was one battleship analog at each of the two other attacking points, their ugly, misshapen appearance a blot against the stars. He counted five cruisers and destroyers holding back for the moment, waiting either to swing around the rear later or to provide reinforcements as needed.

Dozens of Yuuzhan Vong fighters launched to intercept the Imperial forces, spewing plasma. Led by Luke Skywalker in his XJ3 X-wing, the TIE squadrons were equipped only with lasers, so stutterfire was not possible. Instead they attacked two or three at a time, the multiple laserfire having a similar effect and overloading the dovin basals of the skips. Yammosk telemetry enabled them to target the central control ships.

Surprised, clearly expecting less efficient resistance, the Yuuzhan Vong warriors began to scatter, either destroyed outright or repulsed. It wasn't long, though, before the war coordinators in the capital ships reassessed the situation and increased the muscle behind the push into the system. Proton explosions blossomed like white flowers in the vacuum, while magma bolts cut red lines across the void.

"Fall back, Skywalker," Pellaeon ordered through the comlink in his breath mask. "I think you've made your point."

"I'm going to stay out here a while longer, Gilad," came the reply.

"Just you be careful, Luke," he heard Mara pipe up from the *Jade Shadow*, where she and Danni Quee waited on the sunward flank with *Protector*. The healer was on *Widowmaker* with the giant lizard and himself, a half-dead old man who was supposed to be running the show. If the situation hadn't been so serious, Pellaeon might have found the whole thing seriously amusing.

"How's Jacen coming along?" Luke asked.

"He's getting results," Mara said. Her grim tone prompted Pellaeon to take a look.

Jacen Solo, the boy Jedi who had come so delightfully close to besting Moff Flennic, was on *Right to Rule*. In the hours since regrouping at Yaga Minor, thousands of MSE-6 mouse droids had been modified with the Yuuzhan Vong–detecting algorithms the Galactic Alliance had developed and sent scuttling from ship to ship throughout the fleet, identifying three Yuuzhan Vong infiltrators. In analyzing the communications these infiltrators had received from within the fleet, Jacen had been able to expose more than a dozen sympathizers. None had been confronted directly, but all had been posted to the *Right to Rule* and individually summoned to a "staffing meeting" with the intention of seeing their activities brought to an immediate end.

Jacen had set up the meeting in a conference room that looked perfectly innocent, but had in fact been heavily modified with some of the most sophisticated security devices the Empire had to offer, via which Pellaeon was able to follow the proceedings over the monitors set up in his room. Also, nearby, a squad of stormtroopers stood ready to rush in to Jacen's aid, should he require it. It was a risk, perhaps, to have such a concentration of the enemy in one area, but Jacen felt it was less of a risk than having the same enemy scattered throughout various ships when they were exposed. It would have been harder to coordinate their rounding up, whereas having them all contained in one room presented a controlled situation, more easily contained if something went wrong.

The traitors arrived one by one, staggered at two-minute intervals to ensure that they wouldn't meet in the corridor outside and suspect the trap they were walking into. Jacen sat patiently at the front of the room, saying nothing as each one entered.

The disguised aliens were the last to enter. The first came into the room a full five minutes after all the traitors had been seated. She breezed easily in, noting those seated around the large table in a single glance. Her expression was unreadable, and so human that Pellaeon could scarcely credit that it wasn't in fact her real face, but rather an example of the biotechnological masks the Yuuzhan Vong called ooglith masquers. She was, to all appearances, a tall, plain woman with long, gray hair tied back in a severe bun, with nothing remarkable about her at all.

But there was something in the way she hesitated slightly when she caught sight of her human sympathizers that convinced Pellaeon she wasn't all she appeared to be.

"Greetings, Fiula Blay," Jacen said from the front. He continued to lean against the podium as he spoke, his casual demeanor oozing disrespect. "Won't you take a seat while we wait on the arrival of the others?"

The woman glared at him, but did as she was asked without comment. Pellaeon noticed the beginnings of fear in the eyes of four of the spies as they recognized the leader of their particular resistance cell.

"What's going on here?" one of them demanded. "You have no right to keep us here like this!"

"*Keep* you here?" Jacen repeated with an exaggerated frown. "You make it sound as though you were prisoners. Why should you think that?"

The man swallowed but said nothing more.

"You've been called here so we can have a little chat," Jacen went on. "That's all."

"Fine," another said sharply. This one wore the uniform of an intelligence coordinator. "Then let's get on with it, shall we?"

"When we're all here," Jacen said calmly.

"We haven't got time for this," he went on angrily, making to stand. "In case you haven't noticed, there's a war going on out there!"

Jacen stood up straight and took a step forward. "That's precisely why we're here," he said, his eyes leveled evenly at the traitor.

The man returned to his seat with a grunt of complaint and fell silent.

"You could at least tell us who you are," said a third, a female security officer.

"Can't you guess?" Jacen said.

The door opened at this point, and the second of the Yuuzhan Vong entered, this time in the disguise of a portly corporal seconded from the *Relentless*. He, too, hesitated when he saw the group gathered before him, but like Fiula Blay he kept his expression tightly controlled.

"What is the meaning of this?" he asked. "What am I doing here? I should be out there, where I'm needed—"

"All will be explained," Jacen said, pointing to an empty seat. "Please, sit."

The tension within the room mounted as everyone waited uncomfortably for the last of the infiltrators to arrive. Nothing was said, but the body language of those around the table spoke volumes. Pellaeon estimated that perhaps eight of the eleven sympathizers had already figured out what was happening, with the remaining three probably just having the beginnings of suspicion in their gut. It showed in their furtive eye movements, their flushed expressions, and the way they squirmed uneasily in their seats. The only ones who didn't flinch or show any concern were the two disguised Yuuzhan Vong. What was going on in their minds was anybody's guess.

Finally, the door hissed open and the third Yuuzhan Vong walked in. An enormous man with shoulders as wide as a Wookiee's, "Torvin Xyn" took in the scene instantly, his expression breaking into a snarl as soon as his eyes fell upon Jacen.

"Jeedai!" he hissed. "I can smell you!"

A number of those seated started to stand as Torvin Xyn's skin peeled away from his face, revealing the scarred and snarling visage of the Yuuzhan Vong beneath. The skin covering his chest and arms rippled, and suddenly there was an amphistaff in his hands.

Jacen took a step back toward the podium. "There is no need for this," he said. "Nobody need be harmed!"

But even as he spoke, the Yuuzhan Vong let loose an unintelligible roar and launched himself at Jacen. Almost inaudible beneath the alien's deafening war cry was the distinctive *snap-hiss* of Jacen's green-bladed lightsaber extending. He brought it up between them in a bright blur, sweeping in an arc to deflect the intended blow to his neck from the amphistaff. Then, shifting his weight back onto his right leg, he moved to one side, just enough to miss the charge of the giant alien. The Yuuzhan Vong swept his amphistaff down and around to cut at Jacen's legs as he passed but the Jedi Knight was already off the ground by that point, kicking outward with his left leg to knock the alien off balance. Amphistaff and lightsaber clashed again as the two other spies burst out of their disguises and joined the fray. Realizing they had been discovered, the human sympathizers fell about in a panic.

Any thought that the enemy still had the upper hand was soon dispelled when the door burst open and the squadron of stormtroopers filed in, the snouts of their blasters trained on the aliens. Security droids swooped in behind them. A quick succession of shots brought down two of the Yuuzhan Vong infiltrators. Exposed without their vonduun crab armor, they died with their hideously scarred visages snarling. The final warrior fell when he raised his amphistaff high into the air in readiness to bring it down on Jacen's head, and the young Jedi proved to be too fast. Thrusting his own weapon up high, he managed to block the Yuuzhan Vong's strike when the warrior had barely started the downward swing, then seemingly effortlessly brought his lightsaber down onto the Yuuzhan Vong's torso. Such was the force of the blow that his weapon cut almost halfway through the alien's barrel chest before coming to a halt.

Jacen stepped back from the smoking corpse of "Torvin Xyn," wiping a forearm across his sweat-beaded face as he turned to the panic-stricken traitors clustered together away from all the fighting. A few were jabbering apologies and pleas for mercy, lost in the babble of so many people trying to speak at once.

"There's no point protesting your innocence," Jacen said loudly. When the noise settled he let his lightsaber fizz out, replacing the handgrip on his belt. There was a look on the young Jedi's face that surprised Pellaeon, as though the fighting he'd just been involved in dismayed him. And yet, at the same time, there was a rock-steady certainty there, as well. "Your quarters have been searched and your movements monitored. Your guilt is beyond question. The only question remaining is whether there are any more of you that we should know about."

The cold-eyed intelligence coordinator took a step forward. "Jedi scum," he said, spitting on the floor at Jacen's feet. "You've only delayed the inevitable."

"Permanently, I hope," Jacen said, unflustered. He looked around the room. "Anyone else have something to say?"

No one answered, but Pellaeon noted two who looked as though they might under different, more private circumstances. With a gesture from Jacen, stormtroopers took the prisoners away for interrogation.

The young Jedi sagged back into a chair when everyone had gone, pulling back the sleeve of his robe to speak into a wrist comlink.

"Mission accomplished," he announced tiredly.

His voice came over the private link at the same time as Pellaeon heard it via the microphones in the dummy interview room.

"Well done, Jacen," Mara Skywalker said from *Jade Shadow*. "Are you all right?"

Pellaeon watched on as the Solo boy examined the back of his hand. "Just a nick," he said. "I'll be fine." He glanced around at the Yuuzhan Vong corpses. "This wasn't necessary. They had a chance to come peacefully."

"Did you really think they would?"

"You never know." He half smiled. "Maybe sending their most dangerous and aggressive warriors in to be killed by us will eventually reduce the gene pool, breed a more temperate Yuuzhan Vong."

Pellaeon had never had occasion to laugh in a bacta tank before, but he couldn't help himself now. "Victory by natural selection? An interesting game plan, Solo."

"Requesting permission to fall back behind the mine rings, Grand Admiral," Captain Yage interrupted.

Pellaeon had been keeping half an eye on the disposition of the battle while watching Jacen's handling of the spy situation. The Yuuzhan Vong fleets had engaged on all four fronts, with the fighting fiercest where they'd first entered the system.

"Permission granted," he said. As the frigate began to drop to a lower orbit around Borosk, Pellaeon switched to a general command channel. To the numerous generals, captains, and commanders to whom he entrusted the details of the battle, he said: "Commence fallback. *Rule* and *Protector* battle groups first, then *Stalwart* and *Relentless*. Orbital control, activate the mines as soon as the bulk of the enemy comes within range. Ground, make sure the targeting systems concentrate on the smaller ships, where possible; the shields and mines should keep the capital vessels at bay for us to deal with. And remember: we're playing a waiting game. The more we can bleed them, the more they'll hurt."

A series of affirmatives returned over the line. With no Yuuzhan Vong infiltrators left among the Imperial forces, Pellaeon felt sure that the fallback of his fleet would appear as an unruly retreat to the rigid-minded warmaster behind the attack. He was confident that the fully charged turbolasers and cannons waiting for them down on Borosk below would convince the Yuuzhan Vong of their mistake.

Then, at last, the battle proper could truly begin.

Saba hissed as a slave carrier appeared on the edge of the scope, emerging from the planet's atmosphere. Her tail whacked agitatedly against the floor as the sight of it brought back the memory of the destruction of her own planet.

Captain Yage looked up. "What is it?"

The Barabel pointed at the screen. The carrier had come out of hyperspace well back from the front and was lightly protected. Its tentacles whipped at vacuum like hungry space slugs snapping for food. Where it had been a flattened sphere before, it was now fatter.

Fuller, Saba thought.

"They are confident of success," she said. A terrible hunger gnawed at her belly.

"Maybe they have cause to be confident," Yage said

grimly. The solid woman turned aside for a moment to call instructions to the crew scattered throughout the ship. The bridge of *Widowmaker* was busy in a productive, controlled away, but still noisy to a Barabel's ears.

"This one can feel them," Saba said, closing her eyes and reaching out through the Force. Past the many nearby life-sources that comprised the planet of Borosk and the massed navy of the Empire, and beyond the empty gulf of the attacking Yuuzhan Vong, she felt a concentrated scar in the Force—a scar that itched from pain and fear. She sensed suffocation, imprisonment, claustrophobia, darkness—all the things she had failed to notice when her own people had been taken because of the emotions of anger and rage she had been unable to control. The concentration of those feelings now was too intense to ignore—so intense, in fact, that her head reeled from it. But she would not turn away. She couldn't. She needed to embrace this pain, share in it, in the hope that doing so would somehow alleviate some of the guilt she carried.

Hunt the moment . . .

The people inside the carrier had been stuffed in like animals being taken away for slaughter. The chances were that many of them would die before they ever reached their destination. As appalling a thought as that was for Saba, she knew that from the Yuuzhan Vong's point of view it did make sense. To them, these beings *were* little more than animals, so what did it matter if a percentage of the stock was lost in transit, as long as enough survived to fill the armies at the front?

But Saba Sebatyne was a Jedi, and she could not stand by and allow it to happen. She had to do something—something that could make up for the deaths of all those Barabels she had killed.

How better could they be remembered?

"This one would speak to *Jade Shadow*," she said to Yage. The captain frowned uncertainly, but made arrangements with her comm officer.

"Over there," she said, pointing to an empty comm station.

Conscious of the eyes of the crew upon her—possibly the most obvious nonhumanoid many had seen up close for years—Saba moved to the station and spoke softly into the link: "Mara, this one haz a plan."

There was a slight delay before Skywalker answered. "You have my attention, Hisser," she said. "Whatever you have in mind, it has to be better than taking potshots and watching Luke's retrothrusters."

"Do you see the slave carrier? This iz the prize. If they lose this, the battle will be hollow for them."

"You're saying we should take it out? Saba, we can't do that. It's full of—"

"We do not destroy it," Saba cut in, then paused as she considered the audacity of what she was about to suggest. Her stomach rumbled. "This one wishez to liberate it."

There was an even longer silence this time. "Wait a second," Mara eventually said. On the scope, Saba saw *Jade Shadow* disengage from the battle, closely followed by Master Skywalker's X-wing. "I'm going to patch you into the command ring."

The holoprojectors flickered into life, revealing the faces of Mara and Grand Admiral Pellaeon. Saba moved to allow Captain Yage to take the seat.

"Did I just hear right?" Pellaeon asked.

"Saba wants to free the people trapped in that slaveship," Mara said.

"And what do you think of that?" the Grand Admiral asked.

"I think that's a worthy objective," Mara said.

"Which is not to say it's *practical*," Pellaeon countered.

"No, but Saba makes a valid point. Taking that carrier ship might save a lot of lives, Admiral."

The ageing Imperial nodded, sending wisps of thin white hair swaying in the fluid around him. His expression was mostly hidden behind the breath mask.

"So how would it be done?" he asked. "It's on the other side of the Yuuzhan Vong fleet."

"Exactly," Saba said. "Attention iz forward, on the attack. The rear will be vulnerable."

"We'd still have to get past their interdictors," Mara pointed out. "And it wouldn't stay vulnerable long. There are an awful lot of capital ships out there. An assault party would soon find itself surrounded, Saba, a long, long way from backup."

"And they won't bring it forward until they are certain we've lost," Luke said, inserting himself into the conversation via the comm unit.

"Could that be the way?" Pellaeon asked. "We're on the retreat, anyway."

"Too risky," Yage said. "We'd have to basically give them Borosk before they'd believe us, and there's no guarantee we'd ever get it back."

Pellaeon nodded again, and Saba received the distinct impression that he was treating the discussion more as a theoretical exercise than a serious proposal—although she also sensed that he would like someone to make it work.

"We require a sacrifice," she said. "And we muzt deliver it directly to the target."

"I don't understand," Yage said, turning slightly to look up at the Barabel leaning over her. From so close, the woman's scent was pungent in Saba's nostrils, but not offensive.

"They will guess that we know what the slaveship iz. Perhapz that iz why they have produced it so early in the battle. They use it to enrage us, to challenge our honor. They are saying, *You are slavez already. It'z only a matter of time.*" Saba's blunted claws unsheathed at the insult. Embarrassed by the reflexive action, she hid her hands behind her back. It seemed she could put the Jedi into the Barabel, but she couldn't always take the Barabel out of the Jedi. "We attack it, az they are daring us to."

"But if they're daring us, then that means they'll be expecting us to respond," Mara said.

"Yez. And we will lose."

"I think I'm beginning to follow you," Yage said. "We send in some sort of assault ship to take on the slave carrier. It gets knocked out of the picture, but not before acting as a diversion for another attack, right?"

"No," Saba said. "It *iz* the attack. If the ship iz not utterly destroyed, itz crew will be bounty. They will not waste it."

Pellaeon chuckled through his breath mask. "Emperor's ears—are you suggesting what I *think* you're suggesting? You don't mean 'sacrifice': you mean *bait*."

"From the inside," Saba said, nodding enthusiastically, "this one will be best placed to take over the ship. It iz not a warship, after all. It iz a glorified freighter. It will rely on otherz to defend it. At worst, disabling it will allow the cargo to be unloaded more easily."

"That's the next problem," Yage said. "Where does *that* happen?"

"Right there," Mara said. "When Saba has killed the ship's brain, it's just a matter of getting the captives somewhere safe."

"This one iz thinking of an old trick played on Barab One," Saba said. "The best way to poison a bonecrusher iz to feed it live hka'ka that has eaten poisoned vsst. The bonecrusher doez not taste the poison until itz meal iz over—and then it iz already dead." She shrugged her heavy, scaled shoulders. "It iz not an honorable way to hunt, but sometimez it iz better than dying."

The Grand Admiral's expression sobered. "If you succeed, it'll be the wildest stunt I've ever seen—and you'll seal the gratitude of the Empire forever. Turning my back on the people the Vong captured was one of the most soul-destroying things I've ever had to do. It's a burden I'll be happy to be rid of."

"Luke?"

"I presume you'll want to be involved, Mara," Master Skywalker said, ignoring the concerned whistle from R2-D2.

"*Jade Shadow* would make an ideal poisoned vsst," she said. "And it has a tractor beam that I know will come in handy."

"You can count me in, too," said Danni, her head appearing over Mara's shoulder.

"Are you sure?" Mara asked, frowning slightly.

"Saba and I have worked together before," she said, "and this'll be another great opportunity to see Yuuzhan Vong biotechnology at work up close."

"Too close for my liking," Yage muttered. "But it's your choice, I guess."

Pellaeon's eyes were dancing behind the translucent shell of his visor. He was clearly seeing 3-D views hidden from those watching his hologram. "If we're going to do this, then let's get moving," he said. "Every minute delayed is another minute my pilots are out there getting killed. We have a lot to put in place in a very short time, and I think I might've found our—what was it, Saba?"

"Hka'ka," she supplied.

"Yes," said Pellaeon. "You Jedi might be crazy, but

those are Imperial lives you're saving. I don't want anything to go wrong. Is that understood?"

Remembering the recent massive and tragic losses of her own people, Saba could only nod solemnly.

Nom Anor woke to the sound of screams and the realization that, even in the depths of Yuuzhan'tar, he would never be safe.

Years of backstabbing—sometimes literally—his way toward the top had taught him to be a light sleeper. It was a habit that had served him well, saving his life more than once in the years before his exile. But even here, in the bowels of the planet, he slept with the coufee he had carved from a discarded flake of coral within reach at all times, and the socket containing his plaeryin bol always half open. If anyone was fool enough to attempt attacking him during the night, they would wind up dead within moments of intruding in his sleeping quarters.

This reflexive response had almost brought one of his new companions to an unfortunate end a week earlier. Quite unexpectedly, considering he had done nothing to curry her favor, he'd been visited in the dark hours by Niiriit Esh. In his usual semiconscious state he had sensed her presence and leapt from his sleeping mat, limbs instinctively adopting an attacking stance and his coufee whipping out to slash his attacker across the throat.

He had barely reined in the attack in time. The faintest of lambent glows had revealed the shock in her eyes—as well as the hurt. Silent in her mortification, she had hurried from the room, her simple shift swishing against the shell walls as she retreated to her chamber.

In the couple of heartbeats after she had fled, he realized with some embarrassment that she had almost certainly been unarmed, and that there had been no intentions of hostility in her actions. Far from it.

But that had been then; *this* awakening left nothing in doubt: he and the other Shamed Ones were under attack.

From the commotion outside, Nom Anor knew that the scream that had awoken him had been the sentry, Yus Sh'roth, being killed. It was a shame, he thought idly; the former shaper had been a vital member of this community of Shamed Ones. Nevertheless, Nom Anor neither had the time or the desire to grieve. The fact was, Sh'roth's death scream could mean life for the others, because it gave them time to ready themselves for the invaders—whoever they were.

Maybe, he thought, it was nothing more than a loner that had inadvertently stumbled upon the camp and been surprised by Sh'roth; or perhaps even just another band of Shamed Ones hoping to make a silent raid while the camp slept, trying to steal some food—

But, no. He was fooling himself. The sound of amphistaffs cracking left no doubt in his mind that these attackers were warriors. Their camp was too deep to have been fallen upon by some passing patrol, which meant only one thing: these warriors, these trained killers, had been deliberately sent to wipe it out.

The certainty was more than enough to spur Nom Anor into action. He quickly gathered his things and left his humble dwelling, knowing as he did that it was unlikely he would ever return. Outside he was almost bowled over by someone dashing past in a wild panic, heading down the long, spiraling corridor that ran the length of the disused ventilation shaft. Probably I'pan, he thought, given the wily thief's knack for getting out of difficult situations.

Waiting in the shadows a second longer, Nom Anor listened carefully for the sound of anyone pursuing I'pan. But there was none. All he heard were distant footfalls and muffled cries. He didn't know how many warriors there were, but it was clear they had the upper hand. The cavern was quickly filling with the sound of the Shamed Ones' massacre.

Not this Shamed One, Nom Anor swore to himself, turning to follow I'pan down the corridor into the depths of the shaft where the chuk'a hibernated, and wishing his former companions speedy passages to the afterlife—if one awaited them. The Shamed Ones had, without question, saved him from what had been a very difficult situation when he'd fled Shimrra's wrath. He had lasted longer than expected by eating granite slugs, but eventually he would have succumbed to this alien environment and died—at the hands of a predator, or from something as simple and stupid as drinking poisoned water. He owed them his life and, thanks to their stories about the Jedi, there was every chance he owed them his future, too.

But what future would he have, he asked himself, if he were to charge up the corridor now and throw himself at a squad of fully armed warriors? He was just one against an unknown number.

He had owed a few people his life before. He owed no one a death.

With that in mind, he pulled a lambent from the wall and headed off down the gentle, curving slope in the direction I'pan had taken. Before he'd even taken a dozen steps, though, a high-pitched shriek brought him to a halt. He stood still for a moment, looking back in the direction of the scream, and knowing in his heart that it had come from Niiriit Esh. He hesitated for what seemed like an eternity, his newfound sense of responsibility causing within him a tremendous conflict. Niiriit might have been Shamed, but she was still a warrior, and she would never have run away from a battle. She would have fought to the death, for honor, for Yun-Yammka, for—

He shook his head vigorously. This was all wrong, he told himself. He was still thinking of her in terms he knew from the world above. But she was no longer a warrior; she was a *Shamed One*. She wouldn't have given her life to Yun-Yammka, the Slayer; she would have sacrificed herself to save her friends, as the Jedi did. Her memory deserved the truth, even if it still felt wrong to him.

He turned and continued down the passage, practically smelling the blood lust of the killing squad chasing him into the darkness.

The hulking mass of an old *Katana*-class Dreadnaught lumbered out of Borosk's lower orbits, where it had been lurking unnoticed since the beginning of the battle. Saba was familiar with its type; she knew her history well. It was a survivor of the Dark Force fleet that Admiral Thrawn had used so effectively against the New Republic. Reclaimed and refitted with centrally computerized slave-rigging units, it operated with a bare minimum of crew. Even so, its sluggish hyperdrive and weak shields had left such vessels sorely outclassed by more recent ships, and Saba was surprised to see one still operating. She wasn't the only one.

"That heap of junk isn't going to get us very far," Mara had said upon seeing it.

"That's exactly what you're supposed to think," Pellaeon had replied over the comm. "And besides, it's not supposed to."

By then, Saba had changed ships and changed into one of the brown, lightly armored jumpsuits that had become standard for Jedi Knights going into close combat with the Yuuzhan Vong ever since the mission to the worldship orbiting Myrkr. Danni Quee had also slipped into one and was sitting nervously with Saba as they listened in on the discussion about the ship that would ferry them into position. Saba's claws twitched in readiness, filled with a primal need to strike back at the ones that had taken her people from her.

How better could they be remembered?

"I've been saving it for a suicide strike," the Grand Admiral had gone on to explain. "It's designed to die twice. The first time, what the enemy sees is selective field failures and shaped charges designed to make it look like the engines have failed. Then, when it looks like it's adrift in vacuum, it comes back to life and takes everyone by surprise."

"You hope," Mara had put in wryly.

Pellaeon had shrugged in his tank. "That's the plan, anyway. We've never had cause to use it before."

"The difference between a fake death and a real one is slim," Mara had commented.

"I am aware of that," he'd said soberly. "That's why the crew complement has been reduced to the bare minimum. We found some old combat droid brains mothballed in storage. Emperor Palpatine recovered them when Governor Beltane's SD project fell in a heap, decades ago. Since there's never been an SD-Eleven and we needed every resource we've got, I figured we could combine the two and create something new. This ship is pretty much capable of flying itself to the target, maintaining a convincing semblance of attack, keeping its crew alive while the outer shell 'dies,' then commencing the second, covert operation in accordance with new instructions. There's plenty of room on the inside for stabilizers and inertial dampeners; it's basically just a hollow shell. Ordinarily we'd crew it with a squadron of TIE fighters and some troopers, blow the shell when surprise can be maximized, then retreat, if possible. But I'm sure we can make room for other cargo."

On the way in, Saba knew, "other cargo" meant *Jade Shadow* and a reduced TIE fighter contingent. If all went according to plan, the Dreadnaught—originally *Braxant Brave*, but hastily renamed *Braxant Bonecrusher* in honor of her plan—would cram its empty heart with liberated slaves. A rapid repressurization unit had been installed at one end of the massive space; *Jade Shadow*'s tractor beam would help capture the slave carrier and its contents; force fields would keep the air and cargo in long enough for the ship to jump to safety while *Jade Shadow* and the fighters covered its back.

That was the plan, anyway. It was, as Pellaeon had suggested, almost crazy enough to work. Saba kept her thoughts carefully away from what she would like to do to the Yuuzhan Vong if the chance arose. Instead she concentrated on the people in the slaveship. They were what mattered. Not her. Not what she had lost.

"All in place," came Jacen's voice over the secure comlink. "Ready for you to dock, Aunt Mara."

Jade Shadow's thrusters fired to jockey it into the same orbit as *Bonecrusher*. "All systems go?" Mara asked.

"Initial jump locked in; the drives are hot. We're ready when you are."

Jacen had wanted to be involved in the mission as soon as he'd heard about it. Pellaeon, however, had advised against it.

"You should stay behind," the Grand Admiral had said. "That's where a responsible leader belongs."

Jacen had seemed mystified by this. "But I'm not leading anyone."

"One day you will," Pellaeon had said, "and you owe

it to those who follow you to be there for them, both during and after a campaign."

The comments had been a compliment to Jacen's character, but it didn't seem to compensate for the idea of being left out of the mission. While he obviously appreciated the Grand Admiral's confidence in him, he still did not want to be left behind. In the end, he had eventually forced a compromise. He would be the human brain behind the droid minds during *Bonecrusher*'s elaborate ruse, hidden away inside the Dreadnaught shell, where it was safe, and from where he was currently directing the operation. As sophisticated as the SD combat droids had been, they were no match for a Jedi, and Saba felt better knowing that she could trust the Dreadnaught to do what it was supposed to do with Jacen behind it. Once she and Danni were in the slaveship, she wanted to know that there would be somewhere to escape to on the way out.

Danni checked her pressure seals for what seemed like the thousandth time as *Jade Shadow* nudged its way into *Bonecrusher*'s ordinary-looking flight deck. They had enough air for six hours. If they weren't out by then, they would need to locate pressurized areas on the slaveship, or find alternate ways to breathe.

"It'z okay," Saba told Danni, who had moved from nervously checking her suit seals to rummaging through her instrument pack, making sure she'd not left anything behind. "Remember yammosk hunting."

"That was easy compared to this." Danni looked much younger with her hair pulled back into the hood of the jumpsuit; at barely half Saba's mass, she wouldn't have even passed for a Barabel child. But Saba was under no illusion as to what the woman was capable of. She had survived the Yuuzhan Vong on numerous occasions. Some people had even joked that she was a good-luck charm. Saba didn't know about that, but she did know that the woman was Force-sensitive, and that had to work in their favor.

Her breaths came in long, deep waves, filling her with an energy she hadn't felt for months. The thought of the challenge was exciting and unnerving at the same time. She told herself that she was equal to it, but she knew that it didn't matter if she wasn't. She had to try. It was the only way she would ever be free.

A series of deep clangs announced that *Jade Shadow* had passed through the flight deck's fake inner hull and docked with the heavy grapnels designed to withstand the shaking the Dreadnaught would receive during the early stages of its mission. Over Mara's shoulder, Saba could see two rows of closely packed TIE fighters cradled in cushioning energy nets. The fake flight deck was filled with older TIE fighters piloted by less sophisticated droid brains, designed to act as decoys during the initial attack.

"Breaking orbit," Jacen said. The ship might have been old, but its inertial dampeners were first-rate. Saba felt nothing at all as its drives engaged. "Heading for the jump point."

"Fly well, *Braxant Bonecrusher*," came Grand Admiral Pellaeon's voice over the comm. "We'll keep them as busy as we can for you down here."

"Thanks, Gilad," Mara said. "Just make sure you're still around to pick up our pieces afterward."

"It will be my pleasure to return the favor."

Saba felt a stirring through the Force as though Luke and his departing wife were communicating in private—and then there was nothing but the silence of hyperspace. Her connection with the living universe was gone. They were on their way.

"First jump engaged," Jacen said.

"Trim optimal," interceded a droid voice, deep but with

jarring, nasal overtones—the voice of the droid brains doing the job normally done by thousands of crew. "Projection optimal. All systems optimal."

"ETA?"

"Seven point five-three standard minutes," the droid replied. "Perfectly optimal."

"I don't suppose *above* optimal is an option, is it?" Jacen asked.

"Good question," Mara said, pushing her hair back from her face as she leaned back into her molded flight seat. "If we could shave off a few seconds, that could only be a good thing."

"Anything other than optimal would be wasteful," the droid replied.

Saba sissed slightly at the droid's annoying pragmatism.

"I can't help wishing we had a few of Lando Calrissian's YVH droids here to lend us a hand," Danni said as she looked up from adjusting the webbing of her pack.

"You're not the only one," Mara said sourly. "They might show those SD brains that they've got more to worry about than being precisely on schedule. Obsolescence is a terrible thing for a droid, you know."

Jacen chuckled, but the droid remained silent. Saba hissed again and settled back to wait, her claws retracted and tail relaxed, to all appearances a perfect example of Jedi patience. Only another Barabel would have recognized the signs of nervousness she was actually displaying: the slight stiffness to the scales down her back and the restless extension and retraction of her inner eyelids. Not even her Jedi training could completely remove her anxieties.

Hunt the moment . . .

The tunnel extruded by the chuk'a ended in a complicated series of whorls and loops, all of them easily large enough to admit an adult. There were no rooms as such, just random chambers spawned like bubbles in blorash jelly where the chuk'a had meandered to a halt. The lambent Nom Anor held high in his hand sent strange colors and oily reflections dancing all around him. The going was difficult, and Nom Anor stepped carefully on the slippery surface, wary of sharp edges. He wasn't sure how far the torturous passages led; all he knew was that the top of the chuk'a itself was to be found at the very lowest point of the passage. There its soft tissues would be exposed and sensitive; there lay his means of escape.

As he wove through the basement of the place he had briefly called home, he became aware of the sound of breathing. At first he thought it might have been his own echoing back, but the faint thudding noise that accompanied it suggested otherwise. He smothered the lambent in his fingers, turning the light it cast a dull red, and followed the sounds to their source.

Creeping around a jagged hairpin bend, he saw a huddled figure crouching on the floor of a dead end, dressed in the familiar rags of a Shamed One. Nom Anor felt his body sag in relief as he exhaled heavily. For a moment he had feared it might be a warrior sent to cut off escape.

"I'pan, you fool," he said. "You almost—"

He stopped when the figure turned to face him. It wasn't I'pan at all. It was Kunra.

The disgraced warrior half rose to his feet, holding a chunk of yorik coral in his right hand. It was black-stained in the reddish light.

"What are *you* doing here?" Kunra asked, making no attempt to hide the bitterness he held for Nom Anor.

"I could ask you the same thing," Nom Anor said. "But I imagine we're both here for the same reason."

The warrior looked down, then back up at Nom Anor.

"That *is* the chuk'a cap, isn't it?" Nom Anor added, indicating the bloody patch by the warrior's feet.

With its job done, the shell-excreting chuk'a now blocked the rest of the shaft and acted as plug, keeping any subterranean dwellers from coming up from below—as well as preventing anyone from going down. Opening that plug would allow him, and Kunra, to get away before the warriors reached them, and with any luck they might not follow them down into the darkness.

But the creature's "cap" was anchored securely into the side of the shaft, and getting it to withdraw those anchors wasn't easy. There was a soft, spongy layer of flesh just below the hardened cap, and somewhere beneath that was the nerve connected to the creature's right ganglion network. Once that nerve was stimulated, the cap's multiple pincers that were thrust into the rock would retract defensively, causing the chuk'a to fall. From the blood on Kunra's hand and around his feet, Nom Anor guessed he hadn't had much success doing that.

Kunra nodded in response to Nom Anor's question. "But it's not responding. I can't reach it."

"Let me try." Nom Anor moved forward, handing the lambent to the warrior and pulling the homemade coufee from his belt. He did this slowly, making sure Kunra had a chance to see the blade before stooping over to examine the fleshy portion of the shell-making beast. Then he set about digging for the nerve with the point of his coufee. It wasn't easy; he was distracted the whole time, constantly wondering whether Kunra would vent his dislike of the ex-executor by bringing the piece of yorik coral down on the back of his head.

"I can't see," he said. "Move the light over here."

The light wobbled as Kunra shifted, then steadied at a more useful angle. Nom Anor breathed an internal sigh of relief. *We are allies again,* he thought. *For now, anyway. But there are still things I need to know.*

"Did you lead them here?" he asked without turning to face Kunra. "The warriors?"

"No!" The shock in Kunra's voice that such a thing could even be suggested left no doubt in Nom Anor's mind that the ex-warrior was telling the truth. "What would make you think such a thing?"

Nom Anor shrugged. "You and I were the only ones who got away, and I know I didn't call them." He glanced up. The ex-warrior's face was a mess of half-finished scars and internal anguish.

"It wasn't me," Kunra reasserted. "I don't know why they're here. I escaped because—" He hesitated for a second then forced out the words: "I was with Sh'roth when they came. While they fought him, I—I ran."

Nom Anor studied Kunra a moment longer, then returned to his work with barely a nod of acknowledgment. *I ran.* That explained everything: why Kunra had been the only one given enough time to escape, *and* why he was Shamed in the first place. Warriors didn't run, no matter what the circumstances; judging by the look on Kunra's face, this clearly wasn't the first time he had displayed cowardly tendencies. He was probably lucky to have escaped the first time with just a Shaming.

"Then what brought them here, do you think?" he asked. He couldn't help but wonder if someone else had betrayed him to the authorities. If Shimrra had learned of his existence, sending such a band of warriors to finish him off in the dead of night was exactly the kind of thing he'd do.

"What else?" Kunra said, more animated after the change of subject. "The one thing the high castes are afraid of, of course: the heresy."

Nom Anor admitted to himself that the idea made

sense. The priests would tolerate the Jedi sect as much as Shimrra would the Jedi themselves, perhaps even less. The Shamed Ones preaching it would be the enemy within, and rooting them out would be a priority. But if that *was* the case, then why had he never heard of such cleansing raids through the underworld of Yuuzhan'tar before his fall from grace? He assumed the answer to that lay in the nebulous way the message spread: even if Shimrra captured a convert, that one would only lead him to two or three others, who would in turn lead him nowhere, or in circles. There was no clear trail—as Nom Anor himself could attest. He had tried to find it, and failed.

Perhaps his own inquiries had, for the first time, established a clear trail to follow. He might have brought premature death down upon his fellow Shamed Ones by trying to find a way to use their beliefs to his own end. If so, the irony wasn't lost on him. Without them—and without a way out of the bottom of the shaft—he might very well find himself caught in a trap he had inadvertently laid for himself.

Frustration made him stab deep into the chuk'a cap over and over again, until his right arm was buried in it up to his elbow, black with gore. Finally he felt the creature respond with a spasm, and knew he had to be close to the nerve. He twisted the blade deeper, and for his effort felt a tremor ripple through the chuk'a. Another twist and the tissue around his hand tightened like muscle pulling taut. Fearing his fingers might be broken—or worse, that he might lose the only weapon he had left—he hastily pulled the coufee from the cap. A spurt of dark blood followed it, and the shell around them shook even more.

Kunra looked relieved.

"You've done this before?" he asked, the beginnings of a smile on his scarred lips.

Nom Anor was about to confess that in fact he had never done anything like this in his life, when the floor suddenly fell out from beneath them, consigning them both to the depths of the vent.

Not far from *Jade Shadow*, Jacen Solo's thoughts were very much focused on the present, not the future. In the minutes remaining till the end of jump, there was so much to do: systems to familiarize himself with, droid brains to program, decoy strategies to scrutinize, along with innumerable other checks to be made on an unfamiliar system. It was time-consuming, but necessary. Once he gave the order to jump, then the mission would truly be under way, and there wouldn't be time to make sure everything was in order.

Sealed in the cockpit of a flightless TIE fighter that was in turn wrapped in an energy web dense enough to stop a comet—all of it huddling inside the belly of *Braxant Bonecrusher* with *Jade Shadow* and numerous TIE fighters—he was electronically patched into the mind of the Dreadnaught and able to oversee its every move. He felt like a Phindian puppeteer, using tricks of light to cast shadows many times larger than himself onto a screen. Jacen only hoped the Yuuzhan Vong would be fooled by the illusion. If they weren't, the Dreadnaught wouldn't last long, and the mission would turn out to be very short indeed. It packed only the one surprise; once that was gone there would be nothing else. All they'd have to rely upon then was luck. And while good fortune was one of the things his family was famous for, it was not something he wanted to base the success of this mission upon. The death of Anakin had proven once and for all that luck did not stay in one's favor indefinitely.

The seconds ticked by as he continued his last-minute

checks. The chores were complicated, but they only occupied the analytical part of his brain. Another part—the more intuitive section that he usually assigned to the understanding of his place in the Force—turned to Danni and Saba in *Jade Shadow*. As he observed them and their own preparations from a distance, he suddenly realized just how little he was really adding to the mission itself: he was there mainly just to double-check what the SD brains would be doing. Nevertheless, he still believed it was important for him to be around for at least part of the mission. And he believed it for reasons that, until now, he had kept hidden even from himself . . .

Danni's nervousness touched him deeply. She didn't have a lightsaber or a full Jedi's training in the Force; she would essentially rely on Saba throughout this mission into the belly of the slaveship; but she was still going, and her courage made him like her even more. He vividly remembered the moment they had shared while waiting for Captain Yage to board *Jade Shadow*. There had been something there, a connection of some kind. Had that been the result of boredom? he wondered. Or was it evidence of larger, genuine feelings? There was no denying he'd had a mild, juvenile crush on her shortly after rescuing her from the Yuuzhan Vong on Helska 4, but that had been a fleeting and insignificant thing. He had put it down to mere emotions affected by circumstances, nothing more, and so had effectively buried the impulses. But now those feelings were back, and what troubled him more than anything else was how it had taken so little to rouse them.

When the mission was over, he would have to examine the situation more closely. And delicately, of course. He had proven himself as a pilot, a warrior, and—some would say—a Jedi, but when it came to matters of the heart, he was a definite novice.

"Jump complete," the droid brains announced, snapping him out of his reverie.

"Er—halfway there," Jacen said quickly to the others, worried that any hesitation might somehow reveal something of his thoughts. His fingers flew over the controls, calculating then laying in the second jump. The layout of the instruments in the TIE cockpit was different from what he was used to, but not radically dissimilar.

"That sounds just *optimal*," Mara said from the cockpit of *Jade Shadow*, not far from where he was sitting.

"Correct," the droid brain said. They hadn't been programmed to recognize sarcasm.

Jacen's course matched that of the droid brains. Unless the slaveship had radically altered position, they should come out practically on top of it.

He okayed the jump. According to the instruments, the drives surged back into life; thanks to the energy web, he felt as though they'd remained completely stationary.

"On our way," he informed the passengers of *Jade Shadow*. "We'll be there soon."

"In seven point four-seven standard minutes," the droid brain informed them. "Tactical circuits engaged. TIE decoys ready for launch. Shield generators programmed. Hull detonators primed."

The droid brains cycled through their precombat checklist once every minute with no variation. Jacen found himself half hypnotized by the steady mantra, and his mind began to wander again. His thoughts turned to Danni once more, and he called up a view of *Jade Shadow*'s cockpit, where she and Saba waited with Mara for the mission to truly begin. Her breathing became heavier as her tension increased. But there was an edge of excitement to that tension—and it was infectious, too. He could feel his own heart beating a little faster, and his palms began to sweat . . .

He was thankful when the droid brain announced their imminent arrival. He busied himself with double and triple checks to *Braxant Bonecrusher*'s systems, ensuring everything was locked down nice and tight—including himself.

"Here we go," he said over the comlink. "Hang on. This is going to be rough."

"I'm sure you'll look after us, Jacen," his aunt said. He smiled uncomfortably at her confidence in him.

Not if I don't focus on what I'm doing, he thought to himself.

"Five seconds," the droid brain announced. "Status: optimal. Three. Two. One."

The white of hyperspace streaked and became stars as the Dreadnaught barreled back into realspace with all the subtlety of an asteroid. Sensors swept the immediate area, searching for the slaveship. Once it was found—almost exactly where predicted—the Dreadnaught's cannons and batteries locked on and began firing at the tentacles. At the same time, the squadron of decoy TIE fighters launched from the flight deck and swooped in to attack.

This was a crucial phase in the operation, and Jacen couldn't help but feel anxious. The attack had to be stiff enough to convince the Yuuzhan Vong that it was a serious threat, but not so stiff that it would seriously damage the slaveship. The last thing they wanted to do was burst it open and destroy its contents.

But there seemed to be little danger of doing that. The slave freighter was armored against attack, and its tentacles were tough. It wasn't equipped with plasma guns to defend itself, and its dovin basals weren't responding the same way as those on combat vessels, but coralskippers soon launched from nearby vessels and powered hard to intercept the attack. Jacen watched the views on the screens surrounding him with apprehension, fists clenching uneasily: it was impossible not to be nervous so deep in enemy territory, with so little standing between success and destruction.

But then, that was the point. They were pretending to be a suicide mission, and the Yuuzhan Vong would instinctively accept it as such. It fit perfectly into their philosophy. The arrogance of the species didn't allow them to learn from their mistakes, it seemed—or at least accept that others thought differently from them.

The droid brains were in their element here. Scattered throughout the ship but linked by a high-speed network, they fired turbolasers and bolstered shields while broadcasting objectives to the simpler TIE fighter brains. Their reports were uniformly flat-toned and perfectly objective. Even when a freak missile squeaked through the shields and took out one of their own, the pitch of reporting didn't vary. This was battle, Jacen thought, and losses were expected. The droids probably regarded the jolting and jarring of the Dreadnaught as an indication that they were doing their job properly.

Two TIE fighters were destroyed almost instantly when the skips arrived; another three fell within the following minute. The remainder of the fighters managed to cripple one of the slaveship's tentacles, while *Bonecrusher* dispatched three coralskippers using the random-stutter technique Jacen had programmed into the droid gunners. For a brief moment it looked like they might hold out longer than anticipated, but then fortune's tide turned and the TIE fighters were destroyed with deadly precision.

Within minutes, the last one had been picked out of the sky by two converging streams of plasma. Barely had the burning cloud of wreckage dissipated when the attack turned on the Dreadnaught itself, pounding it from every direction. The droid brains brought the craft about, as though intending to flee. Skips swooped around it, firing round after round into its shields. Explosions rocked the ship as one by one the shields were permitted to fail. Debris sprayed into space as one of the hyperdrive engines blew, rattling Jacen in his protected roost like he was nothing more than a die in a cup. Even through the hull of the Dreadnaught, the energy web, and the TIE cockpit shell, there was still enough leftover energy to give him a shake. The steady thrum of *Bonecrusher*'s generators stuttered as the Dreadnaught's course began to twist back upon itself.

That was all the encouragement the Yuuzhan Vong needed. Sensing the kill, they sent streams of plasma fire into the weakened points along the hull. Quad batteries exploded; deflector shield projector bays burst into flames as air leaked out of decompressing decks; the Dreadnaught's rounded, almost beaked nose burst open as though its command decks had been breached. Artificial gravity failed along with the remaining drives. Then the reserve power generators took a direct hit, blowing an enormous hole in the side of the ship, venting air and even more debris into the vacuum.

Then it was over. Generators shut down and—since Jacen was there to bring them back when required—the SD droid brains shut down with them. Something groaned deep and long as the Dreadnaught settled into a state of inactivity. The clanking and rattling of debris escaping through gashes in the outer hull sounded like garbage being ground and mangled in a compactor.

Eventually total silence fell in the secret heart of the ship. Jacen unconsciously held his breath, sensing the TIE fighter pilots and his crewmates in *Jade Shadow* doing the same. This was the moment that would determine whether the mission failed or succeeded. If the Yuuzhan Vong didn't believe the ship to be truly dead, then they certainly soon would be.

To the rest of the universe, the *Braxant Bonecrusher* looked as though it had spent its fighters in a failed attack and been taken out itself. With everything powered down, there would be no reason to suspect that another squadron waited within for the word to launch, along with *Jade Shadow*, Jacen in his TIE cockpit, and the droid brains. Everything depended on this illusion remaining intact.

Jacen had only two holocams on the hull transmitting data back to him. He kept his eyes on the views—one above the breach in the Dreadnaught's back, the other from the stern, looking along the ship. Stars rotated around the Dreadnaught; the last explosion had given it a convincing tumble.

It was Mara who finally broke the silence. "Anything, Jacen?" She spoke in barely a whisper.

"Nothing conclusive yet," he returned equally as quietly. "They're not firing, which is a good thing, but the slaveship isn't visible at the moment, either."

"This one iz convinced by the quiet," Saba said.

Jacen listened. It was impossible to hear through a vacuum, so what the Yuuzhan Vong were doing would be impossible to detect aurally. But there was a quality to the silence that suggested Saba was right: the Yuuzhan Vong had called off the attack. What happened next was not yet known, but there was really only one possibility.

"Okay," he said. "Everyone take your positions. I'll click you when I have something definite."

Jacen reached out into the Force. *Good luck,* he sent to Danni and Saba. If they received the thought, they were too busy to respond.

He picked up a slight electromagnetic hum as the yacht's air lock cycled through, but he doubted anyone outside the ship would notice. And if they did, they were likely to put it down to the wreckage settling. Ships took time to die all the way through. There might be pockets of mechanical life still ticking futilely away. There might even be survivors . . .

A shadow moved across the screens in front of him. He stiffened, even though he knew what to expect. *Braxant Bonecrusher*'s slow roll around its center of gravity brought the slaveship gradually back into view a minute later—and, sure enough, it was looming much larger than before.

Jacen clicked once to confirm that everything was going to plan. A second later, a powerful jolt ran through the Dreadnaught. For a second he thought that that one almost imperceptible click might have given them away, until he realized that what he'd in fact felt was the dovin basal of the slaveship grabbing on to *Bonecrusher*.

Everything's going according to plan, said Mara. His aunt had sent out a bubble of both encouragement and reassurance to everyone on board.

Another jolt followed, accompanied by the sound of twisting metal. He feared for the structural integrity of the ship; without the inertial dampeners, it wasn't used to such stresses on its frame. Thankfully, though, it held.

When everything settled down again, the stars were no longer moving as fast, and the slaveship was rotating, too, anchored to the hull of *Bonecrusher* by the Yuuzhan Vong's version of artificial gravity. It was coming at them tentacles-first, like something out of a nightmare.

He clicked again, this time speaking into the comm.

"They've got us," he said. "And our friendly slaveship is moving in fast."

"Any sign of the ships?" Mara asked.

"I think it's safe to assume that most of them have gone back to their capital vessels," he answered. "They seem to have left just enough to—"

A voice over the comlink cut him off. Although not allowed to transmit, the Dreadnaught's receivers were still intact.

"This is Commander B'shith Vorrik," said an abrasive Yuuzhan Vong voice. Jacen was initially nonplussed. The villips the Yuuzhan Vong used to communicate among themselves didn't transmit over electromagnetic frequencies, unless they were modified by an oggzil. The only reason they would use one of those would be to speak to the enemy—and that was confirmed with Vorrik's next words: "All infidels will surrender immediately, or be destroyed."

Jacen's heart sank. The commander knew they were there. The plan had failed; it had all been for nothing!

Wait, Jacen, Mara sent, sensing the despair welling up inside of him.

"We have no intention of surrendering to become *slaves*," came another voice over the receiver.

The growled words came from Grand Admiral Gilad Pellaeon. Jacen almost laughed out loud in relief: the Yuuzhan Vong's ultimatum had been addressed to the Imperials, not *Braxant Bonecrusher* at all.

"Surrender the Jedi you harbor among you," Vorrik continued.

Jacen chuckled grimly to himself. Clearly the tactics they had introduced to the Imperials hadn't gone unnoticed.

"Why should we turn on those who help us?" Pellaeon replied.

"What good is the help if it results in your destruction?" Vorrik responded.

"You attacked us without provocation," Pellaeon shot

back. "It would seem our destruction was always your intention."

"The presence of the Jedi is provocation enough," Vorrik growled. "Your resistance is provocation! Your very *existence* is provocation! Now, power down your weapons, infidel, and surrender."

"I have a better idea," Pellaeon said evenly. "Leave the system now while you're still in a position to do so."

Jacen knew that the Grand Admiral was playing for time—either that or he wanted to *seem* as if this was what he was doing. With the Dreadnaught powered down around him, there was no way of telling the disposition of the Imperial forces, but he assumed that Pellaeon was still working to the original plan: to make it appear as if they were in retreat. B'shith Vorrik's announcement was probably nothing more than an attempt to hurry things along.

The Yuuzhan Vong commander's laugh boomed out from the receivers. "If you were counting on the cowardly attack to our rear flanks to change the course of this battle," he said, "then you should know that it has failed. Your survival, now, fool, rests solely upon *my* goodwill."

Grand Admiral Pellaeon hesitated just long enough to give the impression that this news had rattled him.

"I don't think there's an atom of goodwill in the entire Yuuzhan Vong culture," he said. There was a tremor in his voice. Jacen had to admit, the Grand Admiral was playing his role well. "We would sooner die than submit to you, Vorrik."

"Then so be it," Vorrik said, laughing again. "And may Yun-Yammka devour your bodies as well as your souls."

The Yuuzhan Vong commander added something more, but Jacen stopped listening. A faint *click* had

indicated that Saba and Danni had arrived in position
and were preparing to cross over to the slaveship.

Cross over . . . Jacen shook his head. If that wasn't a
euphemism, he didn't know what was. He felt Mara
joining him in wishing Saba and Danni luck as somewhere on the damaged hull of *Braxant Bonecrusher* they
prepared themselves for what they had to do.

He felt them leave, felt their rush of apprehension as
the tentacles took them. Then their Force-signatures
were muffled among the many trapped in the belly of the
slave freighter. They were completely out of his reach
now, and the situation out of his control—as was Pellaeon's fight around Borosk. The only thing he could do
from here on in was wait for a sign, and hope.

When the mouth of one of the slaveship's surviving
tentacles came groping for her, Saba Sebatyne almost felt
her courage desert her. A two-meter-wide, well-muscled
sphincter nosing through the holes in the Dreadnaught's
hull was enough to make anyone think twice.

Pellaeon's minions had appropriated a number of ca-
davers from the nearest Star Destroyer's morgue and
scattered them around the intended blast hole. Saba felt
dismay for the families of the dead soldiers, but she also
knew it was necessary if they were to pull off this mission. A dead ship with no dead bodies might have
aroused suspicions and put their plan in jeopardy.

The tentacles didn't waste time with the bodies, though,
passing over the dead tissue to continue searching for
something more useful. They poked deeper into the punctured hull, looking for anything alive—anything at all.
Danni blanched behind her faceplate as one fumbled
blindly closer, but she didn't back away.

Nor did Saba. Putting her faith in the Force, as well
as her pressurized jumpsuit, she pushed out gently from

her hiding place in the direction of one of the tentacles. With surprising speed, the tentacle noticed her and swung around to take her. Her body tensed as she remembered her people spilling out from the slaveship all those months ago, filling the void with six-pointed stars that drifted lifelessly from the ruptured wall of the ship. She closed her eyes and forced the memory down; now was not the time to be reliving such grief. She needed her wits about her; she needed to focus on the assignment at hand.

"For this one's home," she whispered. "For this one's people."

She forced her muscles to relax as she was engulfed by the maw of the tentacle and swept along a slippery, ribbed tube toward the hold of the ship. *Hold? Who am I kidding?* It was the slaveship's belly, and right now she was being *eaten* by it, her body pummeled by every muscular surge of the tentacle.

The contractions around her grew stronger as she approached the end of the tentacle. She wondered briefly if Danni was following, but didn't have time to check; she was too caught up in the moment and what she was experiencing to sense anyone else. Still, she wanted to reach back and feel for Danni, just to be able to *touch* her and find some reassurance. Just to get a hand to her right now would have made the discomfort that much easier to deal with.

Then, abruptly, the ride was over, and she was spat into what felt like a thick mass of jelly. She was knocked repeatedly across the face and body by the large number of hard lumps in suspension, so much so that she feared for the integrity of her faceplate. But when she finally came to a halt, she was relieved to find it was still fully intact.

She gasped for air and felt a pain in her ribs. Nothing

seemed to be broken, but she was definitely bruised. All around her was a uniform, infrared glow—unfortunately too diffuse or muffled to see by. She spread her legs to orient herself and felt objects pressing in all around her. Soft on the inside and firm in the middle, the objects felt strange to her touch. Her fingers sought purchase, but they kept slipping in the jelly.

Then something scrabbled at her faceplate, making her jerk backward. Her hands found the torch in her equipment pack and snapped it on. Just enough light came through the jelly to reveal that something leathery and star-shaped was trying to force its way across her face. She firmly brushed it aside and suddenly came face to face with a human.

She gasped with shock, then cursed herself. Of course. She was in a slaveship; what did she expect? The goop around her was probably a softer version of blorash jelly, used in combat to pin an opponent's limbs down. The thing flapping at her face might have been a gnullith, living breath masks for Yuuzhan Vong's pilots. The human floating upside down in front of her—just one of thousands trapped in the jelly—didn't have a gnullith and was, as her questioning hands determined, quite dead. The black-haired woman must have drowned before the gnulliths reached her—or worse, died during ingestion.

A pressure wave rolled through the jelly from above her, and Saba assumed that Danni had just arrived. She moved her powerful legs and arms to propel herself forward, attempting to swim for the outer shell of the belly, but it was impossible to tell if she was making any progress. And even if she was, she had no real idea of which direction she was in fact moving. It was like trying to swim through a sap pool while blindfolded.

She tried climbing instead of swimming, using the people around her for leverage. They all seemed to be in a state of drug-induced unconsciousness, and as such didn't respond when she grabbed hold of them. Again, she wasn't sure if she was making any real progress. For all she knew, she could have been simply pushing the bodies behind her rather than moving along them. Any sense of direction had abandoned her in her free fall. She wouldn't have minded so much had it not been for the gnulliths swimming through the jelly. Everywhere she turned she encountered their strange flapping motions as their slithering air tubes constantly groped for her mouth.

So she gave in and centered herself. Switching out the light and closing her eyes, she sought her innermost point, and *then* she reached out.

The people around her created a concentrated ball of life pressing in on all sides. She was deep within it, and had been heading deeper until she'd stopped. Reorienting herself, keeping her claws carefully sheathed and her tail limp, she used the Force itself to move her through the resistant jelly.

The edge gradually came closer, and she found herself reaching for it well before it arrived. It was almost as though she was groping for breath from the bottom of a lake. All of the captives were unconscious, but many of them were fearful and suffering in their dreams; not even sleep could protect them from the trauma of what their bodies were undergoing. The overlapping nightmares were suffocating, and Saba found herself humming a childhood tune she hadn't thought of for years to keep them at bay. It worked, but only just.

When she finally hit the edge of the belly, she clutched tightly at it, allowing herself the time to regain her strength. The interior surface was ribbed, so movement along it wouldn't be difficult once she got going again.

All she had to do was collect her thoughts, orient herself with respect to the ship around her, and then—

Something clutched at her from out of the jelly. She pushed herself between a couple of the immense ribs, kicking out at what she thought to be another gnullith. But it came back, groping insistently for her. For a moment she panicked, completely flustered by the oppressive, grotesque environment. *The same one the last of her people had endured, before . . .* She reached automatically for her lightsaber, even though she knew that lighting it would inevitably hurt the unconscious captives pressing in around her.

Then a light appeared out of the reddish murk. It grew brighter as whatever was grabbing at her found purchase, and pulled. Saba realized with a flood of relief that the thing that had taken hold of her equipment belt was a human hand—and that the hand belonged to Danni Quee.

The Barabel couldn't help it. She laughed at herself, amused by her mistake and buoyed by the fading of her intense but fleeting panic. Her sissing fit continued until Danni's faceplate pressed up against hers and she could see the human woman frowning in concern.

"Saba? Are you all right?" Danni's voice was muffled by the thickness of their masks. "You're shaking!"

"This one iz very glad to see you, Danni Quee," she said, forcing herself to be calm. Given their situation, uncontrolled laughter could be just as detrimental as panic. "How did you know where to look?"

"Through the Force," she said. "Can't you see me that way?"

Saba shook her head. "There are too many people in here with us. I am drowning in their mindz."

Danni removed her faceplate from Saba's and looked around. It was her turn to shiver.

"It's dark in here," she said upon turning back to face Saba. "I'm glad I've got this light."

Saba nodded. "This one iz more glad that you found me."

"Do you know where we are?"

Saba concentrated again. She couldn't feel the alien ship or its Yuuzhan Vong crew, but she could sense the shape that the sac of imprisoned humans made, then work out where they were from that.

"We're past the halfway point," she said. "There iz a bulge that I suspect containz the ship's control centers. It'z not far from here—about a hundred meters or so."

"Point me in the right direction, then, and let's go," Danni said with determination—although it obviously came with some effort. She was as uneasy about the whole thing as Saba was. "The sooner we're out of here, the better."

Saba led the way, propelling herself along the wall by digging her claws into the ribbing and pulling herself forward. Danni followed, using Saba's tail as a guide. As before, Saba had to shoulder aside unconscious or dead bodies on her way, and the extra energy this required soon tired her.

Movement along the wall was certainly simpler than swimming through the jelly, but it still wasn't easy. The interior of the slaveship was muscular and slippery, the surface soft but resistant to her probing digits. The ridges, she decided, were formed by vast muscle fibers wrapped around the hold, keeping the pressure in and allowing it to flex when new additions arrived. It wasn't as tough as yorik coral, small plates of which she noticed had coated the exterior. With the slaves kept unconscious— presumably by a compound delivered via the gnulliths, since contact with the blorash jelly hadn't affected Danni at all—it seemed obvious that the Yuuzhan Vong had ignored any threat from the inside. Saba felt reasonably confident that, if worse came to worst, they could cut through the inner layer and find a way out between the yorik coral plates. But that would mean risking explosive decompression, sending the contents of the belly out into hard vacuum . . .

The image of six-pointed stars tumbling into space flashed through her mind. She fought down the thought angrily.

I won't let that happen again!

Time was passing quickly, so she forced herself to hurry. She didn't know how long the slaveship would hover around the Dreadnaught, sniffing for new captives. There had been a couple of small movements through the ship, suggestive of slight attitude adjustments, so she knew it hadn't made any dramatic moves yet. The moment it left, though, their job would become a thousand times more difficult.

When they reached the bulge, its dimensions became clearer. The bulge was shaped like a volcano, with a round lip surrounding a slight dimple at the top. Feeling her way to the dimple, she was disappointed to find that it wasn't an exit as she had imagined. It was, in fact, an entrance, but not one she could fit through. It was from here that fresh gnulliths were constantly pumped into the vast sac, riding on a gentle current of blorash jelly. Avoiding them proved difficult, and Saba pressed herself as flat as she could against the fleshy inner wall to present as small a target as possible.

Danni pressed her faceplate against Saba's. "This place is getting worse by the minute."

"At least they don't seem to know we're here," Saba replied. "We seem safe enough."

"For now," Danni added.

Danni reached awkwardly for her pack and slid a fat cylinder from it. Saba helped her unscrew its cap and clear away the jelly long enough to activate its contents. Six modified Mark VII scarab droids came to life at the touch of a switch on Danni's remote controller. Each had six legs as long as a human's index finger and two retractable injection fangs. They had high-gain photoreceptors and sensitive biodetectors that had been tuned to Yuuzhan Vong rhythms and pheromones. They didn't normally need remote operators, although their sensors could be accessed from a distance. These had been further modified to give Danni a measure of remote control—since the interior of the slaveship was a completely unknown environment—without jeopardizing their mission. Each scarab would lay a threadlike molecular wire behind it, virtually invisible to the naked eye, which would allow her to keep in touch without using comlink channels.

Heads-up displays in Danni's face mask allowed her to see what the scarabs saw. As she keyed a series of instructions into the tiny droids and sent them scuttling for the gnullith vent, Saba accessed the information and watched, too.

The droids soon found the vent and burrowed into its muscular sphincter. The view through infrared was little different from what Saba saw around her in the hold: lots of indistinct, warm blurs and not much else. But the scarabs slid between the folds of tissue for three meters, nudging gnulliths aside with ease along their way.

The moment the lead scarab began to detect light, it slowed its crawl through the vent. They had clearly reached the end of the narrow passage. Danni instructed the droid to carefully extend a photoreceptor out toward the light, and found a tank filled with clear fluid that was thicker than water and held bubbles in suspension like human saliva. Throughout, the tank was teeming with star-shaped creatures that twitched and writhed in the liquid. This was the source of the gnulliths.

The scarab didn't detect any nearby Yuuzhan Vong biorhythms, so the droid slipped free of the vent and swam awkwardly around the edge of the gnullith pool. Ignoring the scarab's presence, the flapping star-shaped organic masks continued to swim into the vent from the bottom of the pool where, presumably, they were grown. The other scarabs followed the lead out of the pool, fanning out to find different hiding spots. The remote-control view became a mess of six slightly different images of the same place, and Saba cut them back to only the lead droid to keep it simple. The scarab found a promising passage through the bony wall, leaving its siblings behind.

The view became nothing more than a series of close-ups of unpolished yorik coral at very close quarters as the scarab scurried along the narrow fissure. Eventually it came to a dead end, then backtracked until it reached a turnoff it had ignored before and took that instead. That, too, led to a dead end, so the droid went back to another turning and tried that instead. After a few times of doing this, Saba began to feel frustrated. If they didn't find the equivalent of a control room soon, they were never going to be able to rescue the captives. And worse: *they* would end up captives themselves!

"Got 'em," Danni said suddenly, her voice low but excited.

Saba snapped from her pessimism. "Where?"

"Scarab Four." Saba selected the view and watched biorhythm readings glowing in many colors across a view of yet another narrow fissure. The scarab was moving stealthily closer to the end of the fissure, visible just around a turn up ahead. Bright light shone from around the corner, and Saba could hear the harsh sound of the Yuuzhan Vong language in her earplugs.

The scarab instinctively froze the moment it managed to get one of its photoreceptors around the corner for a look, finding itself at about shoulder height in a small control room containing two Yuuzhan Vong warriors. Brutally scarred, although not as extensively as some Saba had seen, they were elbow deep in the sort of organic controls typical for these vessels. On a strangely shaped screen before them, Saba saw something that she suspected represented the wreckage of the Dreadnaught at close quarters. It was hard to say for sure, though, because the biological display wasn't configured to frequencies her eyes were sensitive to.

Danni, however, was more certain. "That's *Bonecrusher*," she said. "At least we know we've still got a way off this thing."

But for how long? Saba thought as she shifted in the blorash jelly, brushing to one side yet another gnullith.

"I'm going to send the other scarabs in to join Four," Danni said. "We'll get them to attack once they're all there, okay?"

Saba nodded. Given that they hadn't been able to find a way out of the hold from within, this had become the human woman's show. Nevertheless, she still had reservations. "Only two pilotz for a ship this big?" she asked dubiously.

Danni shrugged in the jelly. "We're not picking up any other readings," she said. "And the scarabs have covered seventy percent of the volume ahead of us. It's not so unlikely, really. This would be dishonorable work in their eyes: there's no fighting, no victory; just picking up the pieces left behind by the true heroes."

Saba nodded again, more reassured. If that was the case, the attack of *Braxant Bonecrusher* was probably the most exciting thing these pilots had seen for ages. They would be relieved and cocky, and certainly not expecting an attack from within. Their appearance gave some credence to that notion: their armor was ragged, and one of them even had exposed skin showing through the vonduun crab shell.

One by one, the scarab viewpoints began to overlap again. They crowded together in the crack Scarab Four had found, making tiny clicking noises with their thin, metal legs as they watched the aliens going about their business.

"How far can these thingz jump?" Saba asked.

"I'm not sure," Danni replied. "They have their own attack algorithms. I'd probably just get in the way if I told them what to do."

"And you're sure the poison will work?" A range of anti–Yuuzhan Vong toxins had been identified by Master Cilghal; Pellaeon had instructed his security staff to fill the scarabs' poison reservoirs with it before they left.

"No." Danni smiled at Saba through the faceplate in an attempt to lighten the mood. "But we'll soon find out."

She keyed a new series of instructions for the scarabs, and immediately four of them detached their monolinks and scurried from the hole. The fifth and sixth moved forward to report what happened.

Saba held herself still, despite every muscle yearning to strike, and strike fast. For the time they scurried across the wall, the four hand-sized assassin droids remained invisible to them. Then Saba noticed one appear at the top of the display, cautiously creeping across the ceiling. A second one appeared to the right; a third to the left, slinking along the floor like a sinister insect. The fourth was still out of sight, and Saba found herself leaning slightly as if this would somehow afford her a better view.

The Yuuzhan Vong were still deep in conversation, totally oblivious to the scarabs making their way toward them. The scruffier of the pair leaned forward to adjust the trim, causing the scarabs on either side to momentarily freeze in their tracks. The one on the ceiling, however, kept moving, giving cause for Saba to hold her breath in nervous anticipation. What if they heard it? What if they looked up right now? The entire mission could be blown in an instant.

She watched as the scarab crept forward another body's length until it was positioned directly above the other alien. Then, turning ninety degrees and angling its head downward, it released its grip from the ceiling.

The Yuuzhan Vong howled in pain and surprise as the metal fangs of the scarab sank deep into his arm. He stood abruptly, snatching the tiny droid from his arm and smashing it viciously against the wall. The second warrior stood also, looking to see what the commotion from his comrade was all about. As he did, one of the other scarabs launched itself at him, taking him under the armpit where the vonduun crab armor was traditionally weakest, but the fangs didn't dig deep enough for the poison to be effective and the scarab was instantly swept aside.

At first the two warriors were startled by the attack and didn't seem to realize where it was coming from. But it only took a second to recover and get their bearings. Even though they were in what would have been regarded as a dishonorable position for warriors, they were both still formidable fighters, trained by years of torture and self-deprivation to respond instantly to any crisis.

They reached into their armor for weapons. One had only a coufee, but the other had an amphistaff that stirred and spat viciously in his hands. The second scarab droid tried another leap at the one it had attacked, but was easily batted out of the air by the warrior, and this time was destroyed. The third and fourth scarabs quickly joined the fray, one crawling up the uninjured Yuuzhan Vong's leg and trying to plant its fangs into his thigh, the other leaping for his face. The confined space barely seemed able to contain the sudden noise and movement as the amphistaff whirled and scarab fragments smashed against the walls.

Danni bit her lip as she ordered in the fifth assassin droid. It jumped on the back of the unbitten warrior, managing to get a decent purchase. Finding a gap in the vonduun crab armor, it emptied its reservoirs directly into the Yuuzhan Vong's bloodstream. He shouted in alarm as his partner disposed of it with a single, precise slash of his coufee. The strong, slender needles, however, remained embedded in the warrior's flesh. With seemingly little effort or discomfort, he twisted around and yanked them out. Wincing only slightly, he held them up to the light to see. All-too-alert eyes squinted malevolently at the tiny machine.

"The poison isn't working!" There was a nervous panic in Danni's voice.

"*Grakh,*" the Yuuzhan Vong spat, throwing the needles aside. The other struck the biological console in front of him and shouted more angry words in their own tongue. Alarms began to wail as one of the warrior's hands went into the control sacs. A villip everted itself on the console and the head of a distant superior began to add more shouting to the racket.

The droids had failed and the alarm had gone out. Reinforcements would no doubt arrive soon. Saba's heart lurched into her throat as she felt a shudder roll through the ship and realized that the slaveship's drives had just fired at full thrust. In the organic screen, the strangely distorted shape of *Braxant Bonecrusher* began to shrink.

She gripped the flesh of the wall impotently as the crush of bodies seemed to tighten around her. There was nothing she could do but watch helplessly as her only hope of survival receded into the distance . . .

The chuk'a was a simple creature, bred to turn the base compounds found in stone and dust into pearly building material, and when asked to rest its slumber was complete. There was a specific series of stimulations to be applied in order to bring it to life again; the ex-shaper Yus Sh'roth would have been able to tell Nom Anor what they were. He would also have warned against startling the chuk'a out of its hibernation because, under the circumstances, that could only mean disaster.

The dagger in its side wrenched the creature from its sleep, thrusting it into a world of pain—the shock of which triggered a defensive spasm that caused the chuk'a to retract its anchors from the sides of the shaft. The mass of the chuk'a was too great for the bottom of the structure it had built, and to which it was still attached. As a result, the shell on which Nom Anor and Kunra stood gave way, sending them hurtling downward, along with the creature.

Luckily—although it didn't feel so at the time—the slope of the vent provided enough friction to slow their fall. It also made the chuk'a and its attached chunk of shell tumble, sending its two passengers bouncing around inside the small space, smashing against hardened shell and occasionally slashing themselves against sharp edges. Nom Anor rolled himself into a ball to protect his stomach and head and tried to relax every muscle in his body.

Kunra was somewhere nearby, howling in fear as they continued to plummet. Through the shell they could feel the chuk'a frantically scrabbling for a grip on the sides of the walls as they swept past. Its stubby limbs had no success, and fared badly against the unyielding surfaces. With shell to protect it on just one side, it was sorely battered by the tumble and fell silent and limp just moments before they reached the end of the vent.

Nom Anor and Kunra had no warning that it was coming. One moment they were bouncing off the ferrocrete walls; the next they were tumbling in free fall. In its own way, that silent descent was worse than the crashing and bumping. It was impossible to know what awaited them at the bottom of their fall or how far it might be, and there was nothing to check their acceleration.

With a bone-jarring crunch followed by another brief moment of weightless spinning, then a second impact that seemed even more brutal than the first, the chuk'a reached the end of its downward journey. The sound of shell cracking was loud in Nom Anor's ears as the plug broke in two and fell in pieces around the body of the creature that had created it. His remaining momentum carried him several meters across the surface of what felt like a giant bowl. The refuse of centuries crunched and crackled under him as he groaned and rolled onto his side. Every centimeter of him was screaming with pain, as if his entire body had been pummeled by dozens of amphistaffs at once.

When silence had settled around him, Nom Anor struggled to sit upright. It hurt, but he refused to acknowledge it with a groan or a cry. He had learned over the years not to become a slave to unavoidable pain, but to use it as a goad.

With teeth clenched, he moved through the rubble on

his hands and knees to where the lambent had fallen nearby, a lonely star in a world of darkness. He took it and examined the place where they had come to rest.

It was indeed a shallow bowl, but one made of some kind of metal and surrounded by a lip almost a meter high. That was all he could see; the bowl seemed to be hanging in a vast and empty space—a space so large that echoes off its distant walls and ceiling were smothered by the silent shadows. There was no sign of the bottom of the vent, nor of any other wreckage that had followed them down. That meant that the Shamed Ones' nest was still intact. Had it become detached from the vent walls and followed them down, the warriors riding along with it would have been the least of Nom Anor's worries.

The chuk'a itself appeared to be dead. Its mollusklike form had burst and splattered over a large area of the bowl, its body cushioning its passengers and their shell saddle from the bulk of the impact. Lumps of gray flesh oozed clear fluids everywhere he looked, while jagged fragments of shell lay among the organic wreckage, some still settling.

Suddenly, into the quiet, Kunra cried out in pain. Fearful of how far the sound would carry, Nom Anor quickly rose to his feet and circled the body of the chuk'a to where the ex-warrior lay. The Shamed One was on his back, one leg impaled on a chunk of shell. Trying to sit up, Kunra reached for the approaching lambent glow, but the movement was too much for him and he fell back down with another cry.

"Help me," he panted breathlessly when Nom Anor stood over him.

"Why?" Nom Anor felt nothing but contempt for Kunra's pitiable whining in the face of pain.

"*What?*" the ex-warrior spat.

"Why should I help you?" Nom Anor repeated calmly.

"Because I'm bleeding to death!"

Nom Anor directed the light from the lambent over Kunra's extensive injuries. From the way the dark fluid was spurting from the leg wound, along with the alarmingly pale taint to Kunra's skin, it seemed likely that the ex-warrior's assessment of his condition was correct.

"You left your friends to die," Nom Anor said. "Do you think you deserve to live?"

"Do *you*?" It was clear from Kunra's expression that just talking was causing him a lot of discomfort.

"They weren't my friends."

"Niiriit—" Kunra stopped, wincing from a pain that was both physical and mental.

Nom Anor crouched down beside the ex-warrior. "That's been bothering you since I came along—hasn't it, Kunra?" he said, grinning despite the terrible throbbing of his own injuries. "Once I arrived, she had no interest in you anymore. You were no one."

Kunra winced and sucked air through clenched teeth. "You ruined everything," he managed to hiss out.

Nom Anor shook his head. "And you weren't even there for her at the end, were you?" he said. "If you had *really* cared—"

"All right!" Kunra gasped. The blue sacks under his eyes were growing as white as his scars. "I didn't care enough to die with her. Is that what you want to hear? I didn't care *enough*. Just help me. Please! I'll do anything. Don't let me die!"

Kunra's pleading became fragmented and confused. The pulsing from his leg had slowed to a trickle. Nom Anor waited until the ex-warrior had lapsed fully into unconsciousness before kneeling beside the injured man and reaching into the pack he had brought with him, removing the few medical provisions he had pilfered while on his upward excursions with I'pan.

The Shamed One's leg wasn't broken. That was lucky. Nom Anor had decided that he would expend the effort to deal with the wound, but there was a limit to what he could treat. He injected microscopic knuth bugs into the dying man's circulatory system to replace the lost blood. Clip beetles closed the wound, once the coral had been removed. A porrh wash kept harmful germs at bay and a neathlat covered the wound beneath a living bandage. There would be nothing for the pain, though; it wasn't the Yuuzhan Vong way. And even if he did have something, he would not have administered it. He wanted Kunra to be completely focused when he awoke. Focused and *grateful*.

While he waited for that moment to come, he explored his surroundings. The lip of the bowl wasn't uniform all the way around. There was an indentation at a point where a long, exceedingly massive arm led off into the darkness, presumably attaching the bowl to a wall in the distance. The top of the arm was flat and roughly two meters wide; he would have to walk across it, if there was anywhere to walk *to*. Below the bowl there was nothing to be seen at all, and he wasn't about to take a chance on another fall.

As he stood staring into the darkness, he realized that he had passed an important hurdle. He had not just endured the underworld of Yuuzhan'tar; he had endured an attack from his own kind. He was now most definitely a fugitive, and that hammered home the fact that mere survival was not enough. Any peace he found in the catacombs would always be an illusion, whether it was the heresy or his name that brought the warriors down upon him.

Kunra moaned. Nom Anor went over to him and pressed the coufee against the injured man's throat just as his eyes flickered open.

"Understand this," Nom Anor said. "I could have let you die. But do not allow the fact that you are alive deceive you into believing that I won't kill you out of hand, now or in the future."

Kunra didn't appear frightened; he was probably too weak from his injuries to feel anything much apart from shock.

"I'm not fool enough to think that, Nom Anor," Kunra said. Fluid rattled in his lungs as he spoke; he coughed once to clear it, spitting the gray-green mucus into the dust at his side. Then, fixing his wavering eyes on Nom Anor again, he said "I am too aware of your reputation. You do nothing that doesn't benefit your own cause."

"And what is my cause now, Kunra?" Nom Anor emphasized the question by applying increased pressure with the blade.

"You tell me," Kunra gasped.

"I want many things, and in time I intend to get all of them. *Your* time, on the other hand, is decidedly limited. You can either agree to help me achieve these things, or I will kill you now. There is no other option."

Kunra rolled his eyes and attempted to laugh, but the pain was obvious beneath the facade. "I don't suppose I could have a little time to think about it, could I?"

"You have already held me up enough," Nom Anor said coldly. "Choose now, or die indecisive. It matters not to me."

The ex-warrior closed his eyes, then nodded once. "I guess I will help you, Nom Anor."

"Good." He was satisfied that the answer was truthful. Kunra was a coward; he would do anything to save his life, even if it meant betraying himself. Such desperation would make of him a fine bodyguard, for a time.

They would understand each other on that score, at least. "There are just two more things you need to know," he said, withdrawing his blade from Kunra's throat and sheathing it under his belt. "The first is that you will never question my instructions. Not more than once, anyway, for there will be never a second time."

He paused to let the point sink in.

Kunra nodded. "And the second?"

"You will never use my true name again," he said. "If it *was* my name that led Niiriit and the others to their deaths, then I would avoid something similar happening in the future."

"What should I call you, then?"

"I haven't decided upon a name yet," he said. "Amorrn will do for now—the name I used in the upper levels when I visited with I'pan. But I fear that even this might be recognized now. I shall let you know when I have chosen another."

He held out a hand and helped Kunra to his feet. The ex-warrior's leg was tender, but he could walk, at least. Yuuzhan Vong biotechnology was more effective on living tissue than was the machinery of the infidel—or even, Nom Anor suspected, the nebulous Force of the Jedi.

"Where to now?" Kunra asked, standing in a position that favored his good leg.

"Up," Nom Anor stated flatly, glancing into the darkness overhead. "I have some business to attend to there."

Saba's comlink clicked at the same time Danni said: "Wait, Saba! Look!"

Through the remaining scarab's senses, Saba saw one of the Yuuzhan Vong warriors at the controls of the slaveship slip to his knees, then slowly slump over to one side. The second was having troubles of his own. Going to the aid of his fallen comrade, he lost his balance and fell forward, striking his head on the control console. He regained his footing just long enough to stand up again, then he, too, went down in a heap.

"The poison worked!" Danni's words were carried on a barely suppressed and incredulous laugh of relief. "It just took a little longer than we expected it to."

"It doesn't change anything," Saba said soberly. "We're still drawing away from *Bonecrusher*."

The Barabel drew her lightsaber at the same time she opened a comm channel. There seemed no point maintaining a communications blackout any longer.

"Jacen, this iz Saba," she said urgently. "Our cover has been blown. Please acknowledge."

His reply was muffled by the layers of the people and blorash jelly packed in around them. "I hear you, Hisser," he said. "And we already guessed as much. We have contacts closing in across the board, moving in to pick you up right now. Will you be able to get out okay?"

Danni's expression had quickly gone from elation to one of dismay. Like Saba, she knew the only way out would be to cut through the hull, and that would result in the almost certain deaths of all the captives they'd come to rescue.

But maybe there was a way, Saba thought. It was risky and went against virtually every spacer instinct in her body, but it just might work.

She had sworn not to let such a thing happen again . . .

"Jacen, empty the flight deck," she said hurriedly. "Keep *Jade Shadow* in dock and tell Mara to have the tractor beam ready."

Danni's eyes grew wide in the reddish darkness. "Saba, you're not—?"

"We truly have no other choice," Saba shot back sharply. "Now, hang on to something."

Saba pressed the business end of her lightsaber flat against the fleshy wall of the slaveship interior. The sound it made on ignition was horrific as it boiled through flesh to the vacuum outside. The ship quivered as she dragged the blade along the wall, turning a hole into a slit one meter long, then two meters. The tissue resisted parting even when the lightsaber had moved on, cauterizing the edges and killing nerve endings. A great bulge developed as muscles pushed in from all sides, resisting the pressure differential by fighting to keep the lips of the hole together. But Saba kept cutting, bracing herself as best she could against the ribbed flesh, readying herself for the inevitable.

When the rent in the belly wall reached five meters, Saba felt the muscle tremble and give way. The slit peeled open, emptying the contents of the slaveship out into the vacuum in one thick stream

"Saba, what are you doing?" The exclamation came from Mara. "Those people are going to freeze to death out here!"

"No they won't," Saba replied, fighting the current that was trying to pull her through the gap also. The people bumping into her as they were sucked through the hole only made her task that much harder. "The insulation from the blorash jelly should hold for several minutez—long enough for you to get them into the flight deck."

"And what are they supposed to do for oxygen in the meantime?"

"The gnullithz, of course."

"Saba, the gnulliths won't work in a vacuum!"

"They won't be in a vacuum; they'll be in the blorash jelly—which iz where they've been getting the oxygen in the first place." She grunted heavily as a couple more bodies collided with her on their way out. "Trust this one, Mara. Get them to the flight deck az soon as possible and everything will be all right."

I hope, she added silently to herself.

Mara chuckled nervously. "This is a crazy idea," she said. "One only a Barabel would attempt!"

Saba sissed softly to herself, taking Mara's words as the compliment they were intended to be. With both hands on the pommel of the lightsaber, she widened the hole as far as she dared—too much would send the slaves spraying across the sky in an arc too wide for Mara to catch them all; but too small a hole would mean the slaveship wouldn't empty fast enough, giving the Yuuzhan Vong reinforcements time to arrive. After a few moments she snapped off her lightsaber and crawled around the hole to where Danni was clinging desperately to the command bulge.

"Time to get out of here," Saba told her, wrapping around the woman's shoulders an arm that was almost as long as Danni was tall.

"About the only thing going for this plan of yours, Hisser," Danni said, "is that it can't be anywhere near as bad as the way we came in."

"Here we come, Mara," Saba said over the comlink.

Clutching Danni close to her chest, she let go and was instantly swept up by the current and sucked unceremoniously out into space. Limbs from the other captives continued to batter her as they flew out, so she tucked herself around Danni to protect her. Then the slight acceleration she had felt through the slaveship was gone and she was spinning in space, two living people in a clump of about forty held together by the blorash jelly. The stuff stiffened around her as though setting, keeping the pressure in.

"We're out," she said shortly.

"Keep talking," Jacen said. "It'll give us a trace."

"No—get—otherz—" But that was all Saba could manage. The blorash jelly was continuing to set, pressing at her chest and making it almost impossible to breathe, let alone talk.

Trapped and with little else to do but wait, she stared out through the translucent jelly at the galaxy spinning idly around her, wondering if this would be the last thing she ever saw. She thought back to how her own people had spilled from the slaveship above Barab I. Had any of them been conscious to ask similar questions? Or had they been like all the rest of the captives here, unconscious and oblivious to the danger they were in?

As she continued to drift through space, Saba noticed several lights that were brighter than the other stars. The biggest of these was Borosk's sun, spinning lazily around them, while others she imagined to be TIE fighters that had been launched by *Bonecrusher* to make room for the people rescued from the slaveship. As yet there was no sign of attack from the Yuuzhan Vong, which was fortunate.

"Beautiful," Danni ground through a clenched jaw, her eyes fixed on the view of the massive globules of solidifying jelly drifting nearby. The reddish spheres were glittering in the sunlight, spinning around them in a lengthening spiral with its starting point in the side of the rapidly deflating slaveship.

Saba didn't have the breath or the energy to comment. All she could do was stare, and morbidly wonder what would happen to them when the jelly set completely . . .

But the thought was broken when the bubble that contained them jerked suddenly, bringing their gentle roll to a complete and abrupt halt. A sense of falling swept over her, and with immense relief Saba realized they had been picked up by *Jade Shadow*'s tractor beam. Their bubble—along with a dozen or so others—was slowly being drawn down into hold of *Bonecrusher*.

"Got you," Jacen said. There was no hiding his relief. "Are you two okay in there?"

"I'm—here," Danni said with effort. "Not sure—about—Saba."

Danni seemed to be coping with the solidification of the jelly better than Saba was. Maybe, Saba thought as the tightening across her chest worsened, it had something to do with the smaller lung capacity of humans. A Barabel would find it much harder to breathe in higher pressure since it took more energy to inflate the larger rib cage. Danni and the other humans, though, could survive more readily on small, rapid breaths.

Theorizing was all very well. Knowing the problem didn't help her find a solution—especially when she could feel darkness closing in around the edges of her vision. She closed her eyes so she didn't have to think about blacking out, concentrating instead on Jedi breathing techniques to conserve her energy.

This was disrupted when another rough jolt sent them tumbling end over end. Saba thought she could hear Jacen talking, but he sounded far-off and vague. Soon she heard other voices, and she thought for a second that they might be the droid brains joining in on the discussion, but again she couldn't be sure. Everything was too hazy.

Flashes of light coincided with a faint and distant tapping sound, and she knew instinctively that *Braxant Bonecrusher* was taking hits to its reactivated shields. She should have felt relief that she had been rescued, but all she could think of was the other people in the blorash jelly. She just hoped they had been rescued before the Yuuzhan Vong had arrived.

A thrill of fear rushed through her when the flashing abruptly intensified. Surely the Yuuzhan Vong couldn't be *that* close? But no, she thought numbly. These flashes were from laser light, not plasma.

With some effort, her eyes flickered open and she looked around to see what was going on.

"No, Saba," Danni panted from close by. "Keep them— shut. It won't—be long my—scaly friend."

Despite Danni's reassurance, though, it was hard to maintain a Jedi calm with all the flashing going on, as well as the jelly solidifying around her like ferrocrete. But she tried to stay focused just the same.

Her ears detected a faint sizzling-crackling sound that gradually grew louder. The mass of jelly shook violently. She felt the pressure across her body ease slightly, and then a few seconds later ease some more. Soon Danni was squirming out of her grip, and she realized with great relief that she could breathe properly again.

Saba opened her eyes and the world flooded back in. Between flashes of automatic cutting lasers and robot manipulators grabbing at her, she heard droid brains announcing that the release had been achieved with "optimal efficiency," while TIE fighters reported on the defense of the Dreadnaught. And there was Jacen standing above her, tearing chunks of jelly from Danni's jumpsuit, then helping Saba do the same. The Barabel's mind was still fuzzy, and her hands were stiff and unwieldy as circulation gradually returned. It took her several minutes before she could fully comprehend the scene around her.

She was on a landing deck. More than fifty rough spheres of solidified jelly filled the confined space almost to its limit. From the spheres protruded arms and legs, along with the occasional head of the unconscious human captives. Cutting lasers were beginning to work on several of the spheres, releasing the people so they could be treated. She could feel them through the Force: all would need medical attention to reverse the effects of the drugs supplied by the gnulliths, but it looked very much like the majority of them would live.

She laughed out loud as Jacen and Danni helped her to her feet. Danni threw her arms about the Barabel in a show of both relief and gratitude, while Jacen slapped her shoulder plates in a congratulatory gesture. An immense feeling of satisfaction rushed through Saba—so strong was it, in fact, that for a moment she was afraid that her legs would fold beneath her.

"Initial jump locked in," the droid brains announced over the pounding of turbolasers.

"Take us out of here," Jacen said as he turned away from Saba and Danni to return to his disabled TIE cockpit to oversee *Bonecrusher*'s escape. Saba watched him go with a strong pounding in her chest. She could sense Jacen's pride in her. To him, this was what it meant to be a Jedi: to save lives, to protect freedom, to resist evil. She was glad, in a war with so many horrors, to have been able to give him—and herself—something to be proud of.

How better could they be remembered?

Saba opened her mouth fully, sucking in a lungful of the sweetest air she had possibly ever tasted.

"This is Captain Syrtik of the Galantos Guard," announced the leader of the approaching Y-wings.

Blunt-nosed and older than Jag Fel by several decades, the clumsy fighters followed a strictly controlled flight path out of Galantos's gravity well. Their ion engines were outdated but still powerful enough to overtake *Pride of Selonia* on its way to reinforce Twin Suns Squadron. The frigate's turbolaser batteries tracked the Y-wings as they passed, ready for any sign of hostility.

"State your intentions, Captain Syrtik," said Captain Mayn.

"We're here to help." The leader of the incoming fighters sounded grimly determined. "Just tell us who to defer command to and we'll do whatever we can."

"Councilor Jobath finally saw reason, eh?" Mayn said.

There was a slight hesitation before Syrtik's reply: "Actually, Captain, I'm proceeding without orders."

This time it was Mayn's turn to hesitate. "Very well," she said. There was no hiding her surprise. "Link up with Twin Suns Squadron for instructions. We'll be with you as soon as we can."

"Captain Syrtik, this is Twin Suns Leader," Jag said over the comm a second later. "Switch to channel twenty-nine for those instructions."

Jag closely surveyed the battle through his monitors. The two slaveships had closed together to make a smaller target while the reorganized coralskippers maintained a tight defense. The armored blastboat analog was still hanging back, protected by a trio of determined skips.

He changed to the new channel. "Our priority up to now has been to knock out the slaveships," he said. "But that situation has changed. Those scarheads are getting themselves together, so we're going to need to take out that last ship. Whatever's doing the thinking for them, it's in there."

"A yammosk?" Jaina asked.

"I think so," Jag said. Then, for the benefit of the newcomers, he added, "We have jammers in *Selonia*. Until they arrive, though, we'll have to make do on our own."

He paused, frowning at the screen. He had noted the absence of the *Falcon*, but the significance of it hadn't sunk in at first. The battered freighter had quietly looped back to Galantos once the Y-wings had appeared, almost as though it had other business to attend to. It was probably nothing, but he couldn't help but feel uneasy about it. Tahiri was aboard the *Falcon* . . .

He pushed the thought down. He had enough to contend with as it was without adding more to his plate.

"We're going to divide you into three," he told their new allies. "One squadron will come with me to take out the rear ship. Twin Two has already made some progress on the slaveships so she'll keep that up, with help of the second squadron. The remainder will provide distractions as needed."

"You have no specific instructions at this time?" asked a new, slightly tremulous voice.

Jag rolled his eyes as he remembered how precise and organized the Fia liked to be. He had assumed that the fighters would be piloted by species more suited to the interior of a Y-wing cockpit; presumably they had made substantial alterations to the standard couches to accommodate their bottom-heavy physiques.

"You'll be fine," he said. "Just follow our lead, okay? Right, now let's split up." He picked one of the squadrons at random from the rapidly approaching trio. "Blues, you're with me."

"That's Indigo, actually," Captain Syrtik corrected him.

"Sorry, Indigo. Twin Two will take Red."

"Cerise."

Jag shook his head irritably. "All right, then that leaves Green for—"

"Reseda," he was corrected again.

"Okay, then that leaves *Reseda* Squadron for the general approach. Is everyone clear on their part?"

A chorus of affirmatives sounded out over the open line.

"Right, Indigo Leader, switch to frequency seventeen and we'll begin our run."

As the new arrivals swept into the battlefield, Jag took a second to reprogram the diagnostic displays in front of him. The number of ships had more than doubled, and without any idea of how well the Fia could fly, he needed all the technical backup he could get.

"Are you okay with this, Sticks?" he asked on a private channel.

"A-okay," Jaina replied. Her X-wing peeled off to lead her new flock in a tight loop around the slaveships, herding a pair of cautious skips before her. "But let's hope this will be over soon."

"I hear you," he said. "I'm afraid the Fia's pedantry might turn this into the longest melee we've ever been involved in."

"Not what I was hoping to hear, Jag," Jaina said tiredly.

The obvious fatigue in her voice concerned him. He still didn't know the full story of what had happened at N'zoth, but it would have to wait until the immediate problem was dealt with.

He guided his new wingmates around the slaveships and along a rolling strike path toward the blastboat analog. Skips immediately swooped in to deter them, dividing the Y-wing formation into quarters. Two of the old boats stayed with Jag, but they only managed to keep up because he showed restraint and kept his maneuvering to a minimum. As soon as the first of the skips appeared in his targeting reticle, however, he let his instincts take over.

The skip danced across his scopes, narrowly avoiding the stutterfire he sent arcing toward its coral-armored back. Dovin basals snatched energy out of the vacuum, greedily absorbing everything he threw at them. His two wingmates added to the barrage, but they hadn't yet picked up the new techniques. Their input was little more than a distraction. Nonetheless, he appreciated all the help he got.

"Like this, guys," he said, hugging tight to the skip's tail and sending pulses of energy waves at it, then quickly launched a proton torpedo down the throat of the over-loaded dovin basal. The coralskipper exploded into highly energized dust particles that peppered his cockpit as he passed through the remains of the ship.

"Got it?" he said when he was sure there was nothing else on his tail.

"An ingenious technique," one pilot said. "But does the efficacy increase in direct proportion to the irregularity applied to the—?"

"We don't have time for that, Indigo Five," said another pilot. "We can discuss those kinds of details later."

Jag breathed a sigh of relief as he sent a wave of laser-fire arcing into the side of the blastboat. His wingmates did the same, dodging plasma bolts sent in return.

Around Borosk, triumphant battle reports from Fleet Group *Relentless* were more than overshadowed by the terrible losses endured by *Protector* and *Stalwart*. For every battle group that came close to the yammosk-bearing vessel identified by the Galactic Alliance, five more failed and were destroyed. It was a grueling, frustrating situation to watch, and Pellaeon couldn't help but wonder why this was the case. Was it because of an inherent mistrust of the Jedi who had brought these techniques to them, or simply an inability to follow new tactics quickly?

He continued to listen in from his bacta tank on the ongoing battle.

"Blue Three, keep up that covering fire. I'm going in!"

"Red Seven, watch your tail."

"I have a strong lead in sector fourteen, White Leader."

"On your right and above, Green Ten—on your right!"

"I'm hit! Stabilizers failing! Going to—" Then silence, as another life fell to the aliens' plasma fire.

Listening to the babble on the open channel was doing little to ease Pellaeon's mind, but he maintained his vigil because it gave him a taste of the battle as a whole. He couldn't direct each component within it, but there was some value in viewing it from above. Were the front-line troops panicked, excited, reluctant, enraged? Such things could make an enormous difference in the outcome of a conflict, and a good commander was wise never to ignore it.

Overall, his gut feeling was that they were losing ground. The retreat back to Borosk's mine rings had been tactical at first, allowing him to concentrate Imperial forces around the planet and resist the enemy on more fronts simultaneously. He had seen secondhand what had happened on Coruscant when the Yuuzhan Vong had attacked there, and while Borosk wasn't facing as great a force, it also wasn't as well defended. He'd hoped he could hold the planet long enough for the Yuuzhan Vong to lose patience or for their resources to run low. But the navy was losing more than it was gaining. The persistence of the Yuuzhan Vong was quickly taking its toll on the morale of his soldiers, and that directly impacted upon their battle performance. He knew that if this wasn't turned around soon, it could cost them everything.

"Maintain shielding trios as ordered!" one pilot barked.

"Who are we kidding?" another returned. "This is never going to work, and you know it."

"Can it, Gray Four. We've got better things to do than listen to your whining."

A shrill whistle cut across the open channel, requesting his attention on the private line. Pellaeon turned away from the battle and took the call.

"What is it?" he asked wearily.

The voice of Captain Yage replaced the ambience of battle. She had become his de facto aide-de-camp during the fight for Borosk, deflecting unwanted inquiries and making sure only important ones got through.

"I have a report from Lieutenant Arber, sir," she reported crisply. "The GAM has been installed in *Defiant* and is ready for a test run."

"Excellent." Pellaeon felt a grim satisfaction rise in him. Imperial ships didn't carry gravitic amplitude modulators as standard issue; indeed, such devices were rare and expensive. This one had been brought in from a neighboring system as a matter of urgency and reprogrammed by Imperial engineers according to the Galactic Alliance specifications. If all went well, and it jammed the Yuuzhan Vong war coordinator as Skywalker promised, it could prove to be the turning point in the battle.

"Instruct Lieutenant Arber to forgo the test run and proceed directly to a combat run," he ordered. "And inform Captain Essenton that she is to give Arber her full cooperation. She's a cranky old thing, but when she sees what the GAM can do, I'm sure she'll come around."

Yage didn't question Pellaeon's opinion, although she knew as well as he did that no Imperial had actually seen a yammosk jammer in operation. Everything rested on the word of Skywalker and his Galactic Alliance. If they were wrong, the edge he needed to win the battle, if not the war, might not even eventuate.

He watched the Star Destroyer *Defiant* turn about and break from the defensive orbits the other capital vessels were maintaining below the ion mines. A swarm of TIE fighters and blastboats accompanied it, fending off coralskipper attacks and cutting a path through to the cluster of Yuuzhan Vong capital vessels that had been identified as containing a yammosk. The enemy was taking great pains to ensure that this one was at all times defended against previous attempts to knock it out by Fleet Group *Stalwart*.

As before, the Yuuzhan Vong clustered around the yammosk ship like insects protecting their queen, swarming en masse to deflect the attack and stinging the assailants wherever possible. *Defiant* was hammered by streams of plasma bright enough to make the blazing of its ion engines look dim. Its shields were snatched at by dovin basals and attacked from every angle. It retaliated with fire from its turbolaser cannons, stuttering at the new frequencies as it removed entire flying groups of coralskippers out of the sky. The space around it became thick with debris, swirling nebulae of burning gas and fiery remnants flashing with discharging energy. Pellaeon admired Captain Essenton's skill and determination as she flew the Star Destroyer onward, into the enemy's ranks. *Defiant* was like a giant, poisoned dart plunging deep into the heart of the enemy.

As soon as it was in range, Lieutenant Arber activated the yammosk jammer. Pellaeon knew roughly how it worked, even if the precise details were beyond him. The machine broadcast coded gravitic pulses designed to interfere with similar pulses used by the yammosk to communicate with the vessels under its command. Knocking out the yammosk had the effect of removing the mind behind the coralskipper attacks; jamming their signals was supposed to confuse them. Pellaeon thought again of the swarming-insects analogy, imagining the effect to be something like blowing smoke onto a hive to make the insects' movements sluggish.

The effects were obvious and instantaneous. What had been a deadly dance suddenly became clumsy and unco-ordinated. The myriad coralskippers, lacking central di-rection, were forced to rely on their own judgment—and Pellaeon knew well how poor that could be for a single fighter caught in the middle of a large battle. Without access to central command, the battle devolved into hun-dreds of tiny skirmishes.

There were still flashes of order in places as the yam-mosk fought the jamming signals and briefly regained control of some of the battle groups under its influence. But through it all, the pointed hull of *Defiant* continued to stab, firing torpedoes and concussion missiles relent-lessly, committing every spare fighter to a concentrated attack on the group of capital vessels protecting the cen-tral yammosk. The yammosk fought back as best it could. Even confused coralskippers found it hard to miss a target as large as a Star Destroyer. Laser banks were kept busy by a stream of suicide runs focused on the bridge tower; blastboats formed a primary defense around the besieged ship, forcing the attacks to concentrate on certain approach runs and picking off the skips as they came. The Yuuzhan Vong forces weren't directed enough to target the blastboats in response, so the tactic cut huge swaths through the coralskipper forces that were sup-posed to be defending the yammosk.

TIE fighters descended on the target ships, raining down energy upon them that no amount of dovin basals could absorb. At that point, the yammosk knew it was going to lose and began expending the nearby capital ships in fruitless attempts to divert the attack. But real-

izing that putting the yammosk out of action was in fact
the way to ultimate victory, the Imperial forces remained
focused, refusing to be distracted from their goal by any
new tactics. Attack run after attack run peppered the
core vessel until it began to list around the center of its
mass, venting atmosphere and bodies from numerous
holes in its hull. But still the yammosk fought, and the
self-destruction of two of its sister vessels blew enough
energy and matter across the battlefield to momentarily
stall the Imperial attack. The shock wave swept space
clean on all fronts, knocking TIE fighters out of control
and overloading the targeting sensors of *Defiant*'s turbolaser banks. Coralskippers tumbled and flickered like
hot ash over a bonfire.

One TIE fighter pilot who was quicker to recover than
most managed to score a direct hit on the yammosk's
life-support tank, assigning the many-tentacled creature
to the vacuum in a writhing ribbon of ice crystals. The
Defiant turned about, taking out the remaining capital
ships as it went and decimating the enemy remaining in
the area.

Pellaeon couldn't help but be pleased with the outcome. It had been a bold and ultimately effective move,
and it sent a clear message to the commander of the Yuuzhan Vong fleet: *we can hurt you!*

But the battle was far from over, and while the *Defiant*
had been busy, a hole had been punched through the
minefields that *Right to Rule* was only just beginning
to clean up. The demand on planetary turbolasers and
shields was increasing as more and more coralskipper attackers were approaching the ground. If there was another yammosk somewhere in the Yuuzhan Vong fleet, it
would soon take over command of the attack.

Time. That's what it all came down to. Pellaeon didn't
know how long the Yuuzhan Vong's Commander Vorrik

could commit himself to smashing the Imperial Navy, but if his mission had been a simple strike to break the Empire's spirit, then he had gotten himself a much more protracted conflict than he had bargained for.

Captain Essenton of the *Defiant* reported that they had located a second yammosk. She requested permission to target it, and Pellaeon gave it to her. Keeping the pressure on was the most important thing right now, even if it meant opening up the planetary defense to attack. And the more they destroyed, the better their chances were of success. He could feel that the battle was nearing a turning point of some kind. He just hoped it would be in their favor.

Almost in response to his thoughts, Luke Skywalker's voice suddenly came over the receiver. "Admiral, I thought you might like to know that *Bonecrusher* is on its way back."

"And the mission?" he asked the Jedi Master hopefully.

"A success, I'm assuming," came the reply. "I spoke only briefly to Mara before they made the jump to hyperspace, but she seemed satisfied."

Skywalker, probably sensing the mood of the Imperial forces, had fallen back from the front line and docked his X-wing with *Widowmaker*. Watching from the bridge, he had had nothing but a calming effect on Yage's crew.

Pellaeon smiled. "In that case I imagine we'll soon be hearing from our Yuuzhan Vong friends."

"It would be a mistake to become overconfident right now, Admiral," Skywalker cautioned. "The Yuuzhan Vong aren't inclined to retreat, even when the odds are against them."

"They're not stupid, either," Pellaeon said. "If what you say is true, Shimrra simply can't afford to commit to a long campaign here, and Vorrik will know that. Disobeying orders may hurt him more in the long run than running away from a battle."

The Jedi Master didn't say anything to that, but the silence itself was revealing.

"I know what you're thinking," Pellaeon said softly. "Jacen told Moff Flennic that the Empire is nothing compared to the Galactic Alliance; that we're just a distraction. He was right, and that means I am right, too. Shimrra wants to intimidate us, not destroy us, and from Vorrik's point of view he has already achieved that objective. He's flattened Bastion; he's forced us to retreat to Borosk; and he'll probably take a swipe at the shipyards on the way out. He can make a good case that he's done his job."

Another whistle cut across the channel. "Broadcast from the enemy, sir," Captain Yage said.

"Put it over an open comm," Pellaeon said. "I want everyone to hear this."

"—will but delay the inevitable," Vorrik was saying, spitting out the words with even more than his usual bile. "There will be no mercy. None of you will be spared. Your homes will be razed and your remains will be used as fertilizer for our crops! Your worlds will be absorbed into the glorious Yuuzhan Vong empire as it engulfs the galaxy whole. You will—"

"Maybe I'm missing something, Vorrik," Pellaeon interrupted. "But I'm not seeing any evidence of this great plan of yours. We're destroying your yammosks; we've killed your spies; we're taking back those you thought were captives. You don't have the muscle to take *this* planet, let alone the others. Your threats are as empty as your boasts are shallow."

"You will eat those words when—"

"Empty," Pellaeon repeated over the commander's renewed tirade.

"—we turn your abominations into slag and—"

"Empty!"

"—grind every trace of you into the dust from which you were born!"

"*Empty*, Vorrik!" Pellaeon bellowed. The Yuuzhan Vong commander emitted a sound like that of a womp rat being strangled, but he didn't give him the chance to speak. "It's time for you to make good on your promises, Commander: either destroy us or get out!"

"By the gods of my people, infidel, I promise that you will choke on those words!"

"Maybe one day, Vorrik," Pellaeon said, "but not today. You really should have thought twice about this gambit of yours—especially if you didn't have the resources to pull it off in the first place." In the heartbeat between words he lost all hint of mockery and adopted a cold and serious tone. "We have no intentions of surrendering—not now, not ever. You may win the occasional battle against us, Vorrik, but the Empire will always strike back. That *I* promise *you*."

Vorrik began another howl of abuse that Pellaeon ignored. "You tell Shimrra from me that if he wants to get the job done, then he's going to have to send a much bigger fleet—and a more competent commander to oversee it."

He killed the line before Vorrik had the opportunity to say anything further, then relaxed into the soothing embrace of the bacta tank's fluids. He was happy with his handling of the Yuuzhan Vong commander, even if provoking Vorrik was a calculated risk. But his words had been as much for those in his own navy as for Vorrik. If the Yuuzhan Vong commander did decide to defy his orders and stay, Pellaeon wanted to make sure he had the entire navy behind him.

Thankfully, though, within moments of breaking contact, half of Vorrik's ships had begun to withdraw. The other half lay down a pattern of fire designed to deter the Imperial forces from taking advantage of the retreat. Pellaeon's commanders knew better than to jump right in, but they did make use of the opportunity to take the battle to the other side. Planetary turbolasers poured energy at the fleeing enemy, while the *Defiant* sent waves of confounding gravitational fluctuations into the mess of retreating ships. Squadron leaders, too, took advantage of every break in the rearguard action to sneak through and attack from behind.

Then the capital ships were entering hyperspace and the Yuuzhan Vong fleet was committed to withdrawal. The many views available through Pellaeon's breath mask showed Yuuzhan Vong vessels pouring out of the system in battle groups of various sizes. Some were as small as a cruiser analog with coralskippers firmly attached; others consisted of several capital ships flying in synchrony, coordinated by the yammosk still hiding in their midst.

Pellaeon watched them go with a feeling of relief that he knew he shouldn't indulge. He was no navigator, but he'd had plenty of experience at estimating the courses of ships entering hyperspace. Even without seeing the data, he could tell that the retreating fleet was heading to more than one destination.

"Where are they going?" he asked Yage.

"Initial vectors suggest that two-thirds of the fleet is heading out of Imperial territory."

"And the remaining third?"

"Are heading in the opposite direction," Yage said. "We can't obtain a precise fix, but we think they might be heading for—"

"Yaga Minor," he finished for her.

"It would appear so, sir," Yage said. "He probably

thinks he can get away with it while our forces are committed to mopping up here."

Pellaeon considered this for a moment before saying, "Have *Stalwart* press the attack. I'd like to keep their evacuation as undignified as possible. And I want *Relentless* and *Protector* on their way to Yaga Minor immediately. *Defiant* and *Peerless*, too. Flennic is going to need all the help he can get to keep those shipyards safe."

"What about *Right to Rule*, sir?"

Responsible in part for guarding *Widowmaker* and other tactical Imperial vessels, the ageing Star Destroyer had seen little battle from its position in the inner orbits of Borosk.

"It stays," Pellaeon said. "I have other plans for the old boat."

"Yes, sir."

When Yage had gone, Pellaeon opened a private channel with Luke Skywalker. "Well, Jedi," he said, "we did it."

"*You* did it," Skywalker came back. "I didn't do much more than watch, Admiral."

"Which was precisely what was needed," the Grand Admiral countered. He had no intention of allowing the Jedi Master to underrate his own part in this victory. "While we may never take orders from you, Skywalker, I think you have proven today that sometimes it works to our advantage to accept your help."

"The line between the two seems very fine, Admiral," Luke said.

Pellaeon smiled at the world-weary tone in the Jedi Master's voice. He was no stranger, either, to having to reconcile conflicting elements within his own people. Sometimes it took much more than a common enemy to bring old foes together—and although he had just won his first battle against the Yuuzhan Vong, he knew that the war was still waiting. The hardest part was yet to come.

"Indeed it does," he said somberly as he scanned overviews of the Yuuzhan Vong pullback. "Indeed it does."

Another squawk signaled a new entrant to the private channel. Pellaeon accepted it and heard the voice of Skywalker's nephew.

"This is *Braxant Bonecrusher*," Jacen Solo said from the makeshift bridge of the Dreadnaught. "We have a hold full of people requiring urgent medical attention. Please advise."

"*Bonecrusher*, this is *Widowmaker*," he heard Yage respond. "You are instructed to dock with medical supply platform *Hale Return*. Details to follow."

As the battle computers on the two vessels exchanged data, Pellaeon studied the Dreadnaught via long-range scanner. Battered by two successive rounds of enemy fire, its hull was literally smoking in places from where it had been punctured. He knew that part of the plan had been for the ship to give this appearance, but he could tell by the way it moved that some of the damage it had sustained was very real indeed.

"You took some hits," he said.

"No more than expected," said the young Jedi, playing down the severity of their condition. "The trick worked perfectly."

"Well done, Jacen," Luke said. "You did well—all of you."

There was a slight pause as Jacen examined the course data he had received and confirmed the battle droids' trajectory through the milling Imperial Navy.

"What happened to the war?" he asked, sounding both surprised and relieved.

"It went away," Pellaeon said sardonically.

"But not far," Luke added. "And not for long, either."

"Don't worry," Pellaeon continued. "We'll be ready for it when it comes back. The Yuuzhan Vong will rue the day they dragged me into this."

"Don't let your confidence over this one victory cloud your judgment, Admiral," Luke said. "The Yuuzhan Vong will not take this defeat lightly. This is just the beginning, I assure you."

Pellaeon didn't need to be cautioned. "I think you're right, my friend," he said, nodding in the bacta tank. "The beginning of their end."

The word quickly spread through the Fian squadrons, and despite their inexperience and a number of losses, the Y-wings were managing to score the occasional strike against the Yuuzhan Vong attackers. On one occasion, Jag barely had time to notice the skip on his tail before it was knocked out of the sky by a wave of fire from his port side.

"Nice shooting, Seven," he said in thanks, banking to warn off another skip that was trying to get on the Y-wing's own tail.

A barrage of weapons fire announced the arrival of *Pride of Selonia*, following on from a devastating pass over the nearest of the two empty slaveships that were making their way down to the planet to begin the harvesting of the Fian population. The bladder-shaped alien vessel had split along its back and burst like an overripe fruit, causing an ugly spillage of reddish fluid. Jag watched as thousands of tiny, flapping shapes—Yuuzhan Vong gnulliths—escaped from the massive rent in the slaveship, wriggling and dying in the vacuum like flash-frozen birds. Jaina and her Cerise Squadron friends sent a swarm of torpedoes arcing into the breach, then hurriedly retreated as the multiple explosions tore it to pieces.

"One down," she said triumphantly. It was good to hear the assertive tone return to her voice. "How're you doing, Jag?"

Jag returned his attention to the blastboat. It had turned about as though to withdraw, but he wasn't fooled. The Yuuzhan Vong weren't emotionally capable of accepting loss so gracefully. They were up to something, he was sure.

"It's got to be a ruse," he warned his wingmates. "Get too close and it'll—"

The warning came too late, though, as three Y-wings came in tight to strafe the underside of the listless vessel. All of a sudden the blastboat's dovin basals unleashed their combined energy. The flash that followed was so bright it seemed to turn the blastboat transparent before blasting it into atoms. The resulting shock wave took out the three Y-wings and seriously rattled a further five nearby.

Jag sighed once the shock wave had fully dissipated. "Sorry, Indigo," he said. "I should have warned you sooner."

"Not your fault, Twin Leader," Indigo Five reassured him after a slight pause. "We are sorely uneducated in the art of fighting Yuuzhan Vong. We have only ourselves to blame."

A reduced Indigo Squadron swung in to help Jaina finish off the remaining slaveship, while the combined Twin Suns and Reseda Squadrons quickly disposed of the remaining skips. In no time at all, the battle was over, and Jag allowed his grip on the ship's controls to finally relax.

When his heart rate had slowed and he was sure there were no more coralskippers about, Jag contacted the leader of the Galantos Y-wings.

"So tell me, Captain Syrtik," he said, "what happens when you go back? Will you be court-martialed for this?"

"That depends," the stoic Fia said. "Our charter is to protect Galantos from attack, but we are under the direct command of the councilor and his primates. If they charge us with defying a direct order—"

"But *is* that what you did?" Jaina broke in. "Did they really tell you not to help us?"

Jag noted the dangerous edge to Jaina's voice and said nothing. Emotions often ran high in the wake of a battle.

"It depends on how you define *order*," Syrtik said.

"I can't believe those space slugs," Jaina went on. "Here we are trying to save their skins and they have the nerve to—" The unfinished sentence resolved in a heavy sigh. "No, it can wait. But when Mom hears about this, there's going to be trouble."

"I think there's going to be trouble anyway," Jag said. "After all, they did try to keep her prisoner on Galantos—and they may have even intended to trade her for amnesty when the slaveships arrived."

There was nothing but silence down the line. Then on the scopes, Jag saw Jaina's battered X-wing empty its remaining torpedoes into the side of the single ruined slaveship, spraying its contents against the starry backdrop.

"Are you all right?" he sent to her along a private channel.

"No, I'm not all right," she snapped back. "I mean, why do we bother, Jag? What's the point of trying to defend these people when they insist on stabbing us in the back? It just doesn't make any sense!"

"I'm sure Miza would ask the same question, Jaina."

She was silent for a moment as the name of the dead Chiss pilot sunk in. "I'm acting like a child, aren't I?"

"Actually, you're acting like Jaina Solo—and that's nothing to be ashamed of, I assure you."

She laughed softly. "Thanks, Jag."

"Anytime." He glanced at his scopes. The Y-wing squadrons were already heading back to Galantos, their numbers reduced by roughly a quarter. *Selonia* was launching probe droids to investigate the wreckage of the slave-ships while the remainder of Twin Suns Squadron was slipping one by one into its docking bays.

"We have a lot to catch up on," he said. "Maybe we should dock and debrief in person."

She laughed again, and this time it seemed to come more naturally. "Why, that must be one of the most romantic things anyone has said to me in years."

He smiled, glad to hear her sounding more like her old self. "Then it's a date?"

"Sure," she said as her X-wing swung around to match course with his. "Why not?"

On the far side of the planet, well away from the action, the *Millennium Falcon* was slipping into the same orbit as the small yacht that had followed them up from the surface. Tahiri watched on silently from behind Anakin's parents, uncomfortable with the obvious tension in the cockpit. Han was still rankling over being outvoted after Tahiri had suggested they should try to find the yacht so they could learn more about the mystery man who had saved them. Han had wanted to go and join the battle with the others, and while Leia had said she would have liked to have done this also, she ultimately had sided with Tahiri.

"We're a diplomatic mission," she had argued in the face of Han's tight-lipped resistance. "And if diplomacy means retreating from a fight—or cowering around the back side of a planet, as you so eloquently put it—then *that's* what we have to do."

"But they need our help," Han had protested. It was obvious he didn't have much of an argument. He just preferred the fighting to the diplomacy.

"Twin Suns Squadron and Captain Mayn are more than capable of dealing with a small contingent of Yuuzhan Vong," Leia said. Then, more softly and with a reassuring hand on her husband's shoulder, she added, "Besides, in a war, diplomacy can be just as important as aggression. You'd be surprised at just how many deals are done under circumstances like this."

"I thought it was this very kind of thing that made you want to get out of politics," he said, glowering at the controls as he brought the *Falcon* around.

Leia sighed, tired of trying to make him see reason. "Only one of the reasons, Han," she returned.

Before he could respond, she had turned her attention back to the scanners. Tahiri knew that the argument was over. Leia was a strong-willed individual, and she wasn't the kind to waste time bickering with her husband over something that, as far as she was concerned, had been resolved.

Noticing the growing tension in the cockpit, C-3PO had taken it upon himself at that moment to leave, dismissing himself with the flimsy excuse that his activators needed calibrating. Tahiri suspected, though, that this was a standard excuse the golden droid used whenever things got too uncomfortable between his human owners. Tahiri wished she had a similar excuse. If she hadn't been needed, she might have slipped off as well. Her senses were swimming disturbingly after the elation on the landing field and their escape. She felt light-headed, peculiar . . .

Keep it together, she told herself, doing her best to concentrate on real things, not illusions.

Traffic over the planet was light, so finding the yacht wasn't going to prove too difficult. Ion trails led from a hundred or so launches to upper orbit. It was relatively easy to rule out the fighters and the large freighters. Only a handful remained in tight and low, waiting for rendezvous. Tahiri knew instinctively, through the Force, that the being who had rescued them would be waiting for them, as he'd said he would be. Although she didn't know what he had to say, his mention of the Peace Brigade had convinced her that he knew what he was talking about and that they should hear him out. The silver totem she had found in the diplomatic quarters was missing from her pocket, but it was proof that the Yuuzhan Vong had obviously been involved for a while. The arrival of the slaveships wasn't just a coincidence, she was sure.

The fact that she had responded so strongly to the totem still disturbed her. Its presence—or the past presence of its owner, at least—troubled her, nagging as it did at the back of her mind. It surprised her, too. She hadn't realized that she was so sensitive to echoes of the Yuuzhan Vong. Instead of fading away, as she had fervently hoped it would, the nagging was only getting stronger.

No, she told herself firmly, shaking her head and focusing on the task at hand. Reaching out with the Force, she sought any sign of the person she had recognized on the Al'solib'minet'ri City landing field. Then . . .

"There," she said, pointing. The small Corellian craft was hugging the upper atmosphere below. Shell-like in shape, with several small blister ports sprouting thrusters and rudimentary shield generators but no apparent armaments, its engines were silent. "That's it."

"Are you sure?" Han asked. He still sounded moody.

She nodded, feeling with the Force again. "As sure as I can be."

"Millennium Falcon," crackled a voice out of the subspace communicator. It was the same voice Tahiri had heard back on the landing field. "Hailing *Millennium Falcon.*"

"Yeah, we hear you," Han said. "Mind telling us who you are?"

"A friend," came the reply.

"Let us be the ones to decide that."

"Do we know you?" Leia asked.

"We have never met, but you know my kind," the being said. That he wasn't human was becoming increasingly clear to Tahiri, although she couldn't quite pin down his species. There was a faint singsong quality to the voice that she'd heard before, although she couldn't for the life of her remember where.

"What kind is that?" Han asked.

"I apologize for the reception you received on Galantos," the voice pressed on, ignoring the question. "There was nothing I could do to prevent it. I would have warned you when you arrived, had I known in advance you were coming, but by the time I found a way into the diplomatic rooms you were already imprisoned. I had to wait for an opportunity to help you more overtly and a time when it no longer mattered if my cover was blown."

"You're a spy?" Leia asked.

"Not exactly," said the mystery voice. "But I can help you."

"We're already in your debt," Tahiri said.

"Any debt you may have had with me, Tahiri Veila, was cleared when you helped me escape," he said. "And we hold the Solos in high regard for the many times they've helped us in the past. So no, there is no debt. I am simply glad to have met you—and to have made a difference."

"What can you tell us about Galantos?" Leia asked. "Jaina says that the Yevetha are destroyed. Is that correct?"

"Fian probes to N'zoth confirmed that the Yevethan shipyards have been destroyed, but they didn't stick around to look any deeper. The Fia are deeply afraid of their neighbors; what happened here twelve years ago traumatized their culture. The Yevetha may have been routed almost to the last ship by the New Republic, but they were still there, in the cluster, and the Fia always knew that one day they would emerge to try again. Last time the Fia survived, thanks to the help of the New Republic; this time, however, the New Republic might not be able to defend them."

"And the fear of the Yevetha returning would only have grown as the Yuuzhan Vong crisis deepened," Leia put in.

"Exactly. The Fia aren't by nature a warlike species, and they knew their feeble attempts to arm themselves would never be sufficient. If the New Republic lost, who would protect Galantos from the Koornacht Cluster? So when a group approached them a year ago, promising to end the Yevethan threat, you can imagine how very tempting an offer it was."

"This is where the Peace Brigade comes in, right?" Tahiri asked, fighting the disorientation in her mind to concentrate on the conversation. "Resources in exchange for safety."

"That's right. The Peace Brigade took minerals they needed for exchange with other parties, and N'zoth was destroyed—taken by surprise, thanks to the tactical information the Fia gave the Brigaders, who in turn passed it on to the Vong commanders. That way, the Fia hoped to ensure their own safety by dealing with the Peace Brigade. After all, they feared the Yevetha much more than they feared the Yuuzhan Vong, who have yet to make significant impact on this side of the galaxy. That seemed to be it. Galantos was safe at last."

"All without our knowledge," Leia said.

"Courtesy of the communications blackout."

"Was that also part of the deal with the Peace Brigade? Galantos cutting itself off from the New Republic?"

"Yes."

"But why?" Tahiri asked.

"For fear of reprisals," the stranger replied.

"From the Peace Brigade?"

"From the New Republic. You don't take kindly to those who consort with the enemy."

"With good reason," Han said. "I can't believe we spent so much energy trying to save a bunch of mass murderers from a fate they probably deserve. If we hadn't come along when we did, the Fia would be crated up in one of those slaveships right now and headed for one of the occupied worlds. We should have left them to it."

"You don't mean that, Han," Leia said.

"Don't tell me you're going to forgive them for what they did." Han looked as though he couldn't believe what he was hearing. "The Yevetha don't know how to lose. They're as bad as the Vong in that respect—or were, anyway. They would've fought to the last, and the Fia knew it. That makes them as guilty of genocide as the Yuuzhan Vong."

"The Fia were manipulated into it," Leia said. "The Yevetha would have quite happily destroyed the Fia—and all of us, too, for that matter—but I never once heard you advocate their slaughter. The Fia are as much victims in this as anyone else."

"They sure would've been," Han said bitterly, "if we hadn't come by when we did."

"People do stupid things, Han." Leia's lips were thin and white, as though she was keeping her own anger in check. "I'm not saying that I approve of the Fia and their actions, or that I'm not angry at how they treated us. It's just that I can understand them, their fear of losing everything. The Yuuzhan Vong wanted slaves and information on potential threats. The Fia gave them both by pointing out the Yevetha. They also set themselves up as a slave target by getting complacent and cutting themselves off from their allies. But that doesn't make them our enemy. No one deserves to be enslaved, no matter what they've done. We're here to reopen communications and save lives, not here to cast judgment over who *deserves* to live or die."

Han reluctantly acknowledged the point with a grunt.

"Then we showed up," Tahiri said, made uncomfortable by the argument. She felt oddly threatened when Anakin's parents nagged at each other. "Tipped off by you, I presume. A message found its way into the *Falcon*'s computers, telling us where to go."

"Yes," said the voice on the other end of the line. "I had been trying to get word out of the system for some time, but there was no way to tell if I had succeeded. Obviously, I had, and it was acted on at your end. When you arrived, Councilor Jobath panicked and sent an underling to spare him the difficulty of meeting you face to face. Primate Persha also panicked and in turn lumbered you with an assistant. I'm sure Thrum would have liked to find someone else to palm you off onto, as well, but he was the bottom of the ladder, and he handled the situation accordingly. Because you were able to explore the city and seek vital clues, you were soon on the way to guessing the truth."

"It also gave you the opportunity to get closer to us," Leia said.

"That's right," he said. "At first I was able only to leave a note in your escort's flight computer, but I had limited time and I could not explain myself properly. Then when the Yuuzhan Vong arrived, security was tightened even more. The Fia thought the slaveship was just a freighter come to take more resources."

"Except *they* were the resources," Han said with a shake of his head.

"Yes."

"I have to admit," Leia said, "it's a clever plan. The Yuuzhan Vong are stretched too thin to take this region by force. Instead, they rely upon factions within to do half their work for them. It's efficient and deadly—and I don't dare assume that this is the only place they've tried this tactic."

"That *would* be an incorrect assumption, Princess." The voice over the comm was grimly serious. "There are numerous communications blackouts in place in this quarter of the galaxy. Your intelligence networks are aware of many of these—hence your mission. What is difficult to tell is which ones are innocent, and which ones are the work of the Peace Brigade and the Yuuzhan Vong. In some places, the answer is known after the fact, when it's too late. Rutan and its moon Senali, for instance, were politically divided by the Peace Brigade well over a year ago. A few months afterward, the Senali were wiped out by a Yuuzhan Vong force that subsequently turned its guns on the Rutanians and enslaved half the population."

"Rutan was on our list," Leia said to Han.

"Is Belderone?" the pilot asked.

"Yes, actually, it is," she answered.

"Well, thanks to the Yuuzhan Vong, the Firrerreos are now a dead species," he said. "And the Belderonians won't be far behind."

"How could you possibly know all this?" Han asked. "If communications have been down in these places—not to mention here—I don't see how you could have the faintest idea of what's going on."

"Don't you?" There was a distinct smile in the stranger's voice.

"You knew what our mission was without us telling you," Tahiri said.

"And you were able to infiltrate the *Falcon*'s computers on Mon Calamari," Leia added. "Who *are* you people?"

"If I tell you, you won't believe me. Not yet, anyway."

"Try us," Han said, his voice pitched low to indicate that refusal wasn't an option.

The pilot of the yacht chuckled. "Suffice it to say that I'm part of a network. We're not spies, but we do keep an eye on what goes on around us. We have a knack for getting into the places we need to be, and we tend not to be noticed. We don't work for anyone except ourselves, and we don't sell the information we collect; we don't, therefore, pose a threat to anyone except those who try to harm us. We simply gather knowledge."

"But what are you in it for?" Han asked. "What do you stand to gain from it all, if you don't sell the information?"

"I'd be lying if I said that we stood to gain nothing but the satisfaction of helping others." Again, the hint of a smile. "The truth is, we do it to look out for ourselves. We aren't highly trained soldiers or professional warriors. We're not spies, as I've already said. We are, in fact, the sort who get caught between opposing armies, and are squashed as a result. That's partly how we can do the things that spies and soldiers can't do—like get information into and out of regions like this one, where all but the least likely are closely inspected. Neither you nor the Yuuzhan Vong notices us. We are invisible and everywhere. Not much gets by us that we want to hear."

"So why are you helping *us*?" Han asked.

"Because, at the moment, peace in the galaxy revolves around the health of your new Galactic Alliance. And because we're in a position now to actively help you. It's taken us some time to reach this point, but now that we have, you can feel free to assume that we are on your side."

"For the moment," Han added.

"Yes, Captain Solo: for the moment. And as of *this* moment, I must make my way out of this system and file a report while you must choose your next destination."

"Wait," Leia said. "Before you go, I don't suppose you'd be able to help us with that decision? . . ."

Han shot Leia a sharp look. He hadn't been happy about having the first leg of their journey determined by an anonymous note, and he obviously wasn't enamored with the idea of taking further instructions from cryptic strangers.

"You and your people helped us once before," Leia went on, ignoring her husband. "You've exposed an enemy tactic we hadn't identified before. If you have any more advice for us, we'd be glad to hear it."

"Very well," said the pilot of the yacht. "Where were you thinking of going?"

"We hadn't discussed it," Leia said. "I was considering Belsavis. There have been communications problems there in recent months, and it has a history of conflict that the Yuuzhan Vong could take advantage of."

"The Senex and Juvex sectors would be prime targets, it's true, but it may already be too late there. There might be little else for you to do but clean up the mess. More good could be done by going somewhere in the early stages of corruption. That way, at least, you may be able to prevent the situation from developing into anything too serious."

"That's *if* you're right," Han said. "But how do we know you aren't just sending us on some wild gundark hunt? I mean, you could be a member of the Peace Brigade yourself: you're a covert infiltrator; you're part of a galactic conspiracy. This could all just be some sort of elaborate scheme to put us off the scent. The next place you send us could be—"

"A thousand times worse than here," the pilot finished for him. "Yes, Captain Solo, it could be. And in fact it probably will be, for the place I'm suggesting you travel to is Bakura."

"Bakura?" Han echoed. "Are you telling me—?"

"I'm not telling you anything," the pilot cut in again. "In truth, I know little. The information we have gathered there is scant, and many of my normal channels of information have been cut, along with the routes your spies would normally use. This makes us concerned. If the Ssi-ruuvi Imperium is active again, using this time of distraction to make a move on the life forces of the galaxy as it did once before, then it could be serious. They've had a long time to amass a new battle droid army, and to perfect their entrenchment technology."

There was a moment's silence as those in the *Falcon's* crew contemplated the stranger's words. Tahiri was too young to remember the trouble with the Ssi-ruuk, but she'd certainly been taught about it. As xenophobic as the Yevetha, having evolved under similar circumstances in the heart of an isolated star cluster, the reptilian aliens had only just been driven back by the New Republic with the unexpected assistance of the Chiss. Their techniques of mind control and entechment rivaled those of the Yuu-zhan Vong in terms of horror and agony. The peaceful world of Bakura stood between the rest of the galaxy and the Ssi-ruuvi Imperium and had fallen afoul of the aliens once before.

Tahiri didn't know if the Yuuzhan Vong could surprise the Ssi-ruuk in sufficient force to wipe them out, as they had the Yevetha. The Ssi-ruuk had indeed had longer to recover, and had been stronger to start with. If the Ssi-ruuk were able to use entechment to fuel their ships with Yuuzhan Vong life force—or if the Yuuzhan Vong found a way to exploit the same technology . . .

She shuddered. The question of whether the Yuuzhan Vong had a connection to the Force was still open, and she doubted that they would use any sort of *machine* in their quest for domination, but the idea of any sort of marriage between the two hate-filled species filled her with a terrible dread.

Keep it together, she reminded herself. *Don't lose it now.*

"Thank you," Leia said eventually. She had gone slightly pale. "We're grateful for your assistance."

"Yeah," Han added, his defensive skepticism firmly in place. "We'll take it under advisement."

"Will there be someone there like you?" Tahiri asked.

"Someone will contact you," came the reply.

"Who?"

"Someone. Like I said, we are everywhere."

Indices on the local space scopes began to flash; the yacht was warming up its ion drives, preparing to leave.

"Will you at least give us your name?" Tahiri asked.

"Be patient, young Jedi," the stranger said. "We will sing your song one day soon."

Before Tahiri could ask what he meant, the line went dead, and the yacht was heading out of the planet's gravity well.

Tahiri registered Han's snort of annoyance, but it was almost buried under a realization prompted by the stranger's farewell combined with the sound of his voice and the smell she had noted on the landing field. *We will sing your song . . .*

"He's a Ryn!" she exclaimed.

"A Ryn?" Han echoed incredulously. "He can't be."

"He is. I swear it."

"But what's one of them doing in the spy game? They'd stick out like sore thumbs!"

"I guess," said Leia, watching the retreating yacht as it accelerated and vanished into hyperspace, "we're just going to have to find out for ourselves. . . ."

PART FOUR

CONSCRIPTION

It was amazing, Jaina, thought, just how quickly governments could jump when they wanted to.

Within five hours of the destruction of the two slaveships, not only was the link to the nearest deep space transceiver open again, allowing information to once more flow freely into Galantos from the local subspace network, but Councilor Jobath had emerged from his pressing business on the far side of the planet, professing his deep and undying loyalty to the Galactic Alliance.

Jaina could imagine her father's reaction to that. Her mother would have no doubt shared his sentiments, too, but hid her feelings beneath a more gracious and temperate response. Her parents worked well that way, maintaining a pretense guaranteed on the one hand to intimidate the most ingratiating of local governors, but at the same time capable of wooing them without actually using force.

Jaina hadn't seen the exchange, though. After docking with *Pride of Selonia* and having a few minor bruises treated, she had retired to one of the frigate's berths and slept solidly for almost five hours. It had been cramped and uncomfortable, but it was better than trying to sleep upright in her X-wing—even though she'd had hundreds of hours practice doing just that over the years.

In her deep sleep she had dreamed fitfully of Anakin's last mission to the worldship around Myrkr to destroy the voxyn queen, as well as the cold fury she had felt upon his death that had turned her, for a time, to the dark side. While her body rested, her mind relived the fear that Jacen, too, had died, and the aftertaste of *that* awful grief she would carry with her for the rest of her life, she was sure.

But even as she was dreaming, she found herself wondering: *Why now? Why here? What is the dream trying to tell—?*

She woke with a start, sucking air in sharply as a hand gripped her shoulder and shook.

"What—?" She rolled over, eyes blinking open to peer up at the dark blur leaning over her.

"Relax, Jaina, it's just me." Through the haze of sleep she recognized Jag's solid, calming presence as he sat down on the edge of the narrow bunk beside her.

"Jag?" She sat up, brushing loose strands of hair back from her face. She yawned, knuckling her eyes. "You want to be careful, you know. People will talk."

"Let them," he said. "Besides, you *do* know where you are, don't you?"

It sank in then that she wasn't in her quarters on Mon Calamari, but instead tucked into a space in a communal bunkroom, with little more than a flimsy curtain separating her bunk from the fifteen other identical beds. She had a better chance of finding a Kowakian monkey-lizard at the helm of a starship than of getting any privacy here.

"Why are you waking me up?" she asked after orienting herself. "Has anything happened?"

"No," he said, laughing. "You requested a standard field nap, and I volunteered to do the dirty work when time came to wake you up. It was my opinion that the duty officer should be spared the grisly business." He smiled. "I don't see why he should get to have all the fun."

Her mouth half opened to snap a retort, but the unexpected compliment threw her for a second. Then she shook her head and smiled also. "What do you really want, Jag? If it's a rematch on the dueling mat, then you're going to have to at least give me a minute or two to wake up properly."

He laughed again. "Actually, I came to bring you some news," he said. "About Jacen."

"Jacen?" The last vestiges of sleep vanished; she sat up fully, alarm spiking at the back of her brain. Was *this* why those memories had surfaced? "Tell me," she grated.

Jag did tell her. She learned of Councilor Jobath's turn-around and the reopening of communications. Although she was relieved that the situation on Galantos had been so easily rectified, that was nothing compared to the news that had been relayed from Mon Calamari, once they had regained contact. The Yuuzhan Vong invasion of the Empire had been successfully resisted. After the destruction of Bastion, Imperial forces had successfully turned the invaders back at Borosk and were at the moment forcing them to fight a rearguard action as they retreated. Mara and Luke's mission had been instrumental in the victory, supplying tactics and pivotal aid where required. Rumor had it that they may even have saved Grand Admiral Pellaeon's life in the process.

And Jacen was fine. A moment's examination of the part of her that resonated with her twin would have told her that there was nothing wrong with him. No matter how far apart they were—and at that moment there was more than half a galaxy between them—she would always know if he was in trouble.

She nudged Jag off the bunk, and he turned his back to her as she slid out from under the covers. Jaina quickly slipped her flight uniform on over her underclothes, silently promising herself a serious shower at the earliest opportunity. "You can turn around now."

"Where are you planning to go?" he asked. "You're still off duty, remember? Your parents are asleep. Your fighter is being repaired."

She faced him, hands on hips. "Then why wake me in the first place? Couldn't that news have waited until I had woken up by myself?"

"Well, I just thought—" He fell silent, clearly embarrassed.

"Maybe you really did want that rematch," she said lightly. Then she took his arm and led him out of the crew quarters. "For now, though, let's just walk, okay? Even if it's only as far as the mess. I've a feeling I'm going to be ravenous once all of me wakes up."

She was right; barely had they entered the cramped main access corridor running along the spine of the frigate when her stomach began to rumble and she had a terrible craving for one of the altha protein drinks Lando Calrissian had taught her to enjoy when she was younger. *Pride of Selonia*'s cook droid had a limited repertoire, however, and she had to settle for a bowl of bland, glutinous nutrient soup and a glass of flavored water.

Jag, sipping from a steaming mug, filled in some of the blanks while she ate. She learned about the proposed next stop to Bakura, and the mysterious source of that information. The source was a completely unknown quantity, and it concerned her that her parents were taking such a decision on faith. Their experiences with the Ryn called Droma and his family weren't enough to ease her mind regarding the trustworthiness of the entire species. Given that the mysterious stranger wasn't Droma—and Tahiri assured them that he wasn't—there was still a big question mark over his motivation. If it was a genuine lead, then acting on it quickly could save a great many lives. And if it was a trap, at least they wouldn't be going in blind. She couldn't really imagine the Bakurans allying themselves with the Yuuzhan Vong or the Peace Brigade, though; not given all they owed to the New Republic and the Jedi.

"What about Syrtik?" she asked when Jag had finished updating her. "What's happened to him?"

Jag's pale green eyes seemed to glint with amusement. "Would you believe he's been nominated for a military honor? Jobath has been really on the spot. Syrtik's a national hero, the people love him, but at the end of the day he did disobey orders not to get involved. Jobath has to go along with it to save face, but he certainly doesn't like it." He shrugged. "So everything turned out for the best in the end, eh?"

"Not for the Yevetha, it didn't," she said, distractedly scooping some of the soup onto her spoon.

His expression sobered. "I know; I'm sorry. I read your report. It's brief but to the point."

Jaina vividly remembered the last words of the Yevethan pilot before he blew up his ship, preferring death—not only for himself, but for his species—rather than be rescued by aliens and become contaminated.

Run from them if you like, he had said about the Yuuzhan Vong, the destroyers of his civilization, *but it will do you no good. There is no safety anywhere.*

Even though the tide had turned for the Galactic Alliance, the war had been so long and they had lost so much that she sometimes found it easy to believe that the galaxy would never know peace again. And even if it did, it was unlikely that life in it would ever be the same, no matter what the outcome.

"I'm sorry about Miza," she said, regretting her snap assessment of the Chiss pilot's shortcomings. What had she known about him, really? Nothing, except that he'd flown well and occasionally irritated her. She didn't know how old he was, if he had family back home, or whether he had someone special who would mourn him. She didn't even know if he and Jag had been friends, but she felt the urge to tell him she was sorry anyway, because she *was* sorry.

"It wasn't your fault, Jaina," Jag said. His hand came over the top of hers in a gesture of reassurance.

"Falling afoul of an ambush while simply trying to help someone," she said, shaking her head sadly. "It seems like such an inglorious way to die."

"I don't think there are necessarily any *good* ways to die, Jaina."

"He'll be missed, won't he?" she asked.

"Of course," he said. "For his good points as well as his bad."

Jaina nodded. "And now the squad is one short."

"After only our first mission, too," he said somberly. "Not a good start, is it?"

She turned her hand beneath his, locking their fingers together and squeezing. He squeezed back, but with obvious reservations. She sighed, feeling guilty for having ruined the good mood he'd been in.

"I'm sure everything will be okay, Jag," she said. "I know this is a strange way to run a squadron, but once we've ironed out the bugs—"

"That's not what concerns me, Jaina," he said. "I actually think we work well together. But if what your mother says is true, if the Vong have been reopening old wounds in order to exploit the aftereffects ..." He trailed off uncomfortably.

"What, Jag?"

"Well ..." He shrugged and pulled his hand away from hers. There was something on his mind; she didn't need the Force to see that. "It may be nothing, but the New Republic and the Chiss haven't always been on the best of terms. After Thrawn—"

"Thrawn was an Imperial. We know the difference."

"But to *us* he was a Chiss, Jaina. The Expansionary Defense Fleet has been struggling for decades to protect our borders. Using the Empire as a tool, Thrawn made more progress in a few years than all the others combined. Yes, he may have overreached at the end, but still, when the New Republic finally defeated him, there were many among us who mourned. That's partly why we tend to side with the Empire. It's not just because we're closer to them than we are to you along most of our borders. There's still resentment."

"You're telling me the Chiss might work with the Yuuzhan Vong against us?"

Jag shrugged. "No, I'm not saying that. There will always be some who would rather hear a convincing lie than an uncomfortable truth. The right words in the wrong ears might have repercussions for the Galactic Alliance."

"Great." She pushed her bowl of soup aside, her appetite suddenly spoiled. "And that's Uncle Luke's next stop, after the Empire."

"I'm sorry," he said, looking down awkwardly at his hands. "It's probably nothing. I didn't really want to worry you about it."

There was something in the way he said this that made her study him more closely. "But there's something I *should* be worried about, isn't there?"

He glanced up, and she could see the uncertainty in his eyes. Without saying a word, he removed something from his pocket and placed it on the table between them.

Jaina felt her stomach frost the moment she looked down and saw it. The last time she had seen anything like this had been on the worldship around Myrkr, before Anakin had died. There had been Yuuzhan Vong temples there, some larger than most cities; each had featured gruesome effigies to their cruel and insatiable gods. One in particular stood out. In her worst nightmares, like the one she'd recently awakened from, she saw a particular face looming at her out of the dark, graven from coral slabs that rose scores of meters high into the air.

The fact that this particular image was made from a silvery bonelike substance and was barely larger than her thumb didn't matter. The face was the same: it was Yun-Yammka, the Slayer.

Jaina looked up at Jag; he was watching her closely.

"Where did you get this?" she asked, unable to keep the anger and disgust from her voice. It took all of her effort to resist snatching the thing from the table and throwing it down a garbage chute. It was an abomination, an incitement to horror. As far as she was concerned, no sane individual would ever want to own such a thing. "Where did it come from?"

There was no escaping the accusation in her tone.

"It came from Tahiri," he said with some apology. "She dropped it when she collapsed on Galantos."

The frost quickly spread to Jaina's heart, and for the longest time she didn't know what to say.

The coufee came up so quickly that Shoon-mi didn't even have a chance to see it. With the blade across his throat, he was dragged back into the crack leading from the anonymous sub-basement to the access tunnel that led deeper into the underground.

"Who has betrayed us?" hissed a voice in his ear. "Who sent the warriors to kill I'pan and Niiriit?"

Shoon-mi flailed wildly but was unable to break free. The blade of the coufee was so sharp he didn't even realize it had cut him until he felt the blood trickling down his chest. He stopped wriggling, then, panting heavily and fearfully.

"Kunra!" he called out, but the word came out as barely more than a gasp.

The shamed warrior stood nearby in the center of the basement, unmoved by Shoon-mi's plea for assistance. Instead of coming to his help, Kunra merely folded his arms across his chest to watch coldly.

"Who has betrayed us?" Shoon-mi's attacker repeated, allowing the coufee to bite a little deeper into the flesh.

"It wasn't me!" Shoon-mi cried desperately, realizing that no one would be coming to his aid. "I swear it wasn't!"

In an instant the coufee was gone, and a knee in his back pushed him sprawling to the ground. He pressed at the cut on his throat with his hand, fearful that his lifeblood was flowing away.

"You'll live," growled the one who had cut him. The figure stepped from the shadows to loom over him. The coufee was held menacingly by his side, its blade darkened with Shoon-mi's blood. "And you will tell me what you know."

Shoon-mi stared up into the horrible, one-eyed visage. "Amorrn?" His voice trembled.

Nom Anor nodded slowly, pinching the coufee blade between two fingers and wiping the blood from it. "But this is no time for reacquainting ourselves," he said. "You have ten seconds to tell me what I want to hear, or this blade will open your veins and drink from your filthy—"

"It wasn't me, I swear!" the Shamed One repeated frantically. "It wasn't any of us! The warriors weren't looking for Niiriit or the others. They were looking for thieves! Supplies had gone missing and they guessed that one of the underground groups was responsible. Yours was the third they hit that night. They wiped all of them out. Not just you; not just Niiriit. We didn't know in advance so we couldn't warn you. It happened too quickly." Shoon-mi scrabbled desperately backward in the dirt as Nom Anor loomed over him. "I'm telling you the truth! Please . . ."

"We're making too much noise," said Kunra, who still hadn't moved.

Nom Anor ignored him. "Just thieves?" he hissed. "Nothing to do with the heresy? Nothing to do with *me*?"

"No, just thieves." Shoon-mi continued to back away from Nom Anor. "I wouldn't lie to you, Amorrn. I'm telling the truth!"

The coufee disappeared as Nom Anor fixed the whimpering Shamed One with a look of distaste. "Do not ever call me that again," he said. "It is a name that belongs to someone else."

Weak with relief, Shoon-mi slumped against a wall while his attacker moved away to think.

Not the heresy. Not me . . . Nom Anor's mind spun. All through their long ascent to the basement levels, he had felt safe assuming that the attack had been politically motivated—if not against him then certainly against the ideas I'pan was propagating. Kunra had set up the meeting with Shoon-mi as a first attempt to find out who had betrayed them. And when they knew who it was, Nom Anor would have killed without hesitation.

But if he hadn't been betrayed, if the attack had simply

been a case of bad luck, then that changed everything. Neither the heresy nor he was being actively hunted. He could breathe easier for a while, could stop imagining regiments of warriors at every turn, waiting to ambush him. He could pause long enough to think and decide what needed to be done next.

He almost chuckled aloud at the irony. The warriors might not have been hunting him specifically, but it was still he who had brought death to Niiriit and the others. He and I'pan had been stealing with some regularity from the upper levels, using access codes he remembered from his years as an executor. The thefts, clearly, had not gone unnoticed, and the killing party had been sent in to the underground to mop up anyone likely to be responsible. He had brought death down upon those who had saved his life just as surely as the warriors who had actually wielded the amphistaffs.

He looked at Kunra. Through the gloom he could see the ex-warrior's stoic expression, and wondered if behind that impassive stare he wasn't coming to the same conclusions.

Nom Anor stepped forward and extended a hand to Shoon-mi, who eyed it uncertainly for a moment before nervously taking it and allowing himself to be helped to his feet. Resisting the powerful urge to stab Shoon-mi through the heart, then dispatch Kunra just as quickly, Nom Anor manufactured an expression of relief and let it wash over him.

"We are safe, then," he said, speaking as much to Kunra as to Shoon-mi. "If what you say is true, then the warriors won't be hunting us. As long as the thefts cease, we should be able to live unharmed. Yes?"

"There have been no more thefts," said Shoon-mi, nodding. "The way of the *Jeedai* is safe. No one has betrayed us—and no one will! You have seen yourself the way we spread the message. You know that we are careful who we choose to hear it. The word is safe."

The Message. Nom Anor paced across the room, conscious of Kunra's eyes tracking him every step of the way. He had heard the Jedi heresy referred to as *the message* on occasions before and thought it a suitable euphemism. Whichever word was being obscured—*Jedi, insurrection, hope*—the nature of it was the same. The message was anathema to Shimrra, and that was all that mattered to Nom Anor.

But it was becoming increasingly clear to him that at this rate the message would never reach Shimrra directly. It had been irrelevant to the warriors who had attacked the communities in the underworld of Yuuzhan'tar; heretics, if the warriors even knew they existed, ranked lower than thieves in terms of priorities. For the message—as well as Nom Anor—to reach Shimrra, it would have to break out of the underground, and it would have to do it soon.

"Perhaps we are too careful," he said, thinking aloud and testing their responses as he spoke. "We hold our revelations close to our chests, much like the priests guard their secrets. We hide the light under cloaks of fear and timidity so that no one else may see it. As long as we continue preaching to the converted, we will never grow, never be strong like the Jedi are strong. The millions like us who deserve to know that there is a better way to live, a freedom that counters everything we have ever been taught—they will remain forever in the darkness. Perhaps the time has come, my friends, to shine our light into the darkness."

Shoon-mi looked even more nervous than before. "But if we speak openly about the *Jeedai*, we will be killed!"

"You're right, Shoon-mi," Nom Anor said, turning to face him in the shadows. "We *would* be killed. Therefore we must find new ways to spread the message, to recruit new followers. But we must expand only through the ranks of the Shamed Ones before we dare take our message higher up. As we stand now, we are weak and poorly organized; we will never make a difference like this. We must find strength and take our fate into our own hands—and when we are strong, then we may break free." He came to stand in front of Shoon-mi and placed his hands on his shoulders. The Shamed One continued to tremble beneath his grip. "To gain everything, my friend, we must *risk* everything." His one eye bored deep into Shoon-mi's own eyes until the Shamed One had to turn away in discomfort. "Are you with me?" Nom Anor whispered close to Shoon-mi's ear.

The Shamed One nodded uneasily. "I-I shall do what I can, of course," he said. "I don't know how to fight, but I do know lots of people."

"Good," Nom Anor said, nodding and smiling his pleasure at the Shamed One's response. "That is indeed good. Word of mouth is our greatest weapon right now." He turned to face Kunra. "And what of yourself? Are you with us, too?"

The ex-warrior's eyes glistened in the gloom. This was the crucial moment, Nom Anor knew. If Kunra defied him, he would have to kill both of them and start again from scratch, finding and infiltrating another cell of heretics to turn to his vengeful cause. He might never find one so perfectly primed for the task.

The ex-warrior hesitated, shuffling uncertainly from foot to foot.

"Decide," Nom Anor prompted as he placed a hand inside his robes. Almost eagerly, the pommel of the coufee found his fingers.

Kunra's gaze fell to the robe as he nodded slowly. "I am with you," he said. "For Niiriit and I'pan, and for all of those who have died, I am with you."

But not for me, Nom Anor thought. It didn't matter, though. The ex-warrior's compliance would be enough for now. The task ahead of him would be difficult, and he needed all the help he could get, in whatever spirit it was offered. The heresy as it presently existed was disorganized and internally inconsistent, and would never get any farther than the Shamed Ones. He would need to give it momentum if it was to serve his purposes. Several circular references had developed through numerous retellings; some stories took place on different planets, with different names, at different times. He would need to refine the tale so it suited his needs best, and spread it efficiently enough so it would eradicate the other versions, if only by sheer volume.

It was a long shot, he knew, but it was the only one he had. Nom Anor had dealt with religious fervor before, on Rhommamool, and he knew how to turn a smoldering thought into flames of resistance. But did he dare do it among the Yuuzhan Vong, his own species? This was rank heresy, after all. The Jedi, no matter what good they might do for the Shamed Ones, were still *machine users*. His conscience—atrophied though it had been by years of treachery—continued to nag at him.

But not for long. He had tried unsuccessfully to climb the social ladder imposed by Shimrra, despite being resourceful and intelligent. If he was ever to succeed, he would have to find another way to climb that same ladder that had refused to let him ascend.

Shoon-mi began to say something, snapping him out of his thoughts. "Amorrn—"

"I told you not to call me that!" he snapped. He had

told Kunra that a time would come when he would need to choose a new name; perhaps that time had come now. He needed one to carry him in this new direction.

Shoon-mi took an anxious step back. "Then—then what should we call you?"

Nom Anor thought about this for a moment. What name *should* he choose? Certainly one that would symbolize the work he needed to do in order to ensure his survival, and one that Shimrra would recognize also.

He smiled, then, at a thought. There was a word from an ancient tongue, rarely spoken except in the older worldships. It had connotations for all castes, no matter which god they worshiped. Its meaning was an unmistakable stab at Shimrra, and would be recognized as such by the Shamed Ones he would have to rely on to make the dream possible.

"From now on," he said to his first two disciples, "you shall call me Yu'Shaa."

There was a moment's silence; then Shoon-mi stepped forward a pace, his face creased in consternation.

"Yu'Shaa?" he echoed. "The *prophet*?"

Nom Anor smiled, nodding. "The Prophet."

When Grand Admiral Pellaeon convened a brief meeting on the bridge of the Imperial Star Destroyer *Right to Rule*, twenty-four standard hours after the battle of Borosk, all the surviving Moffs attended, along with those navy admirals and senior officers not committed to the defense of the Empire from the retreating Yuuzhan Vong. Jacen agreed with Pellaeon that there would be a brief period after Vorrik's defeat during which it would be safe to tie up so many leaders from across the Imperial Remnant; not until the Yuuzhan Vong had regrouped and obtained new orders from Shimrra would there be any serious counterattack from the enemy. The strafing of Yaga Minor on their way out had been little more than an afterthought, easily repelled.

For those Moffs who disagreed, who thought that now was the perfect time to consolidate their strongholds against both the Yuuzhan Vong and a Grand Admiral who would dare defy them, Pellaeon circulated a rumor that anyone not in attendance would forgo the right to navy defense. The Yuuzhan Vong was a problem the Empire had to confront as a whole, and the composition of that whole had to be determined as quickly as possible. No one was compelled to attend, but everyone knew the consequences if they didn't.

That there would be retaliation, Jacen didn't doubt. B'shith Vorrik had been humiliated in front of both his army and that of his enemy. Somehow, the Yuuzhan Vong commander *would* return. It was just a matter of how soon that would be, and how much of a force he would bring with him.

Jacen stood to one side with Luke, Mara, Saba, and Tekli, making their presence known but not contributing to the discussion. It was another calculated provocation engineered by Pellaeon. Luke had expressed reservations about flaunting the old enemy before so many Moffs, but through the Force Jacen could tell that the Jedi Master was secretly enjoying the situation.

When everyone was seated, Pellaeon rose from his chair and stood before those assembled.

"The reason I have brought you all here is quite simple," he said, forgoing the formalities of introduction. "I wish to share with you a realization I have come to, and to tell you what I intend to do about it."

Pellaeon walked around the table with hands clasped behind his back. It was a simple psychological ploy, intended to intimidate those seated by forcing them to either crane their heads around to see him or stare dumbly forward at nothing as he talked. It was a cheap trick, but Jacen understood that the Grand Admiral needed every advantage he could get.

Gilad Pellaeon had donned his full battle uniform, and his general appearance had been cleaned up prior to the meeting, but there was no hiding either his age or the fact that he had recently been on the verge of death. He would carry a slight limp for as long he lived.

"In the last forty-eight standard hours, the Imperial Navy has fended off the greatest threat it has ever faced." He studied the Moffs before him with penetrating eyes. "You've seen the reports and studied the breakdowns, so I'm sure you can understand the significance of what happened at Bastion and, hopefully, will have some appreciation of the seriousness of the decisions we must now make." He paused further for effect. "Until we rebuild Bastion, the Empire is temporarily without a capital; the Moff Council has lost several of its most important members and, with them, I suspect, its short-term cohesion. Many of our citizens have been enslaved by the Yuuzhan Vong, and our borders are no longer safe.

"But the threat we have repelled is not the Yuuzhan Vong. It is something far more insidious. Indeed, we didn't know we were facing it until the very last, when it was almost too late to fend it off. That threat can be summed up in one word. It is a word that has more fear for me than extinction. It is *irrelevance*."

Jacen caught a flicker of annoyance as it passed across the jowled face of Moff Flennic. For a moment he thought Flennic might interrupt, but the Moff remained silent, brooding.

Pellaeon had completed a circuit of the table and returned to where he started. He put his palms down on the table and leaned forward. "When we first heard about the Yuuzhan Vong," he said, "we blithely observed their passage through the galaxy and assumed that when they didn't attack *us*, they did so out of caution. We were too strong, too determined, too *superior* for them to risk a confrontation. We believed ourselves to be too formidable an opponent. But when we sent support to the Battle of Ithor, we saw just how strong the enemy's fleets really were. Afraid that we would be unable to defend ourselves, we pulled in our heads and dug in, waiting for an attack that never came."

He straightened now, his expression briefly betraying his weariness. "And it never came," he said slowly, "because we simply didn't matter to the Yuuzhan Vong. We weren't considered a threat. We had demonstrated an unwillingness to become involved in someone else's fight, and a propensity for sitting back and watching our neighbors being destroyed. Why *should* they attack us? We weren't hurting them; if anything, we were making their job easier. In effect, we made ourselves irrelevant, and for that I feel the greatest shame of all."

Pellaeon looked up and caught Jacen's eyes. An understanding passed between the two men that sent a shiver down Jacen's spine. Pellaeon was talking about war, but the same principle could be applied to all aspects of life. The greatest crime a being could commit, against itself and those around it, was to withdraw from the living. Jacen had seen this when his father had withdrawn from his mother after the death of Chewbacca; he had felt it in himself when he had retreated from battle to find an answer to his doubts; and he was seeing it now, on a much larger scale, in the actions of the Imperial Remnant. Life was involvement; being part of the Force meant participating in the evolution of the galaxy. It was not just sitting back and observing. The only question of importance that anyone *truly* intending to live needed to ask themselves was, *how* did one become a part of that process?

Unfortunately, the answer to that question still eluded him.

"Well," Pellaeon went on, "we've been attacked now. No one could've missed that. But does that mean we're relevant?" He shook his head. "No. It means that Supreme Overlord Shimrra took a moment to stamp out a potential threat lingering around his rear lines. A *potential* threat, mind you, not an *actual* threat. The force he sent wasn't sufficient to disable us, even with surprise on its side, but it was nothing compared to the resources he committed to Coruscant. B'shith Vorrik, furthermore, is no Tsavong Lah or Nas Choka. Had we really mattered to the overall war, Shimrra would have wiped us out years ago, not tried now as an afterthought.

"But we refused to roll over and be destroyed, even when we were grievously injured. We insulted the enemy as he retreated, and we liberated some of those taken captive. We showed them that we are not easy prey, and that we will not be so easily dismissed.

"If Shimrra didn't consider the Empire a threat before, he will now. How *long* he considers us a threat, however, is entirely up to us."

"And why is that?" Moff Flennic asked, obviously unable to contain his disapproval of being lectured at any longer. Jacen could feel the resentment radiating from the man.

"Isn't that obvious, Kurlen?" Ephin Sarreti said from across the table. The Moff, recently released from a medical barge evacuated from Bastion, sported one arm in a sling and a dour expression. "If we sit here expecting to defend our territories indefinitely, we'll all be dead within months."

Pellaeon nodded. "And giving Vorrik time to petition another strike force from Shimrra—fresher, larger, and certainly more eager for our blood—would be suicide. We remain a threat only so long as we remain alive."

Flennic inclined his head slightly. "I can't help but feel apprehensive about the alternative you're about to propose."

"It's the only alternative that I can see," Pellaeon said softly, regarding each of the Moffs around the table before continuing. "We must take the fight to the Yuuzhan Vong."

A murmur of unrest immediately rippled around the room, but it was Moff Flennic again whose voice was heard. "You would have us leave our worlds behind?" he asked disbelievingly. "Undefended?"

"Not entirely," the Grand Admiral said. "Every planet would retain a token defense force—at least enough to repel the sort of attack Yaga Minor suffered."

"But not enough to repel a serious invasion," came a woman's voice from the far end of the table.

Jacen recognized the woman as Moff Crowal from Valc VII, a system on the very edge of the Unknown Regions.

"If the Yuuzhan Vong are kept busy elsewhere, there won't *be* one," Sarreti pointed out.

"Can we be absolutely certain of that, though?" Flennic countered hotly. He faced Pellaeon. "Admiral, you are gambling with our very lives here!"

"Isn't that what all leaders must do in times of war?" he returned. "I'm offering you a chance of victory as opposed to the certainty of our destruction. Mark my words: if we do nothing, we *will* be destroyed."

"If, as you say, we can't beat the Yuuzhan Vong here," Moff Crowal said, "then how do you propose we beat them on their own territory?"

Pellaeon nodded. "A fair question," he said. "And one that has occupied my mind these last couple of days."

"Go on then," Flennic said. "Give us your answer."

"There is only one possible answer." The ageing Grand Admiral took a moment to look around him—a staged moment of reflection, Jacen knew, but effective. The man was clearly a veteran of these types of meetings, and could employ all manner of body language to strengthen his argument. "In order to survive intact, the Empire needs to see itself objectively; it needs to cultivate a certain distance from its immediate past and see itself in the context of the wider galaxy and its history. We are not alone here, as much as we might sometimes like to pretend we are. We cannot avoid what is happening outside, as the Yuuzhan Vong have so convincingly demonstrated. For too long have we kept to ourselves; for too long have we ignored what is going on out there in the wider galaxy. We have remained content to direct our attention inward, at our own navels.

"I do not exclude myself from this criticism, either," he went on. "There have been times I could have fought harder to do what my gut told me was right. That I didn't will be my undying shame, because it was almost our undoing. But I will not let it happen again."

"*You* will not?" Moff Flennic mocked. "Grand Admiral, I trust we are coming to some sort of point here. If you have gathered us together to dictate your terms, then please get on with it so that we can vote on your dismissal and put this behind us forever."

Pellaeon smiled, and held the smile a moment longer than was comfortable. There was something in the silence around the table and the way the Moffs glanced at one another that told Jacen that Pellaeon had taken the gloves off. Now was the moment to deliver the message he'd gathered them all to hear. Mara must have felt it too, for he heard her take in a deep breath in anticipation and hold it.

"As Grand Admiral of the Imperial Navy," Pellaeon said, "I am formally advising the Moff Council that at our earliest possible convenience we must strike a formal agreement with the Galactic Federation of Free Alliances to share military resources in order to repel the threat of the Yuuzhan Vong from the galaxy." He had to raise his voice to be heard above the hubbub that immediately filled the room. "Furthermore, I advise that this agreement be ongoing after the immediate threat has passed. The only way to survive in the future is to turn our back on the past. As much as some of you may dislike to hear it, it is time for us to make peace with one another."

Flennic was the first to his feet. "Join the Galactic Alliance? Have you gone mad? You can't believe that any of us would ever agree to this!"

"I don't need your agreement, Kurlen." Pellaeon spoke softly, but his voice carried over the howls of dissent. "When I say that I am advising the council, I am only following a formality. This is the way it will be, because this is the way it *has* to be. I am simply saving you the need to think it through for yourselves."

"This is treason!" another Moff gasped.

"It's common sense," Ephin Sarreti countered.

The Grand Admiral nodded his thanks to Sarreti for the support the Moff was giving him. "My loyalty to the Empire is as strong as it has ever been," he said. "I will do what I must to ensure its survival."

"By forcing us to submit to *them*?" A finger stabbed at where the robed Jedi stood off to one side. "We have spent our lives fighting this scum, and now you wish us to—"

"Be mindful of your words, Moff Freyborn," Pellaeon interjected firmly. "These 'scum,' as you call them, saved my life back at Bastion—as well as saving the Empire from an early grave."

"A grave they dug for us in the first place," Flennic snarled. "At our peak we would never have fallen to the Yuuzhan Vong as they have. We would have sent them back from whence they came—impaled upon their own amphistaffs!"

"Do you really believe that, Kurlen? We weren't able to resist a handful of Rebels, so how would we have resisted the massed might of the Yuuzhan Vong?" Pellaeon's stare was cold and hard. Clearly visible behind the Grand Admiral's bluff, mustachioed appearance was the man who had faced down far worse threats than a hostile Moff Council. "Your reasoning is both faulty and circular—and it is precisely the kind of reasoning that has brought us to these straits. The Empire is foundering not from forces exterior to it, but as a result of its own internal weaknesses. Our current circumstances are our own fault; it is foolish to lay blame elsewhere for our own failings."

"The Empire will never surrender to the Galactic Alliance, Admiral," Flennic said firmly. "And I cannot believe you would ever consider this after all your years resisting their insidious advance!"

Instead of responding angrily, Pellaeon just chuckled. "Like it or not, they have ruled the galaxy for almost as many decades as we did—and with less bloodshed and military expenditure, I might add. Right now, they are the one thing that stands between us and enslavement and death at the hands of the Yuuzhan Vong, and it is time we acknowledged that. And we need to do it *now* before we bury ourselves beneath old grudges and an inability to accept reality."

"I refuse to accept defeat," Flennic said, still on his feet and regarding Pellaeon with undisguised contempt. "And I don't regard that inability as a *dis*ability, either. The Empire is strong; we proved that—*you* proved that—by repelling the invasion. Why, on a day when we should be celebrating our victory, are we contemplating the end of the Empire?"

"First," Pellaeon said, "allying ourselves with the Galactic Alliance isn't the same thing as dissolving the Empire. That should be obvious even to a child, Kurlen. They're not asking us to surrender our sovereignty; nor will we. We will simply combine forces to our mutual benefit. Second, as I said earlier, the Empire exists today only because of luck: luck that the Yuuzhan Vong didn't attack sooner, and luck that the emissaries from the Galactic Alliance came along when they did to show us how to fight effectively. Third, if we don't fight back now, the Yuuzhan Vong *will* return and strike us down without any mercy whatsoever. If we don't drive them back and join with our neighbors to *keep* them back, then no one will ever be safe again. And this Empire we hold so precious will completely cease to be. If you can't accept that argument, Kurlen, then you'll have to learn to accept your irrelevance to the council instead."

Flennic's eyes narrowed. "Are you threatening me?"

Pellaeon's response was almost shocking in its bluntness. "Yes, Kurlen, I am," he said. Then, eyeing each of the Moffs present, he added, "The council will unanimously accept my proposal, or I will take the entire fleet with me when I leave."

The shock of his pronouncement provoked gasps of astonishment and dismay among those who had, perhaps, thought that Pellaeon could be talked around, or at least placated with a slightly softer alternative. No one had seriously considered that their Grand Admiral might gamble the Empire itself over something so outrageous as allying themselves with their old enemies.

Jacen felt a spike of animosity from Moff Flennic in the Force at the same time he saw the blaster come out of the fat man's robes. In an instant, everyone's attention in the room had gone from Pellaeon to the weapon aimed at him.

"This is treason of the worst kind, Admiral," Flennic said steadily.

Jacen was about to use the Force to whisk the blaster from Flennic's hand, when he felt Luke's hand touch his arm.

Pellaeon faced the blaster as calmly as he had faced Flennic's criticism. A dozen stormtroopers stationed at the exits rushed forward with their blasters raised to shoot Flennic down, but Pellaeon waved them back.

"How strong are your convictions, Kurlen?" he asked. "Are you prepared to die for them?"

"You can't threaten us, Admiral!" The Moff's voice was even and calm, but Jacen noted that the blaster in his hand had begun to waver. "*We* are the Council of Moffs; we appointed *you*. We can always appoint another Grand Admiral to take your place—one who won't lead us down such a treacherous path!"

"Another warlord choking on remembered glories, you mean? There aren't many left, Kurlen. Our numbers have dwindled in futile attempts to reclaim something that was taken from us long ago. The galaxy isn't ours by right; we have *lost* it. The sooner we accept that, the sooner we can begin to understand what role exists for us now. And if that new role is to be part of the Galactic Alliance, then so be it. It has to be better than extinction. I for one am sick of fighting a war we can never win— and against the wrong enemy, what's more."

For the first time, Pellaeon's reserve slipped. Jacen saw real passion warring below the surface, like the molten core spinning under the crust of a civilized planet. And it wasn't lost on Flennic, either.

"This is madness," the Moff said, appealing now to the rest of the council. "Are you all just going to stand by and let him destroy everything we've managed to salvage?"

"It's better than being dead, Kurlen," Sarreti said.

"Or enslaved," Moff Crowal added.

Flennic winced as though he'd been mortally wounded. "You, Crowal?" he said. "*You* believe this nonsense?"

"It's not nonsense, Kurlen," she said. "I argued against joining the Galactic Alliance when the enemy wasn't on our doorstep, thinking that if we didn't provoke the Yuuzhan Vong, they would leave us alone. But that proved to be a mistake."

"No." Flennic's gaze swept the faces before him, assessing the expressions and weighing up what support remained with him. Pellaeon watched patiently as he came to the only possible conclusion. "No . . ."

The Moff's certainty faltered, and the blaster dropped. He seemed on the verge of capitulating when a dangerous look came to his eyes and his fingers around the blaster's grip tightened.

"No!" he cried. "I *will not* submit!"

The blaster came back up.

He's going to do it, Jacen realized. *He's going to shoot Pellaeon!*

Ignoring the pressure of Luke's hand on his arm, he gathered the Force around him in order to act—but he was too late. The blaster cracked at the same time as he felt the flex of someone else's invisible will, and he saw the gun fly out of Flennic's hand and clatter across the floor. The blaster's bolt discharged harmlessly over

Pellaeon's shoulder. The Grand Admiral hadn't even flinched.

Two stormtroopers were at Flennic's side in an instant, each taking an arm as they arrested him. He struggled in vain against them, staring wildly at the Jedi standing beside Pellaeon.

"You!" he yelled. "You and your vile mind tricks have poisoned us!"

"Nonsense," Mara said, stepping forward. "We use our powers to save lives, not waste them—unlike you, Moff Flennic."

The dark tone to her voice made it clear who had saved Pellaeon.

"You are not the only one here who served under Palpatine," she continued. "I have changed, and so has the Grand Admiral. And I suspect that you must have, too, for our former master would never have tolerated such idiocy in one of his servants. What were you thinking? That Yaga Minor would become capital now that Bastion has fallen? That you would lead the council? Don't be a fool, Flennic."

Flennic's glare at Mara was cold and piercing, but Jacen could tell by the way he relaxed in the grip of the guards that her words were getting through.

"Stand down, Kurlen," Pellaeon said quietly. "Stand down now and abide by the will of the council, and I swear that no action will be taken for what has happened here today."

Flennic's face twisted as he gathered his injured pride and anger and swallowed them both. Jacen suspected that it wouldn't have tasted good at all, and would have burned going down.

The Moff looked from Pellaeon to Mara, then back again. "Very well," he said quietly. "I give my support to your proposal of allying ourselves with the Galactic Alliance. But I stand by my opinion, Admiral."

"As it is yours to stand by," Pellaeon said, nodding sagely. Then he took a few steps toward Flennic, fixing the corpulent Moff of Yaga Minor with a steely gaze. "But hear this, Kurlen: you have pulled a weapon on me this day, an act of treason that under normal circumstances would be punishable by death. But these are not normal circumstances, and so I am prepared to overlook your insurrection. However, from this moment on you would be wise to be mindful of your actions. Because if you so much as *breathe* in a manner that I think is treacherous, then I *will* have your head. Is that understood?"

Moff Flennic swallowed thickly, but didn't speak. He could only nod mutely.

With a glance from the Grand Admiral, the stormtroopers released their grip on the Moff. Then Pellaeon returned to his place at the head of the table without another word.

Mara crossed the room and collected the discarded blaster, then stepped over to Moff Flennic and handed him the weapon. He accepted it with some surprise, his brow creased in puzzlement.

"Personally, Kurlen," she said, "I prefer my allies to be armed."

With that she faced the Grand Admiral.

"If it's all the same to you, Admiral, I think we should take our leave now," she said. "I imagine there is still much that needs to be discussed here, and given the general feeling toward us in this room, it might be easier for you to do this without us here."

The Grand Admiral acknowledged Mara with a curt bow. "Thank you," he said. Then, with a glance to the other Jedi standing there, added, "for everything."

One by one the Jedi filed from the room—Luke, Mara Saba, Tekli, and Jacen—leaving the Grand Admiral alone with the Moffs to go over the details of his plans. As the rest of the party continued to move down the corridor, Jacen paused outside to look back briefly into the room. Already the discussion was becoming heated again, with those gathered around the table gesticulating wildly as they raised their voices to make their opinions heard on the matter of the Empire's new allies.

The door hissed shut, muting the ongoing debate. Jacen turned to catch up with the others, only to find Mara still standing there waiting for him.

"You look worried," she said.

He swallowed a sound that might have been a laugh, but could just as easily have been an exclamation of annoyance. "Try as I—or Gilad—might," he said, "I find it hard to believe that anyone in that room will ever really regard us as allies. Despite everything we did for them, they still hold us in such mistrust."

"Not all of them." She shrugged. "We've made a lot of progress today—"

"I know, I know, and we'll probably end up with some kind of shallow alliance in place before long. But . . ." He gesticulated vaguely in lieu of actually finding words for what he wanted to say. "Is that enough?"

"Maybe," Mara said. "And maybe you're right. Maybe it won't come to anything more than pretty words from an ugly mouth. But when it comes to the fight against the Yuuzhan Vong, I'll happily take a shallow alliance over none at all."

"True." He offered a half smile in the face of his aunt's optimism.

Mara chuckled at the effort. "That's just the way things are, Jacen," she said, putting an arm around his shoulder and guiding him with her to join the others. He didn't resist her. "Sometimes it's harder to make a friend than it is to fight an enemy."

EPILOGUE

Two days later, Luke watched from *Jade Shadow*'s cockpit as the Imperial Navy reassembled for its mission Coreward. Advance scouts had found the location of B'shith Vorrik's rear guard, and Pellaeon was keen to press home their advantage and push the Yuuzhan Vong back even farther.

"You'll require an escort on your mission into the Unknown Regions," Pellaeon said from the bridge of *Right to Rule*, his image displayed in miniature by the holoprojector between Luke and Mara.

"We're quite capable of handling ourselves, Admiral," Mara said.

"Think of it as a gesture," Pellaeon replied. "A political act rather than a military one."

"A gesture of unity?"

Pellaeon nodded. "Something like that."

Mara grunted unhappily. "What exactly did you have in mind?"

"Captain Yage has volunteered the services of *Widowmaker*, and I have given approval. She's one of the best officers I have. She'll give you support if you need it, but she won't get in your way, I assure you. You can count on her to be discreet."

Luke knew that Yage was a good choice; she had proved herself to be very pragmatic and open-minded.

"We don't really know what we're heading into," he said, "so we won't make a point of refusing the offer."

"You never know," Pellaeon said, smiling. "You might even be glad you accepted it, one day."

Luke smiled in return, then asked, "You have the information from Moff Crowal?"

"I have. We'll download it to your navicomputers in a second. She's supervised numerous scouting missions into the Unknown Regions, some of which made contact with civilizations there. One of her ethnologists has an interest in comparative religions and has recorded a number of myths and legends prevalent among most cultures. One of the more interesting legends is that of a wandering planet, known to appear in systems briefly and then flee when approached. Does this sound something like what you might be looking for?"

Descriptions of Zonama Sekot were nonexistent beyond what Vergere had told Jacen, but they knew without a doubt it could move of its own volition, employing massive hyperspace engines mounted deep in its crust and powered by the planet's core. Luke doubted that there would be two such planets in the galaxy.

"Can you tell us where it was last seen?" he asked.

Pellaeon shook his head. "All we have are the stories, I'm afraid. But I can tell you where these stories hail from. Since it's not a universal fable, you might at least be able to trace some sort of path."

"That might work," Mara said, glancing over the hologram to Luke. "If we could get enough information like that, then we should be able to work out where it's been."

"But what happens when you find it?" the Grand Admiral asked. "If the legends are right, it's only going to run away again."

"That's something we're just going to have to deal

with when the time comes," Luke said. "If the time comes, that is."

"Either way," Pellaeon said, "it looks like you're going to have your hands full."

"No more than you'll have, convincing Vorrik to stay away from your home," Luke said.

"That should be easy compared to getting up in front of a certain Princess to tell her that the Empire has changed its mind."

"You won't be talking to Leia," Luke said. "She's dealing with other things at the moment." They had received a brief update of his sister's activities on Galantos when communications had been normalized after the attack. It concerned him, the way the Yuuzhan Vong were beginning to mop up lesser threats around the edges of their territory, regardless of the strength of their grip on the center. Even if the center fell, the peripheries could still suffer major damage before the threat was eradicated.

"One of your Jedi friends, then," Pellaeon said. "I'm sure they have things nicely in order on Mon Calamari."

"Not the Jedi, either," Luke corrected him again. "We're staying well out of politics this time. I have come to the opinion that the Force is best at guiding an individual, not a nation of any size. The forces that direct a cell to grow aren't appropriate for the plant as a whole—and are maybe even destructive. The last thing we want is another Palpatine."

"A wise move, I think," Pellaeon said. "But whom should I talk to, then?"

"Head of State Cal Omas," Luke said. "Or Supreme Commander Sien Sovv."

"The same Sovv who cost you Coruscant?"

"His reputation is undeserved, as he has recently proven," Luke defended. "And even if it was, we need someone like him to lead us to the right kind of victory:

only someone who has faced losing everything can sympathize with a defeated enemy."

Pellaeon chuckled this time. "Skywalker, you're getting more dangerous the older you get. I hope I'm not around to see what you're going to be like when you get to be my age."

When *Jade Shadow* had recharged its weapons banks and Captain Yage had moved alongside to coordinate their departure, Luke took a walk to stretch his legs, and to find Jacen. Passing through the passenger bay, he found Tekli and Saba playing a dice game. To human eyes, the faces of the dice looked black-on-black, but they were readable in infrared, and both aliens saw well into that spectrum. There was a heady odor to the bay, reflecting the fact that it had been home to too many people for too many days. With *Widowmaker* along for the ride, Luke hoped there might be more opportunities to stretch their legs in the long journey ahead.

He smiled down at them on his way through, and was about to leave when he was stopped by Saba.

"Master Skywalker?" she said, standing.

"Yes, Saba?"

"This one . . ." she started, with something approximating embarrassment in the way her spiked heels scratched at *Jade Shadow*'s metallic floor. The vertical slits of her eyes blinked before she spoke again. Then, with quiet sincerity, she said, "This one iz glad that she came on the mission."

He smiled gently. "This one is glad you came, too, Saba," he said. "Your stunt with the slaveship has done more for our reputation among the Imperials than anything I ever did."

" 'Crazy,' Grand Admiral Pellaeon said."

"That we are." He touched Saba's shoulder and felt

her thickly corded muscles tense beneath her scales. "Consider them remembered," he said softly.

She nodded. "And the hunt continues."

Tekli indicated for Saba to continue with the game. The Barabel crouched down again, her large clawed hand collecting the black dice and rolling them across the deck. Luke left them to it, glad that the unlikely pair had found friendship with each other.

Once the door had closed on the passenger bay, Luke searched the immediate vicinity of the Force for some indication of where Jacen might be. He sensed his nephew deeper in the ship—in fact, he was about as far away as someone could get from the rest of the crew without actually leaving *Jade Shadow*. Luke imagined that Jacen probably just wanted some privacy, which he would happily give to him once he'd made sure everything was all right with the young man. It was only as he rounded the corner to where the power couplings interfaced with the reactor outlets that he heard voices, and realized that Jacen was not alone. Three paces later he was confronted with a sight that brought him to a halt—more from embarrassment than anything else.

Jacen and Danni Quee were standing close together by an open hatchway. Danni's hand was lightly touching Jacen's cheek, and she was saying something to him in a low and intimate voice. Luke couldn't hear what was being said, thankfully, but just seeing them would have been bad enough as far as Jacen and Danni would have been concerned.

He quickly tried to duck back around the corner before he was noticed, but it was too late.

Jacen looked up, and Danni turned to follow his gaze. She hastily pulled her hand away as they stepped apart. For a few uncomfortable seconds, nobody spoke, and no one's eyes met.

"I'm sure Mara would have something appropriate to say at a moment like this," Luke ventured into the awkward silence.

Jacen nodded. "Probably something about not being able to expect privacy on a starship," he said.

"I'll leave you—"

"No," Danni said quickly. "Really. It's all right." She brushed back her hair and, indicating the open hatch, smiled. "We can check out that dodgy surge arrestor another time, if you like."

Jacen nodded once, then Danni stepped past Luke without another word, leaving the two men to talk.

"I'm so sorry," Luke said when she had gone. "I had no idea that—"

"No, it's okay," Jacen cut in. Clearly feeling awkward with the situation, he turned away from Luke, shutting the hatch with a gentle push and then affixing the bolts to hold it closed. For a moment his face stayed averted, but when he did finally turn around, Luke could see that he was smiling. "Actually, you probably did me a favor. I'm not very good at this sort of thing."

"Really?" Luke said. "You surprise me."

"In fact, I'm pretty dreadful."

"Well, I'm afraid you've probably inherited that from your mother's side of the family," Luke said. "That includes me."

"You seem to have done all right for yourself, Uncle."

"Oh, better than all right," he said. "But it took a lot of trial and error along the way. Getting a relationship to work is almost impossible—even without people like me getting in the way. There's no right or wrong way to tread; the rules are made up as you go along and can change without warning." He smiled. "Trust me when I say that it makes being a Jedi look easy."

"Maybe that's why the Jedi of old never married and had children," Jacen said.

"Maybe." Luke thought of his son, far away and, hopefully, safe. "I hope Ben turns out to be smarter than his father. Or at least more perceptive."

Hatch sealed, Jacen said, "I'm not sure that would be possible."

Glad that his nephew held no ill feelings for the intrusion, Luke clapped the young man on the back and led the way back to the cockpit. Danni made a good show of looking nonchalant as they passed, and Jacen managed to only slightly flush.

Mara looked up as they entered. "What kept you?"

"We just got talking, that's all," Luke said.

His wife frowned at him, but then her eyes widened in realization.

Mara studied Jacen carefully as the young Jedi dropped into the navigator's seat behind her. If he noticed her scrutiny, he didn't acknowledge it. Instead he kept his eyes on the view from the forward sensors, studying the ships arrayed around them.

"An Imperial escort," he said with a chuckle. "Who would have ever thought it possible?"

"These are indeed strange days," Luke said, slipping into the copilot's seat beside him.

Widowmaker was visible as a solid icon accompanied by several smaller shapes, gradually docking. Pellaeon had been true to his word—and then some. They were getting not only the frigate, but a squadron of TIE fighters as well. He'd heard a rumor that the droid brains of *Braxant Bonecrusher* had also volunteered to serve with Jacen again, but they had been turned down. The battered Dreadnaught needed some time in dry dock before its long-term flight worthiness was assured.

Mara seemed about to say something when a subspace message came through, flickering to life on the holoprojector.

A staticky image of Han appeared before them, with Leia at his shoulder.

"Hey, kid," Han said pleasantly, his mouth lifted at one corner in the smile that Luke had come to know all too well over the years.

"Is everything all right?" Mara asked.

"Fine," Han returned. There was some distortion to the voice, and the image kept losing cohesiveness, but considering how far it had come the quality was excellent. "Just thought we'd drop a line before we head off. After this, who knows when we'll get the chance to speak again?"

Luke forced a reassuring smile, fighting back a sudden apprehension about his journey. The Unknown Regions were large and contained hundreds of millions of stars. How long it would take to find Zonama Sekot was impossible to tell, but he knew it was going to take a lot of luck and a strong faith in the Force to find one planet out of so many.

"Soon," he said, "I hope."

"Where are you headed?" Mara asked of the fuzzy holograms.

"Bakura," Leia said.

"Bakura?" Luke's apprehension shifted and intensified immediately.

"Hey, relax," Han said. "It's not like we're going in alone. We've got *Pride of Selonia* to watch our backs. We're going to be just fine, kid."

Luke smiled again, and this time it came easier—even though the thought of trouble at Bakura made his skin crawl. The right people were going there to fix it, if there *was* trouble to be found.

"I hope you have better luck than you did with the Yevetha," he said. "How's Tahiri?"

"She says she's feeling fine," Leia said. "There was an episode on Galantos, but she seems to have bounced back. She might need a little bit more rest, I think, before she puts the pieces together."

Leia turned away, then, as if her attention was attracted by something off to one side. She turned back again a couple of seconds later.

"We've just had word that *Selonia* is ready to leave," she said, "so we're going to have to say our good-byes."

"That's okay," Mara said. "We're just about to leave, also."

"You take care, Luke," Han said, with his cocky half smile.

"You, too, my friend," Luke said. "Good-bye, Leia."

"Good-bye, Luke," his sister said. "And may the Force be with you all."

Mara waved. The image crackled and died, and silence once again filled the cabin. Luke sat back in his seat with a weary sigh.

"Luke?" Mara said. "What's wrong?"

"I'm not sure," he said. "These good-byes just feel . . . different, somehow."

His wife's hand came over to rest on top of his. "We'll see them again soon enough," she said. "You'll be fine once we get going."

Her hand left his and joined the other flickering over the controls, completing her preflight checks. Luke smiled at her reassuring words, but they didn't convince him. Something was still troubling him and he couldn't quite put a finger on it. Was it just the mention of Bakura? Or had it been the look on Leia's face when he'd asked about Tahiri?

She might need a little bit more rest, Leia had said, *before she puts the pieces together.*

Together, not *back* together. Yet he hadn't spoken to Leia about Tahiri before they'd left. His gut feeling was that there was nothing to worry about, in the long run, but Leia had looked concerned.

He wasn't sure what to make of that.

Most probably, he decided, his unease came from seeing Ben by hologram earlier—the harsh reminder that his son was growing up fast thousands of light-years away while he was off on some crazy mission to find something that might not even exist. He could only hold tight to the faith that Vergere had known what she was talking about. Because if she did, the fate of more than just Ben could be at stake.

Word came over the comm unit that the last of the TIE fighters had just docked in *Widowmaker*'s flight deck.

"We're ready when you are," Mara said, then turned to him. "Artoo has laid in a course for a planet called Yashuvhu." Luke's much-traveled R2 unit whistled confirmation from the droid station behind them. "Imperial first-contact specialists list it as nonhostile, and our specialist in comparative religions has listed it as one of the places that's heard of Zonama Sekot."

"*Our* specialist?" Luke echoed.

Mara looked up at him. "Dr. Soron Hegerty," she said. "You did know she was coming along, didn't you?"

Luke shrugged. "Never heard of her, actually."

"She was flown in from Valc Seven especially to advise us on local folklore that might help us trace Zonama Sekot," Mara said. "Captain Yage assured me that you knew about this."

They exchanged a long glance before Luke finally laughed. "Sounds to me as though someone might be trying to play both ends against the middle," he said.

"Still, it should stop the trip from becoming boring, don't you think?"

Mara didn't smile, but he could see amusement in his wife's deep green eyes.

"*Widowmaker* is at your command," Captain Yage said when the frigate's hyperdrive engines had cycled through a routine warm-up sequence. "Course laid in; all systems green. Just say the word, Mara."

Mara glanced at Luke, who nodded. She relayed the command, and Luke settled back into the copilot's seat, not needing to do anything with her and R2-D2 at the controls. The stars ahead were bright and too numerous to count. Somewhere within their far-flung tangle was a single world that might be the key to ending the war with the Yuuzhan Vong.

We're going to find you, Zonama Sekot, he thought to himself. *Wherever you are, we're going to find you . . .*

Engines surged and the stars stretched into lines as hyperspace enfolded them. They were on their way again.

Over 2 million copies in print!
Each book a *New York Times* bestseller!

THE NEW JEDI ORDER

Read The New Jedi Order series from start to
finish . . . It's the greatest epic since the
Star Wars movies!

Find out more at: www.starwars.com

Del Rey/LucasBooks
www.delreybooks.com

*Available in bookstores
everywhere.*